Cy   H   E   gles is the auth   ular
Morland Dynasty n   1s, which have captivated and
enthralled readers for decades. She is also the author of the
contemporary Bill Slider Mystery series, as well as her new
series, War at Home, which is an epic family drama set
against the backdrop of World War I. Cynthia's passions are
music, wine, horses, architecture and the English countryside.

Till the Boys Come Home

War at Home, 1918

Cynthia Harrod-Eagles

sphere

SPHERE

First published in Great Britain in 2018 by Sphere
This paperback edition published in 2018 by Sphere

1 3 5 7 9 10 8 6 4 2

A CIP catalogue record for this book
is available from the British Library.

ISBN 978-0-7515-6561-4

Typeset in Plantin by Palimpsest Book Production Ltd,
Falkirk, Stirlingshire
Printed and bound in Great Britain by Clays Ltd, Elcograf S.p.A

Papers used by Sphere are from well-managed forests
and other responsible sources.

MIX
Paper from
responsible sources
FSC® C104740

Sphere
An imprint of
Little, Brown Book Group
Carmelite House
50 Victoria Embankment
London EC4Y 0DZ

An Hachette UK Company
www.hachette.co.uk

www.littlebrown.co.uk

THE HUNTER FAMILY
of The Elms, Northcote

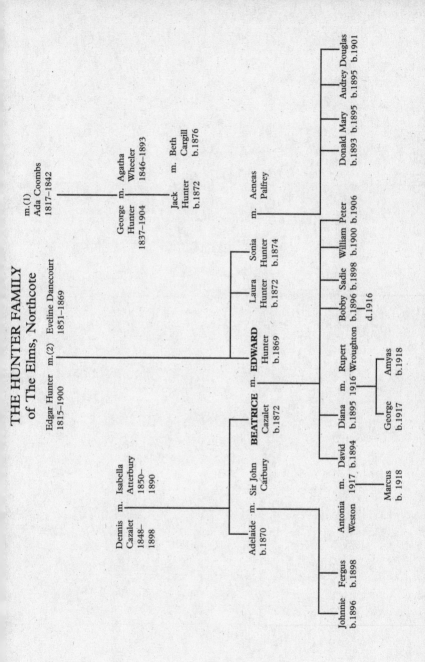

CHAPTER ONE

January 1918

Snow was blowing along Downing Street. The sky was so low and grey there was twilight at midday; but inside No. 10 electric light banished the gloom, and in the State Dining Room, a fire was burning brightly in the fireplace under the massive portrait of George II.

Lord Rhondda, the food controller, had murmured something tactless about coal rationing, but Lloyd George shrugged it off with a droll remark about Rhondda's having made his fortune from coal. Then Bonar Law retold the joke about Rhondda's having survived the *Lusitania* sinking – it was said he was so lucky he bobbed to the surface with a big fish in either hand. Rhondda took it in good part, leading the laughter at the ribbing.

There was a convivial atmosphere around the table, which Edward Hunter found remarkable, given the dire straits the country was in, in this fifth year of the war. Even more remarkable was his being here at all, in a company that included the Prime Minister, the Chancellor of the Exchequer and Field Marshal Haig, commander-in-chief of the British Expeditionary Force. Edward kept his ears open and his mouth shut, as befitted the lowest and least.

At first nothing serious was spoken of: these men, with the weight of the world on their shoulders, needed to relax.

Several amusing anecdotes were exchanged before the war was even mentioned; and then it was only to take light-hearted bets on when it would end.

The Prime Minister put up a hundred cigarettes that it would be finished off in the late summer of 1919, once the Americans had 'got their feet under the table'.

Lord Derby, the war secretary, raised him a hundred cigars that it would be over by next New Year.

'But where will you *get* a hundred cigars, Derby?' Lord Forbesson of the War Office parried. 'Don't tell me you are a hoarder? Rhondda, take note!'

'I've no window to look into a man's soul,' said Rhondda.

'Bonar, back me up,' Lloyd George appealed. 'Summer 1919. Late summer.'

'I'll not bet on the war,' Bonar Law rumbled. 'On a horse, mebbe. What's going to win the Guineas in April, Derby?'

'*My* filly, of course,' said Derby.

'Man, that's what you said last year, but Vincent took it with Diadem!'

'A fluke,' Derby said, waving a hand. 'Vincent was lucky. You may put your hat on Ferry.'

'Unpropitious name,' remarked George Barnes. 'Ferries are damned slow.'

'Not mine. She'll win by a length,' Derby insisted.

'Never mind horses, what about *my* bet?' Lloyd George said. 'Sir Douglas – what do you say? When's this war going to end?'

It was a brave question, and the room held its breath. If anyone was aware how bad things really were, it was Haig – and it was well known he'd been at outs with Lloyd George in the past, blaming him for the shortage of manpower and ordnance.

But Edward's patron, Lord Forbesson, who knew Haig well, dropped Edward a wink. Haig was stiff and dour in his demeanour, but it was from an unexpected but deep shyness: underneath, he was a great optimist. He turned his pale blue eyes on the Prime Minister and said, 'Oh, I'm with Lord Derby. We'll be out of it by the New Year.' An eruption of protest and comment followed. When it died down, he added, 'One way or another.'

Edward almost shivered. The idea that they might lose the war had never been entertained, however bad things had sometimes seemed. But now they were going to have to fight on without Russia.

Driven to its knees by revolution and misgovernment, starvation and lack of equipment, Russia had signed a cease-fire with Germany, and was negotiating for peace at Brest-Litovsk on the Polish border. The Russians had been unreliable allies, but by keeping the Germans occupied on the Eastern Front had taken some pressure off the Allies. Once they were out of the war, Germany could direct its undivided attention to the Western Front.

The mood around the table sobered. Haig said that the next four months would be critical. 'Germany's moved seventy-five thousand men back from the Eastern Front,' he said. 'More to come.'

'But surely,' Lord Derby said, 'they won't risk their whole reserve in an all-out attack?'

'It would be a gambler's throw,' said Haig, 'but we can't rule it out.'

'You're all right for guns and ammunition,' Lloyd George asserted warily. 'We've doubled output from the factories in the past eighteen months.'

'Thanks to the women workers,' Lord Forbesson said. 'Without them, the Royal Ordnance couldn't function at all.'

'Women will always do what's required of them,' Haig commented.

Rhondda agreed. 'They are a great deal tougher than we credit them for. All the same,' he looked around the table, 'we have to take war-weariness into account.'

It was a phrase unknown until recently. The Germans may sicken of the war, the French may falter, but the British lion would never be daunted. Yet, having gone into the war in the highest of spirits and determination, the nation was now wondering how much more it could take.

The casualty lists; the sacrifice of life; the bombing raids on British cities: these were afflictions to be borne bravely. But then there were the shortages, the queues, the blackout, the long hours and the sheer unrelenting slog. Fatigue, anxiety and sorrow – they wore down the spirit. For soldiers, there was the camaraderie of a shared endeavour, the force of duty and the immediacy of danger to stiffen them. But the ordinary people had dreary toil, in hardship and deprivation, with little thanks or praise – and no end in sight.

War-weariness: everyone knew about it, but what could be done about it?

'Well,' said Lord Derby, 'we certainly can't stop now. Germany must be defeated.'

Lord Rhondda turned to Edward. 'What do you say, Hunter? What can we do to improve morale at home?'

It was something he and Rhondda had been discussing, and he saw now why he had been invited to this luncheon – to present, as an outsider, what would probably be an unpopular idea. In politeness, they would have to hear him out. Whether they would agree was another matter.

'We should introduce food rationing,' he said.

There was instant outrage. 'It's un-English,' Milner objected.

'They won't take more interference,' said Barnes. In some ways the worst thing about the war was the ever-increasing regulation of a people who had never had much truck with officialdom

'I fear it would only increase ill-feeling,' said Law, cautiously.

'Just so,' said Derby. 'Set people against each other.

4

Accusations of cheating. Snoopers peering into shopping-baskets.'

'And actually draw attention to the shortages,' Barnes said.

'People understand that there are shortages,' Edward said. 'They "do without" remarkably patiently. What wears them down is the uncertainty. They queue for hours, not knowing whether, when they get to the head of the queue, there will be anything left to buy.'

Haig said, 'My men know what's going on at home. Their wives write to them, and it affects their morale.'

'But it smacks of socialism to me,' Montague muttered. 'Not the business of government to tell people what to eat.'

'Only the basic necessities need be rationed,' Edward said. 'If everyone's sure of getting the same amount of *them*, then there's no competition at the shops, and no bad feeling. It would lift a dark cloud from our ordinary people.'

Lloyd George said, 'No-one likes the idea of rationing, but it may be a necessary evil. How would it work, Rhondda?'

'Prices would have to be fixed,' Rhondda said. 'And it would have to be backed up by the law, with compulsory tickets or tokens, and fines for infractions.'

'Who's going to enforce it?' said Barnes. 'The police won't have time – they're fully stretched already, with so many gone to the Front.'

'There would have to be food inspectors,' said Lord Rhondda.

'God help us,' Barnes muttered, rolling his eyes. 'More busybodies with armbands.'

Edward couldn't help smiling to himself as the vision of Mrs Fitzgerald, the rector's wife in his home village, came to mind. There would never be a shortage, he thought, of people willing to take up the post of interfering with their neighbours.

After more discussion, Rhondda said a further benefit of

rationing was that the general nourishment of the population could be fixed at pre-war standards, resulting in better health. 'And that means increased output. Healthy workers produce more guns and shells.'

'Which brings me, gentlemen,' said the Prime Minister, 'to another point. Recruitment. Sir Douglas?'

Haig said, 'Even when there's no major offensive going on, there's a constant drain of manpower, from accidents and injuries.'

'When do the Americans come in?' Milner asked.

'I can hardly expect them to do much before May or June at the earliest. And the Germans seem likely to attack in the spring. I must have more men.'

'We will have to extend the conscription age,' Lloyd George said. 'We must take boys as soon as they reach eighteen, and send them abroad at eighteen and a half. And raise the upper limit from forty-one to fifty-one. There are plenty of perfectly fit men in their forties – some of them eager to get into uniform, I'll be bound. We might take it as high as fifty-six if we need to.'

The snow had stopped by the time Edward stepped out into the street again. In the muted light, the pavements and rooftops glowed eerily under their white covering. It was bitterly cold. Lord Forbesson left with him, and they walked together to the end of the road. 'Well, that went smoothly,' he said. 'You played your part well.'

'It would have been nice to know I *had* a part,' Edward complained. 'Then I could have been prepared.'

'No, no, you came off quite natural – just what we wanted,' said Forbesson. 'Rehearsal would have stilted you.'

'Do you anticipate much resistance in the House?'

'A few will see it as creeping socialism. I don't like it myself, but with a war to fight, it can't be helped. The important thing is for the lower classes to know their allocation of food is assured, see an end to this damned queuing.' He glanced sidelong at Edward. 'As for the other thing – the upper limit to the conscription age . . .'

'I'm forty-eight. It never occurred to me I might be called up,' Edward admitted.

'I'm fifty-five,' said Forbesson. 'Not that they'd comb me out of the War Office. You won't have to serve, either. You're too important back home. Are you going back to the bank, now?'

'No, the Treasury,' Edward said. 'A meeting about war bonds.'

'There you are, you see,' said Forbesson. 'Can't afford to send *you* to France. Have you had the letter about your knighthood yet? About the investiture?'

Edward felt a curious kind of shyness. He still did not feel he had done anything to earn a knighthood, when men were giving their lives in battle. 'The ceremony is on the twenty-fifth of February,' he said. 'At Buckingham Palace.'

'That's what I heard. I believe the King will be taking it himself. It's this new honour he thought up last year – Order of the British Empire. He's frightfully keen on it. Honours for the fellers who've actually *done* something, not just Buggins's Turn. He'll want to have a little chat with you about your achievements. Better have a few words prepared.'

'Thanks for the hint,' said Edward.

Forbesson smiled. 'Sir Edward Hunter, KBE. It sounds well! Is your good lady excited? I find the memsahibs usually set more store by these things than us chaps.'

'I'm sure she is,' Edward said. 'But she was never one for showing her feelings.'

Ada let Beattie in, and said reproachfully, 'Oh, madam, you're all wet!' It had been snowing again. She helped Beattie out of her coat with a *tch tch*.

Antonia came into the hall as Beattie was trying to take

7

off her hat, fumbling at the pin with frozen fingers. 'You didn't *walk* from the station? You ought to've taken a taxi.'

'There weren't any,' Beattie said. The truth was, she hadn't even looked to see. She had hardly noticed the snow, but she saw now that her shoes were soaked through and her stockings wet to the calf. They would both want to fuss over her, and she didn't deserve it. She didn't deserve their love.

Antonia said, 'You look so tired. You work too hard – and then the journey home. Was the train packed? Did you get a seat?'

'No – yes – I don't know,' Beattie said. It was necessary to distract her attention. '*You* are the one who works too hard,' she said. 'You should be resting. Ada, has she had her feet up, as Harding said?'

The baby was due in April, and Antonia, in truth, looked the picture of health, her eyes bright and her skin glowing. But Ada who, like most unmarried servants, was intensely interested in pregnancy and childbirth, was successfully diverted, and said, 'No, madam. I'm sorry to tell tales, but she was out at the canteen all day. She only got in half an hour before you. I was just going to bring her a cup of tea.'

'Oh, bring me one too, will you?' Beattie said. 'Just what I need.' That got rid of Ada, who bustled off, looking pleased – tea was the panacea for all ills – and she scotched Antonia by asking, 'How's David?'

Antonia answered at length as she followed Beattie into the morning-room. Because of coal rationing, they used it during the day, and the drawing-room fire was only lit after dinner.

'He's very low,' she said. 'He tries to hide it, but I know the signs. He's had pupils all day, and it tires him, but it is better for him to have to make the effort, isn't it, rather than brood?'

'Is it Jumbo?' Beattie asked, letting her tired body down

8

into the chair by the hearth. What a miserable little fire! She stretched her cold wet feet towards the meagre warmth, hoping Antonia wouldn't notice their state.

But Antonia was thinking about her husband. 'He doesn't say, but I think so.'

Jumbo had been David's best friend at school and university, and they had volunteered together in the first month of the war. David was wounded in 1916; Jumbo had been killed in the autumn of 1917. The news had come just as David seemed to be getting better – married to Antonia, his health improving, walking a little more. Jumbo's death had thrown him back into the gloom in which he had existed since shrapnel had shattered his femur and ended his war.

Antonia talked on. Though David was her first-born and best-beloved child, Beattie didn't listen. She nodded and said, 'Mm,' at appropriate moments, and let her mind drift in exhaustion. It was something she was becoming skilled at. She had been all day at the 2nd London General, sitting by Louis's bed, holding his hand while he talked. Her knees grew stiff and her back ached through sitting so long, but he did not like her to leave him for a moment. If Waites, his soldier-servant, had not brought her a cup of tea – God knew where he had scrounged it from – she would have had nothing to eat or drink all day.

He had been talking, talking, about South Africa, his plantation, and their future life there together. She didn't always listen – he had said all of it before, more than once – but gazed at him, loving him, tracing his features with her eyes, remembering their past, grieving for his present helplessness, fretting about what was to come.

She had loved him since she was a young woman in Dublin, just come out, and he was a penniless subaltern up at the Castle. She had loved him madly, unreasoningly, longed for him desperately through twenty years of separation, marriage to Edward and six children; never thinking she would see him again. And then the lottery of war had thrown him into her path.

She had been helpless to resist him; they had pursued a passionate affair in the snatched moments when the army and her duties released them for a few hours. But after the war, he had said – after the war we will go away together, be together for ever. And she had always stopped him, unable to discuss it, unable to contemplate what that would do to Edward, her good and loving husband, and her children.

He had been shot through the head during a night action at Poelkapelle. Somehow he had survived, but the surgeons had removed one eye, and the other was now sightless, the optic nerve severed. He who had been so upright, strong, capable – quintessentially a man of action – was now disabled and dependent. Unaware of night and day, he waited in his own personal darkness for her to come and take his hand. She was all he had, he who had been fearless soldier, world traveller, pioneer and planter. As soon as he was discharged, from the hospital and the army, the decision would be upon her. How could she refuse him? He needed her more than ever. The moment she had dreaded, when she would have to face Edward and tell him, was approaching – screaming down on her like a shell, to blow her life to shreds.

When the time had come to leave for the day, he had clutched her hand harder than ever. His remaining eye was dark-blue – so beautiful! David's eyes! – but blank, his face was as pale as carved wax. The outdoor tan of campaign had faded. *In South Africa*, she had caught herself thinking, *he will grow brown again, riding about the estate.* Oh dear God, South Africa! How could she do it – leave Edward, her children, her whole life?

How could she not?

'You will come tomorrow?' he had said.

And she had said yes, of course. 'You need to rest now.'

'Rest?' he had said. 'From what?'

She had found Waites hanging about outside in the corridor.

'Oh, ma'am, I don't know how to get through to him,' he said, twisting his hands about. 'He just won't understand. I've tried to tell him, but it goes in one ear and out the other. Oh ma'am, can't you tell him, make him see it?'

'See what?' Beattie asked. 'Slow down. You're not making sense. Tell him what?'

'He keeps talking about South Africa, like I was going to go with him. I've looked after him for years, but I belong to the army. As soon as they discharge him, they'll send me off somewhere else. I won't have any say. But he thinks I'll be staying with him. Oh, ma'am, I know he needs me, but I can't help it. Can't you talk to him, please? Make him understand?'

'I'll try,' she said wearily.

She understood that thinking about South Africa was his way of keeping a grip on himself, through the chaos that had engulfed him. And it required him to assume the two people closest to him, her and Waites, would be there with him. Waites had no choice in the matter. And, in truth, neither did she. She must abandon her husband and children, her respectability, the whole structure of her life, because she could not abandon Louis.

'I'll try,' she said again, patted Waites's arm, and went home.

David did not come down to dinner, and Antonia decided to take hers on a tray with him, up in their sitting-room. After dinner, when Peter, the youngest, had gone to bed, Sadie and William went over to the table by the window to play a game of cards, leaving Beattie and Edward alone by the fire. It was a chance for them to talk – if they spoke quietly, they would not be overheard. In a married life blessed with six children, they had learned to conduct their intimate exchanges in that way, whenever and wherever they could. Now, however, it was the last thing Beattie wanted. She was minded to say she was going straight to bed, but could not for the moment drag herself out of the chair. And then it was too late, for Edward, who had been studying her averted face, said, 'You look so tired, dear. Let me mix you a nightcap – it will help you sleep.'

He mixed her a whisky and soda, as he had used to – mostly soda – and brought it to her. His gentleness, his care for her, touched her unbearably. She looked at him with a kind of despair. 'Why are you so good to me?' she said.

He smiled. 'You're my wife. Why would I not be?'

'Husbands aren't always,' she said, and took a gulp of the whisky. She disliked the taste. She preferred it mixed with sugar and lemon, but both were in short supply these days. But whisky and soda was like medicine to her – you took it for the effect, not the taste.

Now she was looking at him, she could not stop. She examined his features, so familiar she barely registered them any more. He was a pleasant-looking man, falling only just short of handsome, his nose and chin perhaps just a little too long. Dark of hair, brown-eyed, sallow-skinned – his beard coming through after this morning's shave was a shadow around his chin and lips. The lips that had kissed hers many thousands of times. She shuddered inwardly at the memory – not in dislike, but in remembering the physical passion that had been between them. She had loved his body, enjoyed his love-making. And they had been good friends, on the whole, as much as husband and wife ever were. Everything had been going along comfortably, until the war. The war had shattered her peace. Her terror for David, when he had volunteered, terror that had proved wholly justified, and then Bobby – oh, Bobby, dead in France, never coming home – had deranged her. She had been unable any longer to give Edward anything, not mind, not body,

12

often not even basic kindness. And then Louis had come back into her life.

And through it all, he had remained the same Edward, kind and good. She did love him, she *did* – but she was in a trap. Yes, a trap of her own devising, but that did not make it any better. She, like Waites, had no choice. He must go with the army. She must go with Louis. And Edward – Edward must be abominably, unjustly hurt. And David – oh God, David! – she must leave him behind, too.

Edward was speaking. She forced herself to pay attention.

'. . . too much for you. I know you will say there's a war on and we must all do our duty, but you need to take care of yourself too. You can't help others if you break your own health. You must rest more.'

'Rest won't help me,' she said, bleakly.

'You must have *some* pleasure in life. A little treat now and then wouldn't harm the War Effort. Lunch in Town. A shopping trip. The theatre – how would you like to go to the theatre? I could get tickets—'

'I don't think I could sit through a play. And then the journey home afterwards – the trains are so slow and so dirty . . .'

'We could stay in Town for the night. Dinner and an hotel. It will be like old times.' When he smiled, his face lifted that extra fraction into handsomeness. Words welled up in her heart. She wanted to tell him; to let everything burst out of her, the whole terrible truth, and have done with it. And while she struggled, he went on, very softly, 'We haven't been very close lately. It's partly my fault – I'm so busy. But I want to take care of you, dearest. I can't bear seeing you unhappy. Let's make an effort to spend time together. The theatre, dinner – we could go away, just for a couple of days. I could make space in the diary . . .'

He wouldn't stop now, she could see that, and she was tired, so tired. She must put an end to this. 'That's a lovely

13

idea,' she said. 'We might manage it in a week or two. Let's see. And now I must go to bed. I'm so very tired.'

He let her go this time, and she hurried away, feeling like Judas.

She fell asleep the moment her head touched the pillow; but as was often the way when going to bed too early, she woke from a profound sleep, thinking it must be morning, only to hear the clock in the hall strike eleven. She lay in the dark, wondering whether she would be able to sleep again; and her bedroom door slowly opened, making a slice of light from the passage beyond. One of the children? Peter was still young enough to seek comfort after a nightmare. David? Her mind jerked fully awake. Something wrong with David? But she heard no voices out there, no commotion.

'Beattie?'

It was Edward. Now he came into the light and she saw him, in his dressing-gown. They hadn't slept together since David volunteered. He had a bed in his dressing-room. What could he want with her? She hadn't moved, and the light had not touched her yet – she could pretend to be asleep. She felt him cross the room, knew he was standing over her. His warm hand touched her hair, gently caressed her cheek. She could wake, let him into her bed, be held by him. He had always taken care of her. Every part of her ached to be comforted. But that would be the worst betrayal of all. He would remember, after she told him the truth, that she had dishonestly taken his comfort, and it would hurt him even more.

'Beattie,' he said again, but it was not a hopeful question. It was a sad and lonely word of departure. And he went away, quietly closing the door behind him.

14

CHAPTER TWO

'Emily!' Cook called out. She looked round impatiently. 'Where *is* that girl?'

'In the scullery,' said Ada, coming back in from the dustbins. 'Doing the knives.'

'She should have finished ages ago. She's so slow, she'd get passed by a snail with bad feet. I want her peeling the potatoes.'

'It's not easy, peeling potatoes with only one arm. I'll do 'em for you later.'

'I'll give her the thick end of *my* arm if she doesn't buck her ideas up,' Cook said. 'And I want 'em now, so's I can boil 'em. I'm going to do 'em soteed for the master tonight, to cheer up the cold beef. He likes a sotee potato.'

'I'll peel 'em and boil 'em for you,' Ada said, going out at the other end, 'when I've done the beds. There's plenty of time.'

Cook went stamping towards the scullery, muttering. Emily had left to become a munitionette, but had returned, begging for her job back, after she had been injured at the factory. The missus had kindly taken her in. Cook was sorry for her, of course, but there never was such a slow, dim-witted and fumble-fingered girl in creation. There was a man with only one arm who sold matches outside the station, and he was bright as a cricket. Even managed to tie his own shoelaces, while Emily, who *had* a second arm, even if it hurt, couldn't even clean a few knives before day turned into night!

'Emily!' she said again, reaching the scullery door. And there was the wretched girl, not working, but sitting and staring into space with her mouth open, cradling the arm that was in a sling. '*Well!*' said Cook – a word into which she could get a world of meaning and menace.

Emily jumped. 'I've nearly done 'em,' she protested. 'Just resting me arm, so I was.'

'I'll rest *you*,' Cook said automatically.

'It hurts awful,' Emily said.

'So do my feet, but you don't hear *me* complaining,' Cook snapped. 'You shouldn't have gone for a munitionette. I warned you but, oh, no – you had to know better. And now look! You young girls are all the same. You never listen. Well, you'd better bring the rest of them knives out here and do 'em at the table, where I can see you.'

She had just got settled when Ada came back in. 'Mrs David says Mr David'll just take soup for luncheon.'

Cook sighed. 'And I'd got a nice bit of fish for him. Soup's not enough.'

'And he probably won't eat that,' Ada said. 'He hardly touched anything yesterday. Got no appetite at all.'

'I expect his leg's paining him.'

Ada nodded. 'But he won't admit it. Doesn't want *her* to worry in her condition. But he's at that Dr Collis Browne's all day long. He told Ethel he'd dropped the bottle and spilled it and sent her out for a new one, but there wasn't any stain anywhere. He'd drunk it all, in my opinion. Course, Ethel plays along with him. Whatever Mr David wants, he gets. He's a ewe-lamb to her.'

Emily's eyes filled with tears. Her arm hurt, but no-one cared. Mr David's leg hurt, and everyone was sorry for him.

Cook looked across at her. 'Look at the mess you're making! And don't use so much powder. It's wasteful. Don't you know there's a war on?'

* * *

16

As she made her way from Chelsea station towards the hospital, Beattie found herself walking faster. However difficult things were, she longed to be with him. After half a lifetime of famine, it eased something in her simply to be near him. She carried a shopping-bag containing twenty Three Castles, two ounces of sherbet lemons, and a block of Trumper's sandalwood shaving soap. She would make the giving of each last as long as possible – have him guess what it was, by smelling it, perhaps. Make a game of it, to wile away the tedium of blindness. And she had gone so far as to look through the newspaper at home before she left, so as to be able to tell him the main events.

She was beginning to be a familiar face around the hospital, and nodded to one or two people as she hurried through. He was no longer in the garden annexe, having been moved to one of the less acute wards – a preparation, she supposed, for being discharged. A date had not yet been mentioned, but she gained the impression that it could not be long in coming. Would the army send him to some sort of convalescent home to acquire the skills he would need to survive in a dark world? Or would they just discharge him and leave him to make his own arrangements?

At the door of the ward she paused an instant, as she always did, to examine him before he knew she was there. Her mind jolted as it took an instant to catch up with her other senses. The man in Louis's bed, the one nearest the door, was a stranger. They had moved him again. A nurse scurried past and she missed her chance to catch her. Then the sister appeared at the far end of the ward, registered her presence, frowned, and came towards her.

Beattie had prepared the question and so said it anyway, though there was something in the sister's face that tried to wither the words on her lips. 'Where is Colonel Plunkett?'

'I'm so sorry,' the sister said. 'I'm afraid it's bad news.'

Beattie's lips were too dry to form any question. The

sister, with an eye of terrible pity, continued: 'There was a sudden change in his condition yesterday evening. He told the nurse that he had felt something like a small explosion in his head, then complained of hearing water running. Soon after that he became vague and confused, and began drifting in and out of consciousness. He died early this morning.'

'Died?' Beattie heard someone say the word, assumed it was her. This could not be Louis she was talking about.

'It was quite quiet and easy,' the sister went on relentlessly. 'He wouldn't have known anything about it. The doctor thinks a blood vessel in his head must have burst, one that was weakened by the bullet.'

Beattie stared, unable to articulate any question. The sister tried to anticipate her. 'He's been moved to the mortuary. Would you like to see him? He looks quite all right – pale, you know, but very peaceful. I find it helps those left behind to see their loved one at rest, free from their suffering.'

'No,' said Beattie. She couldn't bear to hear any more words because they hurt, stuck like knives, doing mortal damage. She turned and walked away, hearing behind her the sister call after her, asking some question. In a panic to escape she hurried along the corridor, misjudging the turn and hitting her hip painfully on the corner of the wall. The pain was good, she wanted it. Above all, she mustn't think.

Outside, she walked, as fast as she could, hurrying so that her legs ached with the effort, bumping into people when they would not move quickly enough, the shopping-bag, with its pathetic, meaningless purchases, thumping against her thigh. World's End, this area was called. There was a public house called the World's End. Oh, God! Almost wildly she turned off the main road, seeking escape. Her mind was repeating words randomly to avoid thought, a meaningless chant to the rhythm of her walk: *Three Castles, World's End. Three Castles, World's End.*

She came to the river. There was a bridge. She crossed

18

it. On the other side, a factory with a huge chimney prodding the sky, belching smoke; low, mean houses; people poorly dressed and work-worn. She walked on, with no idea where she was. That was *good*. She wanted to be lost. She wanted, savagely, never to be found, never to be her again.

There were khaki uniforms gathered in one place: her eye jumped to them, flinchingly. It was a mobile stall serving tea, sandwiches, soup to workers and soldiers, and she veered towards it. Two women were serving behind the counter. She went round to the door and climbed up inside, and began automatically to help. The women looked at her, as if to ask questions, and then, seeing her face, let her be. *Three Castles, World's End.* She poured tea, ladled soup, took money, gave change. She could do this, without thinking, for ever, until the sun went out and the earth turned to coal and went spinning out into the void. *World's End.*

Edward's first afternoon appointment, with Sir Thomas Bromley, was cancelled: Sir Thomas sent round his apologies, saying there was an emergency debate in the House, and he didn't know how long he would be detained. He would make a new appointment for some other time.

So now Edward had two, possibly three hours unclaimed in the middle of the day. Not that he didn't have plenty of work to do, but a sudden feeling of holiday came over him, and he thought of Beattie. She worked so hard, she was so tired, worn down by the war and David's suffering. He wanted to do something for her. The idea came to him that he would take her out to luncheon. She would probably protest that she could not abandon her duties, but he would insist. She needed a break from toil.

And perhaps afterwards he could take her to buy a new frock – to Selfridges, perhaps. She would need something smart for the investiture in February. Mostly she wore things made over by Nula, who had been the children's nurse-maid

19

and was now part-time sewing maid. Thrift was a virtue in wartime, but one was not knighted every day of the week. It would cheer her up, he thought, to buy something new. Women were tough, he knew that with one part of his mind: in some ways tougher than men. But he had been brought up to protect and cherish what custom called the frailer sex. Perhaps they *were* tough, but they should not *have* to be.

'I shall be out for a few hours,' he told Murchison. His confidential clerk lifted reddened, sad eyes, like an elderly hound, from his work as Edward breezed past. 'I can't say where. I shall be back before close of play.' And he was gone.

He took a taxi to Waterloo station, not to waste any of their precious time. He was feeling foolishly excited at the prospect of luncheon with Beattie. Perhaps she would be nice to him, he thought hopefully. A sudden break from routine, a treat, might bring the smile back to her lips, the smile that had first caught and enslaved him so many years ago.

Reaching the canteen, he scanned the faces behind the counter, and his heart fell. She was not there. But perhaps she'd gone only for a moment, on some errand. He went up to the nearest helper and said, 'Excuse me – I'm looking for Mrs Hunter.'

The woman raised her eyebrows and shook her head. 'I haven't seen her,' she said, then looked at her companion, who moved closer, enquiringly. 'Edith! Mrs Hunter? When did we last see her?'

The other woman leaned towards him, eager to be helpful. 'Not for ages. Not since – oh, before Christmas, wasn't it, Addie?'

'Yes, well before Christmas. I don't think she comes any more.'

Edward was impatient with their stupidity. His precious time was wasting away. 'Yes, yes, she works here every day. Mrs *Hunter*. You're thinking of someone else.'

20

The third lady now came over, and the first two looked at her in relief. She was obviously the senior helper, and must take this madman off their hands. 'Is something wrong?' she asked.

'Oh, Betty, dear, this gentleman's asking after Mrs Hunter,' said one of them. 'I told him she doesn't come here any more – well, not for ages, anyway. Do we know where she is?'

Betty looked down at Edward's impatience with a clear, untroubled gaze. 'As a matter of fact, I do happen to know. She does hospital visiting now.'

'*Hospital* visiting?' Edward said, perplexed. There was nothing strange or out of character about Beattie doing hospital visiting, but why would she not tell him of the change?

'Yes,' said Betty. 'Visiting wounded officers in hospital. I happen to know because a friend of mine, Jane Trevor – Lady Aberavon's daughter – is a VAD at the 2nd London General, and she's seen her there, going in and out. She visits blinded officers, I believe – awfully sporting of her. The poor fellows need cheering up so much.'

'The 2nd London?' Edward repeated in bewilderment.

She took it as a question. 'Yes, it's in Chelsea. King's Road. The building used to be St Mark's College. Not far from—'

'Thank you, I know where.' He remembered his manners, lifted his hat, and said, 'Ladies.'

He walked away, puzzled. She had always talked of 'Going to the canteen'. Whenever he asked, 'Are you going to the canteen today?' she had always answered, 'Yes, I must.' Why on earth would she not tell him that she had changed to hospital visiting? Perhaps it was less hard work, physically – could she possibly feel guilty about that? But it must take its toll emotionally. And blinded officers – who could not wish them to be comforted?

He walked over to the taxi rank. '2nd London General, please.'

The driver touched his hat and set off. But after a moment, Edward tapped the glass and said, 'I've changed my mind. Piccadilly, please.'

It would look as though he were checking up on her. If she didn't want to tell him, it would not please her to have him suddenly appear, asking questions. She would tell him in her own time. But the shine had gone off the day. His spontaneous outburst of affection had withered in a late frost, and the blossom was now brown and dead. He would go back to the office. He had plenty to do.

Beattie came back to herself to find that it was dark. The half-painted-out streetlamps were on, a light snow falling through the dim downward columns of light. The surface of the mug of tea she was holding steamed, and the breath of the customer before her, waiting to take it, was smoking in the cold air. She stared blankly at the vapour; then remembered, suddenly, the packet of cigarettes in her shopping-bag. Three Castles. Pain hit her so suddenly and viciously she gasped and almost cried out.

Louis! Louis!

'You all right, love?' the soldier asked in concern. She had frozen with the mug just out of his reach, but now her hand started shaking, and it spilled over a little. She put it down carefully on the counter, and stared around her in bewilderment. She had no memory of how she had got there. One of the other women edged closer. Beattie didn't recognise her; or the other beyond her. This was not her usual place. This was not any place she had ever been before.

Beattie searched her face. 'Where am I? Where is this?' she whispered.

'Lambeth Road,' said the woman kindly. 'Don't you know?'

'I – don't remember,' Beattie said.

22

'You just turned up and started helping,' said the woman. 'We thought you'd had a shock and needed to be busy, so we let you alone. You seemed to know what you were doing, all right.' There was a world of kindness in her eyes. Pity, even. *We've all felt it. We've all suffered. We know.*

No, said Beattie's mind. *You don't know. You don't know what it's like to lose him. Louis! Louis!*

'What time is it?' she heard herself ask.

The woman pointed to a clock hanging outside a jeweller's opposite – the shop closed and boarded up, posters plastering the wooden shuttering. 'Eat Less Bread'; 'Save A Ship'; 'Feed the Guns Week'; 'Women Wanted for War Service'.

The war was still going on. Nothing had changed while she had been away, except that the light of her life had gone out. She felt such an overwhelming wave of desolation that she could not draw breath, as though it were literally a wave and she was drowning. He was gone, and she had to carry on. The war would go on for ever. She was alone.

'It's twenty to five,' the woman was saying helpfully. Then, eyeing Beattie carefully, added, 'In the evening.'

Most of a day had passed in this bleak world since he had left it. Beattie had a feeling of being rushed away from him, as though she were on a speeding train, looking back at some dear and familiar landmark receding into the distance. She couldn't get back to him. She finally managed to drag in a breath. 'I must go,' she said, looking round her wildly.

'Yes, dear, you do that,' said the kind one.

'Where are we?'

'Vauxhall station's just along there. If you—'

But Beattie was out of the stall and walking away, as fast as she could on the slippery pavements – the snow was melting as it landed. Behind her, she heard a man's voice: 'Think I oughter go with her? She don't look the thing to me.'

23

She didn't hear what the answer was, but she walked faster. Her feet hurt, the soles sore with friction. *Louis!* Her mind called and called to him. She didn't know where he was. She was lost.

When Edward arrived home at his usual time, Cook bustled out from the kitchen as Ada was taking his coat, and said, 'Oh, sir, I think there's something wrong with Madam. She came in all pale and worn out and went straight to bed. She wouldn't even take a cup of tea.'

'Is she ill?' Edward asked in alarm. 'Have you sent for Dr Harding?'

Cook hesitated. 'I don't know as she's ill, exactly, sir. More like she's had a shock.'

Antonia arrived, and Edward turned to her in relief. 'What's going on?'

Antonia walked him into the drawing-room, where the miserable little rationed fire was doing its best against the clammy chill of January. It was hard to get it going when the chimney was cold. Irrelevantly, his mind offered him from childhood memory the old chant about logs: *one can't, two won't, three might, four can, but it takes five to make a fire.* He wrenched himself back sternly and said, 'Tell me what's happened.'

'I don't know,' said Antonia. 'She came home about an hour ago, much later than we expected her. Her coat was wet through, and she was white as a sheet, as if she'd had a shock. She wouldn't talk to anyone. I tried to ask her what was wrong but she just walked past me and went to her bedroom. Said she was going to bed.'

'I'll go to her,' said Edward. Questions boiled up, but he thrust them aside. Mostly, he just wanted to know if she was all right.

He tapped at her door, but went straight in. Her room smelt of her – her face powder, the rose-water she rinsed her hair in. It was her room now, not theirs – he had been

24

sleeping in the dressing-room for years now, banished from her arms, for what reason he did not know. It had started when David volunteered. Her terrible fear for her son had broken something, and he had never been able to offer her comfort for it.

The bedside lamp was on, and she was on the bed, under the eiderdown, but fully dressed and sitting up. Not doing anything – that was the worst part. Just staring at nothing, her face white and drawn.

'Dearest,' he began gently, walking towards her.

She looked up, with such pain in her eyes he almost flinched. 'Don't ask me anything,' she begged desperately.

'I just want to help you,' Edward said. He stood beside the bed, looking down at her, aching with the desire to cherish her, to ease her suffering.

'You can't help.'

'Perhaps I can. Can't you tell me what's wrong?' he pleaded.

She shook her head, and then sighed, as though she had been holding her breath under water. A dreadful sound, like a dying exhalation. 'I'm sorry,' she said, faintly.

'You don't need to be sorry. You haven't done anything. I love you – so very much. Let me help you.'

She closed her eyes, as one enduring pain. 'Leave me alone. Please.'

He waited a moment longer, trying not to feel the hurt, hoping she would tell him something, *anything*, to go on with. But she was obdurate, closed to him. *Where has she been all day?* The insidious question popped up in his mind without his volition, and he dismissed it angrily. She needed his compassion, not curiosity. He must be patient with her.

'If you want me, just call,' he said, 'and I'll come. I love you, Beattie.'

She didn't respond, and he went away and left her, closing the door quietly behind him.

CHAPTER THREE

Ada showed Nula into the morning-room, curiosity barely restrained. Mrs David *could* have been consulting about a new dress, but then couldn't she have waited until Nula came in the natural course of things, rather than sending for her? Oh, well, she supposed they'd get it all out of her afterwards in the servants' hall. She went out and closed the door.

Antonia lowered herself heavily into a chair, aware of Nula's professional eye assessing her. 'I'm sorry to be sending for you like this, but I'm worried about Mrs Hunter.'

'Had a bit of a shock, has she?' said Nula. Antonia gestured to a chair, but she remained standing, hands folded before her.

'You've heard about it?' Antonia was surprised.

'Things get about,' Nula said tersely. 'How bad is she?'

'She hasn't left her room for three days. She won't eat. Won't talk to anyone. Won't have the doctor sent for. I don't know what's happened to her, or if she's ill, or – or *what* to do.' She looked up at Nula with anxious eyes. 'You know her better than anyone. Perhaps you could speak to her, find out what's the matter, so we can do something for her.'

Nula gave a tight little nod. 'Very good, madam. I'll go up and see her. You should be resting yourself.' Antonia only gave a sigh, which Nula translated as *somebody has to take charge*. 'Don't you fret – I'll mind her,' she said.

'Thank you,' Antonia said, with profound gratitude.

* * *

Nula entered the bedroom, and went straight to the window to draw the curtains. Beattie was in bed, lying curled on her side. She stirred as the daylight came in. Nula held out the cup and saucer she had brought with her, and Beattie stared at it blankly.

'Tea,' said Nula.

'I don't want anything,' Beattie muttered thickly.

'You're thirsty,' Nula told her. 'Sit up, now, and take it.'

Beattie struggled to a sitting position, and took the cup and saucer, discovering that she was, indeed, horribly thirsty. As she sipped, Nula moved quietly about the room, tidying it. Beattie's eyes followed her, barely taking in her presence. Her mind was clouded with sleep and misery. She had been dreaming – the same dream that had been recurring since the beginning of the war, in which she found herself alone in the house, and though she rang and rang for the servants, no-one came. But now the dream had extended itself: she found a door in the corner of a room that had never been there before. Passing through it, she found herself in a whole extra wing of the house she hadn't known existed, a vast space that seemed to go on for ever. She walked down endless corridors past innumerable closed doors, and gradually came to realise that she was not just alone in the house, but the only person left on earth. In the dream she wept, great floods of tears pouring out of her without effort or cease for the death of mankind and her own solitude. Awake, in real life, she could not cry.

When she reached the bottom of the cup, Nula took it from her, and then sat on the edge of the bed, reading her face. Beattie turned away. 'Don't ask me questions.'

'I don't need to. You can't keep secrets from me,' said Nula. She stared a moment longer. 'It's *him*, isn't it?' Beattie did not respond. 'He's dead.' Beattie's eyes closed. 'Killed in the war,' Nula concluded. 'Well, and there's an end of it.'

'How can you be so—' Beattie began.

'Hard?' Nula said. 'You loved him. But it's you I care about. He's gone, you can't change that, but I have *you* to mind. Three days you've had, and that's more than most people get. Now you're to get up, wash your face, and carry on.'

'I can't.'

'You can, and you will. Do you think you're the only person in the world to lose someone? All over the country women have their hearts broke. These are hard times, sorrowful times, and not just for you.'

'Oh, don't,' Beattie said wearily.

Nula narrowed her eyes. 'You've a husband, and that's something a lot of women would give their hide for. D'you think he won't see this carry-on and start asking himself questions? D'you want to destroy everything? I said that man'd ruin you, and he did, twice, but I'll not let him do it three times.'

Beattie looked at her now, pain and despair in her face. 'What can I do? It hurts so much.'

'You'll do what we all do, take what God hands us and make the best of it. You've a house to run, a family to mind, war work to do – that's enough to keep you busy.'

War work? Beattie looked alarmed. 'I can't go back to the canteen.' It would remind her too much of him.

'Well, who's asking you to? There's plenty to do right here in Northcote. For a start, you can look to that young woman downstairs, who cares enough for you to send for me; she has her own husband to mind and a baby to bring into the world. She shouldn't be working down at the Hastings Road canteen every day. You tell her to stay home, and *you* go instead.'

Beattie was silent a moment. 'Is she—' she began awkwardly.

'She's exhausted. You're damned lucky to have her,' Nula

28

said grimly, 'and you won't for much longer if you don't make her rest. Now get up, child, for the Good Lord's sake. Put on a morning face and don't let people know what's in your heart. At least have some pride, Beattie Cazalet!'

Beattie pushed back the bedclothes and got unsteadily out of bed. She swayed, and Nula steadied her. Their eyes met. 'Nula—'

Nula enfolded her in a fierce embrace. 'Ah, my little love, my baby,' she crooned. 'It'll be grand, it'll be grand, you'll see. The rain passes and the sun comes out again. Just hold on.'

Nula walked into the kitchen, hoping to look inscrutable but with an undeniable air of triumph about her. 'She's getting up.'

'How did you do it?' Ada gasped.

'What was wrong with her?' Cook asked.

'I thought she was dyin',' Emily said, slightly disappointed. 'Wastin' away, like in a story.'

'She had a sick headache, that was all,' Nula said. 'They can lay you out like a corpse, them things – no-one who's never had one can imagine how bad.'

Ethel, making coffee at the stove for David, looked up. 'I've heard of them. Isn't that what they call me-grains? Lady I worked for once had 'em. How come she's not had one before?'

Nula sidestepped the question. 'Her ma was subject to the same, back in Ireland. But she's over it now. She's getting up.'

'What about breakfast?' Cook asked.

'Tea and toast, just,' said Nula, briskly. 'I'll take it up. And an aspirin. And then she'll be right as a cricket.'

'Are you sure?' Ada said. 'It's so sudden. She looked terrible when she came in.'

'You can't keep the Cazalets down,' Nula said breezily.

'Now, get that toast on, and I'll go and tell Mrs David. She'll be glad to have *that* worry off her mind, anyway.'

'Are you quite well now, Mother?' William asked tentatively.

Beattie, sitting in her fireside chair, sewing, felt the question hit the quiet room like a large stone falling into a still pool. The ripples touched Edward, in the chair opposite her, reading the paper, Sadie at the table writing a letter, and Peter on the floor making a model aeroplane. None of them looked up, but she felt their attention bristle on the air. Her 'illness' had frightened them all.

'Yes, quite,' she said. She had concealed her feelings for most of her life; it was just a matter of getting back into practice.

It was three days since her resurrection, but William was still looking at her doubtfully, examining her for visible symptoms of decline, she supposed. She was tired – she felt tired all the time, a symptom of grief – and she knew she looked tired, but she didn't think children really noticed much about their parents, even when, like William, they were a born worrier. 'I had a bad headache for a couple of days, that's all,' she said to reassure him. 'Why?'

He wriggled a little. 'Well, I have something important to ask you – you and Dad – and I didn't want to – you know – if you weren't feeling the thing, upset you.'

Edward put aside his paper. 'What have you been up to?' he asked sternly. 'Out with it! Have you robbed a bank?'

It was a joke – William was the good child, the studious one, the one who would never bring you grief. But Peter perked up at once and said, 'Gosh, have you? Super! What one was it? It'll be topping to have a real criminal in the family! Did you wear a mask? Where's the loot?'

'Be *quiet*, Peter,' said Beattie. 'What did you want to ask, William?'

'We're all ears, old chap,' said Edward.

The assurance seemed to set William back rather than encourage him. He chewed his lip while he tried to assemble his thoughts, standing with his hands clasped behind his back like a naval cadet. He had been growing again, Beattie thought dispassionately. He would never be as tall as David – more the lean and lanky type – but his trouser legs were now half an inch too short.

'Spit it out,' Edward urged.

'Well, you see,' William said, 'we had a chap come to address us at work yesterday, in the dinner break, in the canteen. A chap from the RFC.'

'An airman? Super!' Peter cried.

'Well, he was actually a pilot, but not at the Front. He's responsible for training new pilots. And *he* said—'

Oh, no, Beattie thought. Aloud, she said calmly, 'You're too young.'

'*Please* listen, Mother. You see, this officer said they desperately need more pilots, and even though I'm working in aircraft design, and I know it's important, well, I can do that *after* the war. The real need now is for flyers, and that's something I *can* do to help the war effort. I'll be eighteen in February—'

Edward glanced automatically at Beattie. Of course, as a man, he felt differently about these things. He was proud that his son wanted to go and fight, but she would inevitably think only of the danger. So he said, 'The lower conscription age doesn't come in until April. We can talk about it then.'

'But, Dad, this chap said that you can enlist when you're seventeen in the Reserve, and get started on your training right away, and then you can go straight to France when you're eighteen and a half. Enlisting now would give me a start on the other men. I could be in France, flying, by the summer. And he said the Germans are bound to start something this spring, and we need to be ready. He said it was *vitally important*.' The last words had left him almost breathless, trying to convey the urgency of his desire.

'Well, I suppose he must know what he's talking about,' Edward said. When the Germans signed the peace with the Russians, it followed that there would be hell to pay on the Western Front. He had not talked about it at home, not wishing to alarm them. But anyone who kept up with affairs could work it out for themselves. Sadie was watching him across the room with knowing eyes.

Beattie was trying to contain herself. All she said, at last, was 'Bobby *died*,' but there was a world of meaning in it.

William looked at her earnestly. 'I know, Mother, and that's *why* I have to go, don't you see?' He glanced at the pilot's watch, which looked so big on his wrist. Father had given it to him after Bobby was killed. 'To finish what he began. I know it's what he would have wanted. It's – it's a *sacred trust.*'

There was a silence. Sadie was watching the scene with compassion for all the players. Peter, silently urging parental consent, was gripping his aeroplane so hard he was in danger of snapping it. William was gazing at the parents as though his honour were at stake

Edward realised, with a sudden access of sympathy, that to his son that was exactly what it was. When he said he *had* to go, it was no device of speech. He looked at Beattie. 'My dear? I know he's young, but we've always brought our boys up to consider their duty. I don't really see that we can refuse him, do you? He'll be called up in any case in a few months.'

William's fist clenched in sudden emotion, and he looked at his mother. 'Mum?' he said softly. She winced inwardly at the childhood appellation. 'Please?'

This war will take everything, she thought. It won't stop until it's consumed every bit of us. But what choice was there? 'All right,' she said.

The boys erupted in celebration. Sadie smiled to herself over her letter. Ada came in to make up the fire, and was practically seized by William to be given the news. She, of course, took it back to the kitchen, whence it wafted upstairs and brought David and Antonia down – they had been having a quiet evening in their own sitting-room.

Beattie looked at David with the now familiar mixture of love and sorrow and longing. The lines of pain were etched deep in his face – he looked ten years older than his real age. He manoeuvred awkwardly on his crutch, and Antonia, awkward herself in pregnancy, seemed always just in the right place to give him a steadying touch. He accepted her help automatically, and Beattie felt a pang of jealousy. But she knew her son better than Antonia knew her husband. He was congratulating William, but he was not pleased about it. How could he be? William had a whole working body, William was to go off to war, as Bobby had done, and perform brave deeds and be a hero, while David, the elder, stayed at home and taught little boys their Latin grammar. She knew that he felt a failure.

'Where will you do your training?' Sadie was asking.

'Well, ground school at Reading, first, for theory,' William answered, 'but then you get sent to a training squadron for flight instruction. And that might even be here,' he added, with a hopeful look at his mother, 'because Coney Warren's going to be a training squadron. So you see, Mother, I might be just round the corner!'

As if that made it any better, Beattie thought. The palliative he offered was so absurdly inadequate that it made her smile, and she saw some of the strain leave William's face, thinking she was happy with the decision at last.

A cold February fog gripped Poperinghe, giving the narrow streets a strange hush, but inside Artemis House there was the usual atmosphere of friendly warmth. 'Ack Harry', as it was nicknamed, had no official status, unlike Talbot House, but its fame had spread so rapidly since its opening the previous November that there were comings and goings all day. Every woman who served in any capacity in the war abroad knew that it was a place she could go to be safe, to take a breath: to meet friends, read a book, write a letter or simply chat to a like-minded sister. There was always tea on the brew and a bed for the night, if needed.

A library of books was beginning to be assembled, some donated, some sent from England, some left behind by those passing through. They had been stacked at first wherever there was room, until Laura had decided something more permanent was needed, and a couple of Tommies – borrowed from the army by that indefatigable friend to Ack Harry, Major Ransley – built shelves all along one wall of the dining-room, designated the 'quiet room'. Periodicals and even comics turned up from time to time, and generally lived in the drawing-room until they disintegrated through much handling.

Many of the women who came to Ack Harry were in uniform – there were VADs, QAIMNs, FANYs, WVRs, WAACs – and it was rumoured there would be WRAFs as well, at some not too distant date. Poperinghe was the jumping-off place for the whole Front, for the women's services as it was for the men's. It was said everybody passed through Pop at some point. The sight of women in military-style uniforms was no longer a surprise, and even the most sticklerish army men did not try to deny that they performed invaluable services.

And there were many others not in uniform but doing sterling work all the same, in nursing, driving, catering, cleaning, secretarial and other capacities. And sometimes it was just women travelling for some purpose of their own who came shyly or briskly to the door looking for a home. Laura and Louisa, the founding geniuses, never asked questions. There was a story behind every face, and sometimes the traveller was glad to share it; others passed through silently and left no mark.

On this particular Thursday, the 7th of February, there was a pleasant buzz. In the quiet room, four ladies from the Women's Legion were having a game of whist, making little sound but the click of cards and the occasional soft comment, like 'My trick, I think.' A civilian volunteer was writing a letter, and a local Belgian was reading a book and making notes from it. In the drawing-room, a lively group consisted of four FANYs stationed nearby and two friends passing through from London whom they had arranged to meet at Ack Harry; and an off-duty nurse was at the piano, playing popular tunes by ear, while her bosom friend leaned on the piano-top in deep reverie, quietly smoking.

They had had to allow smoking, and it had caused a sharp disagreement between Laura and Louisa. Louisa thought it would damage their reputation back home, and lead to parents forbidding their daughters to use Artemis House. Laura said it was simply a fact of life that most women working near the Front smoked, and they wouldn't have any customers if they banned it. Veronica 'Ronnie' Mildmay, their new helper, sided with Laura, which had not gone down well with Louisa; but so many of the girls who arrived there lit up without thinking that it would have proved difficult to stop them, and Louisa had given in with bad grace.

'I should have thought you'd side with me,' she complained to Laura, when they were alone. 'I've been your friend much longer than her.'

Laura looked perplexed. 'It's not a matter of *siding* with anyone,' she protested. 'It's just what seems right and practical.'

She was worried that Louisa seemed so often fractious these days. It had been partly for her sake that Laura had suggested starting up Ack Harry, because their previous incarnation, driving an ambulance back and forth from the Front to the hospital, was proving too much for Louisa's

35

health. But she seemed discontented much of the time, and picked quarrels. Laura had the feeling that sooner or later she would give up Artemis House and go back to England, which would be a shame – they had been together in various war enterprises since 1914.

She seemed serene enough just at the moment, however, leaning against the drawing-room door jamb and listening to the nurse playing 'Let The Great Big World Keep Turning'. The other nurse was quietly crooning the words, slightly out of tune; occasional shrieks of laughter from the FANYs made a counterpoint. Laura had just been refilling the urn and tightening the tap, and came to join her, saying, 'God bless the man who invented the urn! Imagine if we had to keep boiling kettles all day long!'

Louisa turned to her with a smile – unusual enough, these days – and was about to say something, when the front door opened and Ronnie came in, fog jewels in her hair, a swirl of mist sneaking in with her. 'I think it's getting thicker,' she announced.

'Well, shut the door, you're letting it in,' Louisa snapped, the smile disappearing.

Ronnie reached behind her and closed it without looking. She was waving a newspaper. 'I just got this from a nice fellow coming out of Talbot House – fresh from London, only a day old. And guess what? The Representation of the People Act has gone through. It received Royal Assent yesterday.'

The piano-playing stopped, both nurses coming to attention. A whispered 'What did she say?' catching-up went on across the room, and by the time Ronnie had opened the paper to the right place and Laura and Louisa had read it, everyone in the room had heard the news.

Laura looked up. 'I can't believe it! After all these years!' It was hard to take it in. She shoved the paper back at Ronnie, flung her arms round Louisa and gave her a mighty hug. 'We've done it! You've done it, Lou, because you did much more for the movement than I ever did. You must be so proud!'

Louisa released herself irritably and grabbed the paper to go on reading, the others crowding in to peer over her shoulder, chattering excitedly.

Laura, most unlike herself, wanted to dance, to jig, to hug people. She compromised by shaking Ronnie's hand vigorously and saying, 'We've got the vote! Congratulations, Miss Mildmay, on being part of the electorate.'

Ronnie was grinning so hard her smile almost reached her ears. 'Congratulations, Miss Hunter,' she replied in kind. 'We've got the vote!'

Louisa looked up. 'You've got it,' she said sourly. 'All men over twenty-one—'

'Over nineteen if they're serving at the Front,' Ronnie corrected.

Louisa ignored her. '*All* men – but only women over thirty, and only if they're householders. So thank you very much. You've got the vote, but *I* haven't.'

Laura tipped her head to one side, puzzled by Louisa's lack of pleasure. Even if she *didn't* have the vote, it was a huge step forward for womankind. 'I'm sorry you sold your aunt's house,' she said, 'but you still have the money. You can buy another one day. Darling Lou, do try to look a little pleased!'

The women from the quiet room had been attracted by the hullabaloo, and were asking questions, so the news had to be repeated and the same joyful exclamations given vent to.

But in the middle of it, there was a thunderous knocking on the front door, and Laura left the circle of celebration and went to answer it.

Standing before her was a corporal driver, and behind him, in the fog, she could make out a large motor-car with some uniformed officers in the back seat, and a very obvious flat tyre. It was a frequent hazard on these roads, increasingly potholed and frequently littered with sharp debris discarded by passing columns.

'Sorry to bother you, miss,' said the corporal, 'but we got a bit o' trouble.'

'So I see,' said Laura. 'Do you want me to change it for you?'

He reeled. 'That won't be necessary, miss,' he said, taking it for a joke, 'but if you was to have such a thing as a torch I could have a loan of? Only it's dark as – as anything, with this fog and all.'

'Of course,' Laura said. 'I'll go and fetch one.'

They kept a torch in the hall-stand drawer for emergency use. She grabbed that, put on her coat and, catching Ronnie's enquiring eye, said, 'Some chaps with a puncture. I'll just give them a hand,' and went out.

The corporal had got out the jack and was putting it in place. With a glance at the greatcoats and caps in the back, Laura said loudly, 'Perhaps your passengers would get out. That would make it easier.'

They obeyed without a word, and stood to one side watching while the corporal got down on his knees, and Laura stood behind him, directing the torch light and passing him spanner and nuts as required. The spare, she noted, as she trundled it up, was not much of an improvement. 'Not much tread left on this,' she commented to the corporal.

'No, miss,' he said sadly. 'Tyres don't last no time at all in these parts.'

One of the officers – the younger one – said, 'You know something about motor-cars?'

'I used to drive an ambulance, and maintain it, too. The first thing I did when war broke out was take a course in driving and motor-repair.'

The corporal tightened the last nut and stood up, brushing

off his knees. 'That's done. Thank you, miss. You been a great help.'

'You have indeed,' said the older officer, coming towards her and offering his hand to shake. He had a faint Scottish accent. 'You may think I was ungallant in not taking your place, but one thing the last four years have taught me is that women can do most things that men can, and delight in showing us so. If I have misjudged in this case, I can only apologise.'

'I was glad to help,' Laura said, amused. She shook the hand, looked up, and registered pale blue eyes, straight nose, white moustache and rounded chin that were hauntingly familiar. There was a slightly quizzical look in the eyes, and the mouth under the moustache was smiling. She had just helped to change the tyre of the commander-in-chief of the British Army.

'Why did you give up driving the ambulance, if it is not impertinent to ask?' Haig enquired.

'She fell to pieces, and we couldn't see immediately how to obtain another vehicle,' Laura answered. 'And I had had an idea to start this place,' she waved a hand behind her, 'so it seemed to be the right time for the change.'

'This place?' Haig looked across her shoulder at the building. 'A.H.' He read the curly initials back-painted on the glass fanlight above the door.

'Ack Harry, sir,' his colleague murmured.

Haig's eyebrows rose. 'Artemis House! Yes, indeed. I've heard of you, of course. I believe you're doing wonderful work.'

'Thank you, sir,' said Laura, flattered their fame had reached so far.

'Providing a service which, alas, the army cannot,' Haig went on. 'But don't think we don't appreciate you. Tell me, is there anything you want? If it can be arranged, I'll see it gets to you.'

'You're very kind,' Laura said, trying desperately to think. An opportunity like this probably wouldn't come again. But they were pretty well set up for most things. Think, woman, think! Don't snub his generosity. There must be something you want. The words seemed to come out of their own accord. 'A gramophone,' she said, and mentally clapped her hand to her forehead. *What did you say that for?* 'We *would* like a gramophone.'

Haig seemed as surprised as she was. 'A gramophone. Well . . .'

She couldn't back down now. 'We were thinking of arranging gramophone concerts, you see, for the women, and for the local people in general. Music can be wonderfully healing to tired spirits.'

'Indeed it can,' said Haig, stiffly. He seemed disconcerted. Probably he had no more idea of how to get hold of a gramophone than she did, thought Laura.

He glanced at his junior, who obligingly tapped his watch and said, 'We ought to be going, sir. The puncture's already made us late.'

Oh, well, Laura thought. Can't be helped.

Haig cleared his throat, rumbled, 'Thank you again, ma'am, for your help,' and hurried back into the car. The corporal gave her a covert grin and a shrug and started up, and the motor disappeared into the fog, just as Ronnie came out to see what was happening.

'Who was that?' she asked, as the taillights winked and disappeared.

'Field Marshal Haig,' said Laura.

Ronnie laughed. 'Of course it was! And was the King with him?'

'Not this time.'

'Ugh, it's horrible out here. Come back in. We're going to have a brew of cocoa to celebrate getting the vote.'

'We haven't got it yet,' Laura said.

'Of course we have – from the moment of Royal Assent. We haven't had a chance to use it yet, but that's no reason not to celebrate.'

Laura linked arms with her and walked back into the house. 'It ought to be champagne,' she said.

'Pity we're a dry house,' said Ronnie.

On Saturdays, from five to nine in the evenings, ladies at Artemis House were allowed to entertain respectable gentlemen in the drawing-room, under supervision of one of the proprietors. So far there had not been many takers of the offer, largely because the visitors were so transient, but on a couple of occasions a girl had used the drawing-room to meet a father or brother in more comfort than was afforded by an hotel or restaurant. But Major Ransley, a surgeon at the local hospital who had helped them at every stage of setting-up, was a frequent visitor on Saturday afternoons. By some alchemy, he managed to get his hours off to coincide with that time more often than could be purely random.

On the Saturday after the great news, he came to visit Laura, Louisa and Ronnie, and they entertained him in the private office. There were no male guests in the drawing-room, so they were not needed there to supervise.

Major Ransley was a great raconteur, and always had amusing tales to tell – or, at least, made everyday occurrences into amusing anecdotes. Even Louisa, who seemed a bit sulky whenever Ransley visited, was induced to smile once or twice. He had just come to the end of a narration, and had sat back in his chair, saying, 'Now it's your turn. Tell me what's been happening to you this week,' when there was a knock at the door.

One of the visitors, a VAD who worked in a canteen, was there, and said, 'There's a parcel arrived for you – a big one. Some men brought it in and left it in the hall.'

They all got up. 'I didn't hear anyone ring the bell,' said Ronnie.

'They just came in,' said the VAD. 'It's a big crate – I don't know how you're going to open it.'

It was indeed a wooden crate about half the size of a tea chest, standing in the middle of the hall where it was in everyone's way. Ronnie walked round it. 'Claw hammer,' she said practically. 'To get the nails out and lever up the lid.' They kept some basic tools in the office, and she went to fetch one.

'I wonder what's in it,' said the VAD. Others had wandered out to see the fun.

'I wonder if it's a bomb,' said one of them.

'Why would anyone want to send us a bomb?' said the first.

'The Germans would. They want to bomb everyone.'

'If the Germans want to bomb us, they can drop one from the sky,' said Laura, and then wished she hadn't. That wasn't a thought to put in anyone's head, this close to the Front.

Ronnie returned with the hammer, and Ransley gently took it from her hand and set about levering out the nails. Ronnie caught Laura's eye and grinned. Some modern women couldn't bear to be helped, but she never minded someone holding a door for her.

The nails were out, the lid was lifted, the straw packing inside removed and, reaching in with his long arms, Ransley lifted out a dark blue leather box.

Laura knew what it was. 'It's a gramophone,' she said with pleasure. So he had kept his promise!

Louisa came forward to examine it. 'It's a beauty,' she breathed, lifting the lid. 'Who on earth sent us this?' She looked sharply at Ransley. 'Was it you?'

'No, no, I assure you. I only wish I'd thought of it.'

Ronnie had lifted out the horn, and said, 'There's another box in here. It's heavy.' It was covered with red leather, and opening the lid revealed a collection of disc recordings. She read the labels. 'All classical,' she said. 'Beethoven, Tchaikovsky, Mendelssohn. Whoever sent it doesn't want us to be dancing.'

'Isn't there a card?'

'Here it is,' said Ransley, finding the envelope that was under the gramophone lid. He handed it to Laura, who opened it and read it out.

'"Dear Madam, I hope you will forgive the delay in sending you the promised gramophone. I had to have it sent from London as there was not a suitable machine to be had in Ypres. I wish you well in your concerts, and in all your endeavours. Yours sincerely."'

'Yours sincerely *who*?' Louisa demanded, beside herself with curiosity.

'It's signed Douglas Haig.'

'Who's he?' Louisa said, and then her eyes widened. 'Not *the* Douglas Haig?'

'My goodness, you do have friends in high places,' Ransley said.

Ronnie started laughing. 'You *said* it was him, and I didn't believe you! Laura changed a flat tyre for him one day,' she explained to Ransley. 'This must be his thank-you.'

'I didn't change his tyre, just held the torch. And this is for Artemis House, not for me. He said we were doing good work and he wanted to help.'

'You never told me,' Louisa complained.

'I didn't think he meant it. And I didn't think you'd believe me,' Laura said.

'What's he like?' Louisa asked.

Laura considered. 'Just the way he looks on the news reels. But a little bit Scottish. I bet one of the records he's sent is "Fingal's Cave".'

CHAPTER FOUR

She had come back to the world. She functioned. She walked,
ate, spoke, worked – but she felt as though there were a
layer of gauze between her and the world, through which
she saw it slightly blurred, heard it slightly muffled, felt it
not at all. She understood, now, the blank look she had
observed in women who had been widowed by the war. You
carried on – but a bit of you had been left behind, the bit
that made the world brightly coloured, immediate, joyful
and painful.

She didn't think anyone else had noticed that she was not
really there. What did any of them know about what went
on inside other people? As long as she filled the space that
was marked 'the mistress' or 'mother' or 'Mrs Hunter',
people looked no further. As for Edward, she had withdrawn
herself from him so long ago, he must be used to it by now.
She tried to look into her heart and see what she felt about
him, but it was too bound up with Louis, guilt and frustration, gratitude and resentment. Mostly what she felt was a
sort of vague relief that she no longer had to hide her daily
actions from him. It was one small burden less to carry.

She had to act normally, and seem to be pleased about
the coming investiture. Once she might have been excited
by the prospect of being *Lady* Hunter. Now it meant nothing
to her. But she was glad that Edward's endeavours were
being recognised, and so when he said – quite casually, as

if it were not very important – that she might like something new to wear for the occasion, she curbed her first response, that she had plenty of clothes already, and told him that it was a good idea.

He seemed pleased. 'You should ring Diana, have her go with you. She'll tell you what's right to wear to the Palace.'

'She's never been to the Palace, as far as I know.'

'But she will go one day. And she knows people who have. Have lunch together – make it a little outing. It will do you both good.'

As he said it, the time he had tried to do the same thing jumped into his head, disturbing him. *Where had she been? Why had she lied to him?* He had wanted to do something nice for her, and instead had received a headful of unwelcome thoughts and horrid suspicions. He hated himself for suspecting her of—

Of what? Of having an affair? It was the only thing a husband or wife had to conceal from each other, wasn't it? But it was crazy, unthinkable. Respectable women in their forties, mothers of large families, mainstays of their communities, did not do things like that. And Beattie, above all, would never, *never* do such a thing. To imagine her with a stranger, after all these years, was impossible.

He had to put it down to war weariness, a *crise de nerfs*. Still, it left him with the unwanted, nagging question: *where had she been that day? And all the other days?* He tried not to think about it, and was so busy he managed most of the time. You had to carry on – but there was a little piece of you in a quiet corner of your mind that cried for attention, like a dog locked in the cellar.

The snow was mostly gone from Highclere, and in Westleigh, down in the valley, the roads were clear, but it was foggy. It appeared as a mizzling prick of rain on the windscreen; and together with the low level of light, it made visibility poor. Mrs Cuthbert was for abandoning the attempt, but Sadie had wound up her nerve for it.

'After all,' she said, 'I will have to drive through rain and fog at some point in my life. And I *do* want to be useful to you.'

'You're useful now,' said Mrs Cuthbert. 'And you don't need a certificate to drive – just the licence.' They had stopped and bought it at the post office on the way to Westleigh. Mrs Cuthbert offered to pay the five shillings, but Sadie didn't think that would be right.

As for passing the Automobile Association's proficiency test: 'People never think girls can do things unless they can prove it,' Sadie said. 'Having a certificate will make that easier. I really wish I'd learned to drive sooner. My aunt Laura went and took a driving course first thing when the war broke out. And now she's in France,' she concluded wistfully.

'Would you like to go to France?' Mrs Cuthbert asked.

'Well, it *would* be an adventure,' Sadie said; then, seeing her expression, added, 'My father would never allow it anyway. And I know the work at Highclere is important. I'd just like to do something *more* for the war effort, that's all.'

Mrs Cuthbert said nothing, but she looked a little troubled. When Sadie had asked her to teach her to drive, she had been delighted with the idea of having another driver at Highclere, where she broke and schooled horses for the army remount service. There was only herself and Podrick, the head groom, but he disliked driving so much it was a punishment to ask him. Her husband Horace was willing in an emergency to pilot the motor-car, very slowly, provided there were no narrow tracks, tight corners or gates involved, but he wouldn't even look at the horse-box. So having someone young, vigorous and steady-nerved to call on would be invaluable. She had been the first to suggest the proficiency test, and Sadie had jumped at the idea – she plainly liked accumulating skills and having certificates to prove it. She had already passed the Red Cross First Aid and Home Nursing examinations; she talked wistfully of acquiring a Royal Aero Club aviators' ticket one day. That seemed in the realms of wishful thinking, but Mrs Cuthbert wouldn't entirely put it past her.

But if Sadie, *with* a driving certificate, left her to try something new . . . Just now Mrs Cuthbert would have been glad to give up the test appointment and go home. It was cold, foggy and damp, and the roads were slippery. She had to operate the windscreen wiper constantly with frozen fingers, and still it was like driving through soup.

But Sadie, with the resilience of youth, said, 'I'm sure it will clear up soon.'

Inside the AA office in Church Street, the examiner glanced at the window and suggested coming back another day. There was a small fire in the office, and its zone of warmth reached as far as his chair behind the desk. Sadie gave Mrs Cuthbert a glance that said quite clearly what she thought him. *Chicken-hearted.*

Mrs Cuthbert spoke for her. 'I think, as we've come all this way, we might as well carry on with it,' she said firmly.

So Mr Beasley had no choice but to put on his coat, gloves, and a deerstalker-type hat with lappets, and follow them out to the waiting motor. He seemed so miserable that Mrs Cuthbert felt obliged to try to converse with him.

'I suppose it is a surprise to you to have ladies coming for the test,' she began.

'I hardly see anything *but* ladies these days,' he said gloomily. 'If the war goes on much longer, I fear we shall see our *patrolmen* become women.'

Mrs Cuthbert suppressed the only retort that came to mind and climbed into the back, Sadie slid behind the wheel, and Mr Beasley got in beside her with an audible sigh. 'Very well,' he said. 'We begin.'

Fifteen minutes later they were back. 'Congratulations, Miss Hunter,' Beasley said, fumbling for the car door handle as soon as Sadie had applied the hand brake. 'You've passed.'

'Are you sure?' Sadie asked anxiously. It had seemed absurdly easy, and she didn't want any omission to taint her precious certificate.

Beasley paused in the act of closing the car door to say firmly, 'I am an expert in these matters, Miss Hunter. It doesn't take me long to tell if someone is proficient. And if you can drive in this weather, you can drive in anything.' The last was added in a mumble, almost lost as he hurried across the pavement to the office.

Sadie and Mrs Cuthbert followed him, and waited while he filled in the certificate, signed it, and stamped it with the official AA stamp. Sadie folded it carefully inside the sulphur-yellow cover of her new licence, feeling oddly flat.

Mrs Cuthbert must have sensed it. 'And now,' she said as they walked out again into the grey, cold day, 'for a cele-bratory tea at the Queen's Head.'

'Oh goody,' Sadie said, brightening. She flourished her licence and certificate, and added. 'And then I can drive you home.'

They had visitors at The Elms on Sunday the 17th. First to arrive was William, most unexpectedly, from Reading, proud in his uniform. When they exclaimed that they hadn't expected a visit so soon, he explained that it wasn't leave, but that they didn't have any lessons at the ground school on Saturday so could do as they liked. After morning parade he had dashed out and jumped on a train. 'I have to be back tonight, of course. But I couldn't resist coming and seeing you all. Only,' he looked awkward, 'I shall have to borrow my fare home from somebody.'

'Didn't you get a return?' Sadie said, surprised.

'On the train from Reading to Paddington, yes, but I didn't have enough left for a return on the Underground.'

'I think we can find a few shillings for you,' Edward said. 'But I am worried that you've run through your money already, when it's only the middle of the month.'

William blushed richly. 'Oh, Dad! I know it's bad, but it's just that – you see, there are a lot of little things to buy when you first get there that you don't reckon on and – and chaps stand you things and you have to stand them back – and . . .' He looked down. 'I suppose I didn't manage awfully well. I'll do better next month, honestly I will.'

Edward suppressed a smile, and said, 'I know you will, my son.' He never had any doubts about William becoming a rake-hell. His conscience had always been an overgrown organ.

Sadie gave him a fierce hug. 'It's so good to see you – I'll give you the fare myself if I have to! Tell us everything! How is ground school? Are the other fellows nice? Do you sleep in a dormitory? What's the food like?'

He hugged her back, laughing. 'One question at a time! The grub's all right, but not a patch on home. What are we having today? I do hope it's roast beef and Yorkshire pudding. I've been thinking about that all the way from Reading.'

'It is,' said Beattie. 'At least, that's what I ordered.'

'And what's for pudding?'

'I can't remember,' Beattie said, perfectly well aware of what was on his mind. 'Perhaps you'd better go and ask Cook.'

'Well, I will, then,' he said, and dashed off to the kitchen, to show off his uniform and be rewarded with a slice of cake to tide him over – getting up early and travelling had made him ravenous.

Edward looked at Beattie with a smile. 'I think he's growing again.'

'That's the army's problem now, not ours,' she replied.

She sounded like her old self, but though her face was composed and serene, her eyes held no spark. Her lips smiled at him, but nothing else did.

The second visitor was Edward's nephew Donald, his sister Sonia's eldest, who had been wounded in December near Armentières, and had now recovered enough to go back to his unit.

'Light duties only for a couple of weeks,' he said, 'and then it'll be back to normal. I haven't told Mumsy that bit,' he added, with a grin. 'She thinks I'll be pottering about behind the line for the rest of the year.'

Sadie thought he didn't look fully fit, but it might only have been his hospital pallor – soldiers were generally so brown. 'I expect pottering is useful to the war effort, too,' she said.

David had come down for luncheon in his cousin's honour. He looked sour, and muttered, 'Some of us would be glad even of that.' But only Sadie heard him.

The third visitor was Christopher Beresford, whom Edward had invited some time ago for luncheon that day. He was with the Ministry of Agriculture, and had worked with Edward for a time in the campaign to encourage greater food production. Their mutual liking had developed to the extent that he was now a family friend, and he had been squiring Sadie for some months. There was soon an eager three-way conversation between Donald, who knew what it was like at the Front, and William and Beresford, who didn't. Peter listened wistfully.

'It'll all be over before I get a chance to go,' he complained.

'That's what Duck says,' Donald said, noticing him kindly. Duck was his younger brother, Douglas. 'He's joining the cadets now he's seventeen, and desperately hoping the war will go for on another year at least.'

'When do you think it will end?' William asked his cousin urgently.

50

The smile in Donald's eyes faded. 'God knows,' he said tersely; and added, 'Not soon.'

After luncheon, everyone went out for a walk around the garden. There were no flowers now, or even lawns – it had all been dug up and put down to vegetables. A garden in winter is not pretty anyway, and this one had few features to attract, but Beresford could not help being interested, and Edward was glad to discuss planting plans and yields in detail. So it was not until they encountered the gardener, Munt, who asked William about ground school, a subject on which the young man could be expansive, that Beresford was able to hang back for a private word with Sadie.

'What do you mean to do with your new licence?' he asked. It had been a topic of conversation around the table. 'You *were* joking about being a driver in France, weren't you?'

She had been, but now said mischievously, 'Why should you mind? It would be the most exciting thing that could happen to me.'

'I'm not sure I want exciting things to happen to you,' he said. 'They could be dangerous.'

'They don't let women anywhere near the front line,' she said, with a hint of impatience.

'I don't know how to break it to you, but front lines move. And the Germans have aeroplanes, from what I've heard. They strafe and bomb.'

'Then it's William you should be worried for.'

'William isn't my—' he began, and paused. He didn't know what word to use. He had been taking Sadie out for some months now, but he was still not sure of what their relationship really was. He liked her enormously, enjoyed her company, and he knew she liked him; but he felt he was on the brink of falling in love with her, and he was not confident that she would welcome that. He had never kissed her. They had held hands once or twice, briefly, but she had

51

always broken the contact first. Their conversations were widely varied and interesting, but impersonal.

He had discussed his problem with his sister Catherine when she was home on leave at Christmas – she was with the FANY out in France. They shared a flat in Baker Street.

'It sounds to me as though Miss Sadie is "not out",' Catherine had said.

'She's nineteen,' Christopher had objected. 'And nobody comes out any more, not now there's a war on.'

'Stoopid! I meant spiritually. Or mentally,' Catherine said. 'She's still asleep. She doesn't know men exist, except papas and brothers and people in officialdom.'

'And which am I?' he asked.

'Brother, I should think.'

'But I don't want to be her brother. What shall I do?'

Catherine examined him. 'You're a darling boy, and not bad-looking, in a wholesome sort of way.'

'Wholesome!' he protested.

'Those freckles and that boyish smile. I mean, you're not Douglas Fairbanks or Ramon Novarro. But any girl would be lucky to get you. Maybe you should just try kissing her. See if she wakes up.'

'I'm afraid life in the FANY is coarsening you, Cat,' he said gravely.

'It may well do,' said Catherine sadly. 'I certainly feel a lot older than when I went away. What's wrong with kissing her, anyway?'

'Nothing wrong with it. I want to, awfully. But I don't want to frighten her off. And her father might not approve. I think he lets me take her out because he trusts me with her.'

'Oh dear, then you really are a brother! It seems a hope-less case.'

Here and now, in the garden, Sadie was looking at him

with those dark brown eyes, waiting for him to finish the sentence. 'William isn't your what?' she asked.

He caught hold of her hand, and drew her closer. 'Sadie, there's something I've been wanting to tell you for a long time. You see, I—'

But she pulled her hand back, turned her head away. 'Please don't,' she said awkwardly.

'You don't know what I was going to say,' he protested feebly. He saw that she knew very well.

'I like being your friend, and spending time with you, but it can't be anything else.'

'Why?' he asked bluntly.

She hesitated. She couldn't tell *him* about John Courcy. And what was there to tell, anyway? John saw her as a horse-mad little girl. It was ironic that it was Christopher who saw her as old enough to fall in love.

'I'm too young,' she said at last. She saw he was going to argue, and added, 'I don't want to – to get mixed up with that sort of thing. Not yet.'

He gave in. 'It's all right. I don't want to rush you. We can just stay friends, until you want something more.'

'I'm sorry,' she said.

'Don't be. I was being a cad.'

She managed a smile. 'You? You wouldn't know how.' And she meant it.

On Sunday the 24th it rained peltingly, torrentially, all day. Sadie kept going to the window to gaze anxiously at the unbroken pewter skies, the dripping trees, the gathering puddles. She was worried about the investiture the next day, and how her parents' finery would be kept dry for the great moment.

'Umbrellas,' Peter said simply.

'But they'll still get splashed,' Sadie mourned. Father would be in morning coat and silk hat, Mother in a dress

53

and jacket of plum silk and a black velvet hat with a hackle. It would be awful if they arrived all draggled and rain-spotted on Father's big day.

But the weather wore itself out in the night, like a storm of weeping, and the 25th dawned calm, quiet, sadly grey, but dry. Everyone gathered in the hall to see them off, and Cook was so moved at the thought of the master becoming a knight, her eyes filled with tears. The word 'knight' had had a powerful effect on Emily, whose imagination fed on stories of gallantry and romance. She thought the master was looking more handsome, suddenly – taller, even. 'He'd look grand on a white horse,' she murmured.

Having waved them down the road, Ada closed the door and the party dispersed. 'Lot of fuss about nothing,' Ethel muttered, heading for the kitchen to pick up her basket.

'How can you say that?' Ada said indignantly. 'It's a great honour!'

'Won't make any difference to *us*, will it? Still having to do more work for the same pay. D'you think *Lady* Hunter's going to get another housemaid to replace Lillian, when *Mrs* Hunter wouldn't? Saving their money to spend on themselves.'

Two spots of colour appeared in Ada's cheeks. 'I won't listen to that sort of Bolshevik talk! You should be ashamed, so kind as they've been to you.'

Ethel didn't answer – feeling, as it happened, a little ashamed at the reminder. She grabbed her basket and headed upstairs.

'That girl!' Ada complained to Cook.

'What's she done now?' Cook asked, sharpening her big knife in preparation for tackling a large piece of beef shoulder.

But Ada was not a tell-tale. All she said was 'The sooner she marries Frank Hussey and leaves this house the better.'

Cook snorted. 'The way she treats him, he'll get fed up and change his mind.'

'But he likes the way she treats him,' Ada said gloomily. 'The big daftie.'

Edward and Beattie arrived at the Palace at ten thirty. Ushers received them and showed them up wide, red-carpeted stairways, past soldiers from the Household Cavalry in full fig, and into the Green Drawing Room. Gradually all those to be honoured gathered, each with an invited guest. Most of the men were in uniform; the women, in their various bests, showed a less homogeneous aspect, and looked at each other with nervous smiles, checking to see if they had got it right. A little before eleven the Lord Chamberlain appeared to conduct the honorands to the ballroom annexe, while the guests were escorted by an usher to the main room, where there were rows of gilt chairs, each with a programme on its red velvet seat, and a military band up in the gallery playing quietly through a programme of light music.

At exactly eleven the King entered with a small entourage of guards and equerries. He looked, in uniform, exactly as he did on the newsreels, stocky and bearded and eerily familiar. The ceremony began. The knighthoods came first, and Beattie watched as Edward walked from the annexe to the centre, bowed to the King, advanced to the investiture stool, knelt and was touched on each shoulder by the King's sword. She found herself unexpectedly moved by it; something inside her contracted as if at a sudden shock, as if she felt the touch of the sword on her own shoulders. Edward, her husband, the man she had shared her life with all these years, was being honoured by the King, and thus by the whole nation. A feeling towards him that had been suppressed for years stirred, disturbing her. She had been mute and numb since Louis died. She did not want to feel again.

Edward rose, and the King spoke a few words to him, then shook his hand – the dismissal. Edward stepped backwards, bowed again, and walked out at the other side. His place was taken swiftly and efficiently by the next man. Once Edward had gone, Beattie had no more interest. She watched the monotonous succession of strangers – enter, bow, medal, handshake, bow, exit – and listened to the boringly soothing music, and could only entertain herself by wondering what the King said to each, and calculating who was spoken to the longest. Edward, she thought possessively, had had quite a good 'go' of the royal attention. She wanted to think him more honoured than all these others.

It was over by twelve. Ushers gathered them up and reunited them with their loved ones in the Picture Gallery. Edward watched her approach with an uncertain look, as though not sure whether she would be pleased for him or not, and she felt a pang of remorse. It must have been hard for him lately to anticipate her mood. She determined to be gay for him, on this day of days. 'Sir Edward, I believe?' she said lightly.

He smiled, and there was relief in it. 'Lady Hunter, I presume?' he responded in kind.

She tucked her hand under his arm. 'Lady Hunter! It will take some getting used to.' They were being politely urged towards the exit. The Palace had done with them. They did not belong here.

'What now?' she asked.

'A taxi to the Ritz, and luncheon,' he said.

'Just us?' she asked. She wasn't sure she could sustain the intimacy so long.

But when he said, 'No, Beth and Sonia are joining us,' she felt guilty, because probably he had thought the same. A husband and wife ought to be able to be alone together. She and Edward used to be good at it. Before the war. The war had changed everything.

Or perhaps he had just wanted to share the moment more widely. His sister Sonia was a good-natured fool, but his cousin Beth was always good company; and he was fond of them both. She decided to believe that that was what it was. They must be the only two of the family who were not busy – it was, after all, a weekday. Diana might have come, she thought, and wondered where she was.

Diana was, at that moment, at home, taking luncheon with her husband. A telegram had been delivered announcing his imminent arrival.

'I wasn't expecting you!' she cried, when he arrived.

'I wasn't expecting myself. But I got a forty-eight, and decided the one thing I wanted to do with it was to see you and George, so I got up at the crack of dawn. I hope you appreciate the effort.'

'I do,' Diana said. She knew he didn't like to get up early, forgetting that in the army he would generally have to. He looked thin, she thought, and there was something different about his face – a firmness, perhaps; a sharper focus. He looked, she decided, like a grown-up, where before he had seemed still a youth.

'Now, we mustn't waste a minute,' he was saying. 'I'm going up to see George and have a bath, while you order luncheon, and have them sponge my uniform and polish my boots. I'll lunch in my dressing-gown. Then I'll get dressed and we'll go out and have some fun.'

'When do you have to leave?'

'Tomorrow after luncheon. But let's not think about that. I have a whole day of civilisation to enjoy.'

'What would you like for lunch?'

'No soup. Chicken or cutlets and some vegetables. Fried potatoes. Whatever sweet they can rustle up. And some cheese.'

'Wine?'

'Tell Heating a bottle of the '02 Latour, and whatever he thinks with the cheese.' He kissed her smackingly. 'You look beautiful, and you smell even better. I can't tell you how

57

horrid the war smells. What were you planning to do, before you got my telegram?'

'Benefit concert in aid of soldiers' widows,' she told him.

'Lucky escape for you,' he said.

Over luncheon she asked him how he had got leave, even for forty-eight hours. 'We've just moved to new billets,' he said, 'and we start training on Wednesday, so there was no need for me for a couple of days.'

'Training in what?' she asked, to show an interest.

'Trench warfare.'

'I thought you already knew how to do that.'

'Ah, but that was when we were attacking. Now the Germans are building up to attack, and we shall have to learn to defend – a whole new skill.'

'But – if the Germans attack, won't it be dangerous?'

He grinned. 'War *is* dangerous, dear – didn't anyone tell you?'

She flushed. 'Don't joke.'

'I wasn't. But defending is easier than attacking, everyone knows that. That's why the Germans managed to resist us all these years. Now the boot will be on the other foot. Don't worry – I lead a charmed life. Now, tell me how it is with you. You are looking very bonny. Is the new little one behaving itself?'

She was accustomed to her husband's odd ways, like talking about pregnancy rather than ignoring the whole process as men were supposed to. 'I seem to have stopped feeling sick,' she said. 'That's probably why I look better. So he isn't being any trouble just now.'

'He? I was rather hoping he might be a she this time.'

'I thought we needed an heir and a spare?'

He waved that away. 'War seems to strip away a lot of nonsense. Dynastic considerations don't seem so important at the Front, somehow. I'd like a little girl to pet and spoil. I'd like to have her sit on my lap and put her arms round my neck and call me "Daddy".' He smiled at her. 'A little girl, if possible, who looks just like you.'

'You say such nice things.'

'It's what I'm known for.'

'You didn't used to,' she mentioned.

'Oh, don't remind me. I was a cad. And worse, an ass. Whatever you think of the world, it's the only one there is, and if you don't try to fit in with it, you hurt yourself and everyone else. I'm making amends now – and you're going to get the full benefit of the new me, I promise.'

She often did not understand what he was talking about, and it no longer bothered her. Like a dog, she listened to the tone of the speech, not the words in it. 'I'd quite like a girl, too. But another boy would be nice, a brother for George to play with. I'd be happy with either.'

'That's a good thing,' he said gravely, 'because "either" is certain to be what you'll get.'

She saw from the gleam in his eye that it was a joke, so she laughed, and said, 'Where shall we go when you're dressed?'

'First we dress you. I don't like that outfit. I want you to dazzle when I have you on my arm. And when I've selected your wardrobe for the day, we'll go and promenade and find out who's in Town, then tea at the Savoy, cocktails at the Café Royale, and gather some friends for dinner and dancing. It sounds like a lot of eating and drinking,' he added, 'so it's a good job you're not feeling sick any more.'

59

CHAPTER FIVE

Luncheon at the Ritz was lively. Sonia, who tended towards somnolence, was wide awake and chatty; Beth was droll, and sparked Edward into animation; and several glasses of champagne loosened and warmed Beattie so that she found herself enjoying the occasion. They were at the coffee stage, lingering over it, while Edward and Beth addressed a fine cognac, when Diana and Rupert came in. Beattie saw them first, and waved to catch their attention, and they came over. But she had seen the look of surprise on Diana's face: they had not known Edward would be here – probably they were looking for their own friends.

Two more chairs were brought, and Diana took a cup of coffee, while Rupert accepted a glass of the cognac, for the purpose, it seemed, of raising a toast to 'our newest knight – and, Lord knows, he deserves it!'

They didn't stay long, and when they left, the party broke up. Sonia invited them all back to Kensington, but Edward said that he must call in at the office for an hour or two, and since Beth had a committee meeting to go to, Beattie said she would go home. She walked with Edward the short distance to his office in Piccadilly, then said there was no point in his escorting her any further. She would go down into the Tube. But he said, 'In your finery? No, a cab to Baker Street at least. I'll hail one for you.' He took her hand and pressed it and said, 'This day would have meant nothing to me if you hadn't been here to share it.'

She ached with the knowledge of her duplicity. A corner of her heart still called pitifully for Louis; but he was gone, and Edward deserved all her attention and loyalty. She determined to shut Louis out of her thoughts from then on, to be the wife to Edward she should always have been. She pressed his hand in return, and said, 'I don't deserve you.'

The warmth in his eyes penetrated her in a way that both pleased and frightened her. She longed to care for him, but was afraid of what it would cost. 'Lady Hunter!' he murmured.

'I keep forgetting that,' she said; and, trying for lightness, 'I wonder if they'll charge more at Hetherington's when they know.'

On the ride through the busy streets, she stared at the crowds passing and wondered about all those people and their lives. So busy, all going somewhere, each a separate universe of cares and joys and responsibilities, friends, families – bereavements. How many of them concealed the agony of loss behind a public face? You had to carry on. She had a sudden sharp sense of peril escaped, a near miss. A shell had been going to destroy her family, and everyone in her personal universe. Louis's death had been the price of salvation.

It was a normal Saturday evening at Ack Harry, and there were gentlemen visitors. In the drawing-room, a rather senior QAIMNS sister was talking quietly in a corner to her brother. Two FANYs were entertaining the male cousin of one of them, casting sidelong looks at the sister as if half afraid she would come over and intervene.

A VAD cook from a canteen in the Grande Place had come shyly to ask if she could bring her fiancé, a private in the ASC, because they had nowhere else to go, since the weather was too miserable for walking about, and it cost too much to keep sitting in restaurants. They now sat in another corner, very upright and ill at ease, but grateful to be in the warm.

And Laura, the official chaperone for the evening, was playing a game of chess with Major Ransley. He was sitting back, exaggeratedly relaxed, with the faint, amused smile of one who has laid a trap and knows his opponent is about to step into it.

Laura surveyed the board with a ferocious scowl. 'I can't see what you've done,' she cried in frustration. 'Dash it, I *know* you've done something, but I can't see it!' His smile broadened, and she looked up in time to catch it. 'It's going to be checkmate, isn't it?'

'In two moves,' he confirmed.

'No matter what I do?'

'Oh, no. There *is* a defence. But you won't see it.'

'It isn't very gallant of you to be so sure.'

'But *do* allow me to be better than you at one poor little thing,' he urged. 'You are so capable in every field, it's daunting for a mere mortal man.'

'Not in *every* field,' she said. 'I can't sing worth a lick.'

'A noble admission. But you play the piano, which more than cancels that out.'

'And I'm not much of a cook.'

'Ah! Now, there you *have* given me slack. As it happens, I'm rather good at cooking. I should—'

At that moment they were interrupted. With another part of her mind, Laura had heard the rap on the front door, but she had also heard Ronnie's voice in the entrance hall, which told her she was dealing with it. There had followed the muffled tones of a man, and now Ronnie was coming towards her, followed by an officer in greatcoat and cap, removing his leather gloves as he approached.

'Laura, you have a visitor,' Ronnie announced. 'He *says*

he's your nephew.' The slight emphasis suggested either scepticism or conveyed a warning, Laura didn't know which.

But the officer removed his cap and said, 'Aunt Laura, what pure pleasure!' and she saw it was Rupert.

She stood up to shake his hand. 'What are you doing here?'

'Just passing through. I've been up to Headquarters, and now I'm on my way back to my unit. Decided to break my journey, thought I'd have a look at the famous Artemis House.'

'Well, it's very nice to see you,' she said, trying not to sound doubtful. She had always been wary of him, knowing his volatility. You never knew what he was going to say next, and in social situations he was like a faulty hand-grenade, likely to go off at any moment and cause havoc. But though there was a twinkle in his eye, and he had called her 'aunt', which she knew he meant as a joke, he had an air of more steadiness than before. Perhaps marriage and fatherhood had slowed him down. 'Major Ransley, may I introduce my niece's husband, the Earl Wroughton? Major Ransley is practically a founding father of Ack Harry.'

'Oh, nothing of the sort,' Ransley protested. 'I was lucky enough to be able to help a little at the beginning.'

'Nonsense! We would never have got off the ground without you,' Laura said robustly.

Ransley offered his hand. 'Captain.'

'Major,' said Rupert, shaking it.

'Sit, join us,' said Laura, and Ransley quickly brought another chair.

Rupert sat, surveyed the board, and said, 'Who's winning?'

'He is,' Laura said. 'I've never beaten him yet.'

'Ah yes,' Rupert said. 'I see the trap. Shall I tell you how to get out of it? Or would that be cheating?'

Laura laughed. 'Tell me! If I don't cheat, I shall never win, and I don't know if I can bear the constant humiliation.'

'She won't allow me one tiny little foothold on superiority,' Ransley complained. 'In solidarity with our sex, captain, I beg you won't help her.'

'Family loyalty must prevail,' Laura told him. 'Or will you pull rank on him and *order* him not to?'

Rupert intercepted the look that passed between them during the exchange, and grew thoughtful. 'I think I had better not interfere. Is your friend Miss Cotton not here?'

'It's her evening off,' said Laura. 'She's in her room, reading.'

'Not joining in the fun?'

'We don't get much opportunity for solitude here,' Laura explained. 'She likes to be alone when she can.'

'I see.' He looked from Laura to Ransley and back, and said, 'Do you know, I think I may have made rather an ass of myself.'

'How's that?' Ransley asked politely.

'Oh, making certain assumptions,' Rupert said lightly. 'And the really amusing part is that I based my whole life's strategy on them.'

'Rupert, what *are* you talking about?' Laura said impatiently.

'Nothing that need concern you, dear aunt,' Rupert said smoothly. 'And, as it happens, it has all worked out quite well. Fool's luck, I suppose.'

'Well, I don't pretend to understand you,' said Laura. She looked at Ransley. 'I'm afraid Lord Wroughton is known for his wit, and the pleasure he takes in confounding people. It's probably best to pay no attention.'

'*Most* unhandsome of you,' Rupert responded promptly. 'Now the major will think me unsound. And we've only just met.'

Ransley looked amused. 'But I know you already by reputation, captain,' he said. 'One of the most dashing young officers of last year's campaigns. I read something about a certain action in Cambrai. You were a lieutenant then. Was it for that that you got your promotion?'

'Oh, they have to give stars to someone,' Rupert said, in the expected throw-away manner.

'I'm sure you deserved it. Are you staying long in Poperinghe?'

'No, I'm quite literally passing through – I have a train to catch in an hour or so. But I couldn't come to Pop without making my number with Miss Hunter.' He gave Laura a civil nod. 'And I'm very glad I did. It has proved a revelation.'

'On what subject?' Laura asked suspiciously.

'Why, on your new venture here, Artemis House. What else?' Rupert said innocently.

'Well, I wish Artemis House could offer you a drink,' Laura said, not entirely convinced. 'But I'm afraid we have only cocoa.'

Rupert shuddered. 'I've survived this long in the war without drinking cocoa, so I had better not break my luck now. And as I don't wish to play Monsieur de Trop to you charming people, I shall take my leave, and see if I can't find a brandy somewhere between here and the railway station.' He stood, and looked again from one to the other with a private and satisfied smirk. 'Glad to have had the opportunity of making your acquaintance, Major.'

'Likewise,' said Ransley, shaking his hand.

'And perhaps we'll meet in London, my esteemed aunt,' Rupert concluded.

When he had gone, Ransley said, 'He does seem a slightly odd young man. But then the best soldiers are often eccentrics.'

'He's not half as odd as he used to be,' Laura said. 'He was sounding quite sensible tonight by comparison. It was the most unexpected thing that he should marry Diana. But it seems to be working out well.' She looked at the chess board and said, 'If I concede the game, will you show me what I should have done? I shall never beat you at chess, I know that. I must fall back on my piano-playing.'

'I will teach you the defence, if you will allow me to show you my only other area of superiority. Male vanity must be allowed to strut occasionally.'

She laughed. 'I know you have many talents. Which were you thinking of? Am I to come and watch you operate?'

'Yes, but not at the hospital. I was referring to my culinary expertise.'

'An unusual skill for a man to lay claim to.'

'The greatest chefs have been men,' he pointed out. 'I don't claim to be on a par with *them*, of course. But will you let me cook supper for you one evening?'

'With the greatest of pleasure – but where? It can hardly be here. It would set a most inconvenient precedent.'

'No, of course not. I was thinking of my billet.'

'Oh,' she said. 'Won't that be— I mean, it might not look—'

He seemed amused. 'Do you think you'll be accused of *Paris-plaging*?' It was a slang and derogatory term applied to nurses who went out with doctors – from their custom of meeting in the hotels of that seaside town. 'I assure you my intentions are honourable. And I share a house with two other officers.'

'I see,' she said, relaxing. 'And do you mean to cook for four?'

'That wasn't my plan.' He grinned. 'The house has a modest but workable kitchen and I'm sure they'll agree to be banished to the sitting-room for the evening and leave it to us.'

'Then it's just a matter of finding a date that suits both of us. Duties permitting.'

'The war permitting.'

'Yes, there's always that,' said Laura.

* * *

It was a Friday morning, the 8th of March, and Edward was sharing the early breakfast table with Sadie and Peter. Unless she had an early appointment, Beattie did not usually come down, but ate later with Antonia and David.

The news that week had been troubling. On the previous Sunday, the 3rd of March, Russia had been forced to sign a treaty with Germany at Brest-Litovsk, and withdraw from the war. The terms of the treaty were deliberately humiliating: Russia surrendered territory encompassing a third of her population, half her industry and 90 per cent of her coal mines. There could be no recovery from such blows: Germany was making sure of Russia's impotence.

The Bolshevik government, of course, had huge problems of its own, simply ruling the country. On the Tuesday, in a symbolic break with the Tsarist past, they had decreed that the capital of Russia would move from Petrograd to Moscow. But such a gesture would do nothing to address the nation's bitter internal conflict and desperate poverty.

For the Allies, it meant that fifty more German divisions would be released to return to the Western Front. Fifty divisions! Edward had long known that Germany was expected to attack as soon as the ground dried out – by the end of March, Haig thought – but he only now understood the magnitude of the problem. *Fifty divisions!* He scanned the newspaper, but without taking in a word. A cold feeling had settled in his stomach. For the first time since the war began, it actually had to be considered that they could lose. And if they lost – my God! The Germans would invade, and the people would resist. There would be fighting on the streets in the towns and villages of Britain. The slaughter and destruction would be horrifying.

To divert his thoughts, he turned to the post, which he had picked up on his way to the table and put down beside his plate. Among the letters was one addressed to Mr E. Hunter. He was not surprised: news of his knighthood would take time to filter through. He slit open the envelope.

It was from a firm of solicitors in Bishopsgate that he had not heard of, and the salutation line read, 'Dear Madam'. With a 'tut' of annoyance, he looked at the envelope again. It was indeed addressed to *Mrs* E. Hunter, but the *s* key on the typewriter was evidently worn and, what with the thickness of the legal stationery, it had not printed fully. He had taken it for a smudge. Some husbands habitually opened their wives' post, but he was not one of them. He began to fold the letter to put it back in the envelope, but his eye had already caught the following line, centred and underlined.

In Re: Louis David Rathvilly Plunkett, deceased.

Plunkett! The name caused him a shock, as though he had touched a live wire. Plunkett, the man whose absence had been a ghostly presence haunting his marriage. But he had not heard or seen the name in many years, and had hoped never to again. Beattie had put him behind her long ago. Why was a solicitor writing to her about him? A sick apprehension gnawed at him. Helpless to stop, now, he read on.

As the executor of the late Colonel Plunkett, who died on the 10th of January at the No. 2 London General Hospital, Chelsea, I write to advise you that you are named in his Will as his sole beneficiary. I should be most obliged if you could find it convenient to call on me at this office to discuss the disposition of his estate.

The place of death was the thing that leaped out of the page at him. The 2nd London General? The person at the canteen at Waterloo had said Beattie had been helping there, on that day he had gone looking for her; had said she hadn't been to the canteen since before Christmas.

68

The 2nd London General at Chelsea. Coincidence? Must be.

But then the date struck him, sinking into his flesh like a barb. The 10th of January. That missing, perplexing day.

Abruptly, he thrust back his chair and left the room, hearing behind him Sadie's voice say, 'Father, is something wrong?'

Beattie was in bed, but awake, lying on her back staring at the ceiling. She sat up as he came in, looking puzzled. Then, seeing the letter in his hand, she said in alarm, 'What's happened?'

He threw it into her lap. She opened it and read it, and a look of sick dismay came over her face. It told him all he needed to know. In the twelve days since the investiture, she had seemed to be coming back to herself; he had hoped that, in time, their relationship would be healed, they would become again what they had been to each other before the war had torn them apart. She might even take him back into her bed. The strength of his hope made the pain of this revelation the more savage.

He said, 'That was the day, wasn't it? When I came home and they said you'd gone to bed. Your mysterious illness. You were there. With him.'

She didn't answer. She couldn't lie any more. It had exhausted her.

'How long?' he asked. 'How long was it going on?'

She found words. 'It wasn't – *meant*. I never thought I'd see him again. It was just chance. He saw me one day at the canteen, when he was passing through.'

'*How long?*'

She didn't answer.

'Every day you said you went to the canteen, you were really with him,' he said.

She made an effort. 'No! Not all – hardly any. We met when he was home on leave, that's all.'

69

'That's *all*?' He shook his head in pain. 'I wondered why you pushed me out of your bed.'

'No, that wasn't it!' she cried. It seemed important he should understand. 'It was only this last year that – that I saw him. I was never unfaithful to you before.'

'But you were in your heart,' he said. She looked at him, wide-eyed. She seemed, as she had seemed to him on other occasions, like a trapped deer, and pity for her rose up in him. He forced it down. 'I didn't know one of his names was David,' he said, in a dead voice.

Her eyes closed a moment, as though he had struck her. Ironic, he thought, since it was she who had wounded him so desperately. He turned away.

'Where are you going?' she cried in panic.

'To work, of course,' he said. At the door he paused. 'I'll stay at the club tonight.'

'But what will I tell them?' she asked. She meant the family and the servants.

'Make something up,' he said. 'You're good at that.'

Work was the great antidote, and he had a busy day. He forgot for great swathes of time; then when he paused for a moment, remembering was like a blow, falling on a place already bruised, the pain sickening. He stayed at the office until nine, then walked round to the club. There a man could be sure of being left alone: convention said that if you did not look up when someone approached, they did not disturb you. He drank two large whiskies, but they did not seem to have any effect, though he had not eaten all day.

Some time after ten he went to the desk to bespeak a room, but instead asked for his coat and hat, and went out into the dark. It had been an impulse, an act purely of escape, but his feet knew where he was going. It was half past ten when he reached Soho Square. He walked up the stairs and rang the bell, and Élise opened the door herself. Her eyes widened at the sight of him, and he felt suddenly ashamed. He should not be here. He should not be troubling her. 'I'm sorry,' he said, and was turning away, but she caught his wrist and drew him in. He heard voices in the background. 'You have visitors. I shouldn't—' he began. But she touched her finger to his lips, stopping him, and closed the door behind him.

In the sitting room there were people sitting, talking. Afterwards he could not remember how many – four or five. She addressed them in rapid French and they got up and, without much surprise, it seemed, went away. Like magic, the room cleared. They were alone.

She stood before him, reading his face. Then she put her arms round his waist, turning her face up to him, and said, 'You do not need to say anything.'

It seemed natural and inevitable that he should kiss her. Her mouth was ready and eager for him, and the long-unsatisfied needs of the body took over.

At some point in the night he woke, and found her leaning up on one elbow in the tumble of her hair, looking at him.

He said, 'She betrayed me.'

She said, 'I know,' though she couldn't have, could she? She reached out and pushed the hair back from his brow, and stroked his cheek tenderly. Then she said, 'You are here now. That is all that matters.' She put herself into his arms, and he felt the warm nakedness of her, skin to skin, the whole length of his body. Some wounds could not be staunched, but the flesh had its own loneliness, and that at least could be soothed.

In the morning, he woke and found her lying on her side facing him, quietly sleeping. She looked younger in sleep, her face smooth and composed. He watched her for a while, remembering the night, her generosity, the exquisite pang of physical release; and her vulnerable beauty filled him with a tenderness that was like sorrow.

Now she was watching him – she had woken. She said, 'Will you go?'

'To work,' he said.

'And then – home?'

He took a long curl of her hair and wound it round his finger. He wished that life were like a cinema film that could be rewound, events changed – another path chosen. But in reality, the road untaken could not be revisited. He hesitated too long to answer her question, and saw sadness settle into her face. Life had to go on. He knew that, and so did she. The night had been an enchantment; but reality sat watching them, just one step back.

'It is no good for you, is it – this?' she said.

'Élise, I can't—'

'I know. I know.'

'It's wrong,' he said helplessly.

'Whatever she has done?'

Oh, this was agony! 'It doesn't work like that,' he said at last.

'And what of me?' She did not ask it angrily, as she might have. She was entitled to be angry. He had taken advantage of her.

'I'm so sorry,' he said. 'I'm so very sorry. I should never have—'

She made a little gesture with her hand, as though catching something out of the air – a feather; a word. 'Ah, no,' she said. 'Don't be sorry. It was me. I made you. I am not sorry. But there must be – a price.'

'*You* should not have to pay it.'

Almost, she smiled. '*You* shall, then. You must not abandon me again.'

He looked at her anxiously. 'What is it you want?'

72

'You shall dine with me once a week, as you used to. It shall be like before.'

'Élise, I *can't*. What if—'

She took on dignity. 'I shall not take you to my bed again,' she said sternly. 'You do not love me. Do you think I have no pride?' He had no answer for that. She went on. 'We shall be friends, as before, that is all. Only friends.'

'But that will be no punishment to me – to dine with you.'

She surveyed him gravely, thoroughly. 'Oh, I think it will,' she said. She cupped his face in her hands and kissed him, long and softly, and he responded with tenderness, undershot with pangs of guilt. And at the end of it she surveyed him again. '*Mon cher ami*. I think it will.'

CHAPTER SIX

The atmosphere in the house was strange, Sadie thought. Nothing in particular had happened, but there seemed an unusual tension, as though they were all waiting for something – some blow to fall. Father was working such long hours, he was rarely home to dinner. Sometimes he worked so late it was not worth his while to travel out to Northcote just to sleep, and he stayed at his club.

It was perfectly reasonable, explicable. Yet for some reason it added to Sadie's sense of unease. She felt as though some terrible danger was approaching. Was it the war? Or was someone ill? Not Mother, not Father, please, God! She wished William were still at home so that she could discuss her feelings with him. She could not talk to Antonia, who was occupied with David and her pregnancy, and Peter was too young. William would have listened and not called her silly or fanciful. He would simply have reassured her.

In the servants' hall, Cook was disturbed because she never knew in advance when the master was dining at home. It suggested some unusual emergency was brewing. There were all sorts of rumours about a big action coming at the Front, and her anxiety, which had been general, on behalf of the country at large, was now personal, since she had a sweetheart out there. Fred. Sergeant Fred McAusland – it seemed silly at her age to talk about a sweetheart, but what else could you call him? Gentleman friend sounded somehow

74

seedy. Fiancé? He had said they would get married after the war, but it wasn't as though he'd bought her a ring, and she didn't want to tempt Fate. No, sweetheart would have to do. He wrote her entertaining letters, and she wrote back to him, but he wasn't allowed to say where he was, exactly, and he didn't talk much about the war in any case. But he was the sort of man who was always in the thick of things. It gave her palpitations to think of him going into battle. They had had enough experience in this house of what war meant, what with Mr Bobby dead and Mr David wounded. Thank God William was only in training. She prayed the war would be over before he got out there. And Peter, at school – surely he was safe. But it still left her with Fred to worry about.

And then rationing was coming in, and she didn't know how that was going to affect her. And Mrs David was swelling up and due to give birth in the next couple of weeks. That was a *good* kind of trouble – except that there was bound to be a trained nurse brought in and, given that all the young ones were off nursing soldiers, it would likely be some old battleaxe who'd turn the house upside down and be demanding special dishes at all hours. As if Cook didn't have enough to do already, and Emily was no more use than ornament. She was out of the sling now, but had no strength in that arm, and was as clumsy as a goat in boots.

The master did come home that night, but it was with a bundle of newspapers and the shocking news that the Germans had launched a major attack that day, the 21st of March, in the Somme region, beginning at 4.40 a.m. with a massive bombardment, the heaviest of the war so far, in which it was thought over a million shells had been fired.

Part of the line under attack was held by the British Fifth Army, which had not long taken over the sector from the French and had not yet had time to strengthen the defences to British standards. The bombardment was followed by a ferocious attack, the weight of which – aided by the foggy morning – took the army by surprise. The line had been penetrated in several places. The casualties were known to be heavy.

The relative quiet of the winter season was over. The war was 'back on'. And war news occupied every mind and conversation.

Frank Hussey, who had once been gardener's boy and now was second gardener to Sir George Pettingel at Mandeville Hall, came to dinner in the servants' hall on Sunday, as he frequently did. He walked in through the garden and stopped for such a long chat with Munt that Cook was almost driven to go down the garden and fetch him. When he did arrive at the back door she dragged him in.

'Oh, Frank! You'll know what's going on. They're saying we been beaten. The Germans've broken our line and our boys are running away!'

The other servants gathered round, knowing that Frank was better informed than most thanks to the discarded newspapers that came to him from the Big House. He used them to line seed trays and add to the compost heaps, but he read them first.

'Don't you go getting yourself in a state, Mrs D,' he said, exuding a large calm. 'Our boys are falling back. That's not the same as running away.'

'Sounds the same to me,' Ethel said bluntly. She was reading Frank's face and, knowing him better than the others, she saw that underneath the habitual calm, he was concerned.

'Look here,' Frank said to his gathered audience, 'the Germans attacked with a new sort of soldier. They call 'em "storm troops". They're trained to come on so fast and hard, they can break the line – like the head of an arrow, see? Then the regular troops come up behind to mop up, so the storm troops can just keep going. Well, our chaps hadn't seen anything like that before, and the Fifth Army wasn't quite ready, so it had to retreat, and then the Third Army, on its flank, had to fall back as well, else they'd have been left out there on their own – what they call "up in the air". But they're fighting all the way. Our boys don't run – put that out of your head.'

Ethel had picked out the words 'fighting all the way'. She said, 'How far have the Jerries got?'

Frank looked at her, wishing she hadn't asked. 'Twenty or thirty miles, I believe,' he said.

Ada gave a little shriek, and Cook cried, *Thirty miles!* In other years, the newspapers had called a British advance of two miles a resounding success. 'Oh, my Lord! How'll we stop 'em? Oh, Frank, what if they come here? They'll do what they did in Belgium!'

The word *frightfulness* hung unspoken on the air. In the early days of the war, as the Germans advanced through Holland and Belgium, lurid stories had abounded, of babies bayoneted, nuns raped, whole villages burned and their occupants shot in mass executions. Four years on, the stories had lost none of their power.

'They won't get this far,' Frank said. 'We got the Channel between us and them. And, anyway, our boys'll never let 'em get as far as the Channel ports.'

Munt had come in behind him, and was surveying the scene with sardonic amusement. He had always enjoyed baiting the women – he had little love for females in general – and the way they were looking to Frank, as if he could save them, tickled him. 'Won't be many of our boys left, be the time they gets that far,' he said. 'Twenty thousand killed the first day, and thirty-five thousand wounded. Gawd knows what we've lost since. How long d'you think we can keep that up?'

'Where d'you get them numbers?' Cook demanded. 'Are you making it up, you horrible old man?'

'Ask *him*,' Munt said, jabbing a finger at Frank. 'Ask lover-boy there. He's the one what reads the papers.'

'We've had losses,' Frank admitted. 'Bad. But we're British. The more our backs are to the wall, the harder we fight. We'll make up the numbers. I heard they're going to be combing out men from the mines and the munitions factories.'

'Who's going to run *them*, then?' Ada asked.

'Wimmin,' said Munt. 'Send you lot down the mines. Won't need canaries, the way you lot shriek all the time.'

'There's already women in the munitions factories,' Ethel said.

'I wouldn't go again,' said Emily, instinctively cupping her bad arm.

'Nobody's asking you to,' Cook snapped. 'Go and stir that gravy and make yourself useful. I got to get the pie out.' She was still worried, despite what Frank said. Their armies had never retreated that far in the war before. Thirty miles? How far *was* it to the Channel? And, above all, where was Fred? Was he in it? Was he all right? She wouldn't know any peace until she had heard from him again.

They talked of other things over dinner – steak and onion pie with a suet crust, and bottled gooseberries and custard. Ethel got up to clear the pudding plates, and Frank helped her, so that they could have a quiet word in the kitchen. His quiet word would have been on the topic of their relationship, but she got in first.

'You say there's nothing to worry about,' she said abruptly, 'but I seen the look on your face. Tell me the truth. Are the Germans winning?'

He paused a moment, assembling his words. 'We never seen nothing like these storm troops. This new way of theirs is hard to defend against. And they got the numbers now – they got all their troops coming back from the east. They're going to throw everything at us, to try and beat us before

78

the Yanks come in. It's bad, and that's the truth. But the Germans winning? I don't think that can happen. Every last man in this country would die before we let 'em win. I'd go, sooner than let that happen. Even old Munt, whatever he says, he'd grab a gun and fight, if it come to it.'

His very determination worried her. If he had something to be determined about, it meant they were in trouble. She said fiercely, 'If they got this far, I'd fight. Any German tried to rape me, he'd get more'n he bargained for.'

'That's the spirit,' Frank said. 'You're a grand girl. I've always said you're one in a million.' He took a breath. 'Ethel, you know what I'm going to say.'

Suddenly she looked tired, and sad, and it hurt his heart. 'Don't, Frank. I can't.'

'You can,' he asserted. 'I want you to marry me, so's I can take care of you. I know you like me. I can't think of any reason you shouldn't marry me, unless you're married already, and I know that's not it. So say you will, lovey, and let's do it before the world falls to pieces.'

'You think it's going to?' she asked, seriously.

Now *he* looked tired. 'I don't know. It's bad out there. Everything's uncertain. Except what I feel for you. Let's grab a bit of happiness while we can. Marry me, Ethel. Please.'

The 'please' almost undid her. She longed to be held in his strong arms and rest herself against his big, sheltering body. Sometimes she wondered why she kept resisting. But then she remembered her shame. And the more she cared for him, the less she could do that to him – let him tie himself to someone like her.

'Don't keep asking me,' she said.

He looked at her a moment, lips pressed together, frowning in puzzlement. Then he shook it off and said, 'All right. Subject closed.' *For now*, he added in his head. He was not one to give up once he'd decided on something. 'What'd you like to do this afternoon?'

'Pictures,' she said. 'The Empire.' This was a new cinema that had opened in Northcote in January. It wasn't as grand and fancy as the Electric Palace, but it saved the fare to Westleigh. 'They got *Cleopatra* on.'

'Theda Bara and Fritz Lieber,' Emily said, coming in with the custard jug. She knew all the films and their casts. 'I'd like to see that. They say it's ever so romantic. That Theda Bara, she's fierce beautiful, so she is. I wish I was a fillum star.'

So unlike Theda Bara was Emily that the old Ethel would have jeered at her. It was a sign of how Frank had softened her that instead she found herself saying, 'I'll bring you back the ticket stub for your collection.'

Easter Sunday was on the 31st of March, and it was raining hard. The government had appealed to essential workers not to take the holiday but to work right through, and with Britain facing possible defeat, the response had been overwhelming.

In the battle on the Somme the Germans had advanced a frightening forty miles: Amiens was almost within artillery range – and Amiens was a vital rail centre. Fresh troops were being moved in, some British and some Australian, to stiffen the defences of the town, for it seemed certain that the German general Ludendorff meant to capture it, and if he did, the danger to the Allied position would be acute.

But Cook was suddenly more cheerful. The news of Australian reinforcements gave her courage. 'Them Aussies'll give 'em what for,' she said. 'Big, tall blokes they are, like the Yanks – not poor little shrimps like our boys.' She felt she was the household authority on Australians because of Fred.

Ada was annoyed by her 'shrimps' reference – her own beau, Len Armstrong, was not big and burly but he was no less a real man, in her opinion. She felt constrained to remind

Cook that Fred was not actually Australian, but had been born in Shepherd's Bush and only went out there as an adult.

Cook was unmoved. 'He looks like one,' she said. 'And he's big enough to be taken for one.' She hadn't heard from him, but she had convinced herself by now that nothing could have happened to him – not to someone like Fred.

Reaching home after a wet walk back from church, Ada found Len waiting for her by the back door, under the meagre shelter of the overhang, at the mercy of drips. She hadn't been expecting to see him until Tuesday, when she would have her half-day. She hastened to hold her umbrella over both of them.

'I'm sorry to bust in on you,' he said, 'but I got something important to say. Have you got time to talk to me? Is there somewhere we can go?'

'Course I got time. Come on in.' The others had gone in ahead, and in the kitchen she said, 'Me and Len want to talk, private. Can we use the scullery?'

Cook had a soft spot for Corporal Armstrong, who was an instructor at the training camp at Paget's Piece, largely because of his fine tenor voice. When he came to visit on a Sunday, he would often entertain them with lovely old songs and hymns. She said, 'Scullery, nonsense! You use the sitting-room. We'll be busy in here, anyway. Emily, stop staring and go and put the umbrellas to drip.'

The servants' sitting-room was a large room next to the kitchen, with the big table where they took their meals, and some comfortable armchairs around the fire where they spent their leisure moments. Ada asked, 'What did you want to talk about, then?'

He said, 'Sit down, Ada dear. I got some news.'

She sat, rather harder than she meant, her hand going to her throat. 'It's bad news, isn't it?'

'I wouldn't call it that, exactly, but it's going to be an

81

upset. The current lot of boys at Paget's Piece are ready, and they're moving out Monday week. Two weeks' brigade training in Hounslow, and then off to France.'

Her hand went down in relief. 'Oh, well, there'll be another lot in to take their place. I know you get fond of 'em, but—'

'No, dear, it isn't that,' he interrupted. 'I been told I got to go with them.'

It took a moment to register. Then her eyes widened. 'You're going to France? To the *war*? To *fight*?'

He gave her a twinkly smile. 'I am a soldier. That's what soldiers do.'

'Yes, but . . .' She had got used to having him around. She had thought he'd be an instructor for ever – safe at home.

'They're desperate short of NCOs. You can train a soldier up in a few weeks, but it takes longer for NCOs, and there's no replacing years of experience. They're making me a sergeant. Well, aren't you pleased?'

She didn't look pleased, but she hadn't really taken that part in. She was still struggling with France. 'Oh, Len!' she cried.

'I know what you're thinking,' he said, 'and I won't spin you any candyfloss. War is war. But it's the inexperienced lads that cop it, rather than old sweats like me. They do say you can't kill a sergeant, not with a spade and pickaxe. So don't look so glum. I mean to come back to you in one piece.'

'Oh, Len,' she said again, in tones of despair. 'I know it's got to be. It's duty and all that sort of thing, but—'

'I know, ducks. But that's not all I came to say. I've got a question for you. I know it's a bit of a cheek, but we been walking out a while now, and what I thought was – how'd you like to get married before I go? I'd like to know I had a wife waiting for me back home – might concentrate me mind more, see, make sure I dodge those whizz-bangs. And

82

if the worst come to the worst, well, you'd get a widow's pension, and all my worldly goods. What do you say? Shall we get spliced?'

A radiant smile made her look younger than her forty-four years. 'Oh, Len, yes! Of course I'll marry you.' He took her hands and raised her to her feet to give her a tender kiss on the lips. She sighed in satisfaction, then asked, 'But where'll we live after?'

'Well, I'm hoping you can stay on here till the war's over. With me being away, you won't want to be separated from your old friends. And it'll keep you busy.' He gave her a twinkling look. 'After the war, I thought maybe we could get a little shop, and live over it. Give us something to do, being as we're probably too old to start a family.'

'I'd like a little shop,' she said shyly. 'But how'll we get married? I mean, when? Will there be time?'

'I thought about that. We haven't got time for banns, but I can get a special licence, and I checked and they'll let me have forty-eight hours' leave, if you can get the time off from your boss.'

'Oh, goodness!' Ada said. 'I'd forgotten about that. I'll have to get permission from the missus to get wed.' Many households wouldn't keep married servants.

'She won't say no, surely – not in the circs,' said Len. 'What about Friday?'

'Friday!' Ada said. It was so soon! After all these years of spinsterhood, suddenly on Friday she'd be a married woman!

'We could have Friday and Saturday together,' Len went on, 'then I got Sunday to pack up at camp, before we go off on Monday.'

The reminder that he was leaving took some of the shine off it. But it was only a dent in her joy. 'Can we tell them in the kitchen?' she said breathlessly. 'They'll be so excited for me.'

* * *

Luncheon was late, after such a momentous announcement. The kitchen erupted with excitement, which Ada tried to dampen down because she hadn't asked for permission yet. But when she walked Len up to the drawing-room to confront the family, the missus said she had no objection to the marriage, and couldn't see any reason Ada shouldn't have the two days off. 'Do I understand you wish to continue with your employment here afterwards?'

'If it's all right with you, madam,' Ada said humbly. 'Until the war's over – what with Len going straight off to France.'

Beattie was only too glad not to have to look for another maid, with the best women going to the factories. And with Antonia about to give birth, she didn't want any more disruption.

Edward, looking tired to death, managed a smile, shook Len's hand, and told Ada there would be a wedding present for her, which made her blush and lower her eyes.

Sadie asked where the wedding would be. Len said they would get spliced at the register office in Northcote. He and Ada would go to a hotel for their two-night honeymoon, and he'd have her back safe and sound on Sunday morning.

Beattie was relieved they would not be sleeping at The Elms as a married couple. Of course, if he got leave at some point, some arrangement would have to be thought about, but for the moment there seemed to be remarkably little awkwardness for her to have to deal with. It inspired a burst of generosity. 'Have you got anything to wear, Ada?'

'Just my best dress, madam. My brown.'

'Why don't you send a note round to Nula, ask her to come and see if there's an old dress of mine she could alter for you?'

'Oh, madam, you're so kind! Thank you,' Ada said, and took Len away to tell the others how nice everyone had been about it, and to discuss the arrangements while they all pitched in to get luncheon back on track.

* * *

When the late 'upstairs' luncheon – pea soup, roast lamb and plum tart – had got to the pudding stage, Sadie cleared her throat for attention, and said, 'I've got an announcement.'

Edward roused himself from his thoughts to say, 'Don't tell me you're thinking of getting married as well!'

Peter hooted with laughter. 'Sadie, getting married?'

'Why is that so funny?' she retorted.

'The only person you'd marry is a horse,' Peter said.

'Don't be silly, Peter,' Beattie reproved automatically. 'And take your elbows off the table. What is it, Sadie?'

'Well, ever since I got my driving licence, I've been wanting to do something with it.'

'You drive for Mrs Cuthbert,' Antonia pointed out.

'Yes, but that's just fetching and carrying. I want to do something more useful. And when I was in Northcote yesterday, I saw a poster up by the station that said the Red Cross urgently want more ambulance drivers.'

It had struck her straight away because almost the first thing she had done for the war effort was to drive wounded officers from the station to Mount Olive hospital – though that had been with a horse and cart.

'So I went round to the depot on the Westleigh Road – you know they're using that old furniture warehouse next to the cottage hospital as an ambulance station? And when I showed them my licence and my certificate they were frightfully bucked and said right away I was just the sort of person they wanted. So I joined,' she concluded, looking round the table for reaction.

'But how will it fit in with Highclere?' Beattie asked. 'Or do you mean to give that up?'

'I can do both. I don't need to be at Highclere so much now they've got so many girls. With the ambulance-driving, you just have to say when you would be available – they're so desperate for drivers they'll take any hours you can spare. So I thought perhaps I'd do two afternoons a week.'

'Do you think you can manage an ambulance?' Edward asked.

'I've been driving the horse-box up at Highclere, and they said an ambulance wouldn't be much different. You have to drive smoothly with horses and avoid potholes and so on, so that they don't slip and fall, and you have to do the same with the wounded, so as not to jolt them.' She tried to read his face. 'You don't disapprove, do you?'

'I think you're very young for such responsibility,' he said.

'No younger than a lot of the soldiers who are getting wounded,' she said.

'That's different,' said Edward. But was it, any more? He had seen it with his sister Laura, that restlessness. To begin with she had worked in an office, the first woman in his family's history to take a paying job, then she'd become a lady policeman, then driven an ambulance, and now was running a hostel horribly close to the Front line. What she would do next he couldn't guess – if they allowed women in the army she'd probably demand a gun and go out to kill Germans. She wanted new challenges all the time. And she was not the only one. When the war was over, how would women ever settle down to domesticity again?

'I believe a person should stick at something once they've started it,' he warned.

'Oh, but I *am* a sticker, Dad,' Sadie protested.

'Driving an ambulance is important work,' Antonia said. 'Where exactly would you be doing it?'

'In Northcote. Meeting the ambulance trains and driving the wounded to one of the hospitals – Walford Road, Mount Olive, that nursing home at Bentley Manor—'

'Dene Park,' Peter added, bouncing. 'That'll be queer, driving soldiers up to Diana's house!'

It had been a way of reducing the death duties after the old earl died, to give up part of the house to the government for use as a hospital. Diana's mother-in-law hated it so much she hadn't set foot in Dene Park since the first patients arrived.

'I can't imagine what Lady Wroughton will think,' Beattie said. 'You, her daughter-in-law's sister!'

'But Mother, *upper-class* girls join the FANY and drive ambulances!' Sadie protested. 'And dukes' daughters and everything join the VAD and nurse.'

Beattie wearied of the subject. 'Well if your father has no objection . . .' She looked down the table at him, and he looked back, but their eyes didn't meet. They were managing pretty well in front of others to carry on as if nothing had happened, though they spoke to each other as little as possible. He worked long hours, and she was engaged for much of the time with war-work, so it was perfectly possible not to meet except at the dinner table, and even then not every day. She had used to think the war was tearing her family apart. Now it seemed it was only the demands of the war that were keeping it together.

'I've no objection,' Edward said. 'I hope it won't tire you too much.'

'Oh, nothing tires me,' Sadie said. 'I like to be busy.'

'I wish *I* could drive an ambulance!' Peter cried. 'I hate being eleven. You're not old enough for *anything*.'

CHAPTER SEVEN

Nula picked out a navy wool flannel skirt and jacket that Beattie didn't wear any more. 'The colour's right for you,' she told Ada. 'It's lovely material, and it won't need much altering – just the waistband let out, and the hem taken up a bit. What have you got to wear under it?'

Ada had a cream blouse with pintucks down the front, which Nula approved. 'Neat and ladylike. And there's a navy velour hat somewhere that used to belong to Miss Diana – I'll find it and steam it for you. I know your Sunday hat,' she had seen it at church often enough, 'and it wouldn't do at all.' She also found an artificial flower, a cream-coloured gardenia, that had once graced an evening gown, which she sewed onto the hat to make it more bridal.

Ada was overwhelmed by everyone's kindness. Cook, who hated sewing, stitched some lace onto Ada's nicest cotton nightgown for 'The Night', any reference to which had Ada's cheeks scalding. Emily took away her best black shoes and gave them the polishing of their life, singing under her breath as she buffed them to a glossy shine.

Antonia gave her a dear little cameo brooch, 'From me and Mr David, with every blessing, Ada dear,' which would look perfect at the neck of her blouse. Sadie gave her a pair of art silk stockings: 'You can't wear cotton ones on your wedding day.'

Even the notoriously grudging Ethel lent her her best black cotton gloves. 'They're nicer than yours.'

Munt's contribution was not to say any of the things that he was bottling up, and judging by the gleam in his eyes, Ada would have been satisfied with that for a wedding gift. But on the Friday morning he came to the back door with a little posy of violets, white and purple mixed, the stalks neatly bound with raffia, for her to carry. 'Not much in the garden these days,' he grunted, 'but you can always find a vilit if you knows where to look.' And he stumped away before she could thank him. He couldn't abide gushing.

All the servants were given the morning off to go to the wedding. Nula and Mrs Chaplin, the charwoman, also went, and Ada's two friends, the Covingtons' maid, Ruby, from three doors up, and Hilda Barnes, who was cook to Miss Freebody down the end of the road. Ada's only close relative, her cousin Maudie, whose husband worked a farm on the far side of Goston, turned up, which pleased her enormously, because she knew, having spent her summer holidays on the farm for many years, that it was an awkward journey, involving three buses.

On Len's side, there was a small but vocal contingent from the army camp; and Len himself, with his uniform sponged and pressed, an army gloss on his boots, and a shave that came close to punishment, was waiting for Ada at the door, looking nervous. But when he saw her, his expression was something she would treasure for the rest of her life. 'You look beautiful,' he murmured, as he took her hand through his arm. 'Mary Pickford's got nothing on you.'

Afterwards they all went to the Station Hotel, where Len had a surprise for her: he had reserved the Gade Room, and Mrs Weaver, the landlady, had put up a nice spread of potted-meat sandwiches, cold sausages and buns, and there was beer and lemonade, and one of the lads from the camp had come to play the piano. It had a note or two missing, and the effect was curiously syncopated but none the less jolly.

'This do must've cost you a fortune,' a worried Ada whispered to her new husband.

'Don't you fret,' he replied. 'I got a bob or two saved up. Anyway, you only get married once. Got to have a bit of a knees-up.'

When the eating and drinking had slowed down a bit, everyone joined in a sing-song round the piano and, by request, Len did a solo rendering in his lovely tenor voice of 'If You Were The Only Girl In The World', sung directly to Ada, holding her hand, and bringing tears to many eyes.

Walking home afterwards, Cook said, 'I think that was the nicest wedding I've ever been at, for all it wasn't posh or anything.'

'Or even in a church,' puffed Mrs Chaplin, who couldn't walk as fast as the others.

''Twas ever so romantic.' Emily sighed. 'When he sang to her, I thought I should die, it was so lovely.'

'It's just a pity there wasn't a cake to cut,' Cook said. 'If I'd had more notice . . .'

'She looked well in that suit,' Nula remarked.

Ethel said nothing. She had been imagining herself and Frank in place of Ada and Len. They'd make a much handsomer couple. And they'd make better use of the room at the Swan in Westleigh, to which Len and Ada were trundling at that moment on the bus. She shivered at the thought and shoved it away. 'I think it's going to rain again,' she said.

Things had been going better at the Front. The German advance had been rapid and frightening, but the land they had captured was mostly the shell-torn wilderness that had been fought over in 1916, difficult to cross and harder to bring up supplies over. Now their advance had slowed as they outran their supply chain. The British and Empire reinforcements brought in to defend the strategic centres of Amiens and Arras were able to hold them off, and after several fruitless attempts to take the towns, on the 5th of April Ludendorff called off the operation.

'We've lost a lot of ground,' Lord Forbesson said to Edward, when he met him in the club that evening, 'but it's not good ground, and Fritz will find it hard to defend when we counter-attack. As we will, make no mistake.'

'Casualties have been high, though, haven't they?' Edward said.

'Approaching two hundred and fifty thousand altogether, dead and wounded,' Forbesson admitted. 'British, French and Empire combined.'

Edward hadn't realised it was so many. 'A quarter of a *million*?' he exclaimed.

Forbesson rallied. 'But they've lost as many, if not more, and they can afford them less. They've lost specialist storm troops, highly trained and irreplaceable. The Kaiser calls it a victory, but all he's won is a few miles of dead ground, and at the cost of his best men.'

'I wish I could be as sanguine as you,' Edward said. 'We've had a bad jolt, and it's not over yet.'

'No,' Forbesson agreed. 'Having to shift our troops to Amiens has left the Hazebrouck route exposed, and it's my guess they'll attack there next. If they could break through—'

'It would open the way to the Channel ports,' Edward finished for him. For a moment he was sunk in silent thought.

Then Forbesson said, 'But I've had word that my boy, Esmond, has come through all right. He was at Amiens. Pretty hot work, but he's got away without a scratch. Dorothy's relieved, as you can imagine. She was singing this morning – first sound she's made in days.'

'I'm very happy for you,' said Edward. Esmond was their only son. 'My cousin Jack's survived too, with just a minor wound.'

'And how is your boy in the RFC? Oh, well, it's the RAF now, isn't it? It'll be hard getting used to the new initials.'

'He did very well at the ground school, and now he's passed on to flying school. He hoped to be sent to Coney Warren, just down the road from us, but instead they sent him to the training squadron at Farnborough.'

'I dare say he'll be having too good a time to be missing home,' Forbesson said. Edward nodded in a rather distracted way, and Forbesson said, 'I say, is anything wrong? You've been looking awfully preoccupied lately. Everyone well at home? Memsahib in top form and so on?'

Edward felt the usual stab of pain at the mention of Beattie. He hesitated – but Forbesson was an old friend, and had done him many services in the past. He reached into his inside pocket and pulled out some papers, laying them on the table. 'This arrived on Monday.'

Forbesson picked them up, but barely had to glance at them. Everyone recognised them now. 'Oh, your call-up papers! Arrived on Monday, eh? April the first. Quite a joke! Well, purely a matter of form, of course. You, of all people, know how to appeal, and you'll be exempted.'

'I've decided I'm not going to appeal,' Edward said.

Forbesson's eyes opened wide. 'Not— My dear fellow, what can you be thinking of?'

Edward could not, of course, tell him the reason: that he could not go on living like this, pretending all was well between him and Beattie, sharing a house with her without any contact or kindness, carrying silently the burden of her betrayal – and of his reciprocal guilt. Every day was agony, whether he went home at the end of it or stayed at the club. He had even – he admitted it to himself with shame – thought about Élise, and the comfort she could offer. She managed, during their weekly suppers, to behave like the Élise of old, lively, warm and amusing, yet he could not but be aware of the tension that lay between them. If he asked her for love, he was almost sure she would relent from her vow, and that was yet another thorn to endure. He must not hurt her again; but though it was by her choice, surely his weekly visits hurt her.

He needed to escape; and here was the means.

He said, 'My duty.'

'Fiddlesticks,' said Forbesson, robustly. 'What you do here at home is far more important – and only you can do it. Any fool can carry a gun and get shot at.'

'We desperately need men,' Edward said with a calmness he didn't feel.

'But, my dear fellow, think—'

Edward lifted a weary hand. 'I've thought, believe me. I don't want to think any more. My mind is made up.'

'Well, I'm damned,' Forbesson said quietly, examining Edward's face. What he saw there evidently convinced him, because he said, 'I thought you were rather too quiet lately. And I suspect there's something else behind this, but it ain't my business to quiz you if you don't want to tell me. But I have to say I'm damned sorry you've come to this decision.'

Edward tried a smile. 'I fancy an adventure, that's all. What poor desk-bound idiot wouldn't want a free trip to France and a chance to shoot at Jerry?'

And Forbesson kindly left it at that.

Len left Ada at the gate of The Elms on Sunday morning, with a brief but intense kiss. 'I won't come in,' he said. 'Running a bit late. Got a lot to do today.'

'And you're off tomorrow,' she said.

'Oh-seven-hundred,' he confirmed. 'We'll be marching through the streets to the station, with pretty girls throwing flowers at our feet.' She didn't smile at the jest. 'Now, don't you fret while I'm away,' he said. 'Don't want you getting worry-lines in your pretty face.'

'Oh, Len! I'm not pretty.'

'Beautiful, then. And I'm coming back. Fix your mind on that. We're going to have a lovely life together.'

She looked at him in despair. 'You'll write to me?'

'Course I will. Chin up – Mrs Armstrong!' The name made her smile, and he took his chance to leave her on the right note. She watched him walk away down the street towards the main road, but he didn't turn and wave. She knew he didn't believe in prolonged goodbyes.

She thought everyone would be at church, but when she went in through the back door, she found Cook there, sitting at the table with a cup of tea and leafing through her recipe book.

'There you are!' Cook exclaimed. 'Come and sit down. Pot's fresh. Get yourself a cup.'

'No, thanks,' Ada said, but she sat down anyway. 'We had breakfast at the hotel not long since. Jolly good one, too – eggs, bacon and sausages. Len had mustard on his sausages, isn't that queer? I mean, at breakfast!'

'Soldiers' habits, I dessay,' Cook said. 'Prob'ly puts sauce on everything, too.' She eyed her companion keenly, looking for changes. 'Well, so you're a married woman now.' Ada had gone through the secret door to that other land Cook knew nothing of. But now there was Fred, and . . . Well, the mind boggled. She had to know. That was why she'd stayed back from church, to have a chance to talk to Ada alone.

'What's it like?' she blurted out.

'What's what like?' Ada prevaricated.

'*You* know. Come on, there's just you and me here. You can tell me – I'll never say a word. Was it – nice?'

Ada stared at her a long minute, lips pressed tight together, cheeks slowly reddening. Cook didn't think she'd answer, but suddenly the dam burst. 'It's *awful*!' she said. 'I was so embarrassed! And having to face him the next morning. I don't know what God was thinking when He made that up.'

Cook was shaken. 'But – but wasn't your Len kind?'

'Oh, he was kind as can be, but . . .' She could not

94

speak of the horrors of intimacy. She didn't even have names for those parts, and nothing in the world would induce her to refer to them. She searched for a sidelong way of expressing it. 'Taking off your drawers in front of somebody. In front of a *man*. Think of that.'

Cook thought. Words failed her.

'The thing that gets me,' Ada went on, 'is there's girls that do it voluntary. For *fun*. Like Ethel. And with strangers! Honestly, if it was anyone but Len, I just couldn't have, never in a million years.' She got up. 'I'm going up to change, and then I'll start work. And I don't want to talk about it any more, thank you.'

'Course not,' Cook said automatically. She was still thinking. She tried to imagine taking off her drawers in front of Fred, and her imagination failed. She'd never considered that part of it. It was – it was just *rude*. It never happened in love stories. Or at the pictures. Geraldine Farrar never took her necessaries off. You never saw Mary Pickford in bloomers. It just wasn't romantic. Even those Obelisks, or whatever you called 'em, had a sort of flimsy nightie-thing on when you saw them lying about eating grapes.

But then there was all those stories and poems that people had written for hundreds of years about love. And love obviously meant the other thing as well. There must be something more to it, surely. If everyone thought it was awful, how would the world keep going?

Maybe Len Armstrong had done it wrong. That must be it. He wasn't so much of a much, Ada's shrimpy little Len. Now, her Fred was a different kettle of fish. Her Fred was big and strong and the sort of chap who knew how to do things proper. He'd get it right, would Fred!

She was happy with the idea for an instant – but then she was right back to the taking off of drawers, and whatever you said, that was hard to get past.

★ ★ ★

95

By the end of March, Major Ransley and Laura had still not managed to co-ordinate a date for him to cook her supper. The action at the beginning of April was taking place at Amiens and not Ypres, but there was still greatly increased traffic through Poperinghe, and both were extra busy. Ludendorff calling off the Somme action on the 5th of April did not slow the flood of wounded coming down, and on the 8th Laura received a note from him, saying, 'Tonight or never. I'm taking a few hours off no matter what, and will pick you up at AH at seven. Don't fail me. We must seize the day.'

Louisa and Ronnie were in the office, going through the accounts. Louisa's face collapsed into a scowl. 'You can't just take off like that. It's not fair.'

'There's nothing fair about war,' Laura replied.

'I think the expression is "love or war",' Ronnie said, with a sly smile.

'Come on!' Laura laughed. 'I'm well past that.'

'You can't go, anyway,' Louisa said. 'It's not your evening off.'

'Oh, Lou! What does it matter?' Laura said. 'We've always been flexible. I gave up my evening off to you last week.'

'That was different. I was sick,' Louisa said angrily. 'You can't change things at the last minute, just because your precious Major Ransley clicks his fingers. It's like him to think he can order everybody about for his own convenience.'

'But, Lou, dear, he's a surgeon,' Laura reasoned. 'It's harder for him to arrange things ahead of time.'

'He could if he wanted. He's just selfish. And arrogant, like all men. *And* interfering. Always trying to tell us how to run Ack Harry, always pushing his nose in where it's not wanted. I'm just sick of it!' And she flung out of the room, slamming the door behind her.

Laura turned to Ronnie, her eyebrows raised. 'What on earth was that about?' she said, half hurt, half embarrassed.

Ronnie pretended to be reading the bills on the table.

'Ronnie, why does she hate him so much? He's never been anything but pleasant and friendly towards her.'

'Why are you asking me?' Ronnie said neutrally.

'Well, you have fresh eyes. And you're good at reading people.'

Now Ronnie looked up. 'She's jealous,' she said bluntly.

'Oh, don't be absurd,' Laura retorted.

Ronnie sat on the edge of the desk, folding her arms, and said, 'You can be blind when you want to be, can't you? You have something you want to achieve, and you just plunge on, regardless. It's an admirable trait in many ways – you get things done – but people can be trampled on the way.'

'I've *never* trampled Louisa,' Laura began.

Ronnie interrupted her. 'What's she doing here? Why is she even in France?'

'Belgium,' Laura corrected.

'Don't evade. You know what I mean. She came here to be with you. She's not natural war-zone material.'

'She was a militant in the Cause,' Laura objected.

'She just helped out at the office,' Ronnie said. 'I've talked to her about it. She didn't go out on raids or throw stones at policemen and get herself arrested. Oh, she believed in the Cause all right, but mostly she liked the companionship of the other women. And when you have a lot of women together with no male influence, you get some very fierce friendships. It's a kind of hothouse that breeds intense emotions. Like a girls' boarding-school – factions, pashes, best friends, squabbles, name-calling. And jealousy. Lots of jealousy.'

'Ronnie,' Laura said patiently, 'this isn't a girls' boarding school. What on earth are you talking about?'

Ronnie sighed, as if at wilful stupidity. 'Lou has a crush on you,' she said, 'and now she thinks you like Ransley more than her.'

'Oh, really!' Laura protested. 'That's so – childish!'

Ronnie shrugged. 'You asked me.'

'But she's a grown woman.'

'Age doesn't come into it. Believe me, I've seen plenty of it. I've been knocking about women's organisations all my life.'

Laura frowned at her in perplexity. 'But what can I do about it?'

'Nothing,' said Ronnie. 'It's Louisa's problem. If you tried to cater to it you'd only make things worse – for both of you. But don't be surprised if she gives up on you one day and goes home.'

Ransley was outside at exactly seven, in a motor-car with headlamps obscured but for a narrow slit. He drove her out of Poperinghe on the north road towards Krombeke. He was concentrating on driving – not easy with so little light and potholes everywhere – so she didn't expect conversation, but after a few minutes he said, 'You're very quiet. Everything all right?'

'Hm? Oh, yes, of course,' she said.

All day Louisa had maintained a martyred silence, and had pointedly absented herself when Laura went up to get changed. Laura wished Ronnie hadn't said anything, for if it was true, it would make things awkward. She and Louisa had been close friends for four years, and shared a house back in London. But if Lou had a *schwärmerisch* sort of crush on her, she would not be comfortable with the closeness any more.

Ransley turned off onto a lane to the left, and soon reached a crossroads around which a few houses clustered. 'This is it,' he said. It had been only a five-minute journey. 'I warn you, it's no great thing.'

'You never saw the ruined cottage we lived in when we drove the ambulance,' Laura said.

He pulled onto the grass before one of the houses. 'Even worse, I haven't been home for two days, so I've no idea what there will be to eat.'

'Now that *is* serious—' Laura began.

'But I have *this*,' he interrupted, reaching behind and pulling out a bottle of wine. 'Vintage claret, liberated from a cellar in Ypres. A grateful soldier gave it to me after I sewed his arm back on.'

'Château Latour? That's a lot of gratitude!' she said.

'He was strictly a beer man.'

They got out. It was silent, as the country is silent at night, and dark – the clouded sky obscured the stars, and if there were lights in any of the houses, the blackout concealed them. The cold, damp air smelt green, with a faint whiff of cow manure, and a little hot oil from the motor. The only nearby sound was the ticking of the engine cooling; but in the distance there was a muttering like summer thunder – the guns at the line, firing intermittently.

'You'd better take my hand. I know the path and its hazards,' he said, reaching out. His was warm and strong, and as it engulfed hers, she felt a small unruly pang in the pit of her stomach. They had shaken hands on many occasions, so why was this different? But it was.

Inside the cottage it was dark. He closed the door behind them and left her by it while he felt his way around to check the blackout curtains were closed. Then she heard other indeterminate sounds, followed by the scritch of a match, and light bloomed in a paraffin lamp on the table. The room jumped into life. It was an ordinary kitchen with a deal table and chairs, a wooden dresser, some cupboards, an earthenware sink, and a range under the chimney.

'Welcome to my palace,' he said.

'Very handsome,' she replied. 'Where is everyone? Your fellow officers?'

'I thought they'd be here,' he said. 'They must be working late. You know how it is when there's a flap on.'

'So, no chaperons?'

'It seems not. Shall I drive you home? Or, if I promise not to ravish you against your will, you could stay?'

'Better see if the range is still alight before you invite me to stay. It looks awfully cold.'

'Oh, we don't keep it in when we're all working. We have a twin Beatrice, and I promise you I'm very nippy with it. The question is, what is there to cook?' He started rummaging in cupboards.

'What can I do?' Laura asked.

'You can open the wine. There's a corkscrew in the drawer of the table. Glasses on the dresser. Lay the table, if you like. Otherwise, just sit and look decorative while I potter.'

With a glass of wine in her hand, she felt suddenly relaxed. This absurdly domestic scene was so far removed from the war and her everyday experience that it gave her a sense of being on holiday. And there was something infinitely endearing about Ransley – the skilled surgeon who worked amid blood and pain and shattered limbs – manipulating tin-openers and frying pans, chopping boards and kitchen knives. Their usual easy converse revived itself, and they talked like old friends as he assembled their supper.

The first course was tinned sardines on toast. 'What would we do without tinned sardines?' he wondered. 'The soldier's oysters. Tommy's caviar.'

The second course she recognised as burgoo, a mess of bully beef and crushed biscuit fried together, a soldier's staple. Ransley had enlivened it by adding chopped onion, diced carrot and a dash of Tabasco.

'Never mind French cuisine. This is trench cuisine,' he announced cheerfully, as he placed the plate in front of her. 'My speciality. I did warn you there might not be anything much to cook.'

'It's delicious,' she said, tasting. 'I'm deeply impressed – to achieve this from such meagre ingredients – and on an oil stove!'

'Oh, Beatrice and I understand each other.' He smiled across the table at her.

'How did you learn to cook?'

'Necessity. There's no sense in being more uncomfortable than one has to be, and I like my grub.'

'You will have to teach me,' Laura said. 'It's a pitiful thing not to be able to cook for oneself. It's just that I've never had to do it.'

'I suspect a lot of people are saying the same thing about a great many activities. The world is changing . . .'

'. . . *et nos mutamur in illis,*' Laura finished.

'Ah, an educated lady. Somehow I'm not surprised.'

He even contrived pudding for them. He cut in two a stub of stale cake, and poured a little brandy over it. 'Always saving enough to have with coffee later,' he said. 'Then, over that, we will pour cream, *et voilà*! Trifle.'

'Where on earth will you get cream from?' she marvelled.

'Out of a tin. It's evaporated milk, really. Soldier's cream.'

'More trench cuisine?'

'From the recipe book of that great chef Monsieur Nestlé. Only the very best for you, my dear mademoiselle. One must have some luxury, or what's life for?'

They chatted on, warmed and relaxed by the food and wine. He made coffee on the Beatrice – 'I make no claims for it. Haven't had any proper coffee in months. This is probably half ground acorns' – and they covered its deficiency with brandy.

When he had lit cigarettes for them both, he said, 'When I wrote "tonight or never", I'm afraid it wasn't entirely a rhetorical device.'

'You alarm me,' she said. 'Not a fatal disease, I hope? You look hale enough. Or a long-lost wife suddenly turning up?'

'I wish it were only that. I'm afraid I'm being transferred. Not very far, but far enough to prevent my popping round in the comfortable way I've got used to. They're sending me to a field ambulance.'

This was not a vehicle, but a mobile medical unit, one of three per division. It provided aid posts and dressing stations, the medical attention closest to the line for the wounded, which meant the medical personnel were in the thick of it, and not infrequently under fire.

'So I'll be moving closer to the line,' he went on, 'and with the Germans on the move, I suspect we'll be kept too busy for social engagements for some time to come.'

Laura was surprised at the depth of her own dismay. 'I'm very sorry,' she said, after a moment. 'I've enjoyed having you round the corner to apply to whenever we need help. We never could have got Artemis House off the ground without you.'

'I'm sure that's not true. You would have got things done, come what may. Allow me to know you a little.'

'Nevertheless, Ack Harry owes you a debt of gratitude.' She tried a smile. 'Very few army chaps would have put so much effort into a resource exclusively for females.'

He got up to fetch the bottle and pour them both more brandy, and when he sat again, he took the chair cater-cornered to her, bringing him much closer. 'I'm interested in Ack Harry, certainly,' he said, 'but I'm more interested in you. Actually, I believe it was for you that I got involved, not for those nameless females.'

She felt ridiculously shy. 'Major Ransley,' she said jokingly, 'are you getting spoony?'

'What a terrible expression,' he said, with a wry smile. 'I admire you very much.' He took her hand and folded it in both his. 'In fact, I think I am falling in love with you. Is that absurd in a man of my age?'

'Your age is pretty much the same as mine, isn't it?' Laura said.

'Now *that* is an annoyingly equivocal answer. Does it mean that it *is* absurd, for both of us, or one of us, or not absurd for either?'

'*That*'s an equivocal question,' she said. 'I'm beginning to think you knew your colleagues wouldn't be here, and that you have evil intentions towards me.'

102

He was serious suddenly. 'Would that annoy you? Or would you perhaps rather like me to have them?'

She crushed out her cigarette, everything inside her jumping. 'Shall we find out?' she said. And she leaned forward to be kissed.

It was a decision perhaps fuelled by brandy, and the knowledge of the parting to come; a decision made in the face of danger, such as was made by men and women every day in war time, with varying consequences. But in the event it turned out to be unexpectedly easy and strangely comfortable.

It seemed perfectly natural to be naked together under the covers of his creaking bed in the small room upstairs with the quaintly sloping roof. The feeling of his skin against hers, and the smell of him – not his hair oil or soap, but the man smell underneath, unique to him – seemed things she had always known. He was a skilled lover, taking care of her; his kisses, slow and addictive, she could not have enough of. They did not speak or make any sound, but they moved in absolute harmony, as though it were the hundredth time instead of the first.

Afterwards, when their breathing had slowed, she lay cradled in his arms, her head on his chest, listening to the steady thud of his heart. Under his clothes he was thin – the effects of war, too much work and not enough time to eat – but his arms and hands were strong, and his skin smooth and hairless. She drifted on the tide of his breathing, wrapped in an absolute happiness. She wanted never to move again.

Which suddenly alarmed her. She was not accustomed to such dependence. She felt obliged to dispel any mood of romance. 'Major Ransley,' she said, 'I fear you are not to be trusted.'

He winced. 'Must you call me major? You're not in the army, you know. Can't you call me Jim?'

'Don't change the subject. You promised not to ravish me.'

'No such thing. I promised not to ravish you *against your will*.'

'Jesuitical argument.'

'It must be said, you seemed to be an intrinsic part of the performance.'

'It was only good manners, when you'd gone to so much trouble.'

After a pause, he said diffidently, 'May I ask you something? Something rather impertinent?'

'I think we've gone beyond impertinence, haven't we?'

'Very well. I – how shall I put it? You—' He stopped and started again. 'I'm not your first lover, am I?'

Ah, she understood. She chuckled. 'If I had been a virgin, it would have been even more reprehensible of you to take me to bed.'

'You could have refused,' he pointed out. 'And you needn't answer my question. I had no right to ask it.'

'I don't mind answering. Yes, I had a lover. A long time ago. Nobody knew about it, of course – my family would have been horrified. Well-brought-up girls didn't do that sort of thing. Though I was in my mid-twenties, and they'd given up expecting me to get married.'

'I can't imagine why.'

'Oh, I was never broken to harness, that's all. Well, he was quite a bit older than me – a client of the office I was working in. I fell rather madly in love with him *before* I discovered he was married.' She shrugged in the darkness. 'I make no excuse. It was wrong. But I wanted him, and I've never been good at being refused what I want. And, like many things that one wants but shouldn't have, it didn't live up to the anticipation. As soon as I had him, I fell out of love.'

'Did he hurt you?'

'Not like that. But once the smoke cleared from my eyes, it all seemed just too squalid. So I broke it off – told him I'd never see him again.' A pause. 'And that is the sum total of my experience. Not a very edifying tale.'

He squeezed her against him a little, a gesture of comfort. 'Do you want to ask me any questions?'

'One day,' she said. 'Not now.'

'So there will *be* a "one day"?'

'Unless you're going to tell me you're married.'

'No, I'm not married. Never have been. Never found the right woman – until now. But there have been . . . experiences.'

'So I guessed,' she said, treasuring the 'until now' for later. She pushed herself up on one elbow to look down at him. He was just a pallor in the darkness – she couldn't see his expression. 'You're going away,' she said. 'I don't know when I'll next see you. I hope that it will be some time soon, but I can't bank on it.'

'You know I—' he began, but she stopped him.

'I'm glad we did this. I feel – very warm towards you. But I'm afraid of loving anyone too much while this wretched war goes on. Can you understand that? I have to hold back.'

'I understand,' he said, though he didn't sound happy about it.

'Don't be sad,' she said. 'You know where I am. As long as you want to go on seeing me, you won't lose me. Just – if you don't mind too terribly much – don't talk about love.'

He drew her down and kissed her, and she felt her resolve weakening. But he said, 'Very well. You know how I feel. I won't talk about it any more.'

'When the war's over . . .' she said.

'Ah, then! A lot of pledges will be waiting to be redeemed on that day.'

CHAPTER EIGHT

The house was quiet when Sadie got in. Peter was not home from school yet, her mother, she knew, was at Hastings Road, and she remembered Antonia had said she was going to be bandage-rolling that afternoon for the Red Cross at the church rooms – something she could do sitting down. Cocking her head, she could just hear the murmur of voices from David's room – his last pupil of the day. The small coat and cap on the hall-stand confirmed the presence.

Nailer came sidling up to her, appearing from nowhere, and leaned against her legs. He was rather catlike in some ways, she thought. She reached down and scratched his head. He must have been turfed out of David's room for some reason. It was the one room that always had a good fire, and he liked to spend most of his day there. She looked at the clock and saw it was just on the hour. David's pupil would be about to leave. She decided to walk upstairs and see if he would like a cup of tea with her.

The door of his sitting-room opened as she reached the top of the stairs, and a small boy came out, stuffing a book into his satchel. David's voice followed him: 'Two more chapters of the *Iliad* for next time. And read Monro's commentary.'

'Yes, sir,' the boy said, and scuttled away. He saw Sadie at the last minute, stopped, stared, seemed about to say something, then ducked his head, gasped, 'Sorry!' and shot past.

David's door was still ajar, and Nailer, who had followed her upstairs, dashed past her and took his chance to squeeze in. David said something – she couldn't tell what, but it didn't sound welcoming. Then she was at the door, looking in. David was in one of the armchairs by the fire, and was tipping something, the source concealed in his fist, into his mouth.

He jumped at the sight of her, then scowled and snapped, 'Shut the door. That bloody boy left it open. There's a draught.'

Sadie closed it, but with her on the inside, which she suspected was not what he'd meant. He was not in a sunny mood; and seeing him, she could tell why. He was white and sweating, and his hand shook as he re-capped the small bottle. 'Did I say you could come in?' he growled. He shoved the bottle into his pocket.

'You're in pain,' Sadie said.

'Thank you for telling me. I would never have known.'

'You don't have to pretend in front of me,' she said.

'You'll bring the hordes in your wake.'

'No, everybody's out. I let myself in. Nobody knows I'm here. Let me do something for you. Would you like a cup of tea?'

'You can get me a drink,' he said. 'Whisky.'

'If that was laudanum you probably shouldn't drink alcohol on top of it,' she said doubtfully.

'When I want lectures from you, I'll ask for them,' he said, glaring. She returned the look steadily, and his eyes shifted away. 'It's just paregoric,' he said, and when she didn't move, he sighed and took out the bottle again. 'Look.'

It was a little flat-sided bottle just four inches tall, with the sort of cap that contains a dropper inside. The label said PAREGORIC all right, in red capitals, and underneath, in smaller letters, *Tincture Opium Camphorate*. The word 'opium' made her shiver inwardly. But paregoric was not nearly as strong as laudanum.

107

He was watching her face. 'The pain's bad just now,' he said. 'Just get me a small whisky.' She turned, about to go down to the drawing-room, but he stopped her. 'In the bookcase, there. Behind the Hebrew dictionary.'

Puzzled, she went and drew out the fat dictionary, and found a flat quarter-bottle of Scotch hidden behind it against the wall. She turned back to him. 'Oh, David,' she said reproachfully. 'Hiding bottles?'

'Stop nagging! Give me the damn bottle, and if you can't think of anything to do but whine, you can get out.'

She brought the bottle and the water glass from the table, watched him pour out an amount, and would have taken the bottle back, but he deliberately put it down by his feet at the side of his chair, giving her a sour look. 'What are you doing here anyway? Shouldn't you be playing with your ponies?'

She decided the best thing she could do for him was to distract him, so she sat, taking her time, in the other armchair. Nailer, who had been sitting staring at the fire, raised one hind leg to his ear for a vigorous scratch, then lay down and settled his nose on his paws with a comfortable groan.

'I wasn't up at Highclere this afternoon,' she said. 'I was driving the ambulance.'

'Oh. Yes. I'd forgotten.'

'There was a notice up on the board at the depot, when I took my 'bus back today. About a course in motor maintenance. I was thinking it might be a good idea to sign up for it. Just in case one got stranded somewhere – it would be nice to know what to do.'

Even a few moments ago he would have given her an irritable reply, but obviously the paregoric was taking effect, for some of the desperate lines in his face had loosened. He said, not entirely pleasantly, 'Engines now, is it? My, my. Our little Sadie, growing up so fast.'

'Not so little. I'm nineteen, you know.'

'I know,' he said, staring at her critically. 'You're turning into a young lady, despite all your horsy activities. And you're walking out with that Beresford fellow, aren't you?'

'I'm not "walking out" with him. We just – do things together sometimes.'

'Does he know that, poor sap? You females, the way you toy with a man's feelings! Like a cat with a bird.'

His first fiancée, Sophie Oliphant, had 'chucked' him after he got wounded, and had married a richer man with the use of both legs. Sadie felt he shouldn't mind about Sophie now, given that he was married to Antonia, who adored him, but it was difficult to argue with him in his moodiness. She changed the subject. 'Would you like some tea now – as well as the whisky, I mean? Because I'm parched for a cup.'

He waved the suggestion away, leaned his head back and closed his eyes. Sadie thought he might be drifting off to sleep under the influence of the paregoric, and got quietly up to leave him. But when she got to the door he called her. She turned back. His eyes were still closed, but he said, in a normal tone, 'Don't keep Beresford on a string if you're not serious about him.'

'You don't know he's serious about *me*,' she argued.

'Oh, I think he is. Take it from one who knows.'

The new offensive started with a huge bombardment on the 9th of April, in the area of the River Lys, with the capture of Hazebrouck its obvious intention, as Lord Forbesson had predicted. From Hazebrouck the roads and railway lines ran to St Omer and then straight to Calais and Boulogne.

The brunt of the first attack fell on a section of the line being held by the Portuguese. They were due to be relieved by fresh British troops but the change-over had not been fully accomplished, and one Portuguese division, left holding a seven-mile stretch of the line, was attacked by eight German divisions. After a desperate defence they were overrun, opening a huge gap. The next day, the Germans extended the attack to the north and overran Armentières, taking virtually the whole of the Messines Ridge, and forcing the British back to hold a perilous line along the River Lys with the aid of the few divisions left in reserve.

If they broke through, it was only fifteen miles to the Channel ports.

Rumour raced about the capital, which for weeks had been seeing the wounded pouring in and young soldiers hardly old enough to shave marching out. Edward, struggling to get his work in a way to be left and to put his affairs in order, heard the talk all around him. There had been near panic in the corridors of the House. Haig, they were whispering, had said that if they didn't get French reinforcements, the Germans could be at the coast within a week.

On Thursday the 11th, the commander-in-chief's Order of the Day made chilling reading. Every soldier was issued with a copy, and they were soon widely distributed.

Three weeks ago to-day the enemy began his terrific attacks against us on a fifty-mile front. His objects are to separate us from the French, to take the Channel Ports and destroy the British Army.

In spite of throwing already 106 Divisions into the battle and enduring the most reckless sacrifice of human life, he has as yet made little progress towards his goals.

We owe this to the determined fighting and self-sacrifice of our troops. Words fail me to express the admiration which I feel for the splendid resistance offered by all ranks of our Army under the most trying circumstances.

Many amongst us now are tired. To those I would say that Victory will belong to the side which holds out the longest. The French Army is moving rapidly and in great force to our support.

There is no other course open to us but to fight it out.

110

Every position must be held to the last man: there must be no retirement. With our backs to the wall and believing in the justice of our cause each one of us must fight on to the end. The safety of our homes and the Freedom of mankind alike depend upon the conduct of each one of us at this critical moment.

Backs to the wall? To the last man? Edward thought. Had it come to that? In the club in the evening, when he had called in for a quick bite of supper before going back to his office – he had too much to do to be able to go home that night – he heard other members talking about it.

'Haig's not the chap to panic. If he says that, you can take it that it's serious.'

'I've heard they're marching the Frogs up, but God knows if they'll be in time.'

'The Hun only needs to break through the line, not roll it up. That's the devil of the position. If he does that, we'll be done for.'

'God help us!'

God help us indeed, Edward thought. He felt a taut frustration that it would be weeks before he – and the others of the new intake – would be ready to go out there. Every man was needed, and needed *now*.

By the time they were through their training, it might already be too late. His country's future was in the balance. He was suddenly fiercely glad he had accepted the call-up, whatever then had been his motives.

Though she was sleeping on the upper floor now, it was Ethel who heard, got out of bed, and came downstairs to find David, a dressing-gown over his nightshirt, crutch under his armpit, dithering on the landing. He greeted her with relief.

'Oh, thank God you came! I was wondering who to rouse.'

111

There was a moan from the room behind him – a quiet one.

Ethel guessed Mrs David was doing her best not to make a noise, for her husband's sake. 'When did it start?' she asked.

'She said she was feeling uncomfortable at dinner,' he answered distractedly. 'That was hours ago. How long does it take? For God's sake, call the doctor!'

'I'll just have a word with her first,' said Ethel. 'Don't worry, sir, it *does* take hours.'

Antonia was sitting up with her legs over the edge of the bed. She reached out and took Ethel's hand as she approached and squeezed it hard. She screwed up her face in pain, but she didn't make a sound. Ethel bore the painful pressure, remembering what it was like. She'd have been glad of someone to hold *her* hand.

When the spasm was over, Antonia said, 'Don't let Mr David worry – it isn't good for him. Do you think I should walk about? I feel as if it might help.'

'Walking's good,' Ethel said. She helped Antonia to her feet. There were voices out in the passage. The mistress had woken, and was talking to David.

Now Beattie appeared in the door. 'Oh – Ethel. What a good thing you're here. I'll stay with Mrs David while you go and wake Peter up – I'll need him to run round with a note for Nula. What a pity she's not on the telephone. Don't let him make too much noise. Then you can get dressed. I shall need you.'

'Shouldn't you be telephoning for the doctor?' David was asking anxiously from behind her.

'When I've spoken to Antonia, and found out what's going on. No point in sending for him too early – there'll be nothing for him to do until the end. Nula and I can manage everything until then.'

'But—'

'It's not an illness, David, it's a perfectly natural process.

112

You mustn't worry. She'll be quite all right. When I've spoken to Antonia you can come and sit with her, but only if you don't make a fuss.'

Her calmness was spreading like a pool of quiet, and Ethel could see that David was reassured – not wholly, you couldn't expect that with a first baby, but a lot.

Ethel thought, as she headed for Peter's room, that with six of her own, and this being the second grandchild, the missus ought to know what was what. It was a pity the master wasn't here. She'd probably have liked to have him around, not that men were any use, except for – what did they call it? – moral support.

'It's funny-looking, isn't it?' said Peter, critically. 'Sort of squashed and wrinkled.'

'It's not an it, he's a he,' Sadie said. 'And I expect you looked like that when you were just born.'

Peter was put in mind of some baby rats he had seen when a school-fellow's pet white had given birth – naked, pink, and blindly flexing their tiny paws. But he thought he had better not give voice to that thought.

Cook had slept through the whole drama. It was only when Emily brought up her cup of tea at six that she learned Mrs David was in labour. By then the doctor had been sent for, and by seven it was all over, Mrs David was sitting up in bed sipping a cup of tea, and a new Hunter had done its initial wailing and was asleep in the cot at the foot of the bed.

Cook found herself unaccountably weepy. Of course, one always shed a tear at births, same as weddings – tears of happiness. But she couldn't help thinking of the terrible situation at the Front, our boys in retreat, the wicked Huns advancing . . . This baby, poor little mite, was a child of war, and his father had already paid a terrible price. If the Germans got to the Channel . . . If they got to England . . .

113

Nula, made unusually garrulous by excitement and weariness mixed, regaled them in the kitchen with an account of the struggle, to which Emily listened with mouth and eyes wide open, until Cook noticed her and gave a loud warning cough.

Ada had listened with a mixture of hope, doubt and fear. She would like – in theory – to have a baby with Len; but she was probably too old. On the other hand, she understood that what they had done together at the Swan in Westleigh could theoretically lead to a baby, and she might at this very moment be on her way to just such a painful and gory struggle as Mrs David had gone through. It was a frightening prospect – though having a little baby to hold afterwards would be wonderful.

Before the end of the day, the news had penetrated the kitchen regions that there was not, after all, to be a nurse brought in. The one Dr Postgate recommended was known to Nula, who said she was an antiquated old termagant and would put the household in a ferment, sour the mother's milk and give the baby colic. She had discussed the matter with Beattie, and it was agreed that Nula would come in daily for the first month to take care of Mrs David, that Ethel would take care of the baby, and a new under-housemaid would be sought..

In the kitchen, Ethel said she'd do anything if it meant getting out of housework, causing Cook and Ada to shake their heads reprovingly. She did not want anyone to guess at the feelings that had stirred when she had held the tiny warm bundle. Her own lost child had been a boy. A fierce determination to protect the smallest Hunter had been woken in her, quite against her will. She didn't like to be attached to anyone. Emotions trapped you and got you into trouble. But when she held the baby she didn't want to put him down, or hand him over to anyone, even his mother.

Beattie was glad it was a boy. She had not thought she

would care either way, but when she had held him, she had known that only a boy would do. David's son. Louis's grandson. Not a replacement but, rather, a *completion*.

She searched the crumpled face for likeness, but he was too new to show the imprint of his line. Oh, baby, born into such a troubled world! She remembered the moment when she had first held David as a new-born. She had not known the uncomplicated joy of motherhood: her passionate adoration of her child had always been tinged with sadness.

Edward had left the club by the time Beattie's telegram arrived, but the porter knew Sir Edward and sent it round to his office at the bank, and there he received the news that his daughter-in-law had given birth to a boy.

Murchison, his elderly clerk, hovering in the doorway, said, 'Not bad news, I hope, Sir Edward?'

Edward roused himself, aware that his face must reflect his inner turmoil. 'No, not at all,' he said neutrally. His grandson. Not his grandson. He loved David, and this was a wonderful thing for him. He liked and admired Antonia, and was truly glad for her. But there was a hollow at the heart of what should have been unshadowed happiness. Oh, it was good that he was going away!

'Telephone my house, will you, and say that I shall be home this evening?'

'Yes, Sir Edward.'

'And send a telegram – no, I'll do it myself.' He did not want Murchison's ponderous good wishes. 'And send in Mr Cruikshank.'

Cruikshank was the manager Head Office had sent him to do his work while he was away: an experienced man in his sixties, safe from being conscripted. There was still a great deal to get through with him. But he sent a telegram of congratulation to Antonia and David, and managed to arrive home at seven thirty bearing flowers and a box of crystallised fruit he had bought at Fortnum's on his way to the Tube. Antonia seemed pleased with the offering, as he kissed her and asked her how she felt.

'Very well,' she said. 'Tired, a little.'

'Proud of yourself, I hope,' he said.

'Oh, yes. And grateful. I never thought I'd be in this happy position.' She smiled deprecatingly. 'Everyone thought I was destined to be an old maid.'

He held the little mite, who was trying to open his eyes, and flinching them shut again after the briefest peep, but he did not manage to feel anything at all about it. Men, he thought, did not have the instinctive response to tiny babies that women did. The interest came later, when they were walking and talking. He managed at any rate to be glad it had happened before he went away. It seemed . . . tidier that way.

He glanced covertly at David, sitting in the armchair on the other side of the bed, his crutches to hand. He thought he looked more than usually worn and dishevelled – perhaps understandably. And he had thought he'd smelt whisky on his breath. 'Have you thought of a name?' Edward asked, to get away from such a troubling thought.

David answered, 'Antonia wanted to call him Bobby, and we did think about it, but it would have to be Robert, and I've never much liked that name.'

'Bobby never really was a Robert,' Edward said. 'I don't think I ever remember calling him that.'

'And then I suggested naming him after Antonia's father—'

'And I suggested naming him Edward,' Antonia said.

'So we compromised on Marcus, because we were reading Marcus Aurelius just before it all kicked off,' David concluded.

'Marcus Hunter,' Edward said. 'It has a certain ring to it.' He wondered what sort of world Marcus would grow up into. And what sort of a man he would be. Would he look

116

like David? It was a painful thought. Tall, big-framed, with that reddish hair and hawklike profile, David didn't look anything like Edward. But the baby couldn't help his heritage, any more than David could. He had always loved David as his own, and he would love Marcus, too. And pray that, at the very least, he would grow up in a world without war.

Edward had not meant to wait until the last minute to announce his leaving, but it had proved harder to come out with it than he had expected. For one thing, he had had so much to do at work to get ready, so many difficult interviews to conduct with the bank, the Treasury, the Food Ministry, the conscription appeals tribunals, with Carnegie, his man of business – with Élise. That was, perhaps, the hardest. She had accepted his decision without protest, but he knew she was wondering if he was running away from her. Her fear for him was in her eyes, and when she lifted her face he could not refuse to kiss her. A kiss goodbye. She did not ask him to write to her, and inwardly he saluted her courage. She must know she might never see him again, but they parted on *au revoir*, not *adieu*.

Since he had made the decision he had hardly been at home; and when he was, he was tired, and it was always late, and he could not contemplate opening the subject just then. He kept putting it off. The sight of Beattie gave him pain in a complex mixture of ways, and though his anger with her was still strong, it fought against years of tenderness and care. His going would hurt her, and one part of him wanted only to make her happy.

And so it got to Sunday, and since he had to leave on the Monday, there was no more time left. It had to be faced. When they got back from church, he asked Beattie to come into his study for a moment. 'I want to talk to you privately.' He would have had to be blind not to see the quick flash of alarm the request caused.

'I must speak to Cook about luncheon,' she said, instinctively evading.

'Please.' And he held open the door, so that she had to walk in.

He closed it behind her, and went over to the window, staring out unseeingly, assembling his words. When he turned, he saw she had stopped just inside the door, like a toy that had wound down, her face a mask of inexpression.

He couldn't think of any way to say it except just to blurt it out. 'My call-up papers came. I'm to report tomorrow for basic training.'

She stared. 'You mean – the army? But you don't have to go.'

'I'm going anyway. I decided not to appeal,' he said. He watched the words filter through her mind.

Then she said bluntly, 'Why?'

'You know why.'

She closed her eyes a moment, as though taking a blow. 'No,' she said. Her hands clenched into fists. 'Please, for God's sake, don't make it that.'

'It's done,' he said.

Now she looked at him in desperate appeal. 'I'll go away, if you want. If you can't bear to be in the house with me.'

'Go where?' he asked in surprise. He hadn't expected her to say that.

'Anywhere. I don't know. To my sister's. To Ireland.'

'Ireland,' he said, flatly. The very word was hateful to him now.

She winced at his tone. 'It isn't—' She drew a breath. 'Wherever you like, then. Just don't think you have to – to immolate yourself.'

'It's not a sacrifice.' He could not bear any more discussion on the subject. She was to blame, yes, but he had betrayed her too. What was needed mostly was to remove the chafed surfaces from rubbing against each other. 'My mind is made up,' he said coldly, so that she should not argue. 'I am going to do my duty. I've put my affairs in order. Your allowance will be paid as usual, and if anything else comes up, Carnegie will arrange for you to draw what you need. Go to him with any questions. He has my full authority.'

'Don't,' she began, a feeble word of protest, like one too tired to fight off an attacker.

He went on inexorably: 'And if – if anything should happen, you will be taken care of – you and the children. Carnegie has all the papers. There would have to be a process of probate, but—'

'Why are you *doing* this?' she cried. 'You don't need to!'

'I have to do my duty.' He knew that wasn't enough, and went on, 'I've seen the lengths some people will go to, to get out of it. It's – contemptible. I won't be one of them. The country needs every man. I'm not a special case. I don't merit special treatment.'

He paused, running out of words, expecting argument or anger from her, which would have primed the pump and allowed him to carry on. But she said nothing, only looked at him wretchedly. He had to brace himself not to go to her.

'Well,' he said at last, 'that's all. I'll tell the others at luncheon.'

Peter was excited that his father was going to the war, and proud, too. It would put him on a par with other boys at school whose dads had gone. He could see nothing strange in it.

Sadie, who understood that he could have exempted himself, accepted the news in troubled silence, looking from his face to her mother's, trying to understand.

Edward had been upstairs to tell David and Antonia – she was still in childbed, and he was having his luncheon on a tray with her. David had heard it in silence, then talked about the war situation, gaining animation, as if his father could be his proxy. He had never become reconciled to the unfinished nature of his own crusade. Antonia had said nothing at first, and when she did speak, it was only to ask if he had everything he needed, and who would be packing for him.

At lunch, Beattie was silent, fiddling with her cutlery, not eating, trying to appear normal. She had brought this disaster on them. If only he could have expressed his anger in some other way. She would have sooner he beat her than go nobly into battle to punish her. What would she do without him? She had never had to ask that question before. He had always been there. What if the worst, the unthinkable, happened, and he didn't come back? *How could she manage without him?*

The rest of Sunday fled by, in a strange, taut atmosphere of mingled anxiety and false joviality. On Monday morning he was up, packed and ready to go before it was fairly light. Beattie had been awake for hours, and went down to the early breakfast Cook had provided. He glanced up from his plate when she came in, but did not speak. She sat at the other end of the table in silence and watched him eating. Only when he laid down his knife and fork and drained his cup, preparing to rise, did she say, desperately, 'Don't go.'

He gave a grim quirk of his lips that was not quite a smile. 'It's too late now,' he said. 'The die is cast.' He pushed back his chair and rose. 'I expect all over the country men who never expected to go are saying goodbye to their wives.'

But you haven't said goodbye to me, she thought. She believed, until the last moment, that he would not part from her without a kind word, if not a kiss; but when he was at the front door, with his bag in his hand, he still had not met her eyes. The servants gathered by the kitchen passage to see him go, wide-eyed and, in Cook's case, tearful; and Sadie, Peter, Antonia and even David came downstairs.

'Take care, Papa,' Sadie said, in a subdued voice.

120

'Kill lots of Germans, Dad,' Peter said eagerly.

'I've weeks of training yet, before I get near a German,' Edward told him, gave a general nod for the household to share between them, and was gone.

CHAPTER NINE

The German attack in Flanders continued; French and British units, somehow scraped together, counter-attacked, slowing but not halting the German advance. More forces were being marched up, those already in the zone of conflict hurried from place to place to plug gaps as they occurred. The army machine was at full stretch, getting food and ammunition to the fighters, sometimes having to follow them from place to place, trying to catch up. These were desperate times.

The new conscription limits were combing out younger and older men, even from previously reserved occupations. Ada was shaking out the front doormat one morning when the postman came up the path. 'Morning, Mr Hicks,' she greeted him.

'I don't know what's good about it,' he said.

'Oh? Something up?' she asked. He was usually so cheerful.

'I got my call-up yesterday. Me, at my age! I'll be gone by the end of the week.'

'Oh dear! I'm sorry,' Ada said hesitantly. You didn't know what to say in a case like this. Everybody had to do their bit. Len had had to go. But Mr Hicks was probably in his late forties, and it must have come as a shock.

'The wife's rare put out,' he said. 'There's our Andy already at the Front, and our Sheila's husband, with Sheila and the nipper living with us while he's away. Every day Mother's on tenterhooks. She says now she'll have me to worry about as well. She'll never have a moment's peace.'

'It does seem hard,' Ada murmured.

'I sometimes think war's harder on the women than anyone. At least once you're in uniform you can *do* something. But just waiting around . . .' He sighed and shook himself. 'Oh well, no sense grousing about it. King and country, and so on.' He handed over the bundle of post, and said slyly, 'Got a wrong 'un there – letter addressed to a Mrs Armstrong. Oughta take it back, didn't I?'

Ada blushed. 'Oh you! You know that's me.'

'The one you've been waiting for, eh? Well, glad to bring a bit of sunshine into somebody's life.'

The letter, when she had a moment to open it, was written in carefully taught elementary-school script, and formally phrased like a classroom exercise – as unlike as possible Fred's saucy scribbles.

My dear Wife,

I write hoping this finds you as it leaves me, in the Pink. We have been in the thick of it, but my lads have acquitted themselves well and I've no complaints. Assure yourself that I am Unhurt, though we are all very weary and very dirty! We are out at rest somewhere near Plug Street, but due to go back in the line shortly, as every man is needed in the current Emergency. You are in my thoughts constantly and the memory of those wonderful two days we had together keeps me going whenever things are uncomfortable. I hope and trust you are enjoying Good Health and I pray this war is over soon so that I can come home to you.

With all my love,
Ever your devoted Husband,
L. Armstrong

It was not much of a billy-doo, Ada thought, and did not even sound like Len, not the cheery, funny, warm Len she knew. Some people would not put themselves down on paper – she was sure her letters to him were even more stilted. But at least it told her he was all right. She kept it in her apron pocket as a talisman.

With more men being taken out of the workforce, and most of the women who were able to work already employed, their places had to be taken by children. In the countryside, they had always been withdrawn from school to help with seasonal farm work; now the towns followed suit, and factories, workshops and even mines filled the gaps with boys and girls. Children weren't allowed to be employed under twelve, but ages were rarely checked, and though the local school inspector was supposed to stop abuses of the law, most of them had been called up too, and those who were left had to cover larger and larger areas. The chances of being caught out were small.

The Hunters' boy, Ginger, proudly gave his notice, saying he was going to work in the shoe factory on the Walford road. 'Makin' army boots. Important job. Can't win no war wivout boots.'

'Good riddance,' was Cook's response to the news that he was going. 'Born to be hanged, that young limb.'

There was no difficulty in obtaining a new boy, a scrub-headed lad called Timmy, who said he was twelve, though Emily said she knew his family and he was really only ten. Cook approved of his respectfulness, born of timidity, but predicted it wouldn't last. 'Boys always end up cheeky,' she said sadly. 'It's the way the Almighty makes 'em. Snips and snails and puppies' tails.'

Munt alone was sorry that Ginger had gone – the lad was strong and had learned a lot. He viewed the new recruit without optimism. Timmy was tall for his age, but pale and limp, like forced celery. Muscles like peas in a hosepipe. And timidity towards Her in the kitchen was not a virtue to Munt. Kitchen and garden shared the boot boy, and the one he was scaredest of inevitably got first dibs. He was going to have to work hard to put the fear o' God into the lad.

Cook might have liked the look of Timmy, but she was doubtful at first about the new under-housemaid, a solid, busty girl called Beryl. She claimed to have worked for gentry-folk before, and her last employer was a respectable old lady, but she had been the sole servant. 'We never had a maid-of-all-work in this house before,' Cook complained. 'House-parlourmaids, that's what Mrs Hunter keeps. *Lady* Hunter, I should say.'

Ada soon surmised that Beryl's old lady had exercised little supervision. The girl was addicted to short-cuts of the sweeping-dirt-under-the-carpet sort. She dusted round ornaments instead of lifting them, didn't move the furniture to sweep under it. Ada was outraged when she caught Beryl one day, while laying the table, spitting on a fork and rubbing it on her apron.

'We don't do that sort of thing in this house!' she cried. 'Go and fetch a clean one!'

Beryl was unmoved. 'I'll soon learn your little ways,' she said, as if it was of no great moment.

However, she was strong, healthy, and – at least overtly – obedient, and Cook told Ada they couldn't be too fussy in wartime, when all the brightest girls had gone to the factories.

'The day I stop being fussy you can screw down the lid,' Ada retorted.

Beryl found Cook's favour by praising her cooking – 'The grub's better here'n any place I've been!' She cleared her plate, no matter what was served, was always ready for seconds, and never minded the gristly bit or the burned end if it fell to her portion. Ethel, observing her, decided it was

125

just a lack of discrimination, that she was simply a gannet who would eat anything.

But Cook, having once taken the compliment to herself, would not give it up, and persisted in thinking Beryl had her points. 'Give the girl a chance,' she said. 'We all got to have a chance.'

The wounded poured back, over thirty thousand a week, to be dispersed throughout the country, wherever there was capacity. They were supposed, where possible, to be sent close to their home, but with such numbers coming in it was not possible to be choosy. Sadie was now driving an ambulance for three afternoons a week, meeting the trains at Northcote station. One day, when she drove up to the front of Dene Park, she was surprised to see Diana following the receiving party out. She jumped down from the cab and claimed her attention.

'Oh, it's you!' Diana said, seeming rather distracted. 'What are you doing here?'

'Driving the ambulance,' said Sadie. 'More to the point, what are you doing here?'

'It *is* my house.'

'Don't tell me you're thinking of becoming a nurse?'

'Don't be absurd. If you must know, my mother-in-law wanted me to come and check on them, to make sure things weren't getting damaged.'

'Why didn't she come herself?'

'She can't bear the idea of Dene being "defiled".'

'Did she actually say that?' Sadie marvelled.

'She has very definite views,' Diana said; and then frowned in thought. 'I hadn't realised things were so desperate. It's awful! Look at these poor men! And there are so many of them.'

'I know,' said Sadie bluntly. 'Every time I meet a train I think the flood must stop soon, but it doesn't.'

'Where do you take them all?'

'Wherever there's room,' said Sadie. 'Yesterday I had to go as far as St Luke's in Walford, and that's eight miles away. It used to be an old people's home run by nuns, until the government requisitioned it. And a couple of days ago I had to take men to a private nursing home out in the country on the other side of Rustington. I did feel sorry for the poor boys, being bumped over country lanes.'

Diana turned to look at the façade of the house – massive, rather grim, designed originally to impress rather than welcome. 'I'm glad, now, that Rupert suggested offering part of the house for a hospital.' It eased her conscience to think that they were doing something for the wounded.

'Have you heard from him lately?' Sadie asked.

'Not for ten days. His last letter said he was somewhere in the Lys Valley, and that's where the fighting is, so I suppose he's too busy to write.'

'How calm you sound! Aren't you worried?'

'Of course I am, but I have to think of the baby. The doctor said fretting is the worst thing for it.'

'How are you feeling? Are you well?' Sadie asked.

'I'm well, but I do get awfully tired. I hardly go out any more. I don't really like people seeing me when I'm like this.'

'Why don't you stay down here, then?'

'I have thought about it. I only stay in Town, really, in case Rupert gets leave.'

'You could go back up if he does. There are such things as telephones. And telegrams,' Sadie pointed out. 'Do come! Nula would love the chance to spoil you. And Mother would love having little George nearby.'

Diana smiled – a tired smile, but it illuminated her beauty. 'I'll think about it.' She looked around. 'It's so green here. It's very soothing.'

Sadie, looking round, saw something else. 'They've

finished unloading me. I have to go.' She started back towards her ambulance.

'How is Antonia?' Diana called after her. 'And the baby?'

'Flourishing. You should come and see.'

'I shall. I have to go up tonight, but I'll call in at home on the way.'

The Germans were advancing relentlessly on Ypres, and in Poperinghe, the locals began to leave. Every day there was a procession westwards past Artemis House, of residents burdened with their worldly possessions, staggering along with suitcases and bundles, some pushing a laden pram or handcart, the luckier with a horse and cart. Some led a goat on a string, or had a wire cage crammed with chickens on top of the load. A small girl carried a cage in which a canary jumped monotonously back and forth from perch to perch in stiff anxiety. Dogs ran behind, or were dragged along on leads; but there were no cats. You couldn't take a cat with you. Left behind, they shook off domesticity as a dog shakes off water. You saw them at night, slipping from shadow to shadow, hunting in the empty houses and barns as if they had never known a caress or a warm human lap.

Troops passed in the hundreds, boots slamming the cobbles, and a steady stream of wounded was being evacuated. Laura thought often of Ransley, in more danger now, nearer the Front. How long Pop would be safe, she had no idea. The guns sounded horribly close.

Oddly enough, Louisa did not seem anxious. Since Major Ransley had gone away, she had been a new person, energetic, calm, even singing about her work. The sound of the shelling growing nearer didn't bother her. 'We have to stay,' she said, when Laura mentioned the possibility of leaving. 'We're needed more than ever.'

As units were evacuated, fewer women were coming in.

Their brother house, Toc H, was overwhelmed, so they decided to allow the Tommies to use Ack Harry, to rest, write letters and take some refreshment. The tea urn was always on the go, and one of them was generally to be found making sandwiches of army ration bully and bread, diverted their way by a sympathetic commander who recognised the good work they were doing.

On the 19th of April Vlamertinghe was shelled, and on the 20th the first shells fell on the easternmost edge of Pop.

On the morning of the 21st, Laura was manning the tea urn, while Louisa and Ronnie were handing out mugs and lighting cigarettes for the latest influx of soldiers: they were all exhausted, many of them having been in the line for weeks without relief.

'You ladies ought to think about leaving,' one of them said to Laura. 'If Wipers goes, there'll be nothing between you and the Jerries.'

'You don't think there's any danger of Ypres falling?' she asked.

He shrugged. 'They're practically up to the walls. Not much keeping 'em out now.'

Hardly had he turned away with his mug in his hand than there was the shrieking scream of a shell, someone shouted, 'Get down!' and the whole house shook as a tremendous explosion burst somewhere nearby. Laura was on the floor under the table, without knowing how she had got there. There was a heavy, desperate rumbling somewhere close by. She heard glass shattering. Lumps of plaster fell from the ceiling. She turned her head cautiously and found herself looking into the Tommy's face, an inch from hers. He had got under the table too. His whistling breath was stirring her hair.

'Blimey, that was close,' he said.

They crawled cautiously out. The air was so full of dust, it was like smoke; but no-one seemed to be hurt. Everyone was getting up, brushing themselves off, listening for the next shell.

'I'm getting out of here,' said Laura's Tommy, 'and if you've got any sense, you'll hook it too. One near miss is all you can count on. Means they've got your range.'

Others evidently agreed: in a few minutes the room had cleared of uniforms like magic. The three women went to investigate the damage, and found that the shell had fallen on the house two doors down, largely demolishing it.

At the sight, Louisa turned pale. 'I never thought—' she began. She clutched at Laura's arm. 'All that happened in a second!'

'It's nasty,' Laura said, reading her mind. It was all very well to say you weren't afraid of the shelling before you had seen the results of a hit.

Artemis House had largely escaped damage. The front upper windows had been broken, half a dozen slates had slipped on the roof, and the chimney was crooked. And there was a long crack down the wall of the kitchen on that side.

'But we're still in working order,' Laura said.

'And don't they say you can't get hit twice?' Louisa suggested uncertainly.

'That's lightning,' Ronnie said. 'We must think about moving.'

'Reluctantly, I agree,' said Laura. 'Let's clear up a bit, and talk about what to do.'

While they were sweeping up the mess, an officer from the local headquarters, passing and seeing their door open, came in to investigate and said, 'What are you still doing here? I thought this whole road had been evacuated.'

Laura tried to explain. 'We're Artemis House. We—'

He interrupted coldly. 'I know who you are. But you shouldn't be here.' Not numbered amongst their fans, Laura thought. 'You ladies will have to leave. The barrage is getting closer all the time.'

130

'Toc H are staying,' said Ronnie. 'I spoke to Captain Strachan this morning.'

'They're army,' he snapped. 'Civilians are nothing but a nuisance when things get hot. You'll simply be in the way. Pack up and get out, as quick as you can.'

He said it like an order, though of course he had no direct authority over them. When he had gone, the three women looked at each other, and Ronnie shrugged. 'I hate to give in, but I suppose we'll have to go.' In the background they could hear the crashing of shells, feel the ground trembling as they exploded on the edge of town.

'I wonder what our patroness will say about our abandoning the house,' Louisa said.

Laura wondered, but did not say aloud, where Ransley was, and how he would find her if she left here.

They abandoned the clearing up, and started to pack. The shelling went on, with some crashes sounding so close they jumped. They would freeze for a moment, listening, to see if they were hit. Then they carried on. There was a lot to be done.

Mid-afternoon, there was a rapping at the front door. They all went to see, and found an army lorry at the kerb, engine running. In the back were a dozen walking wounded, and three nurses had crammed themselves into the cab beside the driver.

Another nurse had done the knocking. 'They've evacuated the hospital,' she said. 'We're the last. You ought to go.'

'We're packing up now,' Ronnie said.

The nurse produced an envelope. 'One of the patients who came down last night from a dressing station gave us this, asked us to deliver it. Is one of you called Laura Huntley?'

'Hunter,' Laura corrected. 'That's me.'

The nurse handed over the letter, and they all flinched as a shell screamed down and exploded somewhere in the next

131

street. The driver, leaning out of his window, said, 'If this is what winning the bloody war looks like, God help the losers! Hurry up, miss.'

The nurse shrugged a goodbye at them, and ran to the back of the lorry. Two Tommies reached down for her, and the vehicle was moving off almost before she had scrambled aboard.

The three women went indoors, shaken by the evidence of panic. In the hall, Laura read the note. 'Army is holding Ypres but enemy skirting it and heading towards Hazebrouck. You are not safe and should leave. We are falling back towards Merville. Not hurt, trust you are the same. Let me know where you fetch up so I can write. Ever yours, JR.'

She saw the point. The army's postal system would always find him, but he would not know where to write to her unless she gave him a direction.

'I think—' she began, when a tremendous explosion sent them all diving. The floorboards seemed to heave, there was a cacophony of broken glass, and a prolonged clattering from the back of the house. Pictures fell off the walls, the tea urn toppled from its table with a mighty crash, taking half a dozen mugs with it, and the piano jangled faintly as if crying in pain. *This is it*, Laura thought vaguely. Dust once again filled the air; there was a long, complaining creak from somewhere in the kitchen area, followed by a further rumbling crash.

At last they lifted their heads cautiously. 'That *was* us,' Ronnie said. 'We've been hit.'

They listened for a moment. Laura found her hands were shaking – reaction, she thought. 'Everyone all right?' she asked. Louisa was sobbing quietly. 'Lou?'

'I'm – all right,' she gasped.

'All right,' Ronnie said. Even she sounded shaken.

'It was somewhere at the back,' Laura said. 'We'd better go and see.'

She got up, but Louisa grabbed her and tried to pull her back. 'No, don't! It's not safe.'

Laura freed herself firmly. 'I think it's just been proved that we're not safe anywhere. We have to see how bad it is.'

A shell had fallen at the back of the house, blasting the conservatory into a mess of matchwood and shards of glass. The rumbling had been part of the wall of the kitchen coming down. There was a massive crater in the garden, shrubs were splintered, trees were gashed and leaning, roots exposed; and the remaining back wall of the house was sagging outwards, like soggy paper.

They surveyed it in silence. 'We'd better hurry,' Ronnie said. 'The rest could come down at any minute.'

Laura headed for the stairs, and Louisa shrieked in protest. 'Don't go up there! We've got to get out!'

'Not without our things,' Laura said. Another shell crashed somewhere near, and Louisa shrieked again. 'We're mostly packed – I'm not leaving everything.'

'I'll help,' Ronnie said. 'You stay here, Lou. We'll only be a minute.'

But Louisa didn't want to stay alone. All three ran upstairs, fearing second by second to feel disintegration beneath their feet, or hear the fateful rumbling of collapse. They grabbed whatever bags were packed, their coats, personal documents, and ran down again, and out into the street. There was a smell of burning in the air. Something nearby but out of sight was on fire.

Pop railway station was in the direction of the shelling: they would have to head the other way. 'We'll have to try and get a train at Steenvoorde,' Ronnie said. It was the next town, ten miles down the road towards St Omer.

'Everyone will want a train,' Laura said. 'They'll be crowded. We might not get on.'

'We'll just have to pull strings,' Ronnie said. Her confidence was reassuring.

Laura locked the door of Artemis House, wondering whether any of them would ever see it again. They put on their coats, redistributed their luggage more comfortably, and trudged forward.

They had only got as far as Abele, the next village, when at the crossroads an army lorry came up the side road from the direction of Bailleul. The driver stopped when he saw them, and said, 'Blimey, *wimmin*!' From the tone of his voice, they could have been Martians.

'Are you going to Steenvoorde?' Laura called to him.

Hearing the accent, he hastily corrected himself, and said, 'Beg pardon, I mean, ladies – but wot you doin' here?'

His companion leaned across him and said, 'Never mind that! You better get up behind, ladies, and we'll give you a lift. It ain't safe.'

So they climbed up into the back with a dozen grinning Tommies, and rode in style in the right direction – away from the shells.

CHAPTER TEN

Young men were flexible; young men were used to being
ordered about; young men had not had time to develop
settled habits. Most of all, young men were able to sleep on
anything that stayed still long enough.

Edward's first week in the army was hell. Well, perhaps
not hell, exactly, but invested with constant nagging discomfort and unpleasantness. The lack of privacy was probably
the worst thing for a middle-aged, middle-class, professional
man. He shared a tent with five others, dressing and
undressing under their eyes; had to wash and shave – in
cold water! – at a sort of communal trough. Army clothes
chafed; the boots gave him blisters; army food was unpalatable – his digestive system reacted with outrage.

He was physically exhausted all the time – at his age,
and having been desk-bound for years, he found the endless drilling and marching that filled their days hard to
endure. He understood that they had to be made fit; he
understood also that the bellowed orders and petty
discipline were meant to get them used to obeying without
thought, something that could save their lives in the battlefield. But he still resented the violence of being shouted
at, and it added to the mental exhaustion that stemmed
largely from being surrounded all the time with hundreds
of other men. What coarse and unlovely creatures men
were when separated from women, with their crude

laughter, their spitting and scratching and farting, their constant, monotonous swearing.

They were mostly youngsters of eighteen and nineteen. In his company – A Company – there was one other man caught by the rise in conscription age, a tall, thin man called Nellist, who was fifty, a chartered accountant. He seemed bewildered at finding himself there, and stumbled through each day with the look of someone trapped in a nonsensical dream. By army custom, the younger lads called them 'uncle', and Edward, at least, was accorded a certain respect for his age and education. They restrained their swearing a little when he was near, did not include him in the crudest of their jokes, and one or two even, shyly, brought questions and problems to him. Nellist did not fare quite so well. They seemed instinctively to perceive his weakness, called him Nelly behind his back, and played minor but tiresome tricks on him.

Their commanding officer, Colonel Craddock, was himself a dug-out, over sixty and fully sympathetic of Edward's plight. 'Comes to something, dragging in chaps like you,' he said on the first day. And later that first week, happening to meet Edward hobbling back across the parade ground from Swedish drill, he stopped him and said, 'I say – er – Hunter, isn't it?'

'Yes, sir?' Edward straightened himself to attention, feeling various things inside him creak, like the timbers of a ship worked by too heavy a sea.

'Yes – um – Swedish PT, was it? Do you find anything helpful in it? Physical jerks and so on?' He had rather bulging eyes and a truly outstandingly large nose, which made it difficult to look anywhere else when he spoke to you.

'No, sir,' Edward said frankly.

'Hmm. Lot of nonsense, really, for chaps like you. Won't do you any good when you're an officer. Going to apply for a commission, I presume?'

Edward hadn't really thought about it, but the idea now planted took hold at once. 'Yes, sir.'

Craddock nodded. 'Quite right! Desperately short of officers. Important to get the right sort of chap. Very good, then, you're excused Swedish from now on. The other uncle – what's his name?'

'Nellist, sir?'

'Nellist, that's it. He's excused too. I'll send Mr Larssen a chitty. Use the time to do some reading – that'll stand you in better stead when you get out to France. Come to my office later and I'll give you some books – fieldcraft and so on. Good stuff. Got your copy of the King's Regs?'

'Yes, sir.'

'Mug up on those. Best friend you can have, King's Regs. Very well, then.' He nodded kindly and walked away.

Relieved though he was to be spared physical jerks, Edward found he now had something new to worry about. *When you get out to France.* At night, in the tent, as he lay sleepless on his uncomfortable camp bed, he'd had plenty of time to regret his impulse to serve, to ask himself, *What have I done?* It had been hard enough to untangle himself from his civilian work, and he'd had protests, quite vehement ones, from the Treasury and the Food Ministry, let alone the bank, which seemed exasperated with him. He had not expected to enjoy army life particularly, but he had thought he would get used to it, and that there might be compensations in the companionship it would afford. But he had never until now considered the physical danger he would be in. Of course one spoke about 'if the worst should happen' but one did not visualise it in detail. *He might be killed.* Worse than that – yes, definitely worse – he might be horribly wounded, maimed, disfigured. He imagined himself without an arm, without an eye, with half his face missing. Blind, or driven witless. One of those poor creatures in a wheelchair with nothing below the knee. *Dear God!* He had sooner be killed than come back like that, and dwindle out his life pitied, having to be cared for.

He had accepted conscription to punish Beattie – and, yes, to punish himself. But for him to come back a legless cripple would be more punishment than he had ever intended.

What have I done?

Lying sleepless on his camp bed, which seemed to develop lumps in new places every night, surrounded by the smells and noises of his fellow men – feet and sweat, snores and moans – he longed for home, for his office, for his club, for the comforts of civilisation and the routines he had developed over decades, which were the oil in the machine of life.

And when he did finally fall asleep, he began to have a recurring dream. He was back in London, trying to get to his club, but he was in a street he didn't recognise, of identical semi-detached villas. He walked down the long, long road, thinking that when he reached the end there would be a high street, which would have shops and buses that would tell him where he was, and then he would find a Tube station and would know how to get to St James's. But when at last he reached the end, there was just another identical street of matching villas, stretching away in the shadowless light of a hot midday. And he trudged on, with the back of his mind telling him he would never find a Tube station. He would never get out.

'Up already?' Cook said in tones of surprise and disapproval. 'Hardly two weeks since she had that baby—'

'"Twas two weeks on Friday,' said Nula.

'She'll be lucky her insides don't slip,' said Cook. 'I remember you telling me when Mr David was born, the missus was six weeks abed.'

'Ah, young women today don't make the same thing of having a baby.'

'Not such a young woman,' Cook pointed out.

'Well, she's up, and that's that,' said Nula. 'Better in my mind she should get up than lie in bed when it frets her to death to do so. I'll keep an eye on her, don't you worry.'

'If you ask me,' said Ada, passing through to the scullery with damp cloths, 'she wants to be up so's she can keep an eye on Mr David. She's afraid he's doing too much.'

The birth of the baby had affected David in strange ways. At first, so it seemed to Antonia, he had seemed daunted by its arrival. He had smiled and said the right things to her, but she knew him very well, and was aware that the smiles did not touch his eyes, and the warm words were hollow. Studying him anxiously, she thought he seemed reluctant to touch the baby, or even look at him, and for the first few days had sunk into a brooding kind of misery. Had the new perfect life brought home to him his own spoiled body? she wondered. Or had he suddenly realised his responsibility for a wife and child, and feared he could not live up to it? Whatever it was, he was not happy, and her own joy at holding her child was shadowed by his strangeness.

But then had come the unexpected – even shocking – departure of Sir Edward, accepting conscription, refusing to appeal against it, though he was needed in London. On the day after the head of the household left, David had seemed to arise a new man. He had been up early, shaved and dressed himself, and instead of having breakfast on a tray with her, he had gone downstairs. 'I'm the man of the house now,' he had told her seriously. 'I have to take care of things.' She had listened to his halting progress down the stairs, and felt anxious, and forgotten.

Later, Beattie had come upstairs to see her, as had become her custom, and had told her that David had said the same thing to her – that he was the man of the house now. 'He's

139

in Edward's study now, looking over the household bills. I didn't like to tell him that I usually deal with them. I thought it was a good thing for him to take an interest. He has seemed . . . she hesitated, '. . . awfully *down* for some time now.'

'Yes,' said Antonia. 'It's hard for him, with so little to do.'

'He has his pupils,' Beattie pointed out.

'Yes, but they don't really satisfy his need to work.'

Beattie rubbed her hands together absently, deep in thought. 'I don't want him doing too much and tiring himself,' she said. 'He isn't strong.'

'Do you think so?' Antonia said in surprise. 'He seems to me very strong – that's the problem.'

Beattie looked angry. 'You don't understand him,' she said. 'It's not to be expected – you've known him such a little time. He can't bear to be pitied, so he'll hide any weakness from you. But I know he's in pain. I don't want you pushing him to do more than he can.'

It was lucky that the baby had started crying at that moment, or Antonia might have made a sharper answer than would have been safe, given that she and David lived in Beattie's house and were dependent on her and Edward. She had swallowed her hurt, and said, 'I would never do anything to harm him.'

Beattie moved her head restlessly, as though avoiding a touch. 'Not intentionally,' she allowed. 'But you don't know him as a mother does.'

Ethel came in with the baby in her arms. 'Time for his feed, madam,' she said, casting a covert look from one to the other. She had not overheard the words, but she could sense the atmosphere.

Beattie had left without another word. Antonia sighed unconsciously as she sat up more, while Ethel, the baby confidently in one arm, moved the pillows behind her to

140

support her. Settled, Antonia held out her arms for her child, and Ethel got him into the right position, and watched jealously until he was feeding steadily. She had never had a chance to feed her own baby. Sometimes she wanted to grab little Marcus and run away with him, as fast and as far as possible. But Mrs David supplied him with mother's milk, so she supposed she had to tolerate her.

She said, 'You mustn't let anything upset you, madam. It's bad for your milk.'

Antonia had looked up from contemplating her baby's perfect head, and smiled, thinking Ethel was being kind.

David sat at his father's desk, his head in his hands. His leg throbbed like a rotten tooth. He was twenty-four, crippled and dependent, unable to support his wife and child, and his father had gone off to war instead of him. Just coming down the stairs tired him – how could he have thought he could take his father's place? It was a joke, and not a funny one.

Antonia had said that morning that she was getting up, though he had thought women were supposed to stay in bed for a month or more after childbirth. He knew why. She wanted to keep an eye on him. Why had he married her? He had thought she would comfort him, but instead she had just given him two more people to worry about, two more people to fail. Sometimes when he was teaching a pupil, and the boy suddenly understood something he had been struggling with, he had a moment of satisfaction that made him forget his troubles. But it never lasted long.

He heard the baby start to cry upstairs, the sound muted by distance. Marcus Hunter. He was that child's father, hard though it was to believe. And he allowed the sound to stiffen him, telling himself not to be such a disgusting coward. Bobby had not flinched from his duty, nor Jumbo. His duty did not happen to include fighting at the Front any more,

141

but it was there to be done all the same. He sat up straighter, took a little brown bottle from his pocket and tipped a few drops into his mouth, and started to go through the papers on the desk. Dad had gone to be a soldier. He must take Dad's place.

Cook was so relieved to receive a letter from Fred, after all the terrible news from the Front, that instead of saving it for when she was in bed, she read it at the table in front of everyone.

Silence fell, and all eyes turned on her questioningly, until her hand flew to her chest and she cried, 'He's not hurt! He's all right!'

'I'm ever so glad for you,' Ada said, and politely resumed conversation with Mrs Chaplin to give her privacy, while Emily, in what passed with her for a whisper, explained who Fred was to young Timmy.

Well My Margaret here I am, your Fred speaking, all in one piece youll be glad to know but cor, what a bunfight! In the line fourteen days straight, not that youd know it was the line, its not like trench fighting! Dash here and dash there, new position every night, creep about in the woods and mostly not know which way the Jerries were, they could have been behind us for all we knew! You find out where they are when they shoot at you, ha ha. We heard there was a flap on back home well, we had the wind up out here once or twice but alls well that ends well, and don't worry, we wont let old Fritz get past us, not on your life, so sleep sound at night love cos well fight to the last man like our c-in-c says. Out at rest now but it wont be long before we go back in. I could do with some of your cooking, its been short commons while weve been dashing about, stew if lucky but mostly cold grub when it manages to find us, cold bacon and biscuit. I been dreaming of your bonzer rock cakes, I cant wait to get home and

sample them! And a lot else besides, you know what I mean!
You be good and save it all for me, ever your Fred.

The last part made her blush and wish that she had saved the letter for later, but knowing he wasn't hurt was such a load off her mind, she looked round the table beaming, making Emily, who rarely saw anything but a scowl, flinch.

Ada intercepted the smile and said, 'Does he say anything about the situation?'

Munt looked up from his plate and said, 'Censor'd black it out if he did. Talk sense, girl!'

'He just says it was hot work but they're all right,' Cook said. 'He talks about missing my rock cakes.'

'We all miss 'em,' Munt growled. 'What kind o' beaver is this, bread and dripping? Time was when we had cake with our tea.' 'Beaver' was what he called the mid-morning snack – what the others, in the local vernacular, called 'lunch'.

'Think yourself lucky there's bread and dripping!' Cook snapped. 'There've been times lately my Fred would've been glad of it, out at the Front.'

'Bread an' drippin's not beaver. Bread an' jam, maybe, just about,' he allowed. 'Reckon I shoulda volunteered when the war broke out. At least they gets jam out there.'

'I wish you had, so's I didn't have to listen to you,' Cook retorted. 'And if you don't want that slice, someone else'll have it. We don't waste food in this house.'

'I'll have it,' said Beryl, eagerly.

Munt ignored her, his eyes on Cook. He folded the bread, inserted it whole into his mouth, and chewed at her defiantly. 'You're an awkward old bizzom,' he said indistinctly, 'but one thing I will say, you do bake a lovely cake. When you can be bothered.'

'Don't know how you think I can bake cakes without sugar!' Cook said, exasperated. 'Haven't you heard of rationing? You bring me the sugar, I'll bake the cake!'

Munt narrowed his eyes. 'S'pose you think I can grow it, out in me garden. Wimmin!' He got to his feet. ''F there's no cake, I might as well get back to work. Here, you, Timmy – come on. Got raspberries to tie up.'

There was a slightly tense silence when they left, which Mrs Chaplin broke by saying, 'I heard tell there was some nice cheese at Sharp's farm. They've not put that on ration yet.'

'Ooh, I like a bit of cheese!' Beryl exclaimed. 'Welsh rabbit – that's my fav'rite.'

'My old mum used to put a bit of onion on top,' Mrs Chaplin said. 'Called it French rabbit. Always mixed a bit o' mustard in, as well.'

Conversation resumed. Ada watched Cook fold her letter and stow it in her apron pocket. She wondered, wistfully, when she would hear from Len again. It was only ten days since he'd written, but she was learning the lesson of women left behind in war, that the relief of hearing your man was all right barely lasted out the day. When there was action at the Front, there was constant danger.

'You won't like me for saying it,' said Beth, 'but I'm glad to see you back here.'

'Aeneas said the same thing. You'd all like to keep me under one of those protective glass domes,' Laura said. 'Like a stuffed bird.'

'A bird of paradise, then,' Beth said. 'Or one of those exotic finches.'

Now Laura laughed. 'Exotic? With my cropped hair and broken nails and all the new lines in my face?'

'Exotic is as exotic does,' Beth countered.

They were lunching at the Ritz, amid a sea of khaki. On the 29th of April, the German offensive on the Lys had ground to a halt. The Allies had ceased to move backwards, and counter-attacks were holding the enemy at a new line.

Huge amounts of ground had been lost, including all of the area before Ypres that had been won at such cost the previous summer and autumn. But Ypres had not fallen, and the advance had been stopped before it reached Hazebrouck. And the Germans now had two large salients to defend, which weakened rather than strengthened them.

Jack had come out of the line a few days earlier, and Beth had had the precious letter that told her he had survived 'with a few scratches, and an insatiable desire for proper food', in his words. According to intelligence, he wrote, it had been problems of supply that again had slowed the Germans. 'They've left themselves pretty exposed – with a salient, open to attack on three sides. Nuts for us! You see we take comfort where we can find it out here.'

'It's been a frightening few weeks,' Beth acknowledged.

'But thank God the defences held, and the Germans didn't reach the Channel,' said Laura. 'I'm only sorry poor Artemis House fell victim. I had an awkward interview with Lady Overton about it – at least, I thought it would be awkward, but she did agree there was nothing else we could have done. Even though Talbot House is staying put.'

'Darling, you're not thinking of going back there? The Germans are not done yet – and the Americans aren't ready to come in. The whole area is frightfully dangerous.'

'Oh, I'm not going back – yet,' said Laura. 'Like the army, to judge from the khaki in here, we're taking time to draw breath, reorganise, and lick our wounds. I dare say a lot of people who've been in the thick of it will be getting leave.'

'God! I hope so! I don't trust Jack and his "few scratches". I need to see him for myself.' She eyed Laura thoughtfully. 'Is there someone in particular you're hoping to see?' she asked.

Laura raised her eyebrows. 'Now why on earth should you think that?'

'Ha! So there is someone! Come on, darling, tell all – this is sensational news!'

'I'll tell you when there's something to tell,' Laura said, laughing at Beth's crestfallen expression. 'For now, I'm dedicating myself to bathing in hot water, trying to get the ingrained dirt out of my hands, and booking an appointment with a hairdresser. Ronnie did the last cut I suffered. I'm hoping a professional might be able to make me look human.'

She had written to Major Ransley to tell him she was safe in England, and giving the direction of her house in Westminster. It was over a week since she had written, and she was trying not to get nervous. She knew how busy he must be, and finding time even to scribble a note must be hard.

But on the morning of the 1st of May, a paragraph in the newspaper sent her stomach swooping nauseously. The headline was ADVANCED DRESSING STATION IS STRUCK BY SHELL, but it was the word 'Merville' underneath that snatched her attention. The information was slight. An advanced dressing station of the British Second Army near Merville had been struck by an enemy shell, causing the death of two of the wounded and one RAMC officer, while two QAIMNS nurses had been injured, one seriously. The dressing station had been on the point of evacuating to a place of greater safety when the incident occurred.

She stared at the words with sick dismay. *Of course* it did not follow that the RAMC officer who had been killed must be Ransley. There might be two or three officers at a dressing station, depending on where and how big it was. And there would be more than one dressing station in the area.

But he had said they were falling back towards Merville. And he had not replied to her letter.

A week was nothing, she told herself sternly. Eight days, nine days was nothing.

Louisa looked up from her part of the newspaper. 'Is something wrong?'

'No – nothing,' she said after a pause. Louisa had always reacted badly to the mention of Ransley's name. 'What are you doing today?'

'Having lunch with Beryl Gibson and Baby Melville. We're going to talk about the next general election and what we ought to do when it's called. Would you like to come?'

'No – thanks. I've some things to do. I ought to see my banker and my lawyer.'

'Sooner you than me,' Louisa said, and went back to her newspaper.

It was not entirely a lie – Laura intended to see them afterwards. Her first call was to Lady Overton's house, where she found herself on the doorstep facing a rather stern butler who did not believe her ladyship was at home.

Since a butler must know whether his mistress was in the house or not, she translated this as 'not receiving visitors', and said, 'Oh, please, ask her if she will spare me just a very few moments, on a matter of importance.'

The butler glanced at her card, seeming to weigh her up, then asked her to step into the morning-room. It seemed a long wait in the quiet house, and Laura had time to feel many things, including a fool; but then rapid footsteps approached over the marble floor of the hall, the door opened, and Lady Overton entered, wearing a curious holland smock over her clothes and smelling faintly of formaldehyde.

'I'm sorry to have kept you waiting,' she said. 'I was doing some research in my laboratory, so you will excuse my strange attire. What can I do for you, Miss Hunter?'

Apologies and justifications flooded upwards towards Laura's lips, but she judged Lady Overton would prefer someone who came to the point and did not waste her

147

time, so she handed her the newspaper cutting without speaking.

Lady Overton took out a pair of spectacles from the smock pocket and read the paragraph. 'An unhappy story. What is it you require of me?'

'I need more information,' Laura said, 'and for that, I need someone with contacts in the War Office. Normally I would have asked my brother—'

'Sir Edward? Why can you not?' The glasses were off now, and the sharp eyes were examining Laura's face.

'He has been called up. He is away in a training camp.'

'Called up?' The fine eyebrows shot up. 'No, nonsense! He must be exempt.'

'He decided not to appeal,' said Laura. 'He felt he had to do his duty.'

'He was *doing* his duty,' Lady Overton said impatiently. 'What folly is this? The work he was doing at the Treasury and the Food Ministry was much more important. Any fool can be shot at.' She noted Laura's expression and said, 'There is no accounting for the pride of men. It is exasperating. But this is nothing to the purpose. What is it you wish to find out?'

Now Laura hesitated. For a woman of her age and settled spinsterhood to be forming an attachment for a man was the stuff of comedy, and she did not want to be laughed at.

Lady Overton said, with a hint of sympathy softening her tone, 'I have no wish to intrude on your private affairs, Miss Hunter. If there is someone in particular you wish me to enquire about, you must give me a name.'

Laura reddened slightly, and plunged in. 'It's a Major Ransley, in the RAMC. He was transferred to a field ambulance just before I left Pop, and he told me in his last note they were somewhere near Merville. And I haven't heard from him.'

148

Lady Overton nodded slightly. 'He is usually a regular correspondent?'

'We've never had to correspond before,' Laura admitted. 'But he's not the sort to be an irregular one. And he did not reply to my letter.'

There seemed to be a long silence, though in truth it could not have been more than a few seconds. But Laura was feeling how foolish it was to trouble this busy woman with her petty worries. Everyone in the country must be waiting to hear from someone, and fearing them lost.

But Lady Overton merely nodded, her cool grey eyes neutral. 'Very well. Leave it with me. I will make an enquiry. But it could take several days.'

'I understand.'

The great lady smiled suddenly. 'It took courage to come and ask me. We none of us wish to appear foolish. Are you on the telephone? Then I'll send a note round to your address when I hear anything. And if you hear from him meanwhile, you'll let me know.'

'Of course. And thank you.'

Lady Overton stepped over to the chimneypiece to pull the bell. 'By the way,' she said, 'have you done with your adventures, or do you mean to go back?'

'I think I shall want to go back,' Laura said, 'when I've had time to rest and sort out a few things.'

'Good,' said Lady Overton. 'Let me know when you are ready. I may have something for you.'

The butler came in, and Laura was shown out into the sunshine. May, the sweetest month, had begun. The grass in the square's garden was vivid, the plane trees were coming into tender leaf, and male pigeons were whirling their exotic dances around unfeeling females. But her heart was mute as a stone in her breast. If he was dead, how would she be able to carry on? All she could think was that she had been right after all to take love when it came on that one evening.

Edward and Aeneas, like the rest of the family, would no doubt have thought it wrong, but they were happily married. A woman in wartime had to take her chances.

Diana had thought seriously of moving down to Dene, but had not put the plan into operation. She was heavy with child and was comfortable at Park Place, and though she would have liked to see her family more often, the effort of moving seemed too great. Then the house at Dene Park was so large, the distances between rooms so great, the formality expected by the staff so much more irksome. Here, Dr Fleming was on hand, and approved of her resting as much as possible. She didn't go out much now, but her few admitted friends knew where to find her. And there was a Boots' Library in Piccadilly: in her newly sedentary condition, she had discovered the joys of novel-reading.

She was glad she had not moved when on the 2nd of May a telegram from Rupert was brought to her in her bedroom before she was up, to say he was on his way home. He arrived mid-morning, looking grubby and travel-worn, but more than that, frighteningly tired and grim. But he managed a smile of greeting, and touched her cheek with a finger in place of a kiss.

'I won't get too near you,' he said. 'I must smell to high Heaven. The first thing I shall have is a bath.'

'Are you hungry?'

'Starving.'

'Do you want to go out to luncheon?'

He eyed her shape, artfully draped in expensive silk. 'I'm not sure I have the energy for a restaurant,' he said kindly. 'Let's eat here. Mrs Baynard knows what I like. Tell Heating to bring up whatever wine he thinks best – he knows my taste. Give me an hour to make myself presentable.'

He was almost out of the room when she said, 'How long have you got?'

150

He turned at the door. It was always the first question, these days, wasn't it? She looked anxious, though she was trying to sound calm. 'It's just a forty-eight pass. Sorry,' he said. 'We're desperately short of men out there. I'm lucky to get away at all.'

'Then – there's going to be more action?'

'You'd better ask the Kaiser.' And he was gone.

Over luncheon, he talked in staccato fashion about the action he had been in. She didn't understand much of it, and decided after a while he was talking for his own benefit rather than hers. He didn't ask her anything about her own life – in honesty, there wasn't much to tell, but she got the impression that while he sat opposite her and looked around him from time to time, he wasn't really seeing her or his house. His mind was somewhere else. He was very thin, and he ate rapidly, as if it didn't much matter what the food was, as long as he got it into his body.

When he had finished eating, he got up suddenly and said he must go and see George, and she put down her fork and rose obediently. They walked upstairs together to the nursery – he slowed his pace to hers with obvious effort and made a joke about putting in a lift. George was just finishing his luncheon, after which he always had a sleep, but the rare appearance of his father had to take precedence. He was shy at first, but Rupert was patient with him and coaxed him out, and soon he was pottering back and forth, bringing his favourite toys for inspection, and chattering away in a mixture of proper words and jumbled sounds. He was at the age of trying to repeat whatever favoured adults said to him, which seemed to charm Rupert. He played with him with a patience that surprised Diana.

But afterwards, once they had left the nursery, a restlessness came over him, and he revolted at staying at home, though he had so little time. 'I suppose I ought to pay my respects to my mother,' he said reluctantly. But Diana said the dowager had already left London for Norfolk. He eyed Diana's shape, and said, 'I think I'll take a stroll around one or two places, see who's in Town. You don't need to come – I'm sure you ought to rest.'

And that was the last she saw of him that day. He went out; in the early evening a message came that he was dining with friends and would be late home. She ate alone, and retired early to her book and bed, and he did not come in while she was awake.

The next morning, he came into her room while she was still in bed, and was going over the morning mail with her secretary. He waved Miss Greengross away, and sat on the edge of the bed. His eyes were bloodshot and his hair unkempt, and he seemed artificially cheery. Diana wondered if he was still a little drunk from the night before. He had that unreliable look about him.

'You look very blooming this morning,' he said. 'My rosy little posy. Healthy and alert. Early night, was it? Ah, the wholesome life – there's nothing like it!'

'How would you know?' she said, a little disgruntled.

'I didn't say I espoused it, only that there was nothing like it,' he said airily.

'Did you have a nice time last night?' she asked, trying not to sound sarcastic – he was capable of walking out if the conversation did not please him.

'I don't think so. I can't entirely remember, but there was noise and drinks. And dancing, I think. And then more drinks, I'm afraid – I remember that bit. Debauchery doesn't really come under the heading of "a nice time", does it? Really, you know, I'd have done better to stay at home with my nice little wife. But somehow I just couldn't.'

'Why not?' she asked. 'I'd have been glad of the company.'

'I'm sorry.' He was silent a moment. The hilarity faded from his face, leaving him looking merely tired. 'I'm not sure I can explain it. It's as though all this' – he waved a

152

hand '– is a dream. Not the sort you have when you're safe in bed at night, but the sort you have after too much laudanum. Everything queerly out of shape and slightly menacing and, at any rate, utterly unreal.'

'I'm real,' Diana said, hurt. Why was he being horrid to her?

'Oh, my dear, you are the unrealest of all,' he said sadly. 'You, with your perfect face and fragrant hair. I come from a place where bodies lie unburied. You walk past someone in khaki, lying face down. You look at the soles of his boots and his outflung hand and you don't know who he is, and you don't stop to find out. He was a person to himself, but he isn't to you. He isn't anything any more, just – litter. And it could be you one day. We're all just things to be shot at, litter wrapped in uniforms, upright today, lying in the mud and forgotten tomorrow.'

'But I wouldn't forget you!' she cried, tears in her eyes.

He shrugged. 'You forgot Charles.'

She began to cry. She felt the baby roll over in her womb, and instinctively put her hands over it.

He watched her for a moment, and she had the feeling he was thinking of getting up and walking out. But then he reached out and laid his hands over hers. 'I knew I couldn't make you understand,' he said. 'I shouldn't have tried.'

'Why are you so cruel?' she sobbed.

'I don't mean to be. I'm sorry. I'm tired, that's all. Don't cry any more. Look here, let's go out. Wash your face and put on your prettiest dress, and we'll go out for lunch.'

'I don't want—' she began.

'Yes, you do. You have to eat. And this place must get on your nerves, shut up here all the time. I know it gets on mine. Up you get, and I'll take you out and show you off, watch everyone envying me my beautiful wife.'

He reached out and wiped the tears from under her eyes with a forefinger. The lines in his face were deep, in the sidelong light from the window, as though they'd been etched with a thin, sharp blade, and his eyes looked defeated. It frightened her to see the change in him.

'I hope the baby's a girl,' he said. 'With as little of her father's bad character as possible. Not long now, my darling. Did I ever tell you how proud and happy you make me?'

She allowed herself to be coaxed from her bed. But she had understood a little of what he had been saying. This house, London, everything around her, was the stage of a theatre, painted and unreal. The other place, where unknown men lay unburied, was the only reality to him. Which meant that this present niceness, easier for her to bear as it was, was only a play. He wasn't really there at all.

And what did that make her?

CHAPTER ELEVEN

Things got better for Edward when they started rifle training. Now he came into his own. He had done quite a bit of shooting, and had been considered enough of a good shot for the old earl, Diana's father-in-law, to invite him several times to Dene Park. Now, instead of struggling, he shone.

Now, when the young lads said, 'I *say*, Uncle!' it was with admiration.

Now, instead of being chivvied by the sergeant-instructor to keep up, he was singled out as an example. 'But don't get cocky. This here target don't move about. Any fool can hit a sitting duck.'

'But that's considered unsporting, Sergeant,' he said.

The sergeant narrowed his eyes. 'What did I say about being cocky? Done sport-shooting, have you? Ducks, pigeons and all that malarkey?'

Edward confined himself to saying, 'Yes, Sergeant,' and wisely didn't mention that ducks flew faster than any other bird known to man, while pigeons were notoriously hard to hit.

'Think yourself no end of a swell, don't you?' said the sergeant. 'Know it all, eh? You'll find out. Think you could kill a man?'

He didn't wait for an answer, but moved on along the line. It was, in any case, a rhetorical question.

But it did make Edward go cold down his back, reminding

him again of what all this was for. *When you get out to France.*
To be shot at, to shoot back. Perhaps it would be instinctive
to retaliate. He hoped it might. Perhaps you wouldn't feel
anything if you killed someone; perhaps only the mild satisfaction of seeing a ninepin knocked over in the skittle alley.
It did not do, he thought, for a soldier to have too much
imagination. He hoped, when the time came, he would not
think at all.

There were also lessons in the use of the bayonet, and
the Lewis gun, not only how to fire it but how to dismantle,
clean and rebuild it. He did pretty well with the latter, having
an orderly mind and a mildly practical bent, but poor Nellist
never once managed to put the wretched thing together
again. He seemed to be falling further behind all the time,
in a constant state of bewilderment that Edward was afraid
was approaching mental breakdown.

On Sunday the 5th of May, he was sent for after chapel
by the colonel, who said, 'Hearing good things about you,
Hunter. Instructors think you're doing all right. Taking
names now for officer cadet school. Assume you want to
apply?'

'Yes, sir.'

'Good show. Reflects well on this camp, enough of the
right sort of chaps puttin' their names forward. Ten from
this intake – excellent score. Board tomorrow afternoon,
fourteen thirty hours. Pure formality. You'll be accepted.
Transport will leave oh-eight-hundred Tuesday morning.'

Edward was surprised at how rapidly things were moving,
but A Company's captain, Horsefall, told him that all training
was being compressed because of the desperate need for
men at the Front. 'You'll be out there in no time,' he said
in his slightly flat and nasal accent. He grinned. 'I 'spect
you'll be glad to hear that, eh? Can't wait to "have a crack
at the Hun"?' It was clear the last words were in inverted
commas. Horsefall had been *maître d'* in a large restaurant

in civilian life, and how he had got to his present position Edward never discovered, but he opined that Horsefall was not a gentleman. He was not liked by the other officers. Perhaps that was why he was confined to training camp.

That evening, Edward wrote a letter home, giving the news. He addressed the envelope to the Hunter Family, and the salutation was 'Dear All'. It avoided having to write to Beattie personally. He kept the tone light and breezy. She had not written to him – he had not expected it, in the circumstances. He had received nothing except a postcard from Sadie, saying all was well and she hoped he was not too uncomfortable. He decided it was his imagination that it had come across to him as somehow wistful.

It was a week before a note came for Laura from Lady Overton, asking her to call at her house. It was early, but she guessed her ladyship was an early riser, and when she presented herself at the house, Lady Overton was in the hall, dressed to go out.

'Ah, I'm glad you managed to catch me. I was just on my way to the hospital. I have a list. Come into the morning-room, Miss Hunter.' Laura followed her in, trying to judge from her demeanour if it was good news or bad. When she turned, her face was unsmiling, and Laura's palms grew damp.

'You – have news?' she made herself ask.

Lady Overton took a moment to assemble her words. 'The field hospital in question had to move suddenly, as you can imagine. With the Germans advancing, our troops falling back, and a lot of casualties, things were a little chaotic.'

Laura managed only to say, 'Did—' Her mouth was dry.

'I haven't a full answer yet,' Lady Overton said patiently. 'You understand that when companies are falling back, information is often held up, or lost, or inaccurate. But what I have heard is that there were two medical personnel killed, a nurse and a medical officer. The nurse's name was Cooper: she was injured and died shortly afterwards. The MO was killed outright. His name seems to have been Raleigh or Rawley, or something like that.'

'Oh, God,' said Laura.

'It's not the same name,' Lady Overton pointed out.

'It's too close for comfort. When it's scrawled in pencil on a scrap of dirty paper, or misheard over a field telephone in a noisy room—'

Lady Overton nodded in sympathy. 'And still you haven't heard from him?'

'No.'

'I'm sorry. But don't give up hope. My enquiry is ongoing. Something more definite could come in.'

Laura thanked her and went away. Something more definite? She didn't know whether it was better to know, or to hope.

On the morning of Saturday the 11th of May William arrived at The Elms when the family was still at the breakfast table, having caught the milk train from Farnborough, with a forty-eight pass in his pocket. The returning hero was hugged and kissed, and regaled with sausages, eggs and fried potatoes hastily summoned from the kitchen.

William had done his first solo flight, and was bubbling over with it – had not made a complete ass of himself, though his landing had left something to be desired, but he hadn't completely pancaked or tipped her on her nose, and the instructor had said afterwards that he had it in him to be a flyer, which had bucked him most frightfully, because he'd thought he would get a wigging, and to fly was what he wanted most in the world.

David had come down, and was drinking coffee while he listened. Sadie could not help comparing the faces of the brothers – William's so fresh and eager, David's careworn

158

and lined with suffering. William had filled out, she thought, since he went away, and his face was now more a man's than a boy's. He looked dashing in his uniform, though it was khaki and indistinguishable from the army's. As officers had to buy their own uniforms, a wearing-out period was allowed. 'And nobody likes the blue RAF uniform, so all the older subs are hoping it'll be changed before they have to buy it.'

'I'd have thought blue would suit you,' Beattie said.

'But it's *such* a colour, Mum. They say the army has a lot of material meant for the Russian Imperial Guard that they bought cheap and want to get rid of. Pale blue and covered with gold – makes you look like a cinema commissionaire!'

When the first flush of conversation had died down, he said, 'What's this about Dad being conscripted? Surely they wouldn't call him up, with all the important work he does.'

It was left to Sadie to answer. 'He didn't appeal,' she said. 'He wanted to go. Said it was his duty.'

'Oh,' said William. He thought. 'Well, that's how I felt. Mind you, I didn't expect Pater to feel the same, at his age, but I'm jolly proud he did. I can't wait to be through training and get out there.'

'He's been selected for officer training,' Sadie said. 'He's transferred to a training school in Oxford.'

'You can't imagine our father as a Tommy, can you?' William said, with a grin. 'A foot-slogger? It's hard enough to imagine him a subaltern! I bet he'll be a major at least by the end of the war.'

'Whenever that is,' David muttered.

Sadie glanced at her mother, and saw in her face the unvoiced thought in the back of her own mind: that her father might not come back. William might not come back. Bobby hadn't.

159

Beattie avoided Sadie's eyes, and changed the subject. 'What would you like to do today?' she asked William.

'Well, I'd rather like to go up to Town,' William said. 'Have a look round, take in a matinée, if there's anything decent on. Perhaps a spot of dancing afterwards.'

Beattie hid her disappointment with a light response. 'That doesn't sound like a programme that includes me.'

William looked apologetic. 'Oh, but, Mum, it's not that I don't want to be with you. We'll have all tomorrow – nearly all of it – till I have to catch my train.'

'Of course you must have some fun,' she said. 'And I'm busy today – two committees. I wouldn't see you anyway.'

'Sadie will go with you,' Antonia said. 'Won't you? They'll understand up at Highclere.'

'Oh, yes, of course,' Sadie said. 'If you'd like me to come?'

'I was hoping you would,' William said. 'It'd be dull work on one's own.'

At that moment, Ada came in to say that the telephone, which they had heard ringing, was for Sadie. She left them, with Antonia discussing with William what he should do in Town, and Peter chipping in with suggestions that would have suited him rather than a young gentleman in uniform.

It was Mrs Cuthbert. 'Oh, Sadie, dear, I'm glad I caught you before you started off,' she said.

'Is something wrong?' Sadie asked.

'Well, I hope it's not too serious. It's John, you see. *Our* John – John Courcy.'

Sadie's stomach fell away with the shock. 'What's happened?' she managed to say.

'He's been wounded. I don't know any more than that at present, but he's at Mount Olive. He arrived yesterday.'

'I was driving the ambulance yesterday,' Sadie said.

'Yes, it's just wretched luck that you didn't see him, but among so many I suppose it's not surprising.'

'How did you hear?'

'A friend of Mary's, or a cousin or something, is a nurse there. She got talking to him while she was settling him in, and of course when he mentioned Highclere she made the connection, and sent a message to Mary.'

'Did she say—'

'She didn't say how he was wounded,' Mrs Cuthbert anticipated, 'but I'm thinking if he was talking to the nurse, it can't be *too* bad.'

Sadie was not so sanguine. She had visited wounded officers at Mount Olive, and knew how the desperately wounded, even the dying, could and did talk, clinging on *in extremis* to the last human contact.

'Will you go and visit him, dear?' Mrs Cuthbert was saying. 'I can't go myself because I've got someone from the Remount Service here for a surprise inspection.'

'Yes, of course I'll go,' Sadie said. 'And I'll telephone you afterwards.'

'Good girl. Give him my love, of course, and tell him I'll visit him as soon as I can.'

'Of *course* you must go,' Antonia said with quick sympathy.

'I'm sorry, William. You should still go up to Town,' Sadie said. 'You don't get much leave – don't waste it on my account.'

'Don't worry about me,' William said. 'Would you like me to come with you?'

'Thanks, but there's no need,' Sadie said. 'I don't even know if he's allowed visitors.'

May, Sadie always thought, was the loveliest month. The hedgerows were bridally white with hawthorn, kex and moon daisies, and the trees were fat with new leaf under an arc of gentian sky. It was the most beautiful day, and the walk up the hill towards the hospital should have been a pleasure. Nailer thought it was. He had hurried after her when he

161

saw she was walking, bustled past her to take the lead, looking over his shoulder now and then to make sure she was still following. His progress was erratic, for his nose became deeply engaged with the thick grass of the verges and the intriguing bottoms of hedges. Then he had to gallop to catch her up.

Sadie was vaguely glad of his company, but her mind was elsewhere. John was wounded. How did he get wounded? Had the Germans shelled the horse hospital? Had they advanced that far? *How* was he wounded? Arm, leg, head, torso? She remembered Lieutenant Tom Piper, one of the officers she had visited back in 1915. It had been a beautiful sunny day like this, the day he had died. It seemed so long ago – a lifetime. She was not the same Sadie. Death and wounds and sorrow – friends, boys she had known all her life, her brothers . . . She had vowed never to forget Tom Piper, but she had not thought about him for years. There had been too many others passing through.

And now John Courcy. In 1915 she would have prayed, *God, please save him, please make him well again*. Now the praying part of her was numb. There were only so many times you could ask. Had it ever made any difference? What would happen, would happen. It was childish folly to think you could change God's mind by pleading.

At the hospital, she parted from Nailer, who didn't even try to follow her in. He knew from the smell this was not a place for dogs. He stood only to see her through the door, then turned away, wriggled under a hedge and was gone.

She was a familiar figure at Mount Olive, and had no difficulty in finding out which ward he was in. Sister Ryman said, 'Oh, yes, I know who you mean. He's on B Ward. He's rather sick, I'm afraid. Of course you can see him. We're always glad when someone comes to visit the ones without a next-of-kin.'

162

'How was he wounded?'

'Bitten by a horse, apparently, and the wound went septic. Come along, we'll see if he's awake.'

Sadie knew the look of an animal with a fever, and she saw the symptoms in John Courcy, lying in the high white hospital bed with his left arm hugely bandaged. Her stomach felt distinctly quavery as she walked towards him.

He turned his head on the pillow as she approached, and a slow smile spread over his pinched and troubled face. 'I was hoping you'd come,' he said, his voice cracked and faint.

For a moment she couldn't speak; but he held out his good hand to her, and she took it. It was like plugging into a source of power. Sick though he undoubtedly was, he was still everything to her.

'I only heard a little while ago,' she said. His hand was dry and hot.

'Horse bit me. Idiotic. Saw all the signs, didn't move quickly enough. Bad shrapnel wound, poor devil. Mad with pain.'

'Was it a bad bite?' Sadie asked.

'Bad enough. Had to sit down.'

'And you didn't clean it out?'

'Not at once.'

'You should have washed it straight away.'

'Wish you'd been there to make me. Told myself. But too busy to stop. Now look what's happened.'

'You look feverish.'

'Sick as a cat.' He shook his head ruefully. 'Damn silly way – get home.'

Infections were terrible because there was no way to treat them. A person's own body had to fight unaided, and if that person was tired and run down – as John obviously was . . .

He squeezed her hand. 'Sadie,' he said. 'Sadie.' She thought he wanted to convey some message to her, something

163

he wanted her to do for him. But he only said, 'Glad you've come.'

She pressed back, and began to say, 'Mrs Cuthbert sends—'

But he squeezed her hand again and said, urgently, 'Sadie!' So she stopped and waited. At length he resumed. 'Think about you a lot,' he said. His eyes were unfocused, and shiny with fever. 'Hell out there. Hell. The horses . . . Suffering. Oh, God! Can't tell you how bad.' He paused again. 'Think about you all the time. Is that wrong?'

What was he saying? Did he – care about her, as she cared about him? Or was it the fever talking?

'Wrong in what way?' she asked unsteadily.

'Older than you. War. Not fair in war.' He tried to wet dry lips with a dry tongue, and automatically she freed her hand to pick up his water glass from the bedside cabinet and give it to him. He drank, and when she had put the glass back, she put her hand near enough for him to take again, but he seemed to be drifting.

'When I first saw you,' he said, his eyelids drooping, 'and that ridiculous dog—'

'Nailer's not ridiculous. He's a first-rate ratter.'

He smiled faintly. 'That's my Sadie. Loyal. Love that about you.'

'Do you?' she said weakly.

'Everything,' he said. 'Everything about you.' His eyes were closed now. She was in an agony to understand him before he fell asleep. 'Shouldn't say anything. Wartime.'

'Damn the stupid war,' she said softly, but with vehemence.

'Sadie . . .' he said again, vaguely.

She leaned over him. 'Yes?' she urged.

He was asleep. She leaned closer, feeling the heat radiating from him. 'You're very sick,' she murmured, disappointed. His skin ticked and twitched with the fever as he slept. She

164

laid her lips a moment against his burning forehead, feeling ashamed of herself for taking advantage of him, even as she felt driven to do it. How did people ever get to the point? she wondered. There seemed so much in the way – even without the war. She thought of Christopher Beresford and Hugh Stanhill, who cared more for her than she for them. The chances of two people feeling the same way at the same time seemed so slight. And she must not refine too much on John's words. It was probably fever-talk. Would he even remember when he woke up? She must never refer to it, unless he did. If she embarrassed him, she would lose even his friendship.

And then she thought, *When the war ends, I'll probably lose that anyway*. He would go back to his life and she to hers, and that would be that. It was a lowering thought.

Laura stood before the looking-glass in the hall, putting on her hat, and called up the stairs, 'Are you ready? We should go, if we're going.'

'Just coming!' the call came back

They were engaged to have lunch with Baby and Tom Melville and some other friends. Laura wasn't in the mood for company, while her anxiety about Ransley was unrelieved – Lady Overton had not come back to her with any news – but Louisa had looked upset when Laura hinted at crying off. So she felt she had to go.

She heard Louisa's footsteps on the stairs, just as there was a loud rapping at the front door. Her mind jumped to a telegram – *Good news or bad news?* – and she stepped quickly to throw it open. For a moment her brain would not take in what her eyes saw, but then she gasped, 'You!' in tones of such gladness and relief that he had stepped into the hall and taken her in his arms before she had had time properly to look at him. They were pressed together, arms around each other, her head on his shoulder, when Louisa reached the bottom of the stairs.

'Well!' she exclaimed in outraged tones.

Laura raised her head to look searchingly at Ransley's face. 'Are you hurt?' was her question.

'No, no! I'm not hurt. Did you think I was?'

'They said a forward station was shelled and a surgeon killed. And I hadn't heard from you.'

'You didn't get my postcard?'

'No. It wasn't your station that was shelled, then?'

'Yes, it was. We weren't quick enough getting away. One of my colleagues, Rowley – awfully nice young chap – and poor Sister Cooper dead. Dreadful business! I sent a field postcard as soon as we got clear, but it's been pretty hectic since then.'

'Excuse *me*,' Louisa said loudly and angrily. 'Much as I adore being ignored, I ought to point out that we're going to be late for lunch.'

Without looking at her, Laura said, 'Oh, you go on, Lou. Make my excuses.'

'You've been thinking all this time . . .' Ransley was saying. 'Oh, my dear!' He touched her cheek tenderly. 'That would have been a dirty trick.'

'It would,' she agreed. 'But what are you doing here?'

'*Excuse me!*' Louisa cried.

'Have to report to the director general this afternoon,' said Ransley. 'And be back by tomorrow night. I'll get a hotel room tonight, but I thought at least we could have dinner.'

'Hotel room? Don't be silly,' Laura said with the first smile of the day. It felt good.

Louisa pushed herself between them. 'Oh no you don't!' she said. 'I'm not having him staying here.'

Laura almost laughed, fatally increasing her friend's rage. 'It *is* my house, dear.'

'You said it was my home as well,' Louisa snapped. 'Don't I have a say?' Laura didn't answer, and Louisa's face darkened.

'I see how it is. I don't count for anything. When he's around, you haven't time for me.'

'Oh, Lou, don't be silly,' Laura said, not unkindly.

'Silly, am I? Well, I'm clever enough to see which way the wind's blowing. And if he stays here, I go,' Louisa declared, arms akimbo.

'Why must you make such a fuss?' Laura said, exasperated.

'If I'm *de trop* . . .' Ransley began gently to withdraw his arm from her. 'I don't want to be a cause of dissent. Why don't I just—'

Laura tightened her grip. 'No, Jim, stay. Louisa's being unreasonable, and she knows it.'

'Am I?' Louisa looked from her to him and back, lips tight, eyes bright with unshed tears. 'I know when I'm not welcome. I'll find somewhere else to live. I've plenty of friends – *real* friends – who'll be glad to share with me. And now I'm going to lunch – and I shall tell Baby exactly why you've chucked!' She jerked away, chin high, and, with an indescribable glare, stopped Ransley opening the door for her. 'I'm quite capable of operating a door-knob without male help, thank you very much!'

He fell back, chastened, and she left, slamming the door so hard it made the drops in the chandelier tinkle in protest.

'Oh dear,' he said. 'Was it something I've done?'

'War nerves,' Laura said tersely. 'She's been a bit strange for a long time now. I really think she had better get away from me – I keep leading her into dangerous adventures, and she doesn't seem able to cope.' She turned back to him, surveying his face. Were the lines deeper? He looked tired. Well, no wonder for that! 'You're really not hurt?'

He smiled, and appeared five years younger. 'I have no new holes in my skin, and no further parts missing. My nerves were stretched somewhat.'

She nodded. She could imagine. 'Why are you seeing Goodwin?' she asked.

Sir John Goodwin had taken over in March from Sir Alfred Keogh as director general of the Army Medical Services.

'I have to report, in the light of the death of my colleagues, on evacuation orders and the general readiness of the field hospital in forward areas. I'm not looking forward to it.'

'What time is your appointment?'

'Half past two. We've time to get some lunch, if you'd like.'

'No,' she said.

'You don't want lunch?'

Her eyes were bright. She smiled. 'We have the house to ourselves. And I don't want lunch.'

She walked with him, her arm through his, down as far as Millbank, where he might get a taxi. 'I don't know what time I'll be finished,' he said. 'Shall we just meet for dinner somewhere? Say, six thirty?'

'The Ritz,' she said. 'Then if you're late I can wait for you without embarrassment.'

'I can't imagine you ever being embarrassed,' he said. He turned his head to smile at her. 'What makes you such a wanton?'

'Is that what I am?'

'You don't seem to have any sense of the proprieties, I'm glad to say.'

'You don't, either,' she pointed out.

'I'm almost fifty, the Germans are advancing, and I have to go back tomorrow,' he said. 'I haven't any time to lose.'

'I'm forty-six, the Germans are advancing, and you have to go back tomorrow,' Laura said. 'I have *nothing* to lose.'

CHAPTER TWELVE

Laura opened the front door to find Louisa outside, looking a little shamefaced.

'Why didn't you use your key?'

'Um – I didn't think you'd—'

'Come in, for goodness' sake. Don't hover on the doorstep.'

'Well, I do want to talk to you,' Louisa said, still hesitating.

'Jim's gone, if that's what you're worried about,' Laura said. 'He went yesterday. Back to Flanders.'

'Oh,' said Louisa, and followed Laura to the sitting-room.

'Where've you been?' Laura asked.

'Staying with Baby Melville. She has a spare room. Were you worried about me?'

Laura missed the hopeful note in her voice as she lit a cigarette. 'Of course not. After Pop, I know you can take care of yourself. Want one?'

Louisa shook her head. 'I wanted to say – I'm sorry. I think I behaved rather badly.'

'Oh, forget it, please. I have.' Laura cocked her head, and smiled. 'I suppose it was rather shocking of me to be discovered locked in a passionate embrace on the front doorstep.'

'It wasn't that. Not entirely. It *was* rather – unseemly. But the truth is, I – I was jealous,' Louisa admitted. She blushed. 'Stupid, I know. Childish. But we'd been together a long time, and gone through so much, and then suddenly you'd got no time for me any more.'

'Now, Lou, don't start all that again,' Laura said impatiently.

'I'm not. But you've changed, you know. I suppose we all have,' she added vaguely. 'Anyway, what I wanted to say was, I think it's time I moved on. Living here – well, it's your house, as you pointed out to me.'

'I didn't mean—'

'No, it's all right. I could find a place of my own if I wanted, but I'm going to move in with Baby and Tom. They've got lots of plans. There's a lot more to be done about extending the franchise so that we have the vote on equal terms with men. And Baby's talking about our joining the WVR.'

'Isn't that rather tame, after Flanders?'

'I think I like tame,' Louisa said. 'Since my brother died, I'm rather off fighting and dying. But the WVR's not all knitting and carrying messages, you know. There's a new group being set up, called the Lady Instructors Signals Company, where you train army recruits at Aldershot in signalling. I think that would be fun.'

'Well, darling, whatever you feel will suit you,' Laura said, the doubt showing in her voice.

Louisa clasped her hands together and looked down at them. 'I don't think you and I are interested in the same things any more,' she said. 'I suppose you'll be going back?'

'Of course. It would be rather feeble to give up, just because one's been bombed out.'

'There you are, you see. I never want to be bombed again.'

'Well, I don't exactly crave it,' Laura said, laughing, then became serious. 'Oh, poor Lou – did I make you do horrid things against your nature? You were never very happy as a lady policeman, either, were you?'

'I liked helping the lost children,' Louisa said. 'I didn't like the drunks and the sordidness.'

'I'm a villain for not realising how unhappy you were,' Laura said. 'Will you forgive me?'

'Don't be silly. There's nothing to forgive. I hope we can still be friends,' Louisa said.

'Always,' Laura said firmly, shaking her hand.

But she found she was feeling a reprehensible sense of relief that she would no longer have Louisa to worry about – a sense of a burden having been put down. She could move more freely and respond more quickly on her own. And what new adventures awaited her? The German offensive was far from over, and every willing hand would be needed out there.

Louisa seemed to hear her thoughts. 'Will you be going back to Artemis House?'

'I don't know whether Lady Overton will want to put up the money for repairs. It was badly damaged. And it will depend, of course, on how the war goes. Pop is still being shelled and Talbot House is pretty much under siege, I hear, so there's no going back there yet. But there's always something to do. I might go back to the ambulances. Drivers are always wanted.'

'When do you go?'

'Oh, not yet. Not for a few weeks, perhaps.'

The beautiful spring weather was a nightmarish background to Sadie's days, gripped as her mind was with John Courcy's struggle to live. She went to Highclere in the mornings and worked with the horses, every sound and smell and action making her think of the horses in France, and their suffering, and the torment Courcy must have gone through trying to save them. And in the afternoons she went to the hospital to sit by his bed. She would have stayed there all day, every day, but they would not let her.

As his body battled the infection, John was up and down, seeming better one day, weak but coherent, relapsing into

171

semi-coma the next, feverish and muttering. On the Wednesday there was talk, which she could not help overhearing – since she was listening with strained attention from the other side of the drawn screens – of amputation. She heard the doctors weighing the probabilities. It came down, in the end, to his heartbeat being still strong. 'We'll leave it another day,' was the decree. 'See how he goes on.'

Sadie, returning to him after the consultation and the dressing change, met his gaze, bright with fever and pain. 'They're talking about chopping it off,' he said bluntly. 'I half wish they would – get it over with. God, what a mess!'

'There's still hope,' she said timidly. But she didn't think he heard her. She suspected he didn't really know that she was there. He started talking again, but much of it was incoherent.

She knew the arguments all too well by now. Amputation was drastic, but sometimes the attempt to avoid it only meant a more radical amputation later. Lose a forearm now, or a whole arm later. Or die. But what would a vet do without an arm? She couldn't bear to think of him maimed, when he had always been so strong and capable. What would he do, how would he support himself?

But if the alternative was death?

In the evening, forced to be away from him, she tried to occupy herself, while waiting tensely for the telephone to ring. He had no next-of-kin, but Mrs Cuthbert had extracted a promise from the sister to inform her if his condition changed. And Mrs Cuthbert would telephone Sadie. In bed at night she lay sleepless, staring at the ceiling, trying to prepare herself for a world without him. Thousands of people had had to do it, since the war began. She had learned to accept a world without Bobby, her darling brother. Life would go on. That was the hell of it. Life would go on with her in it, and all her days would be empty of him.

* * *

On Thursday afternoon she walked up to his bed and found him heavily unconscious, as though sunk back into the pillows. He looked as though nothing would rouse him.

Sister Ryland was suddenly behind her. 'They didn't amputate,' she said, her voice harsh. 'Personally, I think they should have, but I'm only a nurse.'

Sadie tried to reply, but only a dry click came out.

Ryland put a kindly hand on her forearm. 'I think you should prepare yourself,' she said.

He was too weak for them to shave him now, and his wax-white, sunken face was stubbled. 'You mean . . .' Sadie managed.

The hand gripped harder. 'I'm sorry. He means a lot to you, doesn't he?'

'We're – just friends,' Sadie said. Just friends – and that was all they would ever be, because of a bite, a stupid horse-bite. Such a ludicrously unimportant thing to end such a vivid life and tear Sadie's heart out of her body.

Ryland had gone away, and Sadie sat, and possessed herself of the good hand. She loved him so much. *God, don't take him. I won't ask for anything more, but just let him live.* She would live her life never seeing him if she could just know he was somewhere in the world. His hand lay insensible in hers. He did not wake. He did not know she was there.

She stayed later that evening, until the night sister chased her away with scandalised exclamations about routine and rules. The next morning, she was out early, and went to straight to Mount Olive before even thinking of Highclere. She had to know. If he was gone, she must know right away. The porter was so used to her that he paid her no attention, though one or two nurses scurrying past as she trod up the stairs gave her odd glances. There happened to be no-one at the near end of the ward when she pushed in through the double doors, and she advanced without challenge until she could see his bed.

173

It was empty. Her insides seemed to fall away, leaving her feeling sick and cold. He was dead. And she had not even been able to be with him. He had died alone. Grief gripped her, closing her throat, tight and painful.

She had been spotted. A nurse turned and saw her and made a shocked face, and then the night sister came bustling down the ward, saying, 'No, really! This is too bad. I cannot and will not have my ward disrupted at all hours in this way. Are you not aware of hospital rules? Go away at once, do you hear me?' Sadie stood like a stone, unable to speak, hardly able to understand. In fury, the sister said, 'Nurse, come and escort this – this *person* out!'

The nurse had to obey. When Sadie didn't move, she took her arm and turned her. Moving like an automaton, Sadie was walked to the doors. When they had pushed through, the nurse whispered, 'Which one was it you wanted to see?'

Sadie licked her lips. 'Major Courcy,' she managed to say. 'When did – when did he die?' She wanted to ask if it was peaceful, but cancelled the thought. What did that matter? Dead was dead.

The nurse raised her eyebrows. 'Oh, he didn't die! He's turned the corner. His fever was down this morning and he was sleeping peacefully.'

'But – where—' Sadie could hardly speak, made imbecile by churning emotions.

'He's been moved to D Ward, for recovering patients. Why don't you come back later and see him?'

'Yes,' said Sadie, blankly.

'I've got to go – Sister'll skin me if she sees me talking,' said the nurse, and with a flip-flap of the double doors, she was gone.

Although the German offensive in Flanders had been held up, the fighting continued, and the situation on the ground was complicated by the constant thin stream of refugees passing back, and by the increasing frequency of air-raids. On Whit Tuesday, the 21st of May, Talbot House finally closed. It had been struck already by several shells, but had kept going for the sake of the men still passing through; but on that day they were ordered by the military authority to evacuate immediately, and they had no choice but to go.

Laura learned the news from Ronnie Mildmay the following Saturday. Her uncle was a colonel in the 43rd and was therefore more in touch with matters in Flanders. She had lunch with her in a restaurant in Albemarle Street.

'So that's that,' she said. 'No hope of going back there now, if even the Toc H padres have gone.'

'Yes, it's a shame,' said Ronnie. 'Well, when one chapter closes, another opens.'

'Have you got plans?' Laura asked.

'Nothing settled yet, but I'm sure something will come up. Can't sit out the rest of the war doing nothing!'

'That's how I feel.'

'Won't your friend Lady Overton come up with something for you?'

'Hardly "my friend" – but I mean to go and ask her when I've had enough of lotus-eating. Why don't you come with me?'

'Thanks. I may, if nothing's come up by then.' She paused. 'It's pretty bad out there,' she said lightly.

Laura laughed. 'I was *there*. A shell fell on me. I know it's dangerous.'

Ronnie was serious. 'I wouldn't bank on going back to Flanders, Laura. With the Germans still advancing—'

'Yes, and we keep falling back,' Laura said, with dissatisfaction.

'It's the new theory of "elastic defence",' Ronnie said. 'I heard it from a friend of my uncle's, who's in the War Office.

You let your lines bend, so they don't break. Absorb the thrust. Allow the enemy to wear himself out.'

Laura frowned. 'That's just a rationalisation of retreat, isn't it?'

'It seems eminently sensible to me,' said Ronnie.

'But we are giving ground all the time. What happens when there's nowhere left to go?'

'Evacuation.'

'Really?'

'It's being discussed. According to my uncle's friend, the war cabinet's talking about what to do if the French "crack".'

'Crack?'

'Can't rule out the possibility, after the mutinies of 1917. If the French fail, wholesale evacuation of British troops from France will have to be implemented. Contingency plans are being drawn up.'

'I can't believe it,' Laura said. But she could. All through the war, the fear had been of the Germans capturing the Channel ports. Evacuation! There would be terrible losses among the rearguard – and the field hospitals would be almost the last to leave.

Ronnie went on: 'And the U-boats are starting up again. Apparently, the government's going to have to extend rationing. They're just choosing the moment to break it to the public. It won't be popular.'

'Keeping up morale here at home will be difficult, if there's more austerity as well as evacuation,' Laura agreed. These were dark days indeed.

They parted outside the restaurant, Ronnie heading towards Regent Street and Laura making her way to Green Park station. As she turned onto Piccadilly, she was astonished to see Edward coming across the road, apparently having emerged from St James's Street. She waited, but he didn't see her until he got right up to her, and then he flinched in a most guilty way and stopped dead.

'Good gracious, what are you doing here?' she asked. He seemed lost for an answer. She looked across his shoulder at St James's Street. 'Have you just come from your club?'

'I was in Jermyn Street. Having a fitting at Brown's.'

'The military tailor?'

'You can't imagine the difficulty, with so many people wanting uniforms. I'll be lucky if it's finished before I go to France.'

'Oh, Teddy – when?'

'Goodness, I don't know. Weeks. Haven't finished the course yet, by a long chalk.' He tried to change the focus. 'What are you doing here?'

'I've been having lunch with a friend. Aren't you supposed to be in Oxford?'

'I'm on my way back there now. They have to let a fellow out to get his uniform made.' He took her elbow and turned her. 'We're blocking the pavement. Walk with me to the Tube station.'

She slipped her hand through his arm, and said, 'How are they all at home?'

'I haven't been back since I was called up,' Edward said.

Something in his tone made her turn her head. 'I know you're not due leave yet,' she said, 'but I understood officer cadets had a certain amount of free time. And Oxford is no distance.' He didn't answer, frowning under his cap. 'Teddy, what happened?' she asked anxiously. 'Why did you go? Is there something wrong?'

He straightened his shoulders. 'Don't be silly. What could be wrong? We need every man, that's all. They're rushing training through as fast as possible to get new troops out there. I dare say I shall be at the Front before the end of June. Things are pretty bad.'

Laura seemed to read something of his thoughts in his face, for she said abruptly, 'Ronnie was talking about evacuation. We can't *lose*, can we?'

There was no reason to keep the truth from her – she had seen more of the reality of war than he had. 'We *can*,' he said. 'Whether we *will* or not . . .'

'Our boys are worn out,' said Laura. 'I saw them coming through Pop.'

'But Fritz has thrown everything at us twice this year, and despite being outnumbered, we weren't beaten. We have new divisions coming through. And the troops who've had it hardest are being rotated into quieter sectors.' He smiled suddenly. 'The Champagne, for instance – the chaps call it the Sanatorium, because the air and the scenery are so fine, and there's very little action there.'

'I've heard of that. Apparently, Rupert's unit is on its way there – he wrote to Diana about it, and she told Beth, asked her if she knew what it was like there and whether he'd be safe.'

'Rupert's one of those people who always lands on his feet.'

'I hope so. With the baby coming, she's hoping, of course, that he'll get leave. Beth said her Jack is expecting some in June.'

'The Americans should be coming to the line in June, or thereabouts,' Edward said, 'so it may well be that our chaps will be able to be spared. I imagine there's a lot of overdue leave to get through. Meanwhile, I must get back to my training.' They had reached the Tube station entrance, where he halted and turned to her.

She examined his face, wishing she knew the truth, but knowing he would never tell her. 'Are you enjoying it?' she asked instead.

'It's better than being a Tommy,' he said. 'Proper beds and bathrooms – I'm too old to sleep on a camp bed in a tent.'

'You may have to rough it, at the Front,' she reminded him.

'Ah, but not in a tent with five others. And it will be my own camp cot, not army-issue. You can buy some pretty decent ones at the Army & Navy. And all sorts of ingenious travelling kit – a little outlay, and one can be quite comfortable.'

She resisted his humour. 'At the Front before the end of June?' she said. 'Oh, Teddy, be careful.'

He looked at her seriously. 'You know you can't ask a soldier to do that. When this war started, I never envisaged being in uniform. But now I am—' That sentence didn't seem to lead anywhere. He leaned in abruptly to kiss her cheek and swung away, walking so fast she could not have caught him without running. He seemed to have forgotten he had been heading for the Tube. He ran across the road, dodging between the traffic, and she saw him disappear into Green Park.

CHAPTER THIRTEEN

When the old fever hospital of Mount Olive had been taken over for a war hospital, a band of volunteers had worked to make it more pleasant, painting and decorating, and also planting a garden at the back for ambulant patients to take the air. On a bench there, before a round bed full of geraniums and begonias, Sadie sat with John Courcy. Nailer lay at her feet, front paws crossed, content after an extensive inspection of the garden to rest and let the summer airs drift past his sensitive nose.

There was a chess board between Sadie and Courcy. The board was battered, and at some point the black knight had been lost, replaced by a pebble. Sadie was not very good at chess anyway. The pleasure for her lay in seeing John so much better.

Once the fever had gone down, his recovery had been steady. 'It's my good Northumberland blood,' he had joked with her. 'They breed us tough in the Border country.'

He had still been feeble, pale and strengthless when he had said that. Now, ten days after the surgeons had discussed amputation, he seemed almost back to normal. There was about his face still the skinned-rabbit look that Sadie associated with those who had suffered severe trauma, but Sister Ryland said he was eating well, and he was obviously getting stronger every day. The fine weather continuing, Sadie had been spending her afternoons with him out of doors, walking about the gardens, or sitting talking, playing chess.

'Mate,' he said now. 'You weren't concentrating. Where was your mind?'

'I was thinking how much better you're looking today,' she said. 'Out in the sunshine every day, your face is getting brown again.'

'Good thing, too,' he said. 'I don't want to go back to France looking pallid and peaky.'

'When . . .' Sadie began, despite herself. She didn't want to know when he'd be leaving, but of course he would have to go. They needed him over there.

'Dr Tufton said this morning I'd probably be discharged on Monday,' he said, his voice neutral.

'So soon,' she said.

'They could have sent me today,' he told her. 'There's nothing wrong with my arm now. Tufton must like me, to give me the weekend.'

'You have to get your strength back,' Sadie protested.

'It's not as if I'm going into combat,' he said. He looked at her frowningly. 'What was your father thinking, to go for a soldier when he could have been exempted?'

'He *said* he felt he had to do his duty,' Sadie answered doubtfully. She had always felt there was something else behind it, but it was not for her to talk about such private things to anyone, not even John.

John shook his head. 'I can't understand him. God knows, I wouldn't go if I didn't have to.'

'Wouldn't you?'

He stared for a long time at a bee wandering about the begonias. Then he sighed, and said, 'I suppose I would. But he has a wife and family. A man has responsibilities when people care for him, depend on him. War is a single man's affair – or it should be. Soldiers shouldn't have ties.'

As always, Sadie tried to interpret his words. It was a bad

181

habit of hers. Was he warning her? She felt they had become closer this past week, being together without interruption, talking. In the peaceful garden, in the warm sunshine, they had sat close, and her hand had rested, as a young lady's should, within reach of his, ready for him to hold it, if the fancy should take him. But he never had. And yet she had felt that it was not impossible that he might.

'Tell me about Le Touquet,' she said, to get him talking again. 'Not the hospital, the place.'

He thought. 'Big, quiet pine woods. Winding tracks. Large houses hidden in the trees. The smell of salt on the wind from the sea. The town itself is quaint, narrow cobbled streets and tall houses, Victorian-looking. Of course, at the moment it's full of soldiers – there are camps all around, and a couple of big hospitals – and soldiers make a mess of everything. But it must have been nice. After the war, I'd like to take—' He stopped short; and then resumed, his eyes on a distant tree. 'I'd like to go back, see it the way it ought to be.'

What had he been going to say, she wondered painfully, *that he had thought better of?* It had sounded as though it would have been, 'After the war, I'd like to take you there.' She supposed he had been tempted by the feeling of intimacy between them to speak unguardedly, and had pulled himself back at the last moment. She wanted to say to him, 'You don't need to be afraid of me. If you see me only as a friend, I won't presume on anything you say.' But she couldn't help imagining what it would be like, if he loved her, to go to France with him, when the war was over, when they had their lives back.

He had almost lost his. She must always remember that he had been given it back at the last moment, and be grateful.

She tried to ask a question as a friend might ask it, brightly, impersonally. 'After the war, what will you do?'

'What I did before, I suppose,' he said.

'Will you go back north?

'I don't think so. I miss it, my home country, but there wouldn't be much work there.'

'Don't they have farms?'

'I'm not sure I want to go back to farm work. Having concentrated on horses all these years, I've forgotten everything I knew about sheep and pigs. I was thinking of specialising in horses, so I'd have to go where they have a lot of them. And to have a decent practice, I'll need wealthy people with expensive horses.'

'Racing stables?' she hazarded. 'Newmarket?'

'Perhaps. Or hunt stables. The Shires.'

That wouldn't be so bad, she caught herself thinking. Cambridgeshire or Leicestershire weren't quite so far away. She might still see him. Then she found he was examining her expression, and reddened at the folly of her thoughts.

'And what will you do?' he asked. 'After the war.'

'Me?' she temporised, trying to compose herself.

'You are a completely different person from the Sadie of summer 1914. And you won't be able to change back.'

'I suppose I'll have to try to get a job,' she said. Girls used to sit at home and wait to get married. That would no longer be possible.

'With horses?'

'It's all I know.'

'I beg to differ. I think you know a great many things, Sadie.'

When he said her name, it made her insides quiver with something very warm and scary. She wondered, agonisingly, what he *meant* by the nice things he said.

But the next moment he spoke in the other, neutral, voice, and said, 'Shall we play again? We ought to try to let you win a few more games before I leave, to even the score.'

'Don't be silly, I've only won two games altogether. And one of those I'm sure you *let* me win.'

'I'll give you two pawns,' he offered.

'No favours, thank you,' she said, with dignity. 'If I win, I want to win fairly.'

He chuckled. 'That's my Sadie!' he said.

What did he mean? she cried inside, while her hand steadily laid out the pieces again. 'I'm black this time,' she said.

It was bad luck that the Champagne, where six tired and numerically depleted British divisions had been sent to rest, was the point on the line where the Germans mounted their third and most ferocious attack of that spring, on the 27th of May.

The French commander, Duchêne, had not absorbed the philosophy of 'elastic defence'. He could not tolerate a single yard of French soil being taken, and had positioned the bulk of his troops in the forward trenches, with no depth to the defences to allow a falling-back. Troops and artillery were crowded together between the north bank of the Aisne and the steep scarp of the Chemin des Dames plateau. At one in the morning the Germans, in possession of the high ground, began a massive bombardment of gas and high-explosive shells on this easy target, destroying the Allied artillery in the first few minutes. When the enemy infantry advanced at 3.40 a.m., there was no alternative but to fall back; but there were too few bridges to allow a rapid retreat across the river, and those who could not escape were trapped and overwhelmed. For the first time in the war, many thousands of British troops were taken prisoner.

The news was terrifying. The surprise attack had breached the Allied line on a twenty-five-mile front between Soissons and Rheims. The crack German storm troops moved at a tremendous pace, reaching the Aisne in less than six hours, smashing through eight divisions and driving the Allies almost ten miles back to the River Vesle by nightfall. It was the greatest advance the Germans had made in a single day.

Britain had faced defeat twice already this year, and the

enemy had miraculously run out of steam. This time they didn't stop: in another week, the Allied line had sagged twenty miles more, and was back on the River Marne, barely thirty-five miles from Paris, where it had fought so bitterly four years earlier to save the capital. There were rumours that Paris was being shelled and Parisians were fleeing. If Paris was taken, the blow to French morale would be sickening, might lead to more mutiny, or even surrender. And if France fell out of the war, all Germany's resources would be aimed at Britain. They would have the Channel ports, and from there it was only a hop to the coast of Kent, and fighting on the mainland.

It was estimated that fifty thousand Allied soldiers had been taken prisoner, and no-one knew yet what the tally of dead and wounded would be, but it was certainly heavy.

Diana telephoned The Elms early on Sunday morning, the 3rd of June, and Ada went upstairs to wake the mistress, her heart in her mouth.

Beattie had not been asleep. She slept badly, these days, and in summer, when it began to get light at half past three, she was generally awake when the first blackbird spoke, and simply lay, enduring her thoughts, until it was time to get up.

'Oh, madam,' Ada said, 'I think she's crying. I'm afraid it's bad news. She said something about a telegram.'

What else did a telegram mean these days but bad news? Beattie thought. Once they had brought glad tidings of unexpected visits and expected births. 'Hand me my dressing-gown,' she said, pushing back the covers.

Diana *was* crying, and it was hard to understand her. But it seemed that Rupert had been posted 'missing'.

'Oh, Mummy!' Diana sobbed, and an indecipherable clot of words burst out, including something about 'dead' and 'baby coming'.

'You must calm down, darling,' Beattie said. 'I'll come right away, but you must think of the baby and try to stay quiet. Take deep breaths. Have a cup of tea.'

'Tea? Mummy!'

'I'll be there as soon as possible. But remember, you don't know anything for sure yet. People go missing and turn up all the time. And a lot of people were taken prisoner.'

Beattie hung up the telephone and stood a moment at a loss. How she wished Edward were there. He would have supported her; he would have known who to contact at the War Office to get more news. She had never felt so alone.

As she walked up the stairs, Antonia appeared on the landing. 'Has something happened?' Beattie explained. She listened quietly, and said, 'You're going to her, of course. Would you like me to come with you?'

Beattie was surprised, then realised that Antonia, calm and capable, was the very person to have by you in a crisis. She had never liked her, because she had stolen David's love from her, but she appreciated her now as never before.

'No,' she said. 'Thank you, but I need you to stay here and look after everything.'

Antonia nodded. 'He may have been taken prisoner. Or just have been mislaid, temporarily.'

'That's what I told her,' said Beattie. She walked past her towards her room.

Antonia called after her, 'Might be a good idea to pack a few things. In case you need to stay a night or two.'

'Yes,' Beattie said. A shock could bring on an early birth.

'Don't worry about anything here,' Antonia said. 'I'll see to things. And if you want me to come at any point, just let me know.'

Beattie looked back. Antonia was not beautiful or high-born or elegant, or wonderful in any way, not any of the things David deserved; but her ordinary, careworn face was suddenly reassuring and *almost* dear.

'I know you will,' she said. It was curt and awkward, but it was the nearest she had ever come to expressing affection.

★ ★ ★

186

She bought a newspaper at the station, and looked through it for war news. It seemed the Americans had joined the action at last. An American unit had reinforced the retreating British at Château Thierry on the Marne, and had been pounding the Germans with their artillery. Now they had mounted a counter-attack at Belleau Wood in defence of the main road to Paris, and had driven the enemy back.

There was only so much her mind could take in, without Edward to interpret it. She let the paper fall slack to her lap and stared blindly out of the window at the green and sunlit countryside rushing past.

Two gentlemen in the seats on the other side of the carriage, who were also reading newspapers, were discussing the news. She heard them, like voices from another world.

'The tide may be on the turn,' one said.

'Yes, it looks as though the Germans may have been halted,' said the other. 'Good news.'

Was it good news? Beattie wondered. It was so hard to feel anything any more. The Germans may have been halted – but they would start up again.

'When the Americans come in in force, we'll see something,' said the first gentleman, with relish.

'I've heard they're like giants,' said the second. 'Tall, strong, bursting with health and vitality. A different species from our poor worn-out Tommies.'

'They're raw, but their enthusiasm is more than enough to counterbalance their lack of experience,' said the first.

But it will make no difference, Beattie thought flatly. It will never be over. And she stared out of the window, seeing nothing.

Diana had argued herself into better spirits by the time she arrived. 'I'm sure nothing can have happened to him,' she said. 'I spoke to Beth, and she said thousands of our men were captured right at the beginning, and it takes ages to

187

get their names back through the Red Cross. Weeks, sometimes. So it's more than likely he's a prisoner of war. Which will be tiresome for him, but at least he'll be out of it, and safe. They take care of prisoners all right, don't they?'

'Yes, of course they do. Just as we take care of their men,' Beattie said, though she had no idea. But there were rules about it, weren't there? And she'd heard there were inspections by the Red Cross.

'But he won't be able to come home until the war ends,' Diana said. 'Oh dear, the baby will be born by then.'

'You have a loving family to take care of you,' Beattie said. Not to her daughter did she show the bleakness inside her. 'You're not alone.'

'I know,' Diana said, making a brave effort. 'It's just thinking of poor Rupert as a prisoner of war. I don't suppose they have nice quarters or good food. He won't like that at all.'

'He'll be used to roughing it by now,' Beattie said. 'Soldiers have to make do, you know.'

Beth came over, and insisted on sharing the vigil with Beattie. She telephoned friends of Jack's who had contacts in the War Office, and Beattie asked Aeneas to do the same, but there was nothing to be learned yet. 'Missing' was all that was known.

Beattie tried to persuade Diana to come back to Northcote, or even to go to Dene Park, but she refused to leave London until she had definite news of Rupert. So Beattie resigned herself to staying, too.

The news came on the 6th of June that the Germans had definitely been halted, and the offensive was officially over. There had been several successful counter-attacks, and the Marne now marked the front line. It was thought the Germans had suffered heavy losses, especially among their irreplaceable storm troops, and were also having difficulties of supply. They had taken a vast swathe of territory; but on the other hand, they now had to defend two large salients, on the Somme and on the Marne, which would require a heavy investment of manpower.

'On the whole, reasons to be cheerful,' Beth told Beattie. 'We've taken everything they've thrown at us, and we haven't been defeated. And now *they're* worn out. They've lost half a million men this year, and we have the Americans.'

Beattie took Beth's word for it, knowing she understood these things better than her. Cheerfulness was beyond her power, though she did everything to simulate it in front of her daughter. Diana rose and breakfasted late, and Beattie adjusted her habits to fit, using the early hours to write letters, knit and sew. She found Diana's stock of unfinished hospital bags, laid aside in the lethargy of late pregnancy, and worked on them, as well as the baby clothes she was making for the next arrival. She tried to keep busy, but handwork left her mind free to wander over a gloomy landscape – Louis dead, Bobby dead, David crippled, Edward estranged, William about to go to the Front. The war, never-ending. And now there was Rupert to worry about, too. She believed he must have been captured – bad enough, but not the worst.

On the 7th of June, they had just left the breakfast table when the butler, Heating, came in to say there was a gentleman in uniform downstairs asking for her ladyship. 'A Lieutenant Rainton, my lady.'

'That must be Ivo Rainton,' Diana said. 'Lady Tees-borough's younger son. Lady Teesborough is Rupert's godmother, you remember, Mummy? Perhaps he has news. Show him up, please.'

She sounded eager and hopeful, but Beattie had caught something from Heating's expression. She got up quietly and drifted over to stand near Diana's chair.

Rainton was a tall, fair young man in khaki, with his right arm in a cast. He looked pale, and troubled.

189

'Ivo! What on earth's happened to you?' Diana greeted him. 'I don't think you know my mother, Lady Hunter.'

Rainton bowed to Beattie, gesturing to his plastered arm. 'I'm afraid I can't shake hands, ma'am. Got mixed up with an army transport. Broken arm. I'm sorry to burst in on you, Diana, but I was asked by Captain Wagstaffe at Headquarters if I wouldn't do the honours. Well, not honours, of course – don't mean that—' He seemed to have confused himself, and his face took a little colour.

Diana intervened: 'Have you news for me?' She looked at Beattie. 'Wagstaffe is a sort of cousin of Rupert's. He'd realise I'd be worrying.' And to Rainton, 'Do you know what's happened to my husband?'

Rainton's lips moved but no sound came out. He looked as if he'd sooner be anywhere else.

Beattie said quietly, 'Won't you sit down, Mr Rainton? You don't look well.'

Rainton dropped gratefully into the nearest chair, licked his lips, and began, 'I was in the recent action on the Aisne, you see. Same battalion as Rupert, but he's commander of A Company and I'm a sub in B Company.'

'But you saw him? You know where he is?'

Beattie stilled her with a look. 'Be quiet, darling. Let him tell his story his own way. Go on, Mr Rainton.'

Rainton licked his lips again. 'We were in the forward trenches. There was the dickens of a bombardment – never seen anything like it. Then the Jerries charged. We were pretty cut up already by the barrage, and then, when we tried to fall back, we were trapped by the river and there weren't enough bridges. By the time I got across, A and B Companies were down to about forty men, and the only officer left apart from me was Rupert.'

Beattie drew a breath of relief. He hadn't been killed, then.

'So we joined forces, and fell back together. Well, it was

pretty much of a scramble, really, what with the speed the Jerries came on. I was trying to steady the men – it don't do to let them think they're fleeing – and Rupert shouted to me, "Rainton, get the men away in good order." And he told me which way to go. And he said, "I'll mount a rear-guard to give you space."'

'Oh, how brave!' Diana breathed.

'Well, it was,' Rainton asserted. 'Two of A Company had managed to hang on to the Lewis gun, and were toiling a bit under its weight. So Rupert picked four other chaps who were a bit puffed and set up to give us cover with the Lewis and rifle fire. Bravest thing I ever saw. I obeyed orders and took the rest of the men on. But then—'

He gulped. Beattie moved closer to Diana and said quietly, 'Go on. You must finish.'

His eyes went gratefully to her, rather than look at Diana. 'It was a shell, ma'am,' he said. 'The Boche must have been moving their artillery down from the plateau, because we'd been out of range for a while. I heard it, and looked back. We'd got almost to the trees, and we were some distance away, but we'd been going up rising ground, so we were looking downhill, and I could still see the rearguard, crouched down behind some bushes, firing at the enemy. I could see Captain Wroughton firing his pistol.' He drew a breath. 'It was a direct hit.' Beattie felt the words like a blow, felt her own flesh shudder. He looked appealingly at her. 'It would have been instantaneous. They wouldn't have known anything about it. There – there was nothing left when the dust cleared. Not even the bushes. I had to go on. I had my men to take care of.'

'You had your orders,' Beattie said.

'Yes, ma'am. A few miles further on we came on some other survivors from our division with a major in charge, and we joined with them, and fought our way back together for the rest of that day. But later on that day I caught my packet, so I was out of it. Then I found myself back in Blighty and it wasn't until Captain Wagstaffe asked me that I found out no-one knew officially what had happened to Lord Wroughton. So I said I'd come and—' He looked pathetically at Diana.

'It couldn't have been an easy thing to do,' Beattie said quietly. 'We thank you.'

Diana spoke at last. 'He's dead?' she said. Beattie dropped a hand onto her shoulder. 'No, he can't be. You've made a mistake.'

'I'm very sorry,' Rainton said unhappily. 'It's official – the letter will be on its way, but Captain Wagstaffe said, – and I thought, – it would be easier if you knew how it happened.'

Diana shook her head slowly.

'He was a fine soldier,' Rainton said. 'He was wonderful at reading the ground, and taking care of his men, and he was quite fearless in action. Everyone admired him.'

Diana didn't speak, and Beattie took pity on the young man and released him from what must have been a hateful task. 'Thank you for coming and letting us know,' she said, pulling the bell.

Heating must have been lingering somewhere nearby, because he came in almost immediately to show the young man out.

'I hope you'll recover soon from your wounds,' Beattie said in farewell.

Diana raised her head. 'My regards to your mother, if you please,' she said, in a near normal voice.

He bowed, and was gone.

'He's only nineteen,' Diana said, almost conversationally.

'Darling,' Beattie said, looking at her anxiously.

Diana didn't meet her eyes. Her expression was still blank. 'Tired,' she said, after a while. 'I'm so tired.'

Diana couldn't take it in. There seemed no way to think about it, no place in her head that fitted the idea that Rupert

192

was dead. When Charles had fallen, she had understood it and felt it, and mourned him. But Rupert? He had always been so full of life in his own most particular way. He would come home – probably burst in laughing at having hoaxed her. It was a tease, a practical joke, it wasn't real. She had little George, fifteen months old, and a baby on the way to prove that she was married to Rupert, that he was real, that he lived. She was the Countess Wroughton. He had made her that.

She felt as though she were in a dream. People flitted in and out – Cousin Beth was there often, and Aunt Laura. She heard them talking about keeping Aunt Sonia away, because however well she meant, she did tend to gush. She heard them talking about the baby, due in the first week of July. She heard them talk about mourning clothes, and her mother saying there was no need for her to put on black until after the baby was born, since she wouldn't be going out in public. Padmore, her maid, sewed black bands for her. Cards and letters arrived by every post. Rupert's cousin Lady Hexham sent white roses; his sister, Lady Grosmore, sent lilies. Visitors were coming to the door with condolences, friends and Wroughton relatives, but she didn't have to see them. The baby was the excuse. Was it the baby, she wondered at one point, that was creating the protective bubble in which she lived? The question seemed interesting for an instant, then faded away. She couldn't hold on to thoughts. She spent her days flicking through magazines – she couldn't read books, her mind wouldn't grip enough – sewing in a desultory way, eating what was put in front of her, and answering yes and no to questions that she didn't really take in.

Her mother-in-law visited. She heard through the closed door the muted argument about whether she might be admitted, whether she would upset her. But when she came in, the other Lady Wroughton was strangely muted. She looked old and haggard, and she stared at Diana long and hard, but all she said was 'Two sons. Both gone. And they both wanted you. Why? I don't understand it.' And after staring a while longer, she sighed deeply, and went away.

It wasn't until almost a week had passed that anything broke through her guard. On the 13th of June she received a visit from Rupert's man of business, Boardman. He had come to tell her, or rather remind her, that her son George was now Earl Wroughton in his father's place. Unusually, she, Diana, had been named his sole guardian in the will, while the trusteeship had been given jointly to her, Boardman himself, and Rupert's friend and erstwhile best man, Lord Teesborough – Ivo Rainton's elder brother.

Then he said, 'I expect you have been worrying about death duties, but I can reassure you on that point. For the duration of the war, the government has waived them on the estates of those who fall in battle.'

The words were curiously clear and sharp-edged, as though a fog had rolled away. She looked at him, a cold horror gradually sinking through her. 'Death duties?' she said.

'Yes, my lady. The measure was brought in because of the number of families in which father and son were both serving, and it was thought the hardship occasioned should two generations fall within a short period would be excessive, especially given that they were serving their country in the most—'

Diana interrupted: 'He's dead,' she said. *Now* she saw it. The piece slotted home with a hateful click. Rupert was dead. He would never come home. Never laugh and tease her, call her beautiful, hold her in his arms, choose her outfit for her, take her to dinner, sit and chat to her by the fire. He was dead. He was dead. There was no more Rupert. She would never see him again.

'Oh, my lady,' said Boardman, helplessly. 'We will all miss him.'

She saw there were tears in his eyes. It was the last straw. She wept, great sobs ripping out of her, suffocating tears constricting her throat, making her gasp and shake. She wept without restraint, like a kind of madness. Boardman stood helplessly, frozen with horror, until at last he had the wit to ring. Beth, who was in the house that day, had to comfort him and show him out, while Beattie took Diana up to her bedroom.

Jack came home on leave on the 17th of June, limping badly, but when Beth asked him anxiously if he had been wounded, he told her it was only blisters. 'Breaking in a new pair of boots,' he said, 'only to be caught out by a lot more marching than I expected. Thought myself clever to find a bootmaker still in situ in Amiens, then had to go hiking all over the place, to Abbeville, then Doulens and back, looking for a half-battalion we were supposed to join. Humiliating, at this stage of my military career, to be suffering blisters like a raw recruit!'

'Raw is right,' she said, when she saw them. 'My poor darling! How are we going to hit the town if you can't get shoes on?'

He gave a grimace. 'I don't think I've got the energy for hitting the town, or anything else. Lord, I feel old! Can't we just stay home and be comfortable? Get some grub in and pull up the drawbridge?'

'Of course, darling, if you want to deprive all those who love you of your company.'

'You're the only one I want to see. But I'm starving *now* – can you rustle up a sandwich or something?'

'There's only war bread, I'm afraid. The shops aren't allowed to sell any other sort, and Mrs Beales doesn't include bread-making in her culinary skills. It's pretty foul.'

'I'll risk it.'

She looked apologetic. 'And I've used up my butter ration, and the new week doesn't start until tomorrow.'

'I'd forgotten rationing.' Jack groaned. 'I think we get fed better over there.'

'I have things in tins – and I think there's a packet of savoury biscuits in the larder, from that hamper that the Palfreys gave us at Christmas.'

'And what is there to drink?'

'Claret, gin and whisky. Oh, and there's a bottle of champagne.'

He kissed her. 'Things are looking up.'

'Go and change, and I'll assemble something,' she said.

They ended up sitting on the little balcony at the back that looked over the garden, drinking champagne and eating smoked oysters and caviar out of tins with the biscuits.

Jack sighed with pleasure. 'Everything's so green,' he said. The garden was rather overgrown, so there was certainly plenty of grass, plus dense hedges and a large tree in full leaf. 'And not a ruined house or a bloated dead horse in sight.'

'Darling!' she protested. 'Not while I'm eating.'

'You can't think how tired one gets of death and destruction.'

'I can.'

'Oh, I was forgetting – poor little Diana's Rupert.'

'Not so little now. She's very large with child, poor girl. It's so hard, that she should lose her fiancé and now her husband.'

'I didn't know him well, but I heard him talked of as a good soldier,' Jack said. He had heard other rumours, too, but they were not for repeating in front of ladies. 'Is she still in London?'

'No. Beattie persuaded her to go back to Northcote. I think she was only waiting to hear from Rupert anyway, before going down, so there's reason for her to stay now.'

'It'll be a bit crowded at The Elms, won't it – assuming she's taking the nursery and her maid with her?'

'Well, I dare say they'd have managed,' said Beth. 'One always does when it's people one loves. But she preferred to go to Dene Park, as it happens. It will please the dowager to have the baby born there. She's awfully dynastic about it, apparently. Nula has dropped everything to be with her – she's going to live there with Diana until the baby comes. And the family is only minutes away.'

'It's the best place for her. There's healing in the countryside,' Jack said. He sneezed. 'Sorry.'

'You're not getting a cold, are you?' Beth asked.

'No, hay fever more like. This garden's full of grass seed.'

'It's full of grass,' Beth pointed out. 'What's this we've been hearing lately about "Flanders grippe"? Have you seen anything of it?'

'Oh, yes, the Spanish flu, as the Frogs call it – though there's no reason to think it came from Spain. The Spanish aren't even *in* the war. It's certainly been going around the camps – the usual sort of thing, high temperature, muscle aches, debilitation. Knocks you out completely for a couple of weeks. Some people think the Sammies brought it over – the Americans, I mean.'

'Is that what you call them?'

'Well, they like to call themselves "doughboys" – God knows why – but the Tommies call them the Sammies.'

'Tommies and Sammies. How cosy. Why do they think the Americans brought it?'

'Because they're newcomers, I suppose, and it had to come from somewhere. They say American farm workers often get pig flu, and this is a variant of that. But then some of the medical officers think it isn't flu at all, but a kind of malaria brought in by the troops transferring from the Middle East. You pays your money and you takes your choice. At all events, it seems to be giving us a bit of breathing space out there, because the Germans have got it as well, so there's a definite lull in the action.'

197

'Breathing space is probably not *le mot juste*,' said Beth.

'True! Sorry. Can you reach the bottle, and I'll top up your glass.' She passed it over. 'God, England is beautiful!' he said, watching two blackbirds chasing each other through the branches of the tree. 'We need to come home now and then, you know, and see this sort of thing, just so we know it's worth fighting for. Which it is – so very much. And when we've biffed the Boche, there must never be another war. We must find a better way of doing things.'

She leaned over and brushed the silvered hair at his temples with her fingers, and noted the deep lines in his weather-tanned face, and thought what a toll it had taken on him. She loved him so much, it hurt her deep in her chest, and she had to distract herself. 'Men's feet are so funny-looking,' she said. 'All knobbly.'

They were bare, and he had propped them on the bottom rung of the balcony railing. He wiggled his toes for her as they both stared at them. 'Do you remember our mountain-climbing days?' he said. 'Will these feet ever carry me up another peak, I wonder?'

'Don't say that,' she protested.

'I only meant that I think I'll have had enough of hoofing it when this lot's over. The motor-car, that's the ticket. Motor-touring. I predict it'll become all the rage – walking will be right out. Or what do you say to buying a little aeroplane and tooling about the continent by air?'

'Sounds wonderful,' she said. 'We'll be the Flying Hunters.'

'Sounds like a circus act.'

'But you'll have to learn to fly.'

'You will too, so we can share the driving. Where shall we go, do you think?'

And they discussed their future travels in increasingly extravagant terms as the level in the bottle went down.

CHAPTER FOURTEEN

The servants had their dinner at midday, and with Peter at school, William away and everyone else busy with war-work, upstairs luncheon didn't take much getting. Cook was usually able to put her feet up for an hour or so in the afternoon. Beryl, full of youthful energy, went and helped at the Hastings Road canteen for a couple of hours in the afternoon, and Ada usually walked up to the church, where there was always something to do – rolling bandages, sorting clothes for the needy, making up parcels for soldiers at the Front. Cook generally let Emily go out, too, for a bit of fresh air – she always looked peaky, these days. Cook suspected she only went and hung around outside Hetherington's Hygienic Bakery to catch a glimpse of Con Meyer, but at least she got air and exercise walking down to the village.

So Cook had the servants' hall to herself, and liked to settle into her favourite armchair and raise her feet on a footstool to let them cool off after the morning's exertions. Her belief in the therapeutic properties of fresh air did not extend to herself. Usually she would have a bit of knitting in her lap, or her recipe book, to copy in a new wartime formula; but it was hardly ever more than a few minutes before her eyelids drooped and she was away.

So it was a violent shock to be roused from deep sleep by someone kissing her smack on the lips. She let out a yell and her arm thrashed automatically, but her hand was caught in mid-air by a very strong one, and a definitely male voice said, 'Steady the buffs! It's not the German invasion.'

Her wits struggled upwards through the veils of sleep and caught up with her eyes and ears. The second shriek she gave took the form of 'Fred!'

'It's me, all right,' he said cheerfully. 'Nice way to make me welcome, Ma-a-argaret, trying to bash me on the coconut!'

'Ooh, you gave me such a start!' Cook protested. 'I didn't know who it was!'

'Oh, you don't say? How many other blokes kiss you on the lips, then? Nice goings-on while your soldier laddie is far away, fighting the foe.' Seeing she was properly awake now, he took her hands to pull her to her feet and said, 'Come here, woman, so's I can kiss you properly.'

'Who are you calling "woman"?'

'You're my woman, aren't you?' he said, enfolding her. 'Pucker up, my girl.'

Cook struggled against him, though not very much. 'You can't do that here – someone might come in.'

'You don't want me to kiss you properly? All right, I'll kiss you *un*-properly.' And he did.

She emerged briefly, red in the face, to say, 'Fred!' in a scandalised gasp, before being submerged again. The next time she surfaced, she had abandoned the fight, and leaned against him gratefully, thinking how nice it was to have a warm, solid man to depend on. 'What you doing here, anyway?' she murmured; and then, more sharply, 'You're not wounded?'

'No, I'm sweet. It's quieted down so we're working through some leave. So here I am, take me or leave me.'

She smiled. 'I'll take you.'

'Good girl. Got any tucker for a starving bloke? Had nothing since brekker.'

'I'll get you something.'

'Bonzer. And whack the old kettle on, eh? Gor, a cuppa tea that doesn't taste of petrol – what every Tommy dreams of!'

He sat at the kitchen table while she made him sandwiches and tea, and he chatted about his life in France – not the action, but the domestic stuff that he knew would interest and not alarm her, little anecdotes about the 'other blokes', eccentric officers, crazy rules, mishaps, deprivations.

'You said it's quiet out there?' she queried, placing plate and cup before him.

'Quiete*r*,' he agreed. 'Gor, that looks good! Smells like real ham.' He took a huge bite.

'Course it's real ham! What other sort is there?'

'We don't get ham like that. Whatever meat we get, it's out of a tin. Mostly bully beef, but sometimes for a relish they give us Australian boiled mutton.'

'In a *tin*?' Cook cried, hands to her cheeks in horror.

He grinned. 'Makes a change. Always happy for a change. One o' my blokes got hold of a tin of pressed rabbit in jelly the other day. Spread it on biscuits like that foy grass. What a treat!'

'I been cooking a lot of rabbit lately,' Cook said. 'Tasty in a stew with shallots and plenty of herbs, but there's a dreadful lot of bones. I've heard of rabbit terrine – never tried making it, though. Where'd he get it?'

'Red Cross. He was just back from hospital – had the flu.'

'You had a lot of flu out there? We've been hearing stories.'

'Fair bit. Once it hits a unit it spreads like wildfire. Hard to isolate when you live cheek by jowl. Knocks you out for a few days, then you're right.'

'There's a lot of it in London. We've not seen any cases in Northcote yet. They say the Americans brought it over.'

'Could be.' He was too busy eating to go into it.

'As if we don't have enough to worry about,' Cook said

201

indignantly. 'What with rationing, and U-boats sinking our ships. And the air raids – terrible! St Pancras station hit. Paddington station a near miss. The lady that wrote "Keep The Home Fires Burning" got killed in that one, did you know? Fifty killed in London in that raid in May, so I read. It's taking your life in your hands, just going up to Town. I'm just glad the missus has given up that canteen in Waterloo, if the Germans are going to go for railway stations. Evil, horrible people! I wouldn't be surprised if it was *them* that started the flu off.'

'Well, if they did, they got it themselves as well, from what we hear. Worse than us.'

'Serves 'em right!' She met his eyes anxiously. Her indignation was her way of dealing with real fear. 'Fred, we're not going to lose, are we? The Germans keep coming and we don't seem to be able to stop them. Miss Diana's husband was killed in that last thing – you know, what they're calling the Marne. Years of war, so many killed, all those terrible battles, and the Germans still coming. What's going to happen? Where's it all going to end?'

At that moment, the back door opened, saving Fred from having to answer. It was Ada, back from the church. By the time a suitable greeting had been exchanged, he had finished his sandwich, and as Ada went to take off her coat, he said to Cook, 'Let's go out for a walk.'

'Walk? With my feet?' Cook protested. 'Whatever for?'

'I want us to be alone, of course. All right, we'll go to the pictures, then.'

'I can't go out, I got cakes to make and dinner to get and bread to set up.'

'When am I going to get a kiss and a cuddle, then?' he said indignantly.

'My night off's tomorrow. You'll have to wait until then.'

'You make it bloody hard for a bloke, that's all I can say – standing there looking like that.'

'Like what?' she said, startled.

'Like a gorgeous armful. How about a stroll in the garden?'

'Whatever for?'

'There's that bit down the back – all bushes and trees.'

'The shrubbery?'

'I'm very interested in shrubberies, y'know.'

'Are you really?'

'Lifelong interest.' He dropped her a wink. 'Get in the middle of that lot and you can't be seen.'

'Oh, you!' she said, blushing. But she didn't say no.

Laura was restless. Her sense of have fallen out of the strong current of events and into a small stagnant pool was exacerbated by the knowledge that Ronnie had gone back: her aunt in the FANYs had found her a job, supervising a canteen just outside Étaples where everybody from nurses and FANYs to Tommies and Sammies stopped for refreshment and sustaining chat. It was on the main road that ran from Boulogne to Amiens, down which it seemed everyone had to pass at some time, and the fact that Ronnie couldn't cook – 'I could burn water' – didn't matter. It was her management skills that were needed.

There was no possibility of going back to Pop – it was still too dangerous – but Laura felt she must do *something*. She was so bored she even went to a Bedfordite meeting; but there she was pleased to meet Louisa, whom she hadn't seen for some time.

'I've been *tremendously* busy,' she told Laura breathlessly. 'Helping out at a woman and baby clinic in the East End.'

'My dear, I didn't know that was an area in which you were expert,' Laura said mildly. 'What do you actually do?'

'Talk to them, give them advice about where to go for help and so on. We have a wide variety of first-rate leaflets—'

Now Laura did laugh. 'Leaflets? Oh, Lou!'

Louisa flushed. 'It's all very well to make fun, but these

women face terrible problems. You're always talking about *doing* something. Why don't you join us?'

'Not my cup of tea,' Laura said. 'I need the spice of danger.'

'It's quite dangerous enough,' Louisa said. 'Maud Eckersall – do you know her? – got a black eye last week. She was talking to a woman when the husband came roaring in and dragged the poor woman away, shouting he didn't want "ideas put into her head". Poor Maud got knocked down in the mêlée.'

'How shocking,' said Laura.

Louisa frowned, as if she suspected Laura of irony. 'Don't you at least find it appalling that these women don't have the vote, while their husbands have it, however brutish and ignorant they may be?'

'Of course I do, darling, but that's a fight for after the war. It's the Germans that concern me now. I'm itching to get back to France.'

'Then why don't you ask your friend Lady Overton for a job?'

'I have, and she said she'd let me know when she had something, but I haven't heard from her.'

'Well, remind her,' said Louisa. 'You're not usually so retiring.'

It was good advice, and Laura determined to do something about it the next day, but by chance she received a message the next morning, asking her if she could find time to call on Lady Overton at the Southport Hospital at noon.

She duly presented herself at the main entrance, and there was a skirmish with the porter, whose business seemed to be keeping people out rather than facilitating their entrance. Eventually he put her in the charge of a diminutive messenger, adding that 'Her ladyship's a 'oly terror if she's disturbed for nothing.' The warning frightened the messenger a lot more than Laura, and he scuttled ahead of her up stairs and along corridors, and deposited her outside a door with a breathless. 'Here y'are, miss,' before positively running away.

There was no reply to Laura's knock, so she opened the door and found a small and very untidy sitting-room, empty of life. She walked over to the window, and amused herself with watching the street scene below until, at almost twenty minutes past twelve, there was the sound of rapid footsteps in the corridor outside. The door was flung open and Lady Overton came in, dressed in a severe dark suit, and gave a slight start as she saw Laura.

'Oh! Miss Hunter,' she said. 'I do apologise for keeping you waiting. I had patient rounds this morning, and one of them has developed tiresome complications, which delayed me. And I have a list this afternoon and notes to read beforehand, so I'm afraid I must be rather brisk and businesslike.'

'Brisk and businesslike suits me down to the ground,' Laura said.

Lady Overton smiled, lightening her tired face. 'Yes, I imagine so. You are a refreshment to me, Miss Hunter. I wish more women were like you. Now, to the point: do you still wish to go back to France in some capacity?'

'More than ever,' said Laura.

'Then I have a proposition for you. A driver is needed for one of my X-ray ambulances. It is purely a driving job – there is no medical element to it, though of course first-aid training is always useful, given the situation out there.'

'I have a first-aid certificate.'

'Yes, I know. And I know you are not – shall we say? – *unmanned* by danger.'

Laura smiled. 'My family think I seek it out unnecessarily. I don't – but if it comes with a job that needs to be done—'

'Just so. Well, the job of the X-ray ambulance is to get to the patient as early as possible in his journey, to avoid exacerbating his condition through ignorance of exactly what it is.

205

So you would be operating in quite a forward position, certainly as far forward as the casualty clearing station – perhaps, on occasion, the regimental aid post. So there will be a certain risk attached. I have to be sure you understand that.'

'Yes, ma'am,' said Laura. 'I was shelled in Poperinghe. I can't say I enjoyed the experience, but it hasn't put me off wanting to go back.'

'I hoped you'd say that. You will be based in Hazebrouck, and operate in an area roughly between Hazebrouck, Armentières and Ypres. The situation is fluid out there at the moment, so you must take military advice on the ground. You will be under the nominal command of the head of the field hospital, but it is mainly common sense that must guide you. The rest of the ambulance team is experienced, so you may trust them. They have been working together for some time, but they lost their driver to appendicitis, so they're anxious to get back to work. Can you leave immediately?'

'As soon as I've packed,' Laura said, feeling the blood running hot through her veins at the thought of adventure.

'I'll arrange a travel warrant for tonight, then. The train leaves Victoria at eleven-thirty.'

Laura nodded approvingly. That gave her time to do some important shopping before packing – morphine tablets, food staples, soap, cigarettes, extra stockings and so on. 'And I'll telegraph ahead and have you met at Hazebrouck by your team. Your ambulance is named Matilda—' She broke off with a frown of thought. 'I seem to remember that you know at least one member of the team: Lady Agnes Daubeney.'

'Annie Daubeney?' Laura laughed with pleasure. 'Yes, of course, we had a private ambulance together – she and I, Flora Hazlit and Elsie Murray – until it broke down irretrievably.'

The frown cleared. 'Ah, yes, of course. I remember your telling me. I knew there was a connection, but it had slipped from my mind. I'm glad you will have a friend there.'

'I shall enjoy working with Annie again.'

'Yes, she's a dear girl. Very well – I must bid you goodbye now, Miss Hunter, as duty calls. I shall have your papers sent round to your house this afternoon. I wish you good luck, and give you my profound thanks.'

'It is I who must thank you,' Laura said, shaking hands, 'for rescuing me from boredom.'

Lady Overton gave rather a strained smile. 'This war may be many things, but indeed one cannot accuse it of being boring.'

Outside in the street, Laura almost hugged herself for her good luck. Going back to France! Being in 'quite a forward position'! Doing something so absolutely important for the war effort. Working with dear Annie again!

And it had not escaped her that Matilda was stationed in the area where Ransley's field hospital operated. In fact, he might well be the senior officer under whose 'nominal command' she found herself. They might see each other! Things, she felt, could not have worked out better.

John Courcy had been gone over three weeks. Sadie was back to her usual occupations, working at Highclere, driving the ambulance and, in the time left over, visiting the wounded officers at Mount Olive.

There were a lot of Americans among them now, she noticed. The British officers said that they fought like crazy men – 'No difficulty in getting 'em to attack. Getting 'em to stop's another matter!' It meant that they often outran their support, and with more courage than fieldcraft, they took more than their fair share of wounds. They were talked of as lying dead in ranks as they fell – 'Like us in 1915 and '16. They've a lot to learn.'

Sadie was glad to be busy. She had hoped that before they parted John would say something to indicate his feelings for her, but he had left with a cheerful 'goodbye', and had not even asked if he could write to her. She had painfully to accept that her own feelings were unrequited. What she thought she had noticed in him had been her imagination.

And so, on Saturday the 22nd of June, she accepted an invitation from Christopher Beresford to go out for the day in the motor-car he had borrowed from a work colleague. 'A spin through the country lanes, and tea somewhere by the river.'

'That sounds lovely,' she said, trying to mean it.

Beresford arrived to collect her, armed with the gift of a tin of pruneaux d'Agen fourrés – stuffed French prunes. 'It's a regional delicacy,' he explained. 'Awfully delicious, I'm told.'

'Where did you get them?'

'A chap in the department who'd just come back from France brought a whole assortment of things. I picked out those for you.'

'That's very kind,' she said.

'It's been ages since I saw you,' Beresford said. 'Work has been terrific all year, with the U-boat activity and the rationing. And your father leaving has rather thrown a spanner in the works. What on earth made him do it?'

Sadie had grown a little tired of defending her father. 'Duty,' she said shortly.

He coloured. 'I say, you do know that I *can't* go, don't you? I was rejected by the medical board.'

'I wasn't criticising you. It *has* been ages,' she said, to get them past the moment. 'I've been terribly busy too.'

'Tell me all about it,' he said, helping her into the car.

As they pottered through the green tunnels and between bursting June hedgerows, she told him about her recent trials and triumphs, and he told her about his, and it was all very comfortable and nice. She *did* like him. She must put John Courcy out of her mind, and get on with her life without him. Beresford was just the right sort of man for her. They shared many interests; her father liked and approved of him; he was attractive, well educated, had a good job, and it seemed that he was interested in her in more than a casual way. When the war was over, she could imagine him courting her properly, proposing to her . . .

'Penny for them.'

She had to say something. 'I was thinking about – after the war. Wondering what it will be like.'

He considered. 'Pretty much the same, I should think. Things don't change that much, not in a short time.'

'The same as now, or the same as before the war?'

'Before the war.'

'Oh, I hope not,' Sadie said. 'Girls not allowed to do anything, or have jobs, or go out alone.'

'I bet there are lots of women who'd like to go back to not having to do anything.'

'Not me,' Sadie said.

He smiled. 'I know not you. You're an original. I can't imagine what you'll get up to once the war's over, but I look forward to finding out.'

He said it with easy confidence, as though it were a settled thing that he would be there to find out.

He stopped talking, having reached a tricky junction with the main road, and she took the opportunity to study his profile as he concentrated on driving. Yes, it was possible, she thought. She liked him, it was easy between them, they could – make a go of it, as people said. His face was attractive and known to her, masculine and good. She could imagine kissing him. It would be pleasant.

But he was not John. When she looked at John, something in her said, *This one, and no other*. There was no reason to it. It just *was*. It wasn't a schoolgirl crush or a childish fancy, it was real and permanent, and she would never feel like that about anyone else. He didn't want her, and she would make a life without him, because she was not a defeatist or a coward or a fool. But she would never love anyone as she loved John Courcy.

Beresford caught her looking at him, and smiled. 'Nearly there. I thought Marlow – there's a place by the bridge with a terrace on the river.'

'Lovely,' she said, and smiled back.

An officer in khaki was at the door. Ada gave him the blankly polite look proper for strangers, and then her eyebrows shot up and she squeaked, in mixed excitement and dismay. 'Ooh, it's the master! Oh, sir, I'm ever so sorry, I didn't recognise you for a moment.'

Edward swept off his cap and handed it to her, with the valise he was holding. 'I hardly recognise myself, these days.'

Others were appearing, attracted by Ada's squeal – David from Edward's study, Antonia coming down the stairs, Beryl, poking her head out from the drawing-room where she'd been polishing the fire-irons.

'Dad, we weren't expecting you,' David said, crutching forward to shake hands. They inspected each other. Edward was shocked – not having seen his eldest son for some time, he saw the difference in him. When you were with someone every day, you hardly noticed what they looked like. David's hair was going grey at the temples. His eyes were pouched, his face unnaturally lined for one who had just had his twenty-fourth birthday. He spoke with a slight slur, and as Edward stared at him, his hand made a guilty movement to his jacket pocket, and away again. *He's taking something for the pain*, Edward thought. *But why should he feel guilty about that?*

'I thought I'd surprise you,' Edward said. 'Of course, once I was on the train, I realised that if I didn't warn you, you might all be out, and the surprise would be mine.'

Antonia had reached him now, and stretched up to kiss his cheek. 'You're looking well,' she said.

David had been thinking the same. This lean, bronzed man was almost a stranger.

'I feel astonishingly well,' Edward said. 'Where is everybody?'

'Peter's at school, of course, and Sadie's up at Highclere,' said Antonia.

'And Mother's at a meeting, but it's only in the church rooms,' David took over. 'We could send a message and she'd be back in five minutes.'

'No need to disturb her,' Edward said.

'She'll be going straight on to another meeting afterwards,' said Antonia. 'Better send her a message.' She looked at Ada, who jerked into life. She had been gazing at the master almost open-mouthed.

'Timmy's in the boot-room,' she said. 'I'll send him. How long are you staying, sir? Your bed's not aired, and Cook will want to know about dinner and such.'

'I have forty-eight hours, but I have things to do in Town tomorrow, so just until tomorrow morning.'

Ada went away to spread the news, and Antonia said quietly, 'Forty-eight hours? Is it . . .'

'Embarkation leave,' Edward agreed.

The meeting was almost over when Timmy arrived. Beattie scribbled a note for the next meeting, at Mrs Oliver's, and sent him off with it, then finished the business in hand before walking home. By the time she arrived, Cook had provided coffee and shortbread and the three of them were sitting at the morning-room table, Edward telling David and Antonia about officer cadet school.

'It was embarrassing at first, being so much older than the others,' he was saying, 'and of course they call me "Uncle", but I think I've managed to keep up with them and gain a certain respect. It helps that—' He broke off as she appeared in the doorway, stood up, and went slowly to her.

211

Beattie looked at him, wide-eyed. The training had changed him. Most obviously, his indoor pallor was gone, along with the softness of the office-worker, the sly padding of flesh and the desk-bound stoop. He was tanned and lean and hard; he held himself differently; and most of all there was something in his face – a definition. Where before he had had the preoccupied and slightly careworn look of commercial responsibility, now he seemed to be looking outward, alert, ready, like the Hunter of his name. To her unprepared eyes he looked younger – and with an air of power about him. For an unguarded instant, he reminded her of Louis when she had first met him: slightly, excitingly dangerous.

Her mouth was dry. She managed to say, 'How long?'

'I have to leave tomorrow morning. I must get up to Town before I go, check on various things.'

He seemed to come to a decision, picked up one of her hands and then leaned in and kissed her cheek. The touch seemed to shock her. When he straightened, she said, 'Is it . . . You're going to the Front?'

'Yes,' he said. He smiled but it was a stranger's smile. 'They think I'm ready.'

In his study, Edward talked to David about his new role as deputy master of the house. It puzzled him – he could not perceive exactly what it was that David had been doing, but he understood that his son needed a role in life, since he could not go and fight. Cramming schoolboys was not enough to make him feel like a man. Edward listened and nodded, and finally said, 'It's a great comfort to me to know you're here and taking my place.'

'Not that, Father, hardly.' David seemed embarrassed.

'If anything happens to me, you will have to take care of your mother and sister and brothers,' Edward persisted seriously. 'I know I can safely leave everything in your hands.

I would not be happy to go if I thought the burden would fall on your mother's shoulders. She is a wonderful woman, but that sort of thing should not be a woman's responsibility. You have a wife and child of your own, now, so you understand.'

'Yes, Father,' David said, and for a moment a clear look came into his pain-worn face, as though a fog had lifted and he had seen the road ahead of him, which before he had been stumbling along, feeling his way.

Quietly, Edward said, 'How bad is your leg?'

David looked at him, the automatic denial on his lips. But then he swallowed and said, 'Pretty bloody.'

'Do you think you should see someone? You haven't consulted anyone since the army surgeon wrote you off.'

'What good would it do?' David said, his mouth hardening.

'Medicine develops by leaps and bounds during wartime,' Edward said. 'That's a well-known fact. Look at this new reconstruction work they're doing at Sidcup – that chap Gillies – plastic surgery, they call it. The most amazing new techniques, not thought of before the war. And they're adding to them all the time. It's two years since you were wounded – things will have moved on.'

'I don't want any more messing about for no purpose,' David growled, turning his head away.

'At least find out,' Edward said. 'You owe that to Antonia and the child. Don't just throw in the towel. I never took my son for a coward.'

'Coward?' David looked back with a spark of anger that Edward was glad to see.

'Then don't say nothing can be done, when you don't *know*,' Edward said. 'Find out – consult somebody. Whoever is the best in the field. I'll stand the nonsense.' He smiled, checking David's protest. 'I've made a bit out of the war so far. I ought to pay something back. Will you promise me you'll see a specialist?'

'All right,' David muttered at last. And, even lower, 'Thanks.'

'I don't want to see you getting dependent on morphine.'

'I don't—' David began to protest.

Edward squeezed his shoulder. 'Opium, cocaine, whatever it is. That's no sort of life.'

David's hand stole without his will to his pocket, where the little bottle of paregoric nestled. He liked to touch it, like a talisman, when bad thoughts came to him. He looked into his father's newly firm and authoritative face, and felt like a child again. He wanted to fling himself on his father's chest and weep, and have his troubles taken away. 'How did you know?' he asked weakly.

'I know you. I'm your father,' Edward said, and the pang in his heart was no less sharp for understanding that in everything that mattered, in love and care and pride, he *was*. What had been lost by his learning that Louis had begat the boy was between Edward and Beattie, not between Edward and David. 'You are my son,' he said, and it might have sounded redundant in the context of the sentence before, but it meant something more, which needed saying.

'Thanks, Dad,' David said. 'I'll do what you say.'

The day passed quickly. Edward walked down the garden for a long chat with Munt, who was eager to show off his burgeoning vegetables, and seemed almost to have forgotten the far-off days of glorious prize-winning chrysanthemums, roses and dahlias – though Edward noticed a couple of strings of sweet peas lurking among the runner beans. 'Brings the bees,' Munt protested when Edward mentioned them. 'Good for pollination.' And then, staring into the middle distance, he confessed: 'I like the smell. Can't better 'em for scent.'

'A man must have some pleasures,' Edward said.

214

Munt looked sharply to see if he was being mocked. Finding he wasn't, he softened a little towards the master. 'I tucks in a few flowers here and there. Nothing like the old days, but got to keep me hand in, for after the war.'

'Quite right,' Edward said, looking round the neat rows of vegetables where once there had been lawns and flower-beds. The garden was no longer a place for pleasure. No more tennis, no more taking tea on the lawn, reading the Sunday paper under the mulberry tree, impromptu croquet, strolling at sunset arm in arm to smell the stocks and watch for bats. The garden worked for the war effort, like everyone and everything else, and The Elms was both the richer and the poorer for it. 'It'll be a strange world, when we get back to it.'

'That it will.'

Edward met his eyes. 'If we ever do. Things are pretty bad over there.'

'You don't need to tell me,' said Munt.

'Boys of eighteen, and officers like me, with no experience – that's what we're relying on now, to push back the Germans. They're shelling Paris now – *Paris*.'

'We'll come through,' said Munt. 'Things'll get wuss, then they'll get better. The Jerries're wearing 'emselves out, and they got nothing more to call on. We got to hold on, like General Haig said, and everyone do his bit.'

'I'm going to do mine,' Edward said bleakly, more to himself than to Munt.

But Munt said. 'You go. I'll watch 'em for you.'

'Mr David—' Edward began loyally.

'Me, and Miss Sadie,' Munt insisted.

'Sadie?' Edward said, surprised. 'She's only a child.'

'Pick of the crop,' Munt said. 'She's a right one.'

Luckily, Sadie came back for lunch – sometimes she had something up at Highclere with the girls. 'Why didn't somebody

215

telephone me?' she cried. 'I could have come! I was lungeing the new intake, but that could have waited.'

'I didn't think of it,' Antonia said. 'I'm sorry.'

'I forget we have the telephone,' Beattie confessed. 'But you have all afternoon.'

'No, I'm on shift at the ambulance depot,' Sadie said. 'I can't get out of that.'

'Never mind,' Edward said. 'We'll have this evening.'

'Well, tell me all about it over lunch,' Sadie said. 'Is it fun being an officer and telling everyone what to do? Didn't you feel an awful fraud the first time you gave an order?'

'How did you know?' he asked, with a smile.

'Because I did, up at Highclere, when I was made supervisor. But I don't think about it now. I expect it'll be the same for you – though, of course, it'll be a lot more responsibility at the Front.'

'I won't be sent to the Front right away,' Edward said, having regard to the nerves of the family and of Ada who was serving. 'You get all sorts of training over there before you're pitched in at the deep end.'

Dinner that evening was a triumph, though Cook watered every course with sentimental tears. The master was going to France, and who knew what might happen? Bobby, the Hunter she had loved best, had not come home. This evening's dinner must be perfect.

She sent Timmy off on the bicycle to the farm over at Goston where they had watercress beds in the chalk streams. 'And come back past Simpson's and get a pint of cream.' She found Munt surprisingly co-operative when she asked for new potatoes and peas. 'I wish we had strawberries,' she said. 'Ought to be strawberries, after lamb.' But in the zeal of growing vegetables for victory, there had been no room for strawberry beds.

'I know where I can lay me hand on some raspberries,'

Munt said, torn between unwillingness to make Cook's life easier, and the desire to give the master a good send-off.

'Raspberries? Where?'

'Never you mind where. I can get 'em, that's all. I'll poddle off when I got your taties and peas up.'

'All right – but don't you let me down, once I'm counting on 'em,' Cook said sharply. 'I'll make meringues – I'll have the egg whites left over from the mayonnaise.'

She sent Ada to Colston's the fishmonger – neither Emily nor Beryl would have been able to wheedle the salmon out of old man Colston – which was a nuisance because there was a lot to do. And she had to ask the missus for permission to use the telephone, because there was a delicate bit of business to be done to get hold of the lamb from Sharp's farm and persuade them to have their boy Aldis bring it over.

But it all came together, and Cook was as proud of that evening's dinner as of anything she had ever produced. Cold watercress soup, poached salmon with mayonnaise, pink lamb cutlets with new potatoes and peas, and meringues filled with cream and raspberries (Munt had been as good as his word).

Afterwards, Cook was 'sent for', and hurried into a clean apron to go and blush and smile as the master told her what a superb meal it had been. 'I shall treasure the memory when I'm over in France, believe me. It was a wonderful send-off you've given me. I've eaten like a king tonight.'

Cook managed to stammer something in which 'nothing too good' and 'hero' and – mysteriously to Edward – the name 'Fred' featured, and took herself away, well pleased.

After dinner, Edward played at cribbage for half an hour with Peter before he went off reluctantly to bed. Then there was conversation among the rest of them. He was not alone with Beattie until the very end, when everyone else had gone up,

217

and she went round turning off lights, while he finished his last nightcap. When she came back into the drawing-room to check the French windows, he said, 'Would you like a drink?'

She looked startled, and said, 'Oh – no, thanks.'

He drained his glass and stood up, saying, 'Well, I think I'll go up, then.' He had turned away, but she made a sound as though she would speak, and he turned back enquiringly. She was standing straight, her hands down by her sides, clenched into fists, bracing herself for something.

'Not like this,' she said at last. 'Edward, let's not part like this.'

He looked at her for a long moment. 'What do you want of me?'

She hardly knew. What she said in the end was. 'I want you to forgive me.'

His mouth quirked with pain. 'It's not a matter of forgiving,' he said. 'You chose another man. Not me. You chose him.'

'It wasn't like that,' she said. 'I didn't *plan* it. It just happened. He suddenly appeared. After all those years. I – I was overwhelmed. It was like a sort of madness. Oh, *can't* you understand?'

'I do understand,' he said – more truly than she knew. 'But that's not it. All those years we were married, it was him you loved. You never loved me.'

'I *did* – I *do* love you! You're my husband. He was never that.' He shook his head. 'If you go, leaving me like this—' She couldn't complete that sentence, that thought. *If he should die . . .*

'Ah, well, you see, I have to go,' he said, almost conversationally. 'That deed is done. I can't change my mind now.'

'Edward,' she said desperately. 'Isn't there *anything* left? Any feeling for me?'

There was, of course. He still loved her, as much as ever. That was the problem.

218

'I know I did wrong,' she went on into his silence. 'I never wanted to hurt you, never. You've always been so good to me—'

'Please stop,' he said, wincing. 'I wish I could see a way back, but I can't. There isn't anything I can do.'

'You could – we could – go to bed.' He looked shocked, and she gave him a smile that was nine-tenths made of pain. 'We were always good at that.'

'Beattie—'

'We're husband and wife. It's right. It would be a different memory to take away. Not this. Not this – distance. A new start.'

He paused a long time, and she waited, like someone condemned.

'I understand,' he said at last, 'how love can be a madness. I loved you madly from the moment I first saw you. You seemed unattainable. Remote. I always loved that quality in you. That serenity. You were like a creature from another world that this world couldn't touch. But now I know, you see,' he said, and his sadness almost broke her, 'that it wasn't serenity. You really weren't there at all – your mind was elsewhere, with the man you had loved and lost. And now when I look at you, I see twenty-five years of being deceived. You made a fool of me. I'm not sure how one gets over that.' He stopped, and then said, very low, 'I'm sorry.'

He left her then, walked quietly away and upstairs to his room. Beattie stood where she was for a long time, the pain in her chest and throat so bad it was as though her heart were literally being wrenched apart. She wished she could die from it, right there and then, so that she could stop feeling or thinking anything ever again.

CHAPTER FIFTEEN

Everyone was at breakfast the next day when William arrived, having taken the milk train.

'Embarkation leave!' he carolled in greeting. 'I'm off to France!'

Peter wailed, 'Oh, I wish I could stay off school! Can I, Dad?'

'Of course not,' said Edward. He had been intending to leave straight after breakfast, but decided on the instant to take a later train.

'I'll still be here tonight,' William comforted his brother. 'I'll see you when you get back. We'll have a game of something.'

William was elated to be going at last – doubly so, because a few days before, he had thought he was facing another delay. He had gone through the training course eagerly, learning engine-fitting, rigging, machine-gunnery, map-reading and signals, while learning to fly the Avro, the Sopwith Pup, the Spad, and then on to the SE5, the Camel and the Dolphin. Finally he had learned a modicum about permitted aerobatics and how to fly in formation, and felt he was ready to go and put it all into practice. Then, to his dismay, he had been given orders for a school of aerial fighting in Yorkshire.

Not only did he deem this unnecessary – for months he had been seeing young pilots going straight from his training squadron to France, some of them with fewer flying hours than he had – but the rumour was that after fighting school you generally got sent to Home Defence. Whether that was true or not, he didn't know, but he had taken the train northwards in the deepest of gloom.

He found the school packed with airmen, many of them Americans and Canadians serving with the RAF, who were as eager as he was to get to the Front. They were boisterous and amusing companions – but with so many young pilots sculling around the place, he reckoned there would be too few aeroplanes to go round and thus little chance of 'getting up'.

But two days later, the officials, coming to the same conclusion, decided to lighten the load by sending away a batch of those who had sufficient flying hours, and William, with distinct relief, got his orders.

'So I jolly well hope this is the last of the put-offs, and I get into action straight away once I'm over there.'

Edward had a long, serious talk with William, and then picked up his valise, said a quiet goodbye, and slipped out, glad the household had someone other than him to focus on. He had a good deal he wanted to do at his office, the welfare of clients to check on, and he ought at least to drop in at the Treasury and the Ministry. His train to France was the late one, at eleven forty-five p.m., which would still leave him time to get a last meal at his club, and perhaps see a few friendly faces there. And he wanted to call on Élise. He felt he owed it to her.

And so, at half past five, when he calculated she would just have got back from the school of dance where she taught, he presented himself at her door.

She was looking more careworn than he remembered her, and though her face lit at the sight of him, she did not grasp his arm to pull him over the threshold, like an eager child, as she had been wont to do in the past. She surveyed him from a polite distance, and asked if he had time to come in.

'Yes,' he said, feeling guilty. He had not done well by this woman, who had lost so much to the Germans, and ought not to have suffered at his hands too. 'I have several hours. If you are not otherwise engaged, I thought perhaps you might allow me to take you out to supper.'

She regarded him carefully and seriously for a moment, then said, 'We may have supper 'ere. Don't worry, you will not be in any danger from me.'

'I thought you might like to go out for a change, that's all,' he said awkwardly.

'It will be better 'ere, for talking,' she said. 'I will tell Solange.'

Conversation was sticky at first. She was reserved with him, and he was not at ease with her, racked by the memory of the night they had spent together. But gradually they relaxed and found something of their old rhythm. He told her about training school, making it amusing for her, liking to see her laugh. She told him about her teaching. They touched on the war news, the state of the market – he confirmed the financial arrangements he had made for her. He mentioned William's visit, Diana's expectations and the progress of little Marcus – he had grown so much since Edward had been away. And that made him think, inevitably, of David, and thence of Louis and Beattie, which stopped his flow abruptly.

Élise watched him, reading his expression. 'You think of her. It is painful for you, I know. But it is such a small thing—'

'Small?' he cried.

'The world is tearing itself to pieces. Those we love have died 'orribly. More will do so, many more. Yes, it is a small thing. You must forgive her, *mon cher*. She loves you.'

'Why should you think that?' he said roughly.

'What woman could be near you for so long and not love you?' she said.

222

His guilt made his face feel hot. But he said, 'She betrayed me. That was not love.'

'No,' she agreed. 'It was madness, and there is much of it about. Especially in wartime.' She looked away a moment at the fading light outside the window, and said quietly, 'You know what I was before I married my dear Guillaume. I was a dancer. I had many men talk love to me – the sort of love that is mad and exciting. And then is gone – pfft! – like a bubble of soap. I know about men, *mon cher*. I know they demand and take, even when they are talking of devotion. It is hard for a woman not to be swayed.'

Edward struggled with this. 'She chose him. Not me.'

She nodded. 'It is pride, then, with you?'

'No!' he protested.

'People can make mistakes,' she said. 'A mistake happens in an instant. Love is something else. Love is slow and kind and takes a long, long time. You must be kind to her, Édouard.'

'Must I?' he said stiffly.

'The world needs more kindness. Is she unhappy?'

He thought of Beattie, as she was when they had talked last night. (Only last night? It seemed an age ago.) He thought of her plea to go to bed together, and blushed inwardly with shame that he had shown his shock. What must it have cost her to ask? He had thought her, on that instant, a harlot, willing to try anything to get her way. But under Élise's steady gaze he had to try to put himself into a woman's mind. She had sacrificed her dignity and pride in the hope it might bring them closer. What had she said? 'We are married. It is right.'

Then why had she not thought about being married when that man had reappeared? She had gone to him without a struggle.

Hadn't she?

At any rate, it hadn't answered. She had not been going about with the secret glow of a woman in love.

'Yes, she is unhappy,' he said, torn between anger, hurt and compassion.

'Be kind to her, Édouard,' Elise said simply. And she added, very quietly, 'It takes but a moment to be mad.'

He knew she was referring to their night together. And here she was, pleading for another woman. Her generosity shamed him. 'I have not been kind to you,' he said painfully.

She smiled a little, and made a very French gesture with her hands. '*Eh bien*, but 'ere you are, when you might be hanywhere else. So we shall 'ave supper together and say goodbye like friends, *hein*? That is much. That is civilised, *n'est-ce pas*?'

'Civilised!' he said, and laughed, though he felt much more like crying.

David was glad his father had made him promise to see someone about his leg. He had known for a long time that he ought to seek help, but he was desperately afraid in case they said it must be cut off. He didn't think he could face life with a missing limb. Even though the pain and disability he presently endured were severe, he had a deep and unreasoning horror of that sort of mutilation. He thought he would prefer death to amputation.

He hadn't spoken to Antonia about it. He guessed she would sooner have him alive at any cost – that was a woman's point of view. Though she was sensible and her advice was always sound, he could not trust her to be disinterested on the subject.

He had been less upset than he would have expected by the double blow of his father and William both going off to the Front at the same time. To his father he knew it was a duty rather than a pleasure; but he had not seemed pulled down by it – indeed, David had never seen him looking better. William, of course, was wildly elated, like any other young man – as *he* had been when he went off in 1915. But he had felt no sharp pang, only a familiar dull ache: the fierceness of resentment had died down. He didn't know if it had simply worn away with time; that he was ceasing to care. He didn't *think* that, deep down, he was any more accepting of his fate. But there came a point – didn't there? – when you stopped raging against your chains from sheer weariness. Constant pain blunted you to everything else.

He didn't want – oh, he didn't want! – to be examined and poked and prodded, perhaps told 'It must come off', probably told 'There's nothing we can do for you.' Father might think medical knowledge had leaped ahead, but a smashed femur was a smashed femur – no argument. There was no arcane knowledge about that, was there?

Amputation and a tin leg? A lifetime of pain and hobbling, cramming little boys for Eton because that was all he was good for?

There was always the option of suicide. A length of rope was easy to come by, and they were surrounded by trees. A short struggle – the pain could not be much, surely, not as much as when he knocked his leg against something – and it would all be over. Peace and quiet at last. Oh, he had thought often about that!

But there was little Marcus, wasn't there? Suicide brought disgrace. Did he want his son to grow up ashamed of his father?

This bloody war! Those damned-for-eternity Germans who had started it! They had taken his youth and his innocence and all that was sweet and sound of him. He was an old man inside, crabbed and disappointed and without hope.

But there was Marcus. And he had promised his father.

He didn't want to bring Antonia into it until the thing was settled, one way or the other, and, a little to his own surprise, it was to Sadie he turned. In his darkest hours she had always been there, had insisted on visiting him when he would much rather be left alone, chatting to him when all he could do was snarl, unrepulsed by his rejection. And she was changed from the simple child she had been in that summer before the war. She had taken on unimaginable responsibilities, had become, quite simply, someone you could ask for help.

It was a few days before she came to see him at a time when Antonia was absent. She arrived, as usual, prepared to chat about her day, and quiz him about his pupils (he noticed, with a kind of grim humour, that she was always careful to give equivalence to her work and his). He let her talk for a moment, assembling his words and his nerve. She was saying something about American soldiers at Dene Park when he interrupted her. 'I need your help.'

She stopped in mid-sentence, and looked just faintly surprised, more at his grim tone than the words. 'Of course,' she said. 'What do you want me to do?'

'I promised Dad I would see a specialist about my leg, but I don't know how to go about it.' He watched her carefully for any signs of jubilance (meaning she had been wanting him to do that for ages) or worry (meaning she didn't think there was any point) but her expression was merely thoughtful.

'There won't be a specialist at any of the local hospitals,' she said, 'so I suppose it will mean going up to London. Did you have anyone in mind?'

'I don't *know* who is the top man in the field,' he said, with slight irritation. 'That's the first problem. The second is, how the *devil* do I get there? I can't go on the train.'

'It would be awfully difficult,' she agreed. 'Let me think.'

'Dad said he would pay for me to see the very best,' he went on while she thought. 'He said medical science has advanced in two years.'

'Well, that's true,' she said. 'Survival rates of people with serious wounds have gone up.'

'How would you know that?' He scowled at her.

226

'Medical journals, left lying around. Overhearing doctors talking.'

'Can't you ask one of these doctors who I should go to?' he said.

'I could, but they're just army doctors. I have a better idea. Why not ask Uncle Aeneas? Yes, I know he's not a doctor,' she forestalled him, 'but he knows absolutely everyone and, most of all, he's the sort of person who knows how to find things out. And,' she added, before he could interrupt again, 'when he has found out, he can arrange the appointment for you, and send his car to collect you. You know he would – he never minds how much he does for any of us.'

'Yes, you're right,' David said reluctantly. Having asked her advice, he didn't want her necessarily to have such good ideas ready to hand. She was his little sister, after all.

'Of course I am,' she said. 'Do you want me to ring him for you?'

'I'm quite capable of using the damn' telephone, thank you.'

'Just as you like,' she said. 'What does Antonia think?'

'I haven't talked to her about it,' he said.

'Whyever not?'

'I – I don't want her to get her hopes up,' he said awkwardly.

Sadie looked as though she knew that was not the real reason, but she only said, 'She'll have to know at some point.'

'Look, just don't talk to her about it yet,' he said. 'And, yes, will you ring Uncle for me? Ask him to keep it just between you and him. When everything's settled, and I've got an appointment and everything, I'll tell Antonia.'

Sadie smiled. 'Dear old idiot! I'll do it any way you like.'

She got up to go, but when she reached the door, he called her. 'Sadie?' She turned enquiringly. 'Do you think they – they'll cut it off?'

It was stupid to ask her that: how would she know any better than him? He expected her to be automatically comforting – 'No, of course not, don't be silly.' The sound of his own voice asking, putting the hideous thought into the open, sickened him. But she looked at him consideringly for a moment, and said, 'Even if that's what they recommend, you can refuse. They can't do anything without your consent. It will still be up to you.'

Relief washed over him. Why hadn't he thought of that? Of course, there would still be pressure on all sides – doctors, his mother, Antonia – but the decision would be his. And Sadie would support him, whatever he decided. She was a good kid.

'Thanks,' he said.

William shared a compartment on the train with four American pilots, two Canadians and another British young man, who immediately settled himself into a corner, pulled his cap over his eyes, folded his arms and went to sleep. The Canadians chatted quietly together, but the Americans seemed inclined to be friendly, and after some banter among themselves, one stuck out his hand to William and said, 'May as well be friendly if we're stuck in here together. The name's Larry. These characters are Hank, Joe and Kenny.'

William shook the hand. 'Hunter,' he said.

'Pleased to meet you, Hunter. Whadda they call you, Hunt?'

'What does who call me?'

'At home.'

'William. Oh, Hunter's my surname,' William said, catching on.

Evidently, the Americans were not a whale on surnames. They exchanged a doubtful glance. 'Bill?' Larry said tentatively.

William grinned. 'Never in my whole life.'

'No, I guess you don't look much like a "Bill". Mind if we call you Hunt?'

'Not in the least.'

'*Not'n the least*,' Kenny imitated, very badly, but with a grin. 'You Brits slay me, the way you talk. I kinda like it, though. Don't get me wrong.'

'Hunt here's okay,' said Larry, 'but those characters at the aerial fighting school – couldn't figure one word in three of what they were saying. Good thing we left when we did.'

'Yeah,' said Kenny, feelingly. 'Can't wait to get over there and bag me some Kraut planes. Thought they were never gonna let me go. How many hours you got, Hunt?'

Talk became general, about flying hours and various experiences in training, and the Canadians joined in, rather shyly, while the other British officer slept determinedly. Noticing this an hour into the journey, Larry nudged Kenny, gave a meaningful look, and said, 'What say we liven up this cabin, boys? How about a sing-song?'

With wide grins they broke into a raucous singing, and kept it up all the rest of the way to Dover, but the unnamed Brit kept on sleeping, or pretending to. William was a little embarrassed at first, but after a bit he joined in, and found it quite liberating to bellow popular songs at the top of his voice.

At Dover they transferred to a waiting ship, rocking uneasily on the dark sea. Everyone grew quiet. 'This is the bit I don't relish,' said Kenny. 'Sick as a cat coming over from the States.'

'Much shorter crossing, this one,' William encouraged him.

'Yes, but the Channel's rough. And what about U-boats?' said one of the Canadians quietly.

On board, most people tried to sleep, or chatted in low voices. William found himself sharing a bench with Joe, the quietest of the four Yanks, who told him, wistfully, about

229

his life back home – evidently he was missing his mother and sisters. 'Ma's singing, that's what I miss most. She sings about the house all the time. She's Irish, you see, born in a little place called Killarney. Ever heard of it?'

'No,' William said, 'but I've got an aunt and cousins in Kildare. At least, the aunt's still there. The cousins went to America for the war. Carbury's their name.'

Joe's eyes opened wide. 'Carbury? No kidding? There was a Carbury from Kildare in my training unit back home. What's your cousin's name?'

'There are two of them, Johnnie and Fergus,' said William.

'No kidding! I *know* Fergie Carbury. He'd just joined my unit when I was ready to ship out. Nice kid. Fancy you being his cousin! That makes us practically family!'

Joe seemed inordinately pleased with the connection, and William supposed it must be part of his homesickness. He was quite willing to accept the eager young man as temporary family, however, and shook the newly proffered hand and said solemnly, 'As good as brothers.'

Joe seemed touched, and shook with extra vehemence. 'Gee, I hope we get sent to the same unit in France.'

'I hope we get sent to a squadron straight away. I'm sick of all the delays. I want to get to the fun.'

At Boulogne, the organisation seemed very efficient, and everybody who inspected William's papers seemed to know exactly who to send him to next. Gradually, from official to official, the twenty pilots from Yorkshire were filtered out of the mass of arriving servicemen and found themselves on another train, in a shabby carriage with no heating – the night was chilly – which, only half an hour later, jerked into motion and began steaming slowly away. Travel-weariness overcame William's companions at last, and they slumped into sleep, but he felt too wound up to doze.

In the dark, and with the many changes of points, it was hard to be sure, but he was worried that they were heading in the wrong direction, away from the Front. *Not more delays, please!* he prayed. The train moved very slowly, with frequent stops in sidings to allow other traffic to pass. The short summer night was ending, and as a pink light began to suffuse the sky, he discovered that they were rattling along parallel to the sea, which meant, as he deduced from the sea being on their right, that they were heading away from the action.

In the rosy light of dawn they dismounted at a station called Berck, and were bustled into a waiting lorry, which bumped them along some rough lanes until they reached what looked unnervingly like a prison camp. There was a high fence topped with wreaths of barbed wire, sentries stepping about on guard duty, and inside, an array of army huts.

'What is this place?' William asked the driver.

'Pilots' pool,' he answered tersely. 'What'ja fink, it was Butnam Palace?'

'Certainly not that,' William murmured; and to Joe, 'I don't like the look of this.'

'Where are the sheds? Where are the planes?' Joe said in dismay.

They descended from the stuffy lorry into the sharp fresh air of early morning, laced with a hint of salt and, more welcomingly, coffee. Young men – pilots – came out of the various huts and drifted over to inspect the new arrivals.

'Office is shut for another half-hour,' one of them said. 'Better head on to the mess and grab some brekker before the fun starts.'

'Fun?' William said hopefully.

'Form filling,' said the young man. 'That's all the fun you'll get here. Don't you know you're in the pilots' pool? We're all waiting for a squadron. They ought to have a sign over the gate, "Abandon hope all ye who enter here."'

In the mess there was coffee, eggs and bacon, and a

multitude of pilots, all eager to get to the Front, many disgruntled and some depressed.

'Nothing to do all day but hang around. And nowhere to sit at night but the bar at the end of the mess.'

'It's some frightful balls-up in admin. The squadrons are crying out for us, but they can't get the paperwork straight.'

'They've got the single-seater bods mixed up with the heavy bomber mob. Could be weeks before it's sorted out.'

'I'm so bored I'm thinking of transferring to the infantry.'

William found he had lost his appetite. He wandered outside and, seeing a corporal unlocking the orderly hut, he went over.

The corporal cocked a wise eye at him, and said, "Fyou was wanting the CO, sir, he's having his breakfast. Just arrived?'

'Yes, and hoping not to be staying long.'

'Come in, then, sir. We'll see if you're on the list,' said the corporal, with a wink that could have meant anything, or nothing.

In the orderly room there was a cork-board on which were pinned all sorts of lists and orders, and on the desk around the typewriter were pinned-together foolscap sheets, which seemed to be nothing but names – scores of them.

'I wouldn't get your hopes up if I was you,' the corporal said, in a friendly way. 'Everyone wants a squadron, and some of 'em have been here three weeks. But you might be one of the lucky ones, sir. Now, what was it – single-seat fighters? Thought as much. You young gentlemen are always the most restless. What was the name, sir?'

'Hunter,' said William. 'W. E.'

'Let's have a look,' the corporal said, started running his finger down a list, and then looked up sharply, examining his face. 'I knew a Hunter, sir, when I was clerk to a squadron near Arminteers back in '16. Hunter, R. D. Very nice young gentleman. Everybody liked him. Would you be any relation?'

'My brother Bobby,' William said.

'Is that right? You do have a bit of a look of him about you, sir, though you're quite a bit darker. How is he?'

'He was killed on the Somme,' William said.

The corporal looked genuinely sorry. 'Oh, dear me. Deary me. That was a bad time, that year, sir. Lost a lot o' good airmen that year. Your brother, eh? Following in his footsteps, sir?'

'I even have his watch,' William said, pushing back his cuff to show it.

'And keen as mustard to get to your squadron,' the corporal said, detaching one sheet from a list and inserting it into the typewriter. His fingers rattled over the keys for a moment and he unreeled the sheet. 'Well, look here, this is a piece of luck,' he said broadly. 'Your name's right here, sir, on this list of pilots going out today. That's all right, sir, don't thank me. Just luck o' the game, that's all. CO will be signing the orders this morning and the Crossley will be leaving at fourteen thirty.'

William thanked him again, and went outside, suddenly feeling like breakfast. He felt sorry for those who had been waiting for weeks, and especially for the pilot whose name would have to be struck from the list to make the numbers right. But no-one could be keener than him to go and prove himself. And hadn't they said in basic training that there was always room for an officer to use his initiative?

Edward found being in France much easier than the training course. Here, nobody knew him. He was not Sir Edward Hunter, who could have appealed against conscription but hadn't. He was just Lieutenant Hunter. Nobody questioned why he was there – everyone had to do their bit, so why shouldn't he? It was normal.

And his greater age caused no surprise. Nobody called him 'Uncle'. When he was given his platoon, the soldiers under him were mostly eighteen- or nineteen-year-olds, who looked to him for leadership and saw his age as a natural concomitant of command. The only difficulty was their assumption that he knew more than he did. But he had an experienced platoon sergeant, and wisely deferred to him, so they got off on the right foot. Sergeant Fullwell was thereafter dedicated to easing his officer's path rather than showing him up.

It was true that his company commander, Captain Campion, was young enough to be his son. Claude Campion was twenty-seven, but he had the superb self-confidence and ease of manner that came from an Eton education. He had also been a leading light in the OTC and came from an army family: he took issuing orders so naturally, it never occurred to him to consider 'bossing' a forty-eight-year-old a problem.

There was so much to do, so much to learn. Every hour was crammed with things calculated to occupy and exhaust him. There was no time to repine. He was busy, he was useful. He was good at what he was doing: people above him were pleased with him and, more importantly, his sergeant approved of him. The time when he would go into the line and be tested was looming, and he assumed he would be afraid. He knew enough about action and the rate of casualties to know that wounding, capture or death were real possibilities. Shells and snipers there would be; mud, rats and lice, too, for that matter.

But he would not be alone – that was the biggest thing. His men admired him. His fellow officers liked him. The long loneliness of the average working man had been set deep in him, and hardly noticed, for that was everyone's lot, wasn't it? To travel to work, then to work, to travel home, to eat and sleep in preparation for the same thing the next day – that was the condition of man. But here in France there was friendship, among men bound together in a fierce and dangerous undertaking. It was like nothing else he had experienced, for even at public school he had been rather bookish and reserved. He was one of a crowd for the first time in his life. The uniform released him from his self-consciousness. His responsibilities were clear. He was – extraordinary to say – happy.

Only at night, in the moments between lying down on his cot and falling into exhausted sleep, did he have time to miss home, and he did miss it, with a hard and consuming ache. But he did not regret his decision. Out here, he knew that, whatever had been his motives, it had been right. And the fear and horror that dogged many at home were absent here. There was no room for either. The next thing to do was placed before you and you did it, as a matter of course. Complaint was reserved for tough pork and watery Maconachie, irksome duties and petty regulations, annoying habits of brass hats, and running out of cigarettes. No-one complained about facing death. They were soldiers. That was what they did.

CHAPTER SIXTEEN

David lay on the couch in the private consulting room at the Southport hospital waiting for the jangling pain in his leg to subside. The sweat on his face could be attributed to the July warmth – outside in the streets it was brassily hot – but Antonia knew better. She could tell by the line of his jaw that his teeth were clenched, and his hands were gripping the edges of the couch so hard his knuckles were white. If he had not been a man, or perhaps only if she had not been present, he would have groaned.

Sir Duncan Keneally had been the consultant Uncle Aeneas had found, through one of his long chains of connection, and the Rolls had transported David in as much comfort as possible to the Southport. He had liked Keneally at once, a well-upholstered, fatherly sort of man, with a comfortable Edinburgh accent, and less of the usual hauteur of the great consultant. David had worried a little, though, that he was evidently in his mature years, with bushy white hair around a pink top, and little gold-framed half-moon glasses over which to peer at him kindly. Would he have kept up with new techniques and knowledge?

But Keneally had disarmed him straight away by saying, 'Your uncle wanted the very best man in the field for you, Mr Hunter, and I have to tell you I am not that man. Thomas Barnard is the femur man *par excellence*, despite his youth, but unfortunately he is serving His Majesty at the moment, as Major Barnard of the RAMC. And as you are no longer in uniform yourself, he cannot officially attend you. However,' he forestalled David's next comment or question with a gently raised hand, '*however*, Barnard and I happen to be good friends, and he has accepted my invitation to look at an interesting case of mine, in his own time and quite *un*officially. And, no doubt, in a friendly way, he will probably give me his opinion, to see if it coincides with mine. Should you object to that, man?'

David had, of course, agreed gratefully, and in due course a brisk younger doctor, in his late thirties, with very black hair and a very red face, had joined Keneally in the 'prodding and poking' as he thought of it. Barnard had said nothing at all to David, had not even met his eyes, and David guessed that this was part of the protocol. The two surgeons had turned away and had a long, muttered conversation of which David could catch nothing, then both had departed, and a female porter had wheeled him away to have X-rays taken of the leg.

Back in the consulting room, Keneally and Barnard had had another prod and now, on the other side of the room, were having another muttered conversation. With Antonia beside him, he was waiting for the verdict. The sweat was not only from the pain, and the shaking of his hands was not only because he had not had any paregoric for some time. It was – he admitted to himself – mostly fear. He dreaded the detached, benign yet stern look that would accompany the words 'It has to come off.'

He stirred in mental agony, and woke the leg again. Antonia heard his indrawn breath, and unclasped one of his hands from the bed-edge to hold it in hers. 'Whatever happens,' she whispered, 'we'll face it together.'

Just for an instant, he hated her. *You won't have to face anything!* his mind exclaimed. But then the great men turned and came towards him, and he was glad of the warm human hand holding his, because he felt very, very alone.

237

'Well, now,' said Keneally, 'we've had a look at the pictures of your leg, Mr Hunter, and it's no wonder it has been causing you a wee bit of discomfort. A lot of bone fragments in there – splinters that have come away from the original injury.'

David could not speak. Antonia spoke for him. 'Is there anything that can be done?'

'Oh, yes, indeed,' said Keneally. 'I am of the opinion that an operation to remove the fragments would result in a much more comfortable outcome.'

'Could you perform such an operation?'

'I could indeed,' said Keneally. 'After the operation, it will be necessary to put the limb into a specially devised splint to keep the fracture site immobilised and prevent further fragments sloughing off. That will mean you will be bedridden for a wee while, Mr Hunter, but worth it, oh, yes, for the end result.'

'How long?' David asked, in a creaking, unused voice.

'Eight to ten weeks,' Keneally said. 'Let us say ten weeks. Not worth spoiling the ship for a ha'porth of tar, now, is it? After that, another X-ray will tell if we have brought home the bacon.'

Barnard spoke for the first time. 'You will probably always have a limp, but you ought to be able to walk without pain.'

'The new Thomas splint has revolutionised the treatment of femur fractures in the last year or so,' said Keneally. 'It's a great pity it was not available when you took your wound. However, we will do our best for you now, oh, yes, indeed.'

Ten weeks in bed, David thought. But that was nothing, to get his life back. He was so grateful they had not spoken of amputation he felt almost faint. All he could say was 'When?'

'The sooner the better,' said Barnard. He looked at Keneally.

238

'As a matter of fact,' Keneally said, 'I can fit you in tomorrow at my private nursing home in Wardour Street.'

Antonia swallowed. 'So soon?' she said involuntarily. She had hardly had time to come to terms with his going under the knife – there were always grave dangers in an operation.

Keneally looked at her kindly. 'I would rather like Major Barnard to have the opportunity to observe, and it happens that he is free tomorrow, which is my list day there, so if I move a few things around, postpone a few other operations, we can proceed. We had better have it done and over with, don't you think?'

'Yes,' David said. He was looking pale – he knew the dangers too. But to have Barnard there was a great advantage. 'Thank you. Thank you both very much.'

'Tush!' said Keneally, waving away the thanks. 'After the operation, you will require specialist nursing, and I recommend you remain in Wardour Street for the first fortnight. After that, a specially trained nurse at home, if you wish.'

When they were alone together again, David reached for Antonia's hand. 'I wasn't expecting anything to happen so soon,' he said.

'Yes, it's a bit unsettling,' she said calmly. She had herself fully under control now. 'But if it must be done, better not to have a long wait.' He nodded. His eyes looked too big in his white face. 'There's no point in going all the way back home now, is there, if you'll have to be in Wardour Street early tomorrow? Would you like to go to an hotel, or shall we see if Uncle Aeneas can put us up in Kensington?'

'The Palfreys can always put people up,' he managed to say.

So they went there.

When Ethel came through the kitchen with baby-bottles to wash, Peter was there leaning against the table talking to Cook. 'Why aren't you at school?' she demanded.

'Half-holiday,' Peter said. He was watching Cook roll out pastry, hoping for the trimmings. He liked raw pastry – better than cooked, really.

'You should go out and play,' Cook advised kindly.

'I'd like to go fishing, if you could give me a bit of bread for bait.'

'A bit of bread? Why not ask for a gold watch while you're at it?' Ethel muttered, stalking past into the scullery.

'I can't spare any bread,' Cook said. 'What's wrong with worms?'

'Munt doesn't like me digging 'em. He says they're working in the soil. He says it's war-work.'

'Ask at Colston's, then.' Colstons' the fishmonger did a useful side-line in maggots, especially in the summer.

'But they charge a penny for them,' Peter objected, 'and I haven't got a penny.'

'Oh, give him some bread, for goodness' sake,' Ethel snapped from the scullery. 'Anything for a quiet life.'

'Will I do those for you?' Emily could be heard enquiring.

'Not likely. I want 'em done properly.'

Cook sighed and said, 'I'll spare you half a crust, but you make it last.'

Peter beamed. 'Thanks! I'll bring you back the fish.' He took the bounty, and ran before she could change her mind.

'What's wrong with her?' Cook said to Emily, as she came through into the kitchen with the carrots she had been scrubbing. 'She's got that baby all to herself – you think she'd be happy.' Antonia was staying in Town, at the Palfreys', so that she could visit David every day.

'She's worried about Mr David,' Emily said.

'But the operation was a success. The missus said so.'

'That's just the beginning,' came Ethel's voice. 'Any number of things could go wrong. You don't know what you're talking about.'

'You could try having a nice thought once in a while,'

Cook objected. "Stead of spreading gloom and despondency around, like the rector said. The missus isn't worried, or she wouldn't be over at Dene Park. She'd be in Town with Mrs David.'

Ethel appeared at the door, drying a bottle. 'She's taking care of her ladyship to keep her mind off. She can't bear to think about Mr David. She loves him too much.'

'Oh, that's so lovely!' Emily cooed, clasping her hands.

'What? You think she doesn't love Miss Diana – her ladyship, I mean?' said Cook.

Ethel slipped the dry bottle into her apron pocket and went back for the second. She didn't answer until she had dried that, too, and hung the cloth over the rail of the stove. 'Ask me, she's never cared a jot about anybody but Mr David.'

'Oh, no—' Emily began to argue, but Cook silenced her with a gesture.

Ethel crossed to the door, head up, but turned at the last minute to say, 'He's not out of the woods yet, you know. There's infections and shock and blood clots and all sorts. He could still die.'

Cook went cold, but found the spirit to argue. 'How would *you* know about stuff like that?' she said derisively.

'I listen,' said Ethel, and stalked out.

Diana was lethargic and uncomfortable, great with child and suffering from the muggy heat. Nula had moved in, as the birth date approached, and Beattie had been there every day, keeping her poor child company, trying not to think about David.

He had survived the operation yesterday, but that was only the beginning. She knew the dangers as well as anyone. Louis had died after seeming for weeks to be recovering. A broken blood vessel in the brain, no-one knew why. The vicious irony of losing Louis and then losing David was more than she could bear to think about. But Diana she could help, with company, conversation, reassurance. She read aloud to her a great deal, played simple card games, and tried to persuade her to take walks, in the cool of the evening, in the private part of the garden.

Around mid-morning, there was a sense of unusual activity in the house. Beattie was sitting with Diana, reading to her from a romantic novel borrowed from the circulating library. They always had a drink at eleven – milk for Diana and coffee for Beattie, with a biscuit or a little cake – and this morning it was late. When the maid finally arrived with the tray, she looked flustered.

'What's going on, Doris?' Beattie asked her.

'Oh, I'm sorry, madam, my lady, only there's a bit of a fuss downstairs. Her ladyship has arrived.'

She meant Diana's mother-in-law, Beattie realised.

'Only it was quite sudden,' Doris went on. 'No notice except for a telegram, which only come half an hour ago. Mr Worrell's quite put out, not to have everything ready, madam. Will there be anything else?'

'This isn't her usual time, is it?' Beattie asked, when the girl had gone.

'No, she's never here in July, unless there's a good reason,' Diana said.

Beattie went on reading, thinking that, in the merest courtesy, she would have to come and present herself.

But Dene had been Violet Wroughton's home for so long, it was impossible for her to regard anyone else as mistress of it. And instead of coming to Diana, she sent a message by her maid, Pickering, summoning her to take luncheon in the dowager's own suite.

Beattie thought it insulting; and though Pickering had survived almost thirty years in the service of her mistress and had developed a carapace, she looked a little uneasy about her mission.

Beattie said, 'Please tell your mistress that her ladyship prefers to take luncheon here, but will be very glad if she will join her.'

Something flickered across Pickering's face, but she could only say, 'Yes, madam,' though she cast what might have been a look of appeal at Diana.

Diana roused herself. 'No, it's all right, Mummy. It will do me good to have a change of scene. Tell her ladyship we will come.'

'Yes, my lady,' Pickering said, and then, 'Thank you, my lady.' It sounded heartfelt.

'Really, darling,' Beattie said, when she had gone. 'She can't treat you like that. It's your house.'

'Oh, Mummy, don't fuss,' Diana said wearily. 'What does it matter? She'll never change, and I don't care.'

'But you ought to care, or she'll keep taking advantage.'

'I'm too tired to care about anything,' Diana said.

Beattie was silent a moment. She knew that weariness. 'Very well,' she said. 'I won't fuss. Would you like to change? There's just time.'

'Must I?'

'Perhaps just your top. And let Padmore do your hair again. There's such a thing as keeping one's end up.'

Diana gave her a faint smile. 'I don't think I've got an end any more,' she said, but she took the advice.

The dowager still occupied the main suite, while Diana had the cadet suite. Diana could have had her things moved at any time, for the dowager was rarely at Dene, but she liked her rooms, which had windows onto the private garden, and had no urge to be any grander.

The dowager rose to greet them as they walked into her sitting-room. Beattie thought she looked much older than when she had last seen her, thinner and a bad colour; and she seemed just a shade less arrogant, less of a force. Had losing her husband and both her sons trimmed her nails? Beattie wondered. It must be hard to be ousted from her throne so brutally.

She greeted Beattie civilly but without warmth, and Diana with briskness. 'You'd have done better to have the baby before this present hot spell.'

'I didn't know it would be hot. And it isn't due for another week,' Diana defended herself.

'In the doctor's opinion. You should not allow yourself to be dictated to by people of that order. My grandson is looking well,' she continued.

'You've been to see him?' said Diana.

'Of course. It was my first call. He is a thorough Wroughton. I see a lot of Rupert in him. He does not seem to favour you at all. And he has a fine number of teeth. I dare say there was no difficulty. Wroughtons always teethe easily. I can't remember any of my three being any trouble at all.'

Beattie could not restrain herself any longer. To go and see George before even announcing herself to Diana! 'I dare say,' she said, 'the nursery staff would not tell you what trouble there was. And no baby ever teethed without a great deal of crying.'

The dowager directed her eyes at Beattie like headlamps on a rabbit. Beattie stared back, unintimidated. The dowager turned back to Diana, but spoke with a little more kindness. 'And you – how are you? All is going well?'

'I think so,' Diana said. 'I'm uncomfortable, that's all. It's hard to rest.'

She meant it was hard to find a position that was comfortable, but the dowager took it otherwise. 'It must be, with all these people infesting the house. What a mess they've made of the great hall! And the approach – vehicles coming and going, strangers strolling about the park, medical equipment left lying about for anyone to see.'

'It *is* a hospital,' Diana said. 'They don't come into this wing.'

'A small comfort. How long do you suppose that will last? That sort of person always encroaches, if you give them the least encouragement. And now I believe you have *Americans* in the ballroom!'

Beattie almost laughed. It was said so vehemently, almost as if she had found fleas in her bed.

'They are fighting with us in France,' Beattie said, seeing that Diana had no answer.

The dowager did not look at her, but she answered, 'I dislike the accent. And they speak too loudly. Wroughton and I visited America in 1910. I cannot say I was impressed.' Having dismissed an entire continent, she went on to talk about her recent visit to Sandringham, and the old friends she had met there, apparently for the sole purpose of impressing on Diana and Beattie that they did not know any of the people who mattered.

A light luncheon was served, to which none of them did justice. The dowager talked on, carrying all the conversation herself. Diana had never spoken much in her mother-in-law's presence, but Beattie, casting glances at her through the meal, began to be concerned. At last she interrupted the dowager to say, 'Diana darling, is something wrong?'

Diana cast her an anguished glance, and leaned across to whisper, 'I think my waters have broken. Oh, Mummy, the *chair!*'

'Oh, darling!' Beattie said, half touched, half exasperated.

'What is this?' the dowager snapped. 'I do not care for whispering – *most* ill-bred.'

'Diana's labour has started, but she was too shy to say anything,' Beattie said. 'She's afraid she may have spoiled your upholstery.'

'We must get her back to her room,' the dowager said. 'Ring the bell. What arrangements have you made? Which physician is to be called?'

'Nula and I will manage very well,' Beattie said, helping Diana to her feet, and casually dropping her napkin over the damp seat so that she shouldn't see it.

But Diana was beyond upholstery now. 'Oh, Mummy!' she said. 'I'm paining.'

The maid who opened the door took in the scene with a comprehensive glance, and her eyes widened. Beattie snapped her to attention with her orders. 'Fetch Mrs Wilkes to her ladyship's room at once, and send up hot water. And someone to make the bed with the special sheets. Quickly, now.'

She was helping Diana to walk and had already reached the door. The dowager watched them from the luncheon table, frozen there. As they were passing through the door she found her voice. 'A physician! You must send for a physician!'

Beattie looked back, and was struck with a most unwelcome pang of pity. The dowager looked helpless, and lost. There was no place for her in this drama. Her time had passed.

'This house is full of doctors,' she pointed out. 'Should we need one.'

They didn't need one. The second birth was quick and easy. Only an hour and a half from the embarrassment of the ruined chair, Diana was delivered of a small, neat baby, Nula and Beattie managing everything, with the help of one of the housemaids who brought water, towels and sheets, and handed what was required.

'Another boy,' Beattie said, showing him to Diana.

Much less exhausted this time, she was already sitting up, and ready to hold her child. 'But Rupert wanted a girl,' she exclaimed.

'He'd have been happy with either, I'm quite sure,' Beattie said, and laid the bundle in Diana's arms, watching her face for that first wonderful look of awe and love.

246

'He's beautiful,' Diana said. 'Much more than George was at the beginning.'

'He hasn't had such a struggle as George had,' Nula defended the firstborn. 'But he is a little charmer. He's going to look just like his lordship. George favours you more.'

'Have you thought of a name for him?' Beattie asked.

'I was expecting a girl,' Diana said. 'Rupert was going to call her Amabelle.' She gazed at the small face, enraptured. 'I think I'll call him Amyas.'

'Where does that come from?' Beattie said.

'It was in a book I was reading. The one before last. He was the hero. It's rather a good name, I think.'

'If it's a boy's name at all,' Nula muttered. She preferred children to be named after the blessed saints.

'Amyas Wroughton.' Beattie tried it out. 'I think it has something. I don't know what the dowager will think of it.'

'I don't care what she thinks,' Diana said, roused to spirit on behalf of her new son. 'He's my child and it's my house and – and – she can just *put up with it!*'

'Spoken like a champion,' Beattie laughed. 'Still, in courtesy, we'd better send her a message.'

They didn't tell Diana at first, for fear of spoiling her milk, but the dowager had suffered a heart attack shortly after Beattie and Diana had left the room. So she didn't come to see the new baby, though a verbal message was brought by Pickering and, after a couple of days, a rather shakily penned note. They told Diana she had a cold and didn't want to infect the baby, and Diana, wrapped in the cocoon of birth, accepted it, and didn't care anyway.

The heart attack was a mild one, but the dowager remained in bed for two weeks, and did not leave her apartments for many weeks more. Her physician said she must take life more easily from now on, rest more, do less.

Beattie went to visit her. The former dragon had a

shrunken look, but what moved her was the eagerness she displayed for company. She could never be warm, but she showed rather gruffly that she appreciated the attention, and managed to keep Beattie long past the time she had allotted for the visit by striking up a new subject every time Beattie made a move to go.

Edward's commanding officer was Colonel Prewitt Dancer, known by the men as 'Prancer Dancer' because of his rapid, light tread. He was a regular officer, energetic and well thought of. One of his little ways was to try to get to know all his officers, including the 'bloody subs', and in pursuit of this aim Edward found himself invited to dinner one evening at the colonel's headquarters in the next village.

'You'll enjoy it. The Old Man gives good dinners,' said Captain Campion. 'And he's a shrewd chap, worth listening to.'

A car was sent for Edward and three other subalterns new to the battalion. They were young men in their early twenties, and once again Edward felt old as they chattered excitedly about actually meeting the colonel, while he had started the year lunching with the Prime Minister and Field Marshal Haig.

It was a lovely summer evening, the sun low and golden through the poplars that lined the way, the road white with dust, the fields bronzed with the ripening harvest. His thoughts drifted to the news from home: his new grandson, and David's operation, which had gone as well as could be expected. There would be a long road to recovery for him, of course, but he had taken an important first step.

He tried not to think about Beattie. His feelings towards her were as mixed as ever, between pain, anger and guilt. Sadie had written too, a note full of her own spirit – busy, energetic, managing to keep everyone in mind, like a juggler with multiple balls in the air. He remembered Munt saying

248

she was the best of the bunch. Odd that he should have thought that. Sadie said she had been to the theatre with Christopher Beresford. Edward was vaguely glad, thinking that if anything happened to him, Beresford could be trusted to take care of Sadie. Did she love him? But he was a good man, and if she married him, enough of love would follow. Not everyone could marry where passion took them; and if they did, it did not always work out well . . .

What a different world he would go back to, if he survived. He gazed at the passing countryside: the fields, the scattered clusters of farms, each with its muddy yard, straw stack and duckpond, the little streams, the distant smear of woods on the gentle curves of the land. There were lorries and ambulances and staff cars on the road, but there were still plenty of farm carts and other horse-drawn vehicles. And the farm workers in their blue smocks and the women in the doorways of their dank cottages, taking the air, arms folded over their coarse aprons, were part of an older France that the war had touched little. A dog lying in the middle of the road, enjoying the warmth of the cobbles, got up reluctantly and ambled out of the way as their driver sounded his horn; in a farmyard, cows waited to be milked, twitching their dirty tails against the flies. It was all very much as Corot or Monet might have painted it. The only discordant note was a party of Chinese coolies working at clearing a drainage ditch beside the road.

Their destination was one of those square stone houses with the small railed courtyard in front that you find in every village, sitting on the main street a stone's throw from the centre. Inside, it had been expensively furnished when Victoria was on the British throne, but time, and four years of occupation by soldiers, had left it looking shabby and faded. But the colonel's welcome was warm, and they were invited into the drawing-room and offered a choice between gin-and-polly and whisky-and-soda. 'Sorry I haven't any

249

sherry – finished my last bottle when the C-in-C came by,' Dancer said. 'Despite his name, Sir Douglas preferred the grape to the grain, so I couldn't refuse.'

Introductions were made to the colonel's staff, cigarettes were lit and drinks dispensed, and a relaxed atmosphere was established remarkably quickly. Edward, with his long experience of official receptions, was impressed. Dancer was a man of about his own age, a little taller, bulky about the shoulders but lean and light in the flanks, with a little less hair on top but a good deal more in the moustache than Edward. He said a few words to each of the subs, saving Edward until last.

'How's the whisky?' he asked, as an opening gambit.

'Very good, sir,' Edward answered automatically.

'Pity you couldn't get here before Sir Douglas – that was a very decent oloroso. You've met him, I dare say?'

'Just once, sir.'

'Hmm,' said Dancer. He was examining Edward keenly, and he anticipated awkward questions. 'It's *Sir Edward*, isn't it?'

'Not here, sir,' Edward said, with a small smile.

Dancer responded with one of his own. 'Indeed. This is the army. Excuse my damnable impertinence. Couldn't help wondering, though, what it was made you throw up all your hobnobbing with the greats in the War Office and the Treasury to come and square-bash with us common fellers.'

'I was called up, sir,' said Edward. And then, a little stiffly, 'How do you know those things about me?'

'Oh, gossip,' Dancer said lightly. 'You're quite a *cause célèbre*. Anything new to talk about, you see – it's quiet out here at the moment, and we all know one another's stories to the point of nausea.' He paused to see what Edward would say, and when it turned out to be nothing, he smiled approvingly. 'Mum's the word. Quite right. I shan't tease you about it. But I will tell you this, Hunter – it's a bit of

250

a nonsense a chap of your age and experience being a lieu-tenant. Soon as you've got your hands dirty, I shall see to it that you're made captain.'

'Thank you, sir. But I have no experience of soldiering.'

'Nor have most of the officers when they get here. Intelligence is a good substitute.' He changed his stance slightly to include the rest of the room. 'You new officers have joined the war at an interesting time.' Other conversations died as everyone turned to listen to him. 'We're out of the trenches, thank God, and at last we have the opportunity to do some real soldiering. The war of movement, gentlemen, which we've been waiting for and which has been predicted for almost four years, is upon us. Decisions will have to be made on the spot, requiring individual initiative and judgement. The officer who has those will go far. And now,' he concluded as a white-jacketed steward appeared in the doorway, 'let us go in to dinner.'

As Campion had predicted, it was a good one, and Edward appreciated every mouthful, after weeks of army food. It began with actual foie gras, which they ate with water biscuits instead of toast – Edward was pleased to note they were Palfrey's, and silently saluted his brother-in-law's business acumen. The fish course was a fillet of trout, grilled and served with lemon juice and watercress. Then there was chicken *en casserole*, with garlic and little bits of smoked bacon as well as layered vegetables in the dish.

'Too tough to roast, I'm afraid, gentlemen,' Dancer apologised. 'But my cook has an interesting way with stews, and I hope you will find it not unpalatable.'

There followed a savoury of mushrooms cooked in cream, and then a dessert of fruit and cheese.

'French cheese, I'm afraid,' said Dancer. 'Colonel Waverley has the only Stilton in this sector, and I couldn't prise it away from him.'

'Not even for ready money,' said his adjutant, and they

all laughed. 'The French haven't really caught the knack of cheese-making,' he went on. 'They only have two kinds – hard cheese that tastes of nothing, and soft cheese that tastes of altogether too much.' More laughter.

When the dessert was cleared, cigarettes were lit, whisky went round again, and the colonel addressed the general situation.

'Fritz hasn't finished with us yet,' he said. 'We've given him a bloody nose, but our intelligence sources tell us he is working up to another attack in this area – that is to say, somewhere in the Champagne. Obviously, he must try to take Paris – that would be a crucial blow to our French allies – and he is likely to throw everything he has at it. And we, of course, will throw everything back at him.'

There was a murmur of approval round the table.

'Any idea when, sir?' one of the lieutenants asked. He looked as keen as a dog about to go out hunting.

'It could be within a month,' said Dancer. 'In the meantime, I see no reason why we shouldn't all have some fun. The Australians and the New Zealanders have been pestering the enemy with a tactic they call "peaceful penetration" and what we used to call "prospecting" when we were in the trenches. It spreads alarm and despondency among the Boche with relatively little cost to our side, and I don't see why the Dominion troops should keep it all to themselves.'

'How does it work, sir?'

'Wherever the ground is right – that is, freedom of movement is possible, and there is sufficient cover – we slip out in small groups, try to waylay their patrols, infiltrate their lines and cut out their posts. You can slip through their guard, come up behind a post and take it by surprise, kill a few, take some prisoners, capture their guns, advance our line by a little here and a little there. It soon adds up. Best of all, it harries them, puts the wind up them, breaks down their morale.'

There were murmurs of approval for the idea.

'Now,' Dancer went on, 'the tactic calls for stealth, initiative, patience, and individual judgement, and it's as good a way as any that I know of "blooding" you young officers. And we have nothing else to do until the next big push, so we might as well keep busy.'

Interested chatter broke out as the colonel finished. Edward was looking at him thoughtfully, and as Dancer met his eyes, he had an odd feeling that he was thinking the same thing: that keeping busy was a way to keep the nerves at bay.

The thought of 'prospecting' made him gulp with excitement – and a certain degree of apprehension. He had twenty-four young, very young, men in his command, and wondered if he was up to making instant military decisions that might get them killed. But he had a good sergeant, who in a pinch would surely tell him what to do. And sooner or later he would have to make those decisions, either on a clandestine patrol or in the heat of battle. That was what an officer was for.

And better to be doing than sitting waiting to be shot at, waiting for the next big push.

CHAPTER SEVENTEEN

The surgeon in the blood-smeared apron stepped out of the tent, blinked in faint surprise at the sunshine, and slowly drew out a cigarette case. He fumbled out a small, thin cheroot, and began patting his pockets for a light.

Laura stepped forward, struck a match and held it to the end. He puffed until it caught, mumbled, 'Thanks awfully,' and only then looked up to see who had come to his rescue.

'Good God!' he cried. 'How did you pop up from nowhere?'

'I was standing here waiting for you. You had the sun in your eyes.'

'My dear, dear girl,' he said, opening his arms to her. 'Oh, Lord, I'm all over gore. Can't hug you.'

'Better not anyway,' she said. 'Detrimental to discipline. How about a chaste peck on the cheek?'

They drew back to look at each other. 'God in Heaven, you are a sight for sore eyes,' he said.

'Me personally, or just someone with all their limbs intact?' she said shrewdly.

'You've come with the X-ray ambulance,' he concluded, working it out.

'Rather, the X-ray ambulance came with me. I'm the driver, you know.'

'And how are you finding it?'

'That driving Matilda is much like driving Bessie,' she

said. 'The same ghastly roads, the same potholes, the same scramble for cover when a German aeroplane comes over. It's just that with Matilda we go up much closer to the line.'

There was no full-scale offensive going on in Flanders just then, but there was constant hostile activity, and a steady stream of wounded and injured into the clearing stations. The background muttering of the guns grew louder and shriller as they went closer, and there was a danger of being hit by a shell, or even a sniper, as well as from aircraft, so it was considerably more of an adventure. Laura drove as fast as she could between calls, on the logic that it was more difficult to hit a moving target. It was hard on the chassis, but Matilda was younger than Bessie, and where Bessie had been a conversion, Matilda had been built for her work, with rough roads in mind.

'Yes, of course, I was forgetting,' he said. 'Driving in Flanders is nothing new to you.'

'But now I'm solely the driver,' Laura said. 'No stretcher-work.'

'Don't you have to operate the X-ray?' he asked.

'No, the other three do all that. My old friend Annie – you remember her? – and two young Frenchmen.'

He cocked his head. 'Young Frenchmen? Have I to be jealous?'

She laughed. 'I'd find it a great compliment.'

'Why aren't they at the Front? Or rather,' he corrected, as the percussion of a shell shook the ground under their feet, 'carrying rifles?'

'That was a close one,' Laura said.

'Yes. We might have to move tonight,' Ransley said. 'Tell me about your Frenchmen.'

'Dogged on the scent, aren't you? Well, Morgan has a weak leg from infantile paralysis and walks with a limp, and Jean-Marie is missing two fingers on his right hand from an agricultural accident. But they are jolly fellows, and very good at their job. And they cherish me.'

'*Do* they, indeed?'

'I'm their lifeline. Not one of the three of them can drive, so if anything happens to me, they're stuck. Consequently they won't let me do any of the heavy work, and when I've got Matilda into position, I've nothing to do but have a cigarette and chat to any agreeable officer who has time for me.'

'I wish I had time for you right now,' Ransley said, 'but I only stepped out for a moment to stretch my hands. They start to cramp after four or five hours.'

'Oh, Jim!'

'No, no, don't sympathise, or I shall collapse with self-pity, like a blancmange. Where are you based? Where do you go back to at night?'

'We've a billet in Hazebrouck.'

'I'm due for a break two nights from now. If I can get to you, will you let me buy you dinner – assuming there's somewhere in Hazebrouck one can eat?'

'Oh, there's a place or two, but it won't be *haute cuisine*.'

'Anything that doesn't move about on the plate,' he said. He threw down the cheroot stub and ground it out. 'I must get back. *Dearest* girl, you have raised my spirits. I'll send a message to you. Where's your billet?'

She gave him the address, they exchanged another chaste peck, and he disappeared back inside the tent. She didn't like to think of what he had to face in there.

Two nights later, they had dinner in a corner of the Café Cloche d'Or in the rue de l'Église – rabbit cooked with lentils and sausage, followed by some very loose, uncorseted cheese and a dish of cherries. Washed down with a flask of young red wine it was rustic fare, but tasty. The table was small and their knees touched under it.

'We're getting quite a lot of "Diggers" through our hands, these days,' he told her. 'The German wounded talk about them. They don't like them. *Unberechenbar*, they call them. Unpredictable. They've got used to the way we fight, but the Australians, they say, might do anything.'

'And *are* they unpredictable?' Laura asked, carefully easing some rabbit bones to the edge of the plate.

'I understand they're great fighters, but difficult to discipline. Don't like being given orders – used to following their individual whim across a thousand miles of emptiness.' He smiled suddenly. 'We had one fellow in yesterday, and when the nurses stripped him off, he was wearing ladies' underwear – stockings, silk drawers, and a chemise with lace at the throat.'

Laura laughed. 'Why on earth?'

'Apparently there's a shortage of vests and underpants. They're not used to the lice, you see. When they get too lousy, they just throw their underthings away, and then they have to make do with whatever they can find.'

He filled her wine glass, and she sipped, and said, 'I must say I'm impressed with the spirit of the men I've come across. There's none of the gloom and pessimism I've been seeing back home.'

'It's because the organisation supports them. It's all in Carlyle, you know. Military discipline is a miracle that works by faith, he says.'

'What does that mean?'

'Men like structure. It's in our nature to respond to hierarchy, ceremony, taking an oath to perform a certain task. Whether the task is tiresome, the ceremony silly and the officer a fool doesn't matter. I suspect,' he added, 'that women may be *slightly* different.'

'Well, I've never liked being told what to do, it's true. But, Jim, is the structure enough to support a man facing death?' she asked.

257

'We all face death,' he pointed out. 'We know from the start it's a losing game.'

'A little different, surely, to face checkmate when you're three score and ten than when you're eighteen.'

'That's where the soldier benefits over the civilian. Military honour allows him to face death with pride.' He smiled. 'I see you're not persuaded.'

'I'm not sure all those lads I see marching past are so high-minded.'

'Oh, but I think they *are* – and you shouldn't want it otherwise. They are full of good impulses, which buoy them up. They have the resolution to die well. How many, if they survive, will have the resolution to *live* well?'

'You are a philosopher,' she said, with a smile.

'Soldiering tends to breed philosophers,' he said. 'It strips life down to the essentials. Talking of stripping life down, that X-ray machine is a damned useful piece of kit, but I'm glad you don't have anything to do with it. Being inside the van with all those rays bouncing back and forth probably isn't good for you.'

She raised her eyebrows. 'Considering the entire German High Command is trying to kill me every day—'

'Why worry about an invisible ray?' he finished for her. 'Sounds like something from H. G. Wells!'

'I shall say no more. We shall all have other things to think about soon, anyway.'

'How come?'

'It looks as though old Ludendorff is working up to make another attack in Flanders. Chaps coming off the line say there's been a lot of movement on the Jerry side – big battalions being moved in.'

She was surprised. 'I'd heard the attack was going to be in the Champagne again.'

'That's the official line. But fellows here think that might just be a diversion. The Boche have always wanted the

Channel ports, and Flanders is the quickest way to get to them. And if Ludendorff attacks in Flanders, it's going to get pretty hot around here. You'll need your tin hat.'

'So will you,' she said. They looked at each other for a moment, and at last she smiled ruefully and said, 'Doesn't make any difference, does it? We'll both do what we do, whether the shells fly or not.'

'The difference being that I'm under orders. You don't have to be here.'

'Would you leave if you could?' she asked him defiantly.

'Probably not,' he said at last. He folded his hand over hers. 'I wish we could be alone together.'

She pressed back. 'So do I. But think how wonderful it will be after the war, when we have all the time in the world.'

'After the war,' he said bemusedly. 'Will you marry me *then*?'

'Quite possibly,' she said.

'*Possibly?*' he protested. 'Laura!'

'Jim!' she responded with the same intonation, 'don't talk to me now about love and marriage and that sort of thing. There's too much at stake. Who knows what will happen to either of us? If you get killed—'

'If I get killed, I'd like you to have the comfort of having been my wife, and inheriting my estate.'

'Oh, stop!' She screwed up her face. 'Some comfort that would be! If either of us gets killed, I want it to be just as friends. Much less to lose. Much easier to bear.'

'Do you really think so?'

She stared at his thin, tired face, which had become inexplicably so dear to her, and let out a long sigh. 'No,' she said. 'not really. But let me cling to my illusions.'

'Very well,' he said. 'Finish your wine and let's go for a walk. It's a lovely warm night, and I want to find a dark corner where I can at least kiss you.'

She eyed him. 'I suspect you're not talking now about a

chaste peck on the cheek, such as is suitable between those who are merely friends.'

'No, I'm not,' he said. 'But you must let *me* cling to *my* illusions.'

Nula was of the old school that believed a woman should not rise from her bed until six weeks after childbirth. But Diana felt so well, compared with last time, that she was out of bed after ten days, though she did consent not to do very much, and to lie on a chaise longue for much of the day.

She had the baby with her a great deal, gazing at him, trying to trace Rupert's features. She thought that Rupert would have adored him, even though he had wanted a girl. The saddest thing was that now there never would be a girl. All chances were ended. Rupert was gone. She tried not to think of what lay ahead for her, because life seemed so big and so empty. Rupert had made all the decisions. Without him, how could she decide what to do even for one day, let alone the rest of her life?

'Don't worry about it now,' her mother said. 'Things will become clearer in time.'

She had visitors: Antonia, to tell her about David, and to admire baby Amyas with a hungry look, that made Diana wonder if she would like another child. Well, at least she still had her husband. David was depressed, Antonia said. She attributed that to the pain, and the effect of the morphine they were giving him for it. She hoped he would be better when he was able to come home next Tuesday, though at the moment he was saying he didn't *want* to come home. 'He's afraid,' she said simply. 'Afraid it won't have worked and he won't be any better.'

Sadie came, and told her of everyday things around The Elms, of Peter and the servants. 'I do like the new baby,' she told Diana. 'He's a dear little chap.'

260

'You should get married and have some of your own,' Diana said.

No point in thinking about a title or a grand marriage for Sadie . . . Although after the war, if Diana took her in hand, she might spruce up acceptably, and her loving to ride would do her no harm in a certain section of the aristocracy. It would give Diana a project . . .

But Sadie said indifferently, 'I shan't get married. I've missed my chance. I shall concentrate on being a wonderful aunt.'

Diana's friend Obby visited, to tell her that she was going to France. 'I put my name down for overseas service a while ago, but you have to be twenty-three, and I've only just turned. Of course,' she added, with a grin, 'if I'd had any sense I'd have lied about my age in the beginning, but I'm hopelessly honest and didn't think about it.'

'Where will you be sent?' Diana asked.

'They don't tell you till you get there,' said Obby. 'Doesn't matter – it'll be the same anywhere. Except that Rolo's somewhere near Amiens at the moment, and I'd love to see him.' Her brother was a captain now.

The letter was brought to Diana later that day when she was alone. Nula had taken the afternoon off to go and see to her neglected husband and house, and Beattie had gone home as usual. Padmore brought the envelope to her, and Diana was wondering why she had not left it for a housemaid to deliver, when she saw the official frank. Well, she thought, Rupert is dead. They can't hurt me any more now.

'There's a parcel, too, my lady,' Padmore said, offering a small package. She hoped it was not some more of his lordship's effects, overlooked before and now being sent back to upset her lady all over again.

Diana opened the envelope first and read the letter. She looked up at Padmore. 'They've given him a medal,' she said.

261

'My lady?'

'Rupert – Lord Wroughton – they've given him the Military Cross. He's an MC.'

'Oh, my lady!'

'"For gallantry during active operations against the enemy," it says. It's not usually awarded posthumously, but his commanding officer put in for it before they knew he had fallen.' It was for the rearguard action Ivo Rainton had told her about. Ivo must have reported it to the CO.

'Perhaps that's what's in the parcel,' Padmore said, urging it at her.

Diana opened it and found a small velvet box, inside which was the silver cross on its purple-and-white ribbon. She stared at it for a long time; and suddenly, Rupert's face was before her, startlingly clear. He was laughing. For some reason, in her mind he thought the medal a great joke – she didn't know why, but she was sure of it. She heard his voice say, 'What a lot of nonsense! Give it to the baby to chew on.'

And then the image faded, and she felt horribly alone. He really was dead – the medal proved it. Tears rushed up, closing her throat.

'How proud his new little lordship will be of his papa when he understands,' Padmore was saying.

And very far away in Diana's mind, a tiny voice, like a mere breath of wind dying away, whispered, *Take care of my children.* And then that was gone too. The last of him. She forced back the tears, swallowed the pain in her throat. She had a job to do, a responsibility. Rupert's boys. Their father was a hero, and they must grow up to know it, and live up to him.

'Yes,' she said. She got to her feet. 'I must change,' she said to Padmore. 'Come and help me – the lilac silk, I think.'

'My lady?'

'I must go and see Lady Wroughton. She will want to know,' Diana said.

It didn't take any courage. She was not afraid of the dowager any more. It was her duty to tell her, and duty, Diana now found, was a very bracing thing, when you let it be.

William's squadron was stationed at Valheureux, a little to the north of Amiens. From a long straight road lined with poplars, a muddy track led to a farmyard, then a wide, flat field where the canvas sheds, tents and lorry lines stood. Through the next gate was an orchard, with tents and small huts scattered among the trees. Life centred on the mess, a snug wooden building that looked rather like a cricket pavilion, painted green, with a porch along the front, which was joined by a short canvas passage to a marquee where they ate. In the mess was a piano, and a bar, and on the wall a German propellor hung above a board on which were inscribed the names of men in the squadron who had been decorated. There were a great many of them.

'This squadron has brought down more Germans than any other in France,' he was told proudly.

Behind, across the fields, a low, rounded hill was topped with an arc of trees, like an eyebrow over an eye. And when it got dark, the horizon glowed with wavering lights and intermittent flashes – the Front, fifteen miles away. When the wind was in the right direction, you could hear the grumbling of the guns, sometimes a heavy thudding, or the longer chatter of machine-gun fire.

His new home.

His new family were all young men, including two Americans. Even the CO, Major Duberley, was only in his twenties, a lean, very dark young man with a heavy moustache. Despite his youth, he took his responsibilities seriously, and would not allow William to go over the line until he had had some formation and firing practice, and Duberley had had a chance to assess him. William, like any young pilot, was chafing to get to the action. The squadron had been bagging almost a German a day, according to the records. He wanted to be part of that.

'The Germans have got better machines than last year,' Duberley told him, sitting across his desk and twiddling a pen between his fingers. 'These Fokker D VII biplanes are pretty efficient, so you've got to be careful or they'll out-manoeuvre you. Don't try a dog-fight with them until you've got some experience. But it's not all aerial combat. These days we're just as likely to be raiding aerodromes, bombing transport and strafing troops. Harassing tactics generally – anything to annoy the Boche. Risky stuff, but well worth it. These guerrilla attacks by fast single-seaters far outweigh bringing down a few more Fokkers.'

So William practised firing at a ground target, and flying alongside his new colleagues, and only sneaked a little across the line when he was sure he wouldn't be found out. He admired Duberley and didn't want to annoy him. The dangers were brought home to him when a flight-commander was wounded the day after he arrived, and the next day a pilot went missing, later confirmed dead.

The following week another pilot was reported missing, and William was promoted to his first real operation. *Dead men's shoes*, he thought. It had an unpleasant rhythm in his mind; but he was young and soon shrugged it off.

His part in his first mission was minimal: in the protective flight for a raid on an aerodrome at Estourmel, he watched the action from high up, ready to head off enemy aircraft; but they were in and out before the defenders got into the air. The raid was counted a success, but one of the young American pilots was killed. The squadron's rate of attrition, he understood, was not unusual. *Dead men's shoes*, in the RAF, meant rather more than at home.

Colonel Dancer was as good as his word, and sent out his men on as many 'pestering' operations as he could. Edward

264

was soon 'blooded': the first time out had been nerve-racking, but it was surprising how quickly he got used to it. Taking responsibility was natural to him, and his men accepted his authority without question.

On the evening of Saturday the 13th of July, he and his platoon were creeping through a wood, expecting to intercept a German patrol. Edward thought it was rather like stalking deer, which he had sometimes done before the war. You had to have an eye for the country, and be good at guessing where the quarry might be hidden. The 'prospecting' actions of the past week had advanced the line nearly half a mile, but had also broken it up, so that in some places the enemy posts were further forward than others, and you could get round behind them.

Orders were to capture rather than kill, for intelligence purposes. Edward's men did not seem to mind much whether they caught or killed Germans, as long as they were doing them down. 'It's good sport, sir,' one of them told Edward. They hadn't the imagination, thank God, to think of them as people. They were objects to be bowled over, like skittles in an alley.

There was a sharp crack of a stick breaking, and whipping his head round, Edward saw one of his own men shrinking down and looking guilty. He gave the signal to stop, and they froze, like good hunting dogs. The wood was quiet – no birds were singing, which suggested they had been disturbed by something. And then he heard the voices. One of his own men hissed in response and half rose, and he made a furious gesture to still him. The muted voices spoke again; he couldn't hear the words, but the rhythm didn't sound English to him. He gestured his men forward, signalling *slow*, *low* and *quiet*.

The trees thinned, and through them he saw one of their own advanced dumps, which the Germans had evidently found. Two were mounting guard, and beside the dump was a rough dug-out, from which came the murmuring voices. Presumably it was the patrol they had been sent to look for. The voices sounded relaxed – pleased with themselves for having found the dump, taking the chance to rest, perhaps making coffee and having a smoke.

Edward spread his men out, his eyes on the two guards. Someone inside the dug-out called a question, and the guards turned their heads back to answer. Edward dropped his hand, the command to move.

That was the dangerous moment, as they covered the short open space between the trees and the enemy, because it was instinctive for guards to shoot. But only a brave or determined man would do so when he was visibly outnumbered, and the guards were still wavering, not knowing who to aim at, when two of Edward's men outflanked them, came up from behind and seized their guns.

Edward, meanwhile, had reached the dug-out, wanting to overwhelm them before they could realise what was happening. There were six Germans in there, one of whom was a corporal. Two had leaned their rifles against the wall and were examining the contents of a cupboard, the others were holding theirs loosely at their sides. They stared at Edward, in surprise, which turned swiftly to alarm. They all looked terribly young to him – callow, unfinished faces, thin, youthful bodies; two had spots, one had fine dark hairs scattered on his upper lip where he was too immature either to grow a moustache or to shave. At the mere sight of him – an older man, an officer – they put down their rifles and raised their hands.

Or, rather, five of them did. The sixth, the corporal, was carrying his rifle at the ready, and as Edward looked at him, a spark of something came into his eyes, and he aimed it, his finger on the trigger.

The world seemed to hold its breath. Edward felt a shrivelling fear in his bowels as he looked at death. He was alone, having outrun his men.

But he had entered with his pistol drawn, and he heard himself bark, '*Hände hoch!*'

He had done a little German at school – it had been considered the language of culture in those days – but had thought he had forgotten it. Necessity had sprung the words from his deep memory.

The red spark died, the hands relaxed, the world breathed again. Edward felt two of his own men come up behind him, and the last rifle fell to the floor. All six now dropped to their knees with their hands up. They seemed eager to surrender. The one nearest him babbled something, and he didn't need to understand the German to know he was begging for mercy.

Outside, he found his heart beating too fast. All very well to know that the Huns were outnumbered from the beginning. If the corporal had fired, Edward would be just as dead, though they were all killed or captured afterwards. He breathed deeply, and the tight pain of his over-rapid heartbeat eased. Now he felt a strange exhilaration. The sun slanted through the branches, there was a smell of pine on the air, and he was intensely aware of his body, the blood running through his veins, the comfortable interplay of nerve and muscle, a sense of wellness. He was strong, fit, alert. He was alive, and he felt it in a way he never had as a civilian. Or, at least, not since he was young: hitting a six at cricket, finishing Head of the River – dancing with Beattie. He had heard men talk about the power war could have over you: that once you had lain in her arms you could admit no other mistress. He understood, a little.

It was a great thing for William to go out on his first dawn patrol. It meant he was finally accepted as a full member of the squadron, an equal, a useful adjunct and not a nuisance.

They took off in formation in the grey light and flew east into a sky of crystal clarity, polished with light. He thought

267

for a moment of Bobby, and wondered if he had felt this same sensation of utter contentment and joy, just to be up here, to be flying. Nothing else mattered. It was not possible to be afraid.

They were in two flights, with William in the upper, protective one, each in a neat V formation, like geese, as they headed into the rising sun, flying over a ruined and ravaged land. It was hard to believe it had ever been fertile, or normal. Where they crossed the line, the artillery was busy on both sides; and they soon heard the heavy cough of 'Archie' – anti-aircraft fire – and saw his little flowers and puffs below them. They were too high for him, out of reach.

At eighteen thousand feet they turned north-west, and then, suddenly, there was a large enemy formation of Fokker biplanes coming towards them. It was too large for the lower flight to tackle alone. No sooner had the enemy formation broken, scattering to engage, than the leader of the upper flight signalled and dived to attack. William dived too, his heart thundering with excitement.

Within seconds, the neat Vs were no more, and instead the air was full of machines hurtling in all directions in a terrifying tangle. For an instant a Fokker appeared in William's sights, and he heard himself shout something in excitement as he fired at him. He had no idea if he hit him; the Fokker veered off at right-angles, too quickly for him to keep up; instead there was a crackle of fire from behind, shots whizzed past his head, and a glance back showed a Fokker on his tail. 'Dive and zoom,' they had told him in practice. He dived and zoomed, and the shots ceased passing him. He found himself behind another Fokker, and opened up, and thought he saw a bullet or two raise splinters before his quarry swerved away.

Fire from behind. He reacted before he had even registered that now he had seen splinters jump from his own struts. Glance back. There he was, coming at him, a glimpse of the pilot, a helmet and goggles and a slash of white teeth below. More brattling fire. 'If enemy fire is too hot,' Duberley had instructed, 'hard rudder and side slip, dive for home.' They were outnumbered, and being chased away by the enemy. Until they could get clear and re-form the V, it was every man for himself. He pushed the nose down and headed on the shortest course for the British line.

It was not long before he started to feel the engine vibrating in an unpleasant way. There was a rattling sound somewhere, and the revolution counter was wavering slowly downwards. One or some of those last shots from behind must have hit something important. He glanced over the side to check his course, and felt a hollowness in his stomach. They had gone a long way east to meet the enemy and the west wind had pushed them further during the fight. He could see what must be Cambrai off to one side, Valenciennes behind him, and calculated that the lines must be about fifteen miles away. But his altimeter was showing fourteen thousand feet, and he was flying into the wind. And the engine was making a tired, unhappy noise.

He flew on, losing height. Now there was heavy fighting below him, artillery exchange, clouds of smoke, and the air was bumpy with it, causing him to lose more height. He could hear Archie coughing, like an elderly smoker – he was within range, if they spotted him. How far now? He must be near the lines, with all that firing. If only the wind would drop. Five thousand feet. Four thousand. At three thousand, the ailing engine failed altogether and he switched off. Now he must rely on gliding to get him home. The bombardment was suddenly louder without the engine's rumbling.

Suddenly the smoke cleared and the earth was close, coming up rapidly, and he had to concentrate on landing without breaking anything – including himself. He bumped, jumped, found the ground again, jerked about in the rough-ness, stopped, tipping forward then settling back. Relief – he had done that much, at least. He clambered out, the sound of the guns horribly loud, and found he had lost his bearings completely. He couldn't tell which way he was facing, or which way the guns were firing. If he was on the wrong side of the line, he was in trouble. Capture, and spending the rest of the war a prisoner seemed at that moment almost worse than death.

He reached into the cubby-hole behind the pilot's seat to check that the flare was there: it had been impressed on him that if capture was imminent, he must set fire to the aeroplane. But what did 'imminent' mean? Should he do it now, just in case? The concussion of a gun shook the ground under his feet, but which way was it firing? If a German patrol came along, would he have time to set light to the machine before they stopped him? Would they shoot him on sight? He saw himself in a bare cell, with a barred window high up. How long would the war last?

Then a voice behind him said, 'I say!'

He jumped in shock and turned, but surely only an Englishman could say those two words in just that manner. And there was a friendly face, split by an English moustache and topped, yes, by a British cap. It was poking out of a dugout doorway, beaming at him.

William could only manage to say, 'I— I—'

'Come on in,' said the face sympathetically. 'Must have had a bit of a shock. Come in and have a wet.'

William collected the papers out of the cubby and staggered in. 'Where's the Front?' he asked.

The officer gestured. 'About a mile and a half that way. Bapaume's about ten miles to the south-west.'

'Thank God,' William said, and sat down involuntarily. 'I was afraid I was going to be captured.'

'We were just brewing up,' said the officer.

'I ought to telephone, let them know where I am,' said William.

270

'Have a wet first,' the officer said firmly. 'You look as though you could do with a spot of whisky in yours.'

'Thanks awfully,' said William. And whether it was the whisky or the knowledge that he was on the right side of the line, he soon started to feel a lot better, and even to plan how he would tell the adventure in his next letter home.

CHAPTER EIGHTEEN

The Germans attacked in the Champagne on the 15th of July, with massive forces, in two prongs, one on either side of Rheims – a ploy to divide the French.

But the French had learned something from the disasters of the spring, when they had kept all their troops in a forward position. Now there was a new strategy: a line of lightly held trenches and dummy posts created a false front, with the real trenches considerably further to the rear. Thus the Germans' initial bombardment fell largely on empty ground, and when they advanced and approached the real Allied front lines, they were met with a fierce barrage of French and American fire.

The attack to the east of Rheims was stalled on the first day. To the west, the German storm troops managed to cross the Marne, but on the 17th, British and American reinforcements were brought up, and they were halted there, too.

The enemy, the newspapers exulted, had had a great plan, but it had proved a great failure; the French, they said, had never fought more superbly; the grand offensive had lost its momentum and petered out into local skirmishing.

On the 18th, a massive counter-attack began, and fierce assaults on their exposed flanks forced the Germans to begin retreating. They had hastily to move troops from Ypres to the Champagne, giving the Allies in Flanders some long-awaited relief.

The nation needed some good news, for July had seen the spread of the influenza epidemic both to the coal-mining districts of Northumberland and Durham, and to London, where seven hundred people had died in one week. Many cinemas, theatres and dance-halls were closed, restaurants and even some churches were having a thin time of it, the streets seemed emptier, and it was unusually easy to get a seat on public transport.

An increasing number of people wore masks over their mouths and noses when they had to go out. It led to a feeling of isolation and suspicion. One no longer offered a handshake when meeting an acquaintance. Anyone unfortunate enough to sneeze in a public place would rapidly find a space left around him.

Everyone had his own patent prophylactic. Camphor was the most popular – the smell of it was everywhere – along with a new domestic disinfectant, called TCP, which was sprayed around and even gargled. Manufacturers rushed out throat lozenges, the sucking of which would prevent germs entering your system. 'Suck at least four or five a day,' said the Formamint advertisement. The makers of Oxo claimed their product fortified the system against influenza; Brand's Beef Essence would make you too strong to fall sick. Smoking cigarettes was supposed to help, and some factories suspended their no-smoking rules in the hope of keeping their work-force healthy.

'I read that if you wash the inside of your nose with soap and water every night and morning you'll be all right,' Ada said. 'I'm going to try it.' The flu had reached Northcote, and though there hadn't been any deaths yet, it was on everyone's mind.

'Porage, that's the thing,' Cook said firmly. 'Lots of porage.' Whether it was meant to kill the germs or merely boost the system, she didn't specify, but unlike Ada, she was in a position to enforce her regime. She sent quantities of porage to the breakfast table every morning, but had little success in imposing it on other meals.

'Me ma always said you should cut up one of your own hairs and drink it in a glass of water,' Emily said. 'And wear a warm muffler, even if it isn't cold.'

'No,' Ada said earnestly, 'I read in the paper you shouldn't wear a muffler, because it traps the germs inside. You should take brisk walks in the fresh air and breathe deeply. Sort of flush them out.'

Beryl didn't say anything, but her infallible prophylactic was soon sniffed out: a raw onion under the pillow. 'That's what my gran swears by,' she protested, when it was confiscated.

'The whole room stinks of it,' Ada complained bitterly. 'It'll never come out of that pillow.'

'You're all a load o' barmies,' Ethel said scornfully. 'None o' that rubbish helps. Just keep away from anyone that's got it, that's all. And if any of you so much as sniffs, you're not coming anywhere near my baby.'

'You never let anyone near your baby anyway,' Ada pointed out, to her rapidly retreating back. She raised her voice to add, 'And he's not your baby!'

David had come home on Wednesday the 17th. Ethel was glad he was back, but he had brought with him a trained nurse, whom she regarded with suspicion. Sister Horrocks was in her fifties, an iron-haired woman with a middle-aged figure and a brisk manner; she did not try to ingratiate herself with the household. 'I'm afraid I don't suffer fools gladly,' she had said, when she first arrived. It was not an apology.

She referred to David always as 'my patient', even when talking to Antonia, ruled his sick-room with a rod of iron, and seemed reluctant to allow anyone but herself near him.

'She seems to be very efficient,' Antonia complained to Sadie, 'but she makes me feel like an intruder.'

'Perhaps she's trying to protect him from the flu,' Sadie

said. 'She keeps asking me whether I've driven any flu victims in my ambulance. It *would* be awful if he caught it now, when he's just had a serious operation.'

'If that was the reason,' Antonia said, 'I might be willing to forgive her. But it looks like sheer possessiveness.'

Ethel was inclined to the latter theory. Sister Horrocks treated her with a wounding lack of respect, even though she had been his sick-room nurse for so long. *I know I'm not a trained nurse*, she thought resentfully, *but I know his constitution better than anyone*. On the other hand, she approved of her vigilance in the matter of the 'flu. Ethel didn't care how many people in the country got it, as long as it was not allowed in the house with her precious baby and Mr David.

And as Sister Horrocks had no interest in establishing sovereignty over baby Marcus, Ethel was inclined to think her mostly a good thing.

The German offensive was giving rise to large numbers of casualties, especially Americans, and Sadie was busy, working at Highclere in the mornings and driving in the afternoons. It helped keep her mind off the fact that there had been no letter from John Courcy. 'Have you heard anything?' she would ask Mrs Cuthbert about once a week, and Mrs Cuthbert would say, 'No, nothing. But I expect he's very busy.' Sadie was afraid he had abandoned them. He had always written to Mrs Cuthbert. Had she betrayed her feelings for him up at Mount Olive, and embarrassed him? Had he decided to sever his links with them as a consequence?

Having delivered some wounded to the old district hospital on the Walford road one day at the end of her shift, she returned to the ambulance depot, and saw the familiar green jersey of a Wolf Cub stopping the traffic to allow her to turn into the yard. At the beginning of the war, a junior branch of the Baden-Powell movement had been set up experimentally, for boys too young to be Boy Scouts, and it had proved so popular that in 1916 it had been given official status, with all the accoutrements of uniform, sixes, leaders (they were given the names of characters from *The Jungle Book*), activities and badges.

She knew all this from Peter, who had always envied William when, as a Scout, he had done war-work, like defending the reservoir from German invaders. Peter's cry had always been 'Not fair!' that he was too young to join, and he had been an eager recruit into the Cubs.

So she was not terribly surprised to see, as she passed him, that the Cub was Peter. Just inside the yard she stopped and leaned out of the window, beckoning, and he came over and looked up at her. 'Aren't you supposed to be at school?' she asked.

'I'm helping with important war-work,' he said grandly. 'I went to school this morning but they sent us home. They've closed it early for the summer holidays. Because of the flu. To stop it spreading, they said.'

'Oh. Shouldn't they have let Mother know?'

'They gave us a letter for our parents. I gave it to Antonia because Mum was out. She's always out,' he added. 'I'm glad Antonia stays at home with David these days.'

Sadie sympathised. Home seemed less like home when your mother wasn't there. Even she, at her advanced age, disliked coming back to find no-one but the servants. Their mother was kept busier than ever with war-work. 'Lady Hunter' was wanted on every committee – a title at the head was so much better for getting money out of people.

'So I went to the Scout hut and they sent me to help out here,' Peter concluded.

'Well, good for you,' she said. 'And they put you on directing traffic?'

'I'm supposed to be here as a messenger, but they said

276

in between I could show the ambulances where there was a space, cos the yard gets so full.'

'And stopping the traffic was your initiative?' she guessed.

'You're supposed to show it, whenever you can,' he said. 'It *is* helpful, isn't it?'

'Well, it helped *me*,' she said. And, remembering William's obsession when he had been in the Scouts, 'Is there a badge?'

Peter's face lit. 'War Service Badge!' he said eagerly. 'You get it for completing twenty-eight days of war service. And you have to do three hours for it to count as a day. So if I do, say, two afternoons a week . . .' He stopped, costive with calculation.

'Fourteen weeks. Three and a half months,' she helped him out. 'Perhaps you need extra tew in the hols, if you can't do that in your head. You should ask David to coach you.'

'He's not well enough. And I *was* doing it in my head. You didn't give me time.'

'It shouldn't take time, something that easy.'

Peter donned a mantle of dignity. 'Would you move on, please? You're blocking the way.'

She gave him a mocking salute. 'Aye aye, sir.'

'That's sailors!' he called after her as she drove off.

But seconds later he had run after her and jumped on the running board. 'I forgot,' he yelled over the engine noise. 'There was someone looking for you. A soldier.'

She stopped again. 'Who could that be?'

'I don't know. He didn't say.'

'Where is he now?'

'He went away.'

'What did he look like?'

'I dunno. Just a soldier. In uniform. I didn't recognise him.'

'Really, Peter, you could be more helpful!'

But he only stuck out his tongue, and jumped off the

running board. Another ambulance had turned in at the yard, and it was much more interesting to him than his sister's mysterious visitor.

'Some Boy Scout you'd make!' Sadie retorted.

As soon as she turned into Highwood Road, Sadie could see the soldier waiting at the gate of The Elms, crouched down talking to Nailer. Nailer had been with her at Highclere that morning, but when she got back he had disappeared before she went to the depot. Sometimes he rode with her in the ambulance cab, and she liked the company. He was not usually so forthcoming with strangers, but he was permitting the crouching soldier the liberty of stroking his back and even tipping his head for a caress. Whoever the soldier was, he had a way with animals.

He stood up as she approached, but she didn't recognise him. He was a broad-chested, strong-looking young man, uniform smartly pressed, puttees perfect, boots polished, and a very large chestnut moustache, well groomed, which was rather concealing of the features.

She reached him. Nailer abandoned him and came to press against her legs, swearing eternal devotion. *Me? Let a stranger stroke me? Never!*

The soldier grinned underneath the glossy foliage and said, 'Don't you know me, miss?'

She shook her head, searching for likeness. 'No, I'm sorry, I—'

'It's me, miss, Victor. Victor Sowden.'

'Good heavens!' she exclaimed. 'I would never have known you. How you've grown!'

'Army grub, miss. Not much to write home about, but there's plenty of it.'

'And you have a moustache!' He preened it with a hand, evidently immensely proud of it. 'And you're a sergeant!'

That was the most surprising of all. He had been the

278

village's worst tearaway before the war, always in trouble. Born to be hanged, the decent folk of Northcote had said. But Sadie had always had a soft spot for him, in spite of everything. Boys of his sort were usually mindlessly cruel to anything weaker than themselves, but Victor's one redeeming feature had been a love of animals. He never tormented birds or insects, and had even fought bigger boys to stop them stoning a cat, or tying a firework to a dog's tail. And he loved horses.

He'd volunteered as soon as the war started to get away from his drunken father and feckless mother, and it had obviously served him well. Sadie was impressed with the change in him. He held himself like a soldier and spoke to her confidently, but respectfully.

'Yes, miss. Got my first stripe last year, and made up to sergeant last month. Doing all right.'

'So I see. Well, congratulations. What are you doing home?'

'Got leave, miss. Haven't had any in nearly a year. You never know when it's going to come up. Thought they'd send me when Jerry stood down. But when it went quiet they sent us to camp near E-tap for training, and just when the new stunt starts off at Reems, and I'm thinking we'll be wanted there, my leave order comes through, and here I am. I didn't want to take it, but my officer said I'd got to.'

'So I should think,' said Sadie. 'I'm sure you need it, after so long.'

'Well, miss, I wouldn't say we haven't had a scrap or two. We was around Arminteers in the last lot. Cor! That was a picnic!'

'So you've come to visit your family, have you?'

'Nah,' he said scornfully. 'They don't care about me, and I don't care about them. Only me brother Horry, he was the only one't mattered, and he's out in France as well now. He joined the Hussars.'

'Another one who loves horses, is he?'

'He just wants to copy anything I do. But he's doing okay. I'm right proud of him.'

'Well, *I'm* proud of *you*,' Sadie said. 'You've really made something of yourself.'

'It's the horses, miss. I started out a horse-holder, and now I'm in battalion transport with twenty-four men under me. Some of that's lorries and suchlike, but I still get to look after a lot of horses. They make you grow up quick, horses do.'

She thought that the war might have had something to do with it too. He was very young to be a sergeant but, having been in from the beginning, it couldn't be said he didn't have the experience. 'You know that I help train horses for the Remount Service?' she said.

'So I heard, miss. And driving amb'lances. Gor! The things women – I mean, ladies – do nowadays!'

'Things have changed since the war started,' Sadie said. 'I've often wondered what happened to the horses I've had through my hands. I wonder if any of them have come to you. I know you'd treat them well.'

'We do our best,' Victor said, but he looked upset. 'It's the work, miss, even more than the shells and suchlike. It breaks their hearts. And sometimes there's nothing you can do for 'em but put 'em out of their mis'ry.'

She nodded gravely. 'But veterinary facilities are better now than at the beginning of the war?'

'Oh, Lord, yes, miss. Bags better. No comparison.'

'If you were at E-tap,' She pronounced Étaples the soldiers' way for clarity, 'perhaps you might have seen the new horse hospital at Le Touquet?'

'Oh, yes, miss. I've been there a couple of times since it opened, taking my horses in. Ever so fine it is, with all the best kit – operating theatres and slings and suchlike, and they've even got a swimming pool, miss, for thep – thepper . . .'

'Therapy?'

'That's the word.' He grinned. 'Always get me tongue twisted round that one. It's a marvellous place all right.'

'Perhaps,' Sadie said tentatively, 'you saw a friend of mine there. Major Courcy?'

'The major? He's the officer commanding there. I've seen him, but not to speak to, of course.'

'Of course,' Sadie said. She wanted to ask if he had looked well when he last saw him, but naturally she couldn't. It was a contact that was no contact – frustrating.

Victor seemed to understand that she wanted more, and began, 'They call him . . .' Then he stopped, embarrassed.

'Go on! Call him what?'

'Well, miss, not meaning any offence, but they call him Old Corsets, cos he runs such a tight ship. But it's meant affectionate, like. He's very well thought of. Very good with the horses, everybody says.'

Sadie smiled to herself. 'Old Corsets'. Wait till she saw him again – she'd have some fun with that. *If* she ever saw him again. 'Keen on the rules, is he?'

'Orderly I spoke to said, when it comes to the horses, everything's got to be done perfect. But that's right, miss. I'd feel the same way. I don't let none of the men under me get away with nothing.'

'Always run your hand along the neck under the mane, eh?' she said.

He grinned. 'Course, you'd know, miss. Knowing about horses. Under the mane, round the back of the ears. And undo the harness buckles, see if there's dirt under the tongue. You get to know all the lazy tricks. But I won't have any horse neglected – and your major's the same way, it seems.'

'Not my major,' Sadie said sadly. 'Just a friend. Well, I'm very glad to have seen you, Victor,' she went on, 'and to see you doing so well.'

He beamed. 'It's been like starting a new life for me, like

being a new person. I got everything to hope for now. And when the war's over, I can get a proper job and *be* someone. You won't be ashamed to know me then.'

'I'm proud to know you now. And I'll follow your career with interest,' Sadie said, shaking his hand. 'And when I send off horses in future, I shall think of you taking care of them.'

'If they come to me, you can depend on it,' said Victor.

Laura's team was ordered to move from Hazebrouck to Amiens on Friday the 2nd of August.

'Which I suppose means there's a push coming up,' she said to Annie.

'What's Amiens like?' Annie asked the boys – as she and Laura tended to call them, though Morgan was twenty-two and Jean-Marie twenty-one.

'Very fine city,' said Morgan. 'Lots of big houses, very fine cathedral. I was there once with my parents. We went to the theatre. Very grand theatre.'

'Maybe it's not so fine now,' Jean-Marie hazarded. 'The war has been very close.'

'But it's never been occupied, has it?' said Laura. 'So perhaps we'll get a decent billet. With soft beds and hot water.'

'If there's a stunt coming up,' Annie said, 'we'll probably be too busy to notice.'

'A woman can dream,' Laura said with dignity.

Amiens, they found, had been largely emptied of civilians. They noticed the boarded-up shops and shuttered houses and the general lack of pedestrians as they drove in, but when they stopped at the first depot in the town to fill up with petrol, Laura discovered that it was not an exodus of refugees, as she had seen in Poperinghe. The other three had taken the opportunity to stretch their legs, and had walked a little way off to sit on a wall and smoke. Laura came back to them after chatting with the fuel-dump corporal.

'It's a deliberate policy, moving everyone out,' she reported. 'Where you get large population centres you're bound to get spies and informants, and they're guarding against that. Which means there's definitely something big brewing.'

'Well, we knew we weren't moved here for our health,' Annie said.

A horn sounded irritably. 'Oy! Move your bus! Other people want juice as well, you know!'

It was an army ambulance, with a scrub-headed orderly leaning out of the window. 'Sorry,' Laura shouted. 'I'll get out of your way.' And to her crew, 'You finish your cigarettes. I want one myself. I'll pull up the road a few yards, and you can walk down and join me.'

But as she headed for her cab, a motor-car with a Red Cross on the side pulled up behind the ambulance and sounded its horn, too. Behind that, there were two more Red Cross vans.

'I'm going! Keep your hair on!' she shouted, scrambling up.

'*Laura!*'

She knew that voice. She beamed with incredulous delight. 'I'm stopping just down there,' she called, with gestures. He was already half out of the car. He said something to his driver and positively ran to the other side of her cab and clambered in.

'What astonishing luck!' he said. 'I couldn't believe my eyes when I saw you.'

She grinned. 'All the best people come to Amiens at this time of year. Taking the waters, don't you know.'

'According to rumour, there's some big stunt brewing,' Ransley said. 'We haven't been told anything official, just to move activities over to here.'

'It shows there's good in every situation,' said Laura, pulling in at the wide place in the road she had spotted. She switched off the engine, and turned to him. The others would be five minutes finishing their smokes and strolling down, and Ransley's motor had to refuel, behind the ambulance. They had that much time to be alone.

He didn't waste it, gathering her into his arms for a prolonged kiss. The gear lever rather got in the way, but you couldn't be too fussy in wartime.

When they broke apart, he sat back to look at her, keeping hold of her hands. 'Are you well? You look well.'

'I'm disgustingly healthy,' she said. 'And you? You look tired.'

'My dear girl, I've gone so far beyond tired I'm in danger of meeting myself coming back. But it's good to be kept busy. Saves one from missing certain people too much, and worrying about them.'

'If we're both based in Amiens,' Laura said, 'perhaps we might snatch a meeting before the balloon goes up. Any idea when that will be?'

'A few days, I imagine – they'll have got us here early enough to inspect and set up. Not before Monday, probably.'

'Well, then, as soon as I know where we're billeted, I'll send you a message,' said Laura. 'If you can get away, let me know.'

'And if I can't,' he said, with a serious look, 'you must promise to take care of yourself.'

'I will if you will,' she said. There was only so much you could do, and they both knew it. In the mirror, she saw her crew coming down the road. 'Time's nearly up.'

'Don't waste it, then. Kiss me again,' he said.

'I was going to have a smoke,' she teased.

'You can smoke any old time,' he said, gathering her in.

When Annie and the boys arrived, they got down and introductions were made. Annie knew him from her time

284

with Bessie in Poperinghe, but the relationship with Laura was new to her. She didn't comment on it, being too naturally polite. The boys had an eager respect for the medical profession, from their outpost of it, and were flattered when he asked them to show him the X-ray equipment and the portable electricity generator that ran it. So the few minutes passed before the medical motors came up. Ransley hopped into his car with only an intense look at Laura by way of farewell. Moments in a war zone would always be snatched.

Edward's battalion moved in stages, and the last leg was done on foot and by night. It was obvious that a very large movement was taking place – lorries of all sorts, lines of ammunition wagons and guns overtook them. He had been to France as a young man, knew the general layout, and had a good sense of direction, so he was able to guess, when they left Abbeville – which he recognised from the railway station and the truncated church of Wulfram – that they were heading for Amiens. They arrived on Tuesday the 6th of August at a farm on the outskirts. The men were settled into barns and outbuildings, while the officers took over the farmhouse. They could hear the guns in the distance, and the occasional closer crash of a shell. The Germans had held Albert, a town sixteen miles from Amiens, since March, and that marked the effective front line. British guns fired back, making a continual low grumbling, and lighting the horizon with a putrid glow.

In the early evening Colonel Dancer called a meeting of his officers, and they crowded into the farmhouse's inadequate sitting-room, which was soon thick with cigarette smoke. The more senior officers perched on chairs, while the juniors stood rather squashed together behind them. Prancer Dancer, prowling lightly up and down the small space in front of them all, told them about the anticipated stunt, and their part in it. It was obvious to Edward that the whole show had been meticulously planned. Everything and everyone was being moved into position in the deepest secrecy under cover of darkness. Forward ammunition dumps were disguised. Tanks and gun limbers were hidden in sunken lanes and under trees. Surprise was going to be a key element in the offensive.

'We've got two battalions of Canadians in Flanders with orders to keep up a steady flow of signals traffic, to convince the Boche that an attack is brewing there,' Dancer told them. 'The rest are here – moved in a series of night moves to fool the German spotter planes. You'll all be glad to know we'll be fighting alongside Canadians and Australians. Formidable chaps.'

In addition to excellent allies, Dancer told them, they had top equipment. They had at least three hundred Mark V tanks, which would be central to the early stages of the battle – they were very different from the unreliable first models that had appeared in 1916. There were also seventy-two light 'Whippet' tanks which followed up like cavalry on any breakthrough. Communication on the battlefield would be by wireless, which would help the RAF to play an important role both in reconnaissance and attack.

Everything, Edward realised, was going to be very different this time from the attritional grind of the advance across the same landscape of two years before. And the very fighting techniques were different, too. Instead of a battalion being wielded as one crude weapon, now each platoon was self-contained, with its own bombers and Lewis-gunners, so that they could move nimbly and react to evolving situations.

'Once things kick off,' Dancer said, 'I will expect officers to use their initiative. No-one knows exactly what might occur from minute to minute. But you people have the training and the intelligence – and, may I say, the character – to make your own decisions. That's why one British company is worth ten German companies. That is why we will prevail.'

He went on to show maps and diagrams, talked of the ground and of objectives, read out operational orders, told them what their part would be in the overall show. 'The kick-off will be four twenty a.m. on Thursday the eight. We go up to the line tonight, but we'll be withdrawing from the front line ten minutes before zero hour, to leave it free from troops. Secrecy is paramount at that point – no lights, no whistles, no talking. Once we get to the reserve trenches, fifteen hundred yards back, everyone is to keep well down, because our guns will be firing at such short range at the beginning, the shells will be virtually skimming along the ground. I don't want anyone's head taken off at that stage. At zero hour, the first wave of infantry will go in with the tanks and take the red line.' He tapped the map. 'It's a line of old defence trenches. The Germans have occupied them since March. At zero plus one we follow them, and at the red line we pass through them and proceed to the second objective, the blue line, German trenches. That's where you'll meet the first resistance.'

After the general briefing, each company's officers gathered separately to talk about individual orders and responsibilities. At their meeting, crammed into the scullery, Edward could see Captain Campion was tremendously keyed up – but it was a happy excitement. 'The Boche are exhausted,' he concluded. 'A spent force. This operation has been planned down to the last detail. Old Ludendorff doesn't know what's about to hit him.'

They went off to do their last preparations, and Edward thought, *I'm about to go into battle at last.* He had been in action in the Ardres Valley on the 19th of July, but that was just a side-skirmish, and they had not actually seen any Germans, though they had been fired on, and he had lost a man, shot through the arm and sent to the rear. But this was the real thing. He thought of the battles of the Somme in

1916, and of Ypres in 1917. Thanks to his connection with Lord Forbesson, he knew rather more about both occasions than was good for him. *A soldier shouldn't have too much imagination.* Where had he heard that? At dawn on the 8th of August, he would be walking with his men towards an enemy that had proved itself both determined and cunning. He felt the sense of optimism that was running through the whole British Army; and he was ready to believe it would be the turning of the tide, the breakthrough, the beginning of the end. But, inevitably, men would be wounded, men would be killed – and one of them might be him.

Machine gun, or shell. He wondered how much it hurt when bullets struck you, or shrapnel. He knew that the excitement of the moment could blunt pain – you could take a frightful hack at rugby and never know it until the match was over. He supposed it would depend on the nature of the wound, and what happened afterwards. In the hours lying waiting for medical help, one might go through the fires of Hell.

And then there was death. He was not afraid of death, but he didn't want to die, not yet. He had a life back in England – a life that was worth dying for, yes, but one, all the same, he would sooner go back and live. He knew on that instant that he had forgiven Beattie. He loved her, and would never love another woman. What had happened to alienate them was not as important as that simple fact. He wanted to stay alive so that he could go back to Beattie and try to win her back. And for his children's sake.

He remembered Dancer's words about the RAF, and wondered whether William was near, whether he would take part in the coming 'stunt'. He remembered Bobby, and thought, *William must stay safe. Surely God wouldn't take two of them in the same way.*

He went off to collect his men's green envelopes.

* * *

William had already been playing a part in the upcoming operation. As the tanks were moved up in short hops under the cover of darkness, aeroplanes had been sent up every night to fly over the area with throttles open, making as much noise as possible to conceal from the enemy any sound the tanks might make. William had gone up on two occasions, and found night-flying exciting, if rather nerve-racking.

Meanwhile, in daytime, they were keeping up normal flying activity to try to convince the Germans that any build-up they might detect was for an attack in the vicinity of Rheims. And at first light on the 8th, they were to be part of an assault on every German airfield in the area, to knock them out with bombs and strafing, and give the Allies air superiority for the first stages of the offensive. It was another part of the sophisticated battle plan that would make the Somme 1918 very different from the Somme 1916.

CHAPTER NINETEEN

Edward's memories afterwards of the battle were fragmented and dreamlike, for which the fog was partly to blame. The day started with it, thick, white and muffling. When they set off at zero plus one, it should have been full daylight, but instead there was an eerie twilight in which sounds were distorted and directionless. It was impossible to see more than ten yards ahead, which made it difficult to keep a sense of direction; but Edward had studied the maps, and he had a compass. Beyond that he could trust only his senses and his luck.

It was not a quiet fog, like the autumnal mist in the woods at home. There were shells bursting, each briefly lighting the whiteness, then darkening it with smoke, and machine-gun bullets whistling, the more frightening because you couldn't see them, or guess where they were coming from. Sometimes the distinctive rumble of a tank would pass them, without the tank being visible, or visible only as a looming shape more solid than the fog around it. It was enough to stretch the nerves.

They found what he assumed to be the red line without difficulty, but the trenches were empty, the first wave having continued forward. The reason was clear: there had been almost no resistance. There were two or three dead Germans lying over the sandbags – the rest must have fled.

Beyond the red line trenches they were able to follow the

tank tracks, which were somehow comforting, as though their mighty bulk left behind some magic protection. Things began to emerge from the mist in front of them. First it was wounded coming back, some walking, some on stretchers. His men stared, but did not speak to them; orders were to move ahead, no matter what. The wounded did not speak either; they passed in silence and disappeared into the mist behind, like ghosts at cockcrow.

Then Germans began to appear, grey on grey, helmetless and unarmed – the captured being herded back. Edward noticed again how young most of them were. They looked blear-eyed and bristly. Some of them smiled nervously, hope-fully, at the British coming the other way; others looked sullen, staring at the ground or grimly ahead. Few seemed to be wounded.

Now there was a sense of the day lightening somewhere up above as the sun strengthened, but the fog had been reinforced by smoke – you could tell by the bitter smell of it – so it was no easier to see ahead. It was like a theatre curtain, he thought, with players pushing their way through from time to time for their brief moment on stage; but the play made no sense.

The strangest thing was when a team of horses came trotting out, still harnessed together but not drawing anything, and unattended. Four of them only. The leaders flung their heads up warningly, but no-one tried to catch them, and they trotted past, heading eagerly into the mist and Amiens, as though going home.

A little further on, they came on the rest of the scene – a limber, smashed and wheels-up in a smoking hole, two dead horses, and a driver lying face-down in the middle of the road where he had been flung by the blast. He had no legs. Another gunner was trying to drag someone out from under the wreck. He must have cut the unwounded horses loose. Intent on his work, he did not glance up at the platoon swinging by. Edward passed the word back about the dead man in the road, so they should not stumble on him. His cap was missing, and Edward noticed, as one notices details at moments like that, that his hair was wheat-gold in the dust.

They went on. At the blue line, where they had expected to have to fight, the trenches were empty. There were a few more dead lying around, but again most must have run. Edward supposed the suddenness of the attack had shocked and panicked them into fleeing.

They went on. The sun was climbing, the mist and smoke were lifting, it was getting hot. A trickle of sweat from under his cap reminded him that it was August, not October. A German spotter plane went over, and the men looked up nervously. A fleet of tanks went by, and soon afterwards, the enemy shell fire intensified. Perhaps the spotter had alerted the artillery. At any rate, the shell fire was coming too close, and Edward ordered his men to take cover in the shell holes on either side of the road. When the shelling moved away, they emerged and went on. Now the fog had lifted, and as they topped a shallow rise, they could see the ground ahead of them, a landscape of tanks, infantry, artillery, and support units all going forward. It was a heartening sight. Fresh ammunition was going up, and already work details were repairing holes in the road. It was businesslike; it was ordered.

A group of Germans came towards them, unescorted, seeming only too glad to be out of it. They raised their hands and waggled them and cried, '*Kamerad! Kamerad!*' One or two of Edward's men had raised their rifles, but he snapped, 'Leave it!' as one did to a ratting dog. He could see they had no guns. One of the Germans, an officer, was holding his wounded arm. He halted in front of Edward, bowed in place of saluting, and said, 'We wish to surrender ourselves.'

'I am not able to accept your surrender,' Edward said.

His eyes widened. 'But – we do not fight. Look, we have no guns.'

'There is nothing I can do for you,' Edward said. 'I am under orders to advance. You must go further back.' He gestured behind him.

The young man bit his lip anxiously. 'They will shoot us.'

'You will not be harmed,' Edward assured him. 'Keep the hands up. We don't shoot unarmed men.'

The officer looked at him, his eyes white in his smoke-darkened face. He was bare-headed, and his hair was matted with sweat. 'Are you not sick of this war?' His voice, high with pain, seemed to burst from him.

Edward noticed that his uniform was worn pale at the seams. How long had he been out here? 'Go on back,' he said, and stepped round him. One of Edward's men growled something, and he said again, 'Leave it. That's not our spoil.'

They went on. Somewhere ahead there was a tremendous explosion, and briefly they saw the flash of it, a sheet of flame leaping up into the sky. Later they learned that it was an ammunition train at Harbonnières, twenty miles up the road. The Germans were so unprepared for the rapidity of the British advance that the train had come steaming slowly into the station as though nothing was happening. Some approaching tanks had opened fire on it, hitting a powder van. Shortly afterwards, a second train came in, a passenger train bringing fresh troops, which was captured without resistance, but with great puzzlement on the Hun side – and perhaps a little relief.

William's squadron had been busy since first light, bombing the German airfields, and then alternating between spotting for their own side and harassing the other side with machine-gun fire and grenades. The fog had lifted by eight twenty, and from their position up above they could see that all the first objectives had been taken already. It was a resounding success.

William went back to base for breakfast and a wash, and then was back in action. The Germans had flown aircraft in now from their bases further afield, and there were dogfights to enliven the bombing raids and strafing attacks on infantry. He got behind a Fokker and gave him half a drum, and was elated to see the black smoke appear, and the machine start to twist downwards like a falling leaf.

He had never felt so alive. *Bobby*, he thought. *I know what you knew.* He felt as though his brother were there with him in the cockpit, egging him on.

Edward's letter to Beattie was dated the 12th of August.

My dearest Beattie,

This is the first chance I have had to put pen to paper. No doubt you have read about events out here. I am glad to tell you that as far as we can tell, the push has been a complete success. Organisation was perfect and the speed of advance terrific, with the Germans running from our tanks and infantry, so taken by surprise they put up very little resistance. My platoon did not actually exchange fire until mid-morning, when we came on a nest of fleeing Boche who had holed up in a coppice and, in the manner of a cornered animal, tried to bite. We took them, with the loss of only two of my men, one dead and one wounded, sent them back under escort and carried on. During the last few days we have advanced over twelve miles and captured a huge number of prisoners and much booty. So you can guess we have been kept on the move. The village we have reached now has been levelled by the barrage with not a house left standing, so we are not very comfortable, but it is glorious to be caught up in the rush of advance after so long a stalemate. My company commander, who has been out here

for some years, said, 'We are out of the trenches now, and
by God we will not go back in.' I think that sums up the
strong feeling of us all.

I hope you are all well at home, that David is progressing,
and Diana finding comfort with her new child. Have you
heard anything from William? I think about you all a great
deal, but most of all, I think about you, my dearest wife.
Being out here teaches one very quickly what really matters.
I am conscious that I did not behave when we were last
together as I should have. When I come back, my dear,
can we not start afresh? Forget everything that has been
said and done between us, except of course the good things,
our years of happy marriage, and our dear children and
grandchildren. We have so much to be grateful for – is that
not enough foundation on which to build a happy future?
I pray most earnestly that you can forgive me my short-
comings as a husband and a lover, and accept me back,
when I come home, as the man who has always loved you
most tenderly, and always will.

    Edward

Beattie sat on her bed with the letter in her hand, staring
blindly at the wall. Edward, her good husband, whom she
had betrayed, was asking *her* forgiveness. It hurt, dreadfully.
She did not miss, either, the reference to his shortcomings
'as a lover'. That hurt the worst of all, because they had
always been very good together, had enjoyed their intimacy:
it had been one of the strengths of their marriage. It was
she who had withdrawn from him. *He* had not failed *her*.
The shortcoming he referred to was that he was not Louis;
and that he should apologise for that was beyond bearing.

Louis. Her longed-for and lost love. Now lost again, and
this time without hope of reprieve. He was gone into the
black night of eternity, leaving her sick and faint and alone,
beached on the hard white shore of the living. She wished

she had never loved him – wished she had never met him, because meeting him she had loved him, without reason, without intention, something she could do nothing about.

Edward had been her whole life, loving her and taking care of her, her good husband. She ought to wish that she had never met Louis again, that day in Waterloo station, because then there would have been no betrayal. But she could not wish it. She would not give up the memory of those few months together even for the hope of salvation. And, knowing that she would not wish the past undone, she could refute her own contention that there had been no betrayal. She had betrayed Edward with every breath of her life because she had never given him what she had reserved for Louis, that first, blind, unquestioning love.

So, now, was there any way back? She was lonely for Edward, and for her life of before. She wanted to be cherished, she wanted the companionship of a shared life, of planning the future, of the children and grandchildren. She wanted to be normal again. She wanted to be *sane*.

But she had no right to all that. She was unrepentant: therefore she could not be shriven. She was trapped in a nightmare place between worlds, no light, no air, no going forward, no going back. What could she do? What was there that was even possible?

She imagined Edward as she had last seen him – leaner, harder, younger-looking. She imagined him in the battle, holding a gun, leading his men into danger. Exchanging fire. She shivered. That Edward was almost a stranger; and, perhaps because of it, dangerously attractive. Her loins ached. It was so long since a man had held her. Perhaps, when he came back a stranger, she could start a new life with him, as if her old Edward was dead too, like Louis. Widows were allowed to marry again. *Forgive us all that is past, and grant that we may ever hereafter serve and please Thee in newness of life*. The words of the general confession drifted through her mind. But it was not forgiveness she asked for, it was wiping the slate clean.

You couldn't go back. But perhaps you could go forward, with sufficient amnesia on both sides.

Perhaps you had to. What, after all, was the alternative?

The pain and depression of the immediate aftermath of David's operation was something the household had been prepared for. But when the pain had eased, they expected him to perk up. Instead, he seemed to sink into a lethargy, uninterested in anything, lying all day silent and staring at the patch of sky he could see through his window.

'Shock,' Sister Horrocks told Beattie briskly, when she asked.

'But how can it be a shock, when he was expecting the operation?' Beattie asked, baffled.

'I mean it in the clinical sense,' Sister Horrocks said, and refused to explain further. Faced with questions she did not care to answer, she had a way of bustling off and being quellingly busy.

'I *think*,' Antonia said, when she and Beattie discussed it afterwards, 'she means that the *body* was shocked at the interference and – and the *violence* of the operation, and it is having a depressing effect on the mind.'

'But surely the mind controls the body, not vice versa,' Beattie protested.

'I don't know,' Antonia said helplessly. 'The important thing is that she thinks this is a stage of recovery, and *only* a stage. As the healing continues, he will come back to normal.'

Beattie wondered what 'normal' was for David – it was so long since his life had been *that*.

But the reports of the battle of Amiens seemed to get through to him. It was Antonia's habit to read the papers to him, in an attempt to stimulate his mind and bring him back to the world. He did not, to begin with, show any interest, and often would close his eyes and fall asleep. She suspected that sometimes he was only feigning sleep to make her stop, but she stuck at it. And the good news of Amiens definitely roused him. Perhaps it was merely a chance of timing, that he was *ready* to be roused – it was six weeks since the operation – but gradually he hitched himself more upright and listened more intently, asked her to go back and repeat parts, and finally snatched the paper from her hands to read for himself.

'This is more like it!' he said. And when Haig paused the main offensive on the 13th of August he said, 'They'll be fighting over the old battleground now, the Somme – much harder going. The Old Man's learned when to stop. That's as important as knowing when to go on.'

Instead, there was a new offensive by Byng's Third Army between the Ancre and Scarpe. 'He's giving his generals more freedom to use their own judgement.'

The Allies had taken twenty or thirty thousand prisoners and five hundred guns. 'The initiative is in *our* hands now,' he said.

'Do you really think it makes so much difference?' Antonia asked, wondering mostly at the change in his spirits.

'Yes, I do. In the spring, the initiative was all theirs. It looked as though the war was going to drag on until 'twenty or 'twenty-one. Now I doubt it will last beyond next spring. All the Boche can hope for is to hang it out long enough to get a peace by negotiation. They can't possibly hope for a win.'

The news that Edward had come through without a scratch was followed by a field postcard from William saying he was well, which set the household's minds at rest – at least until the next time. David began to get up for a short time each day, and Sister Horrocks said that, with gentle exercise and massage, there was hope that he could make a full recovery.

'After three months,' she decreed, 'we will be able to be confident.' The massage would be important for his well-being for some time to come, perhaps for years, and Antonia asked to be taught how to do it. She longed to be useful to him.

Meanwhile it was August and holiday time. None of the family was going away: Beattie and Sadie had their war-work, and Antonia had David. Peter had the Cubs and, for the rest, his recent spurt of growth had given him long enough legs to ride David's old bicycle – Sadie had Bobby's – and armed with that and permission to wander anywhere in Dene Park, as well as his usual haunts, he was happy to spend his days roaming with whichever of his friends was also at home.

But the servants had to have their holidays. Cook was going to her sister in Folkestone as usual, and this time did not manage to bully Emily into coming as well. 'I don't have to,' she asserted, though eyeing Cook as if she might bite. 'Amn't I old enough to choose for meself?'

'You are not!' Cook asserted right back.

Emily pouted. 'Sure, I'm eighteen years old. Nearly nineteen.'

Cook blinked. Emily was so thin and undersized it was hard to believe she was not the child that Cook had always viewed her as. 'You can't be!'

'I am, and girls are married and have families at eighteen.'

'Don't you even think it!' Cook snapped. 'You're not fit to get married, let alone be a mother.'

'Well, but I'm old enough not to go on holiday with you if I don't want to,' Emily stuck to the main point, 'and I *don't.*'

'Suit yourself, then.' Cook said, gave an offended toss of the head and walked away. *Emily eighteen? Lord bless and save us!*

When pressed by the others, Emily was reluctant to say

where she *was* going. But eventually Beryl got it out of her on a strict promise of secrecy: she was going to Ireland. 'I got enough now for me fare. I been saving up for years.'

'You're going to cross the sea?' Beryl cried in astonishment and some admiration. 'With all them U-boats around?'

'Sure people do it all the time,' Emily said. 'Us Irish are the great travellers,' she added grandly.

Beryl couldn't keep such momentous news to herself, and soon all the servants were remonstrating. Even Munt deigned to notice her purely in order to say, 'We won't be seeing you agen, then. Bottom o' the Irish Sea, you'll be, come next week.'

'I'm not scared,' Emily said, but her fingers crept unbidden to the crucifix she wore under her dress.

'You're barmy,' Ethel said. 'By the time you get there it'll be time to come back. It's a waste of bloomin' money.'

'Two days there and two days back,' Emily argued. 'I'll still have three days. And Ma's going to come across from Banagher on the bus, so I only have to get to Dublin. She's got a cousin in Boyne Street we can stay with.'

'All your savings, for three days!' Ethel said scornfully. 'You want putting away.'

Emily's eyes filled with tears. 'I don't care,' she whimpered. 'I want to see me mammy.' She hadn't seen her for almost seven years.

Ada said she didn't want to go away anywhere. 'I'd sooner stay here, if that's all right with you, madam,' she said to Beattie, 'and perhaps just have days out, when it's convenient.'

Beattie guessed she was hoping that Len Armstrong might get leave and suddenly appear: she didn't want to have gone away somewhere and miss him. 'Just as you please,' she said.

Ethel didn't want to leave Marcus – she suspected that if she went on holiday, she would come back to find another

300

nurse-maid or even a nanny installed and herself ousted. And, anyway, where would she go? She had no friends or family. She said she would take days out when convenient, like Ada, but in fact had no intention of absenting herself for more than an hour or two at a time.

Beryl would take her holiday when Cook came back, going to stay with her family. Her family wouldn't welcome her to that crowded house, another mouth to feed, when they had not long managed to get rid of her, but she planned to spend Cook's holiday abstracting as many things from the larder as wouldn't be missed, and concealing them in her suitcase to make herself acceptable.

On the 20th of August the French Tenth Army attacked on the River Oise and forced the German Ninth Army back several miles. On the 22nd, the British retook Albert, a prize of great sentimental value, though after four years of continuous warfare there was nothing of it left. It was simply a shapeless, jumbled mass of bricks, stone and metal, with the massive and beautiful Basilica merely a larger heap of rubble in the general desolation.

On the 25th the Byng Boys took a village only two miles short of the great prize of Bapaume.

And on Tuesday the 27th, marking eight weeks from the date of his operation, David came down to breakfast. Sister Horrocks and Antonia helped him down the stairs between them, but when he reached the level, he gently pushed them away and walked on his own, with no more than a walking-stick, into the morning-room. Beattie, Sadie and Peter greeted him with applause. He smirked self-consciously, and said, 'I haven't won the Olympic hundred yards, you know.'

'To us, you have,' Sadie said, and went to him to kiss his cheek and whisper, 'My hero!' It was only partly in jest.

Peter jumped about excitedly, but quickly adapted to the

301

new reality, gobbled down his breakfast and asked to be excused. He and Jimmy Covington and Willy Andrews were going to cycle down to Coney Warren to spot planes.

The others settled to the pleasure of a normal breakfast. As Cook was away, there was a hiatus in the flow of porage – the influenza had died down, but she had got into the habit of sending it up every morning. Ada, who was doing the cooking, had recklessly used the bacon ration (they'd have to do without until Friday now) to make sure there was a good showing for David, and as well as that she had cooked his favourite kidneys. Sadie told him he could have hers. She might have been able to get over the taste of kidneys had John Courcy not explained to her, when one of the horses had a urinary problem, what the kidney's function was. There had still been no letter from him, though Mrs Cuthbert had written to him a couple of times. It was almost three months since he had gone back. Sadie was sure, now, that they would not see him again. Despite her determination to be sensible, there was a numb ache in her chest whenever she thought of him.

In the post that morning there was a letter for Beattie from Edward, and a pencil scrawl from William for Sadie which was so difficult to read she could only extrapolate that he had been on a lot of missions and was not wounded, without any of the detail. And there was one for Antonia from her father, which mentioned rather wistfully that it was the traditional holiday month and that he had not seen her or his grandson for a long time. He was glad to hear that David was going on better, but supposed she would not be able to visit him for some time to come.

'But we have lots of empty rooms,' she said aloud. The others looked up. She addressed herself to Beattie, 'Do you think we might invite my father to come and stay for a few days? Once Cook is back – and if I help out with the dusting and bedmaking and so on?'

Beattie felt ashamed for not having thought of it. 'Of course you can invite him,' she said, 'and for as long as he likes to stay. And the servants are quite capable of coping, without your having to do housework. Goodness! Before the war, we used to have people staying all the time.'

'Will he be able to leave the tea-room?' Sadie asked.

'I'm sure he wouldn't have hinted at a visit if he couldn't,' Antonia said.

'I shall be very glad to see him again,' David said. 'We used to have such terrific conversations.'

'And now you're surrounded by nothing but women,' Sadie said mischievously.

'Sometimes, having regard to what you're all doing, I beg leave to doubt it.'

The change in David was very evident in that remark: a couple of months ago, it would have been bitter, resentful; today it was light and affectionate.

Cook came home on Friday night. Ada asked her if she had enjoyed her holiday, and Cook answered, 'Well, I didn't get bombed this time.'

'I'm glad you're back. Mrs David's father's coming to stay, and I expect the missus will want posher food than I can cook.'

'Don't give a person time to get their bags unpacked!' Cook grumbled.

'But Mr David's worlds better. Getting stronger every day. It's a treat to see him.'

'And what about you? Heard from your Len recently?'

'No. But no news is good news, that's what I say,' she said bravely. It was past time for a letter. Len was usually pretty regular.

She had a letter the very next morning. The writing was looser and more untidy than usual, and the first words alarmed her.

303

My dear Wife,

I pen you these few words from the hospital in Étaples, please excuse the scrawl as I am writing propped on my knees. I have been wounded but don't worry, not too bad, just one through the arm, it hasn't spoiled my looks ha ha. Lucky it's my left arm or you wouldn't be able to read this. I copped it from a sniper while on patrol after we had dug in, having put the Hun to flight. They counter-attacked north of Albert, and came on pretty fiercely, but we flung them back to their own lines after heavy casualties. My boys have now been blooded and fought like veterans, I am very proud of them, they are all so young. Everyone is in good spirits, feeling the Hun is now on the run. I hope it will all be over soon so I can come home to you. Don't worry, dearest, the fact that I am in Étaples and not Home tells you they expect me to recover in a week or two and be back to work. I am very well treated and the nurses are Tops. You can write to me here. I think about you all the time and kiss your dear Picture every night. Hoping you are in the Pink,

Your Loving Husband,
Len

It was not just the handwriting that was looser, but the composition. After the stiff little missives she had been used to receiving, this was a veritable outpouring of emotion, and she assumed it was because he had been wounded.

'Len's in hospital,' she told Cook, as soon as they were alone together.

'Oh, my Lord!'

'He says it's not serious,' she said, and explained. 'He says I can write to him at the hospital.'

'We can do better than that,' Cook said firmly. 'We'll make him up a parcel. I got lots of nice stuff in tins, and I'll bake him a cake, and you can put in ciggies and soap and things like that.'

'I've got those socks I'm knitting – they're nearly finished. I can get 'em done if I take 'em to bed tonight. It's just the fold-over at the top.'

'Calf's foot jelly – I've got a jar in the larder.'

'He's not sick, he's wounded, a bullet in the arm.'

'I dare say he needs feeding up all the same, after all that time on army food.'

'Chocolate – I must buy some chocolate. They always like that.'

Happily they planned and packed. Cook was rather puzzled about the contents of her larder, which seemed deficient in some particulars, but she assumed Ada must have used them, and she enjoyed making up the parcel too much to think about it closely.

Mr Weston arrived on Saturday afternoon, full of good humour despite the tedious wartime journey. He hugged his daughter fiercely, extravagantly praised his little grandson, and spent the evening locked in a most satisfying conversation with his son-in-law.

'He seems almost like the David of old,' he said to Antonia, the next morning, when they took a walk around the garden together. 'I think you have turned a corner, my darling.'

'Yes, Daddy. I think so too,' she said, turning to smile at him.

The sunshine striking her face showed up all the new lines in it, and the odd grey hair among the brown curls. How hard it had been for her was written there for him to see. He took her hand and drew it through his arm. 'My brave girl,' he said.

'I'm not brave,' she said. 'It's all those men who go and fight for our freedom. And who suffer for it.'

Women's courage took a different form, he thought; but he knew she didn't like to be praised, so he didn't say it.

'Let's hope everything will go smoothly from now on. And

that little pugilist of a grandson of mine!' The baby had caught him quite a blow when waving his arms about in response to being tickled. 'He's certainly a strong one.'

'I think he's going to be tall, like David. He has very big feet – I believe that's a sign.'

'You're getting some mental stimulation, I hope. It isn't all domestic grind? I'd hate your fine mind to be neglected.'

Antonia laughed. 'Only you could worry about that! But I do read, and David and I discuss the news. And now he's getting better, I expect we'll take up our studies again. How is your work going? Is it still the letters of Pliny?'

'Yes, and it's coming along nicely. In fact, I hope I may be able to have something ready for the publisher early next year.'

'Daddy! I didn't think you'd get it done that quickly, with the tea-room to run single-handed.'

'Well, it's not single-handed, is it? You know Mrs Turnberry's been helping me with it ever since Christmas.'

'I thought that was just now and then,' Antonia said. 'I didn't know it was a regular thing.'

'Oh, she's there almost every day. And she's taking care of things while I'm here, visiting you.'

'That's awfully nice of her. It must interfere with her other activities, having to come over every day.'

'Hmm,' said Mr Weston. 'Well, I did think of that myself. It would be much more convenient if Yvonne didn't have to go home at the end of the day.'

'Yvonne?'

'Pretty name, isn't it?' he said casually.

'Oh, yes, quite pretty. But, Daddy, what would Mrs Bates say if she slept there? I know she could have my old room, but it wouldn't really be proper for her to be staying in the house with you, without a chaperone, now would it?'

He began to answer, then looked at his daughter more closely. 'You minx! You know very well what I'm working up to tell you, don't you?'

She laughed. 'It wasn't hard to guess. And if it's my blessing you're after – yes, Daddy, I approve heartily of your marrying Mrs Turnberry, and I hope you'll be very happy together.'

He looked relieved, and gave her a hug. 'I was afraid you might think it foolish at my age. Or worry that she was taking your place.'

'What a monster of selfishness you must think me,' Antonia said, hugging him back.

'No, I know you're a very superior person. And you'll love her when you get to know her,' he promised.

'I'll love her if she makes you happy – and she seems to. Why didn't you bring her with you?'

'Without an invitation?' he protested.

'Well, invite her now! We'll tell the family at once, and I know Mother-in-law will want her to come.'

He patted her hand. 'Not yet, love. For one thing, she's taking care of the tea-room. And I don't want to overwhelm her when I've only just proposed to her. But you shall meet her before the wedding, I promise you.'

'As soon as David's fully mobile, we'll come and visit you,' Antonia said, and paused, contemplating her own words. 'How wonderful it is to say that. And really to believe it at last.'

On the Sunday, Diana came to luncheon, having herself driven over so that she could bring the two babies – though George, at almost eighteen months, was hardly a baby any more. He was a handsome, sturdy child, and was running everywhere. She brought her nursery-maids, Mildred and Ellen, as well, and after the children had been sufficiently admired in the drawing-room, they were taken to the kitchen to be spoiled, then up to the nursery where Ethel joined them to look after all three Hunter grandchildren together. Marcus, she thought, was far superior to Amyas, but she couldn't help feeling a little warmth towards the young earl, who already had a lot of charm.

Diana was beginning to come to terms with Rupert's death, helped, of course, by the babies. She spent a great deal more time with Amyas than she had with George at the same age; and George was reaching the age where he became interesting as a person. She felt she could see traits of Rupert in him. He loved to laugh, and had learned the trick of pulling Ellen's apron-strings undone when she turned her back to him, which made him giggle wildly. *He's going to be a tease when he's a bit older*, Diana thought fondly.

Dear, faithful Nula helped her, still managing to come over most days to see her, even if only for half an hour. And Padmore, her maid, helped by insisting that she dressed with as much care as before. 'I've my reputation to think of, my lady,' she said. Diana didn't know why it helped to present a perfectly groomed appearance to the world, but somehow it did.

And, strangely, the other Lady Wroughton helped her, too. When she had first emerged from her room after the heart attack, she had looked dreadfully frail – thin to the bone. She seemed to have shrunk, too, to be diminished, though she held herself as upright as ever, but Diana thought now she could see the strain it cost her to do so. Her harsh, big-nosed face was like that of a tired hawk.

Diana had expected her to leave Dene as soon as she was able, and resume her old life, but her physician had told her she must take things quietly, and she found she tired more quickly; so she stayed on in her suite, and Diana became accustomed to seeing her around the place. She liked to see the children, though only for short visits – their energy tired her. One day, Diana was invited to take luncheon with her, not in her suite but in the small dining-parlour. It marked a departure from invalidism and a return to a more normal regime.

The dowager rose – slowly and with effort – from her

chair when Diana came in, and said, 'Come and kiss me, child. I haven't seen you for a day or two.'

Nothing short of her own death would prevent Violet Wroughton dressing correctly, and she was in a smart dress and coat of black figured silk, with full complement of pearls and amethysts, her thinning hair carefully arranged with two jet and pearl combs. She supported herself these days with a long ebony walking-stick topped with a gold dog's head. Diana thought she remembered seeing it in the gun-room, where there was quite a collection of walking-sticks, when she had passed through there once with Charles. The hand gripping the head was bone-thin and roped with blue veins, but still weighted with her usual collection of diamond hoop rings, and a newer mourning band, jet bound with gold and small brilliants. Mourning gems were supposed to be dull, but Violet could not bear a diamond that did not sparkle.

Diana was aware that she was being scrutinised as she crossed the room, and was glad that she could trust Padmore to turn her out correctly. She pecked the offered cheek dutifully, noting the usual smell of Pond's cold cream. The dowager had always despised maquillage, and her maid Pickering had only persuaded her to use the cold cream by claiming it was medicinal. Diana thought that she would have benefited from a touch of lip rouge: her lips and eyelids were the same delicate bluish shade.

'You look tired,' Violet said sharply, gesturing Diana into the chair opposite. 'Shadowed about the eyes. Have you been weeping?'

Diana was surprised by the question into answering truthfully. 'Sometimes. At night. When I think—'

'*Don't* think,' Violet said firmly. 'It is a self-indulgence. People in our position cannot afford it – too many others depend on us. You must be resolute, and when sad thoughts occur, put them out of your mind by concentrating on some duty you have to perform.'

It was the first time Diana could remember her using the words 'our' and 'us' in relation to herself, and she was emboldened to ask, 'Is that what you do?'

She expected to be rebuked for impertinence, but the hooded eyes surveyed her thoughtfully, and she said, 'I have lost a husband and both my sons. But it is harder for you. I am old, and accustomed to loss. And I shall soon be gone myself. You must find a way to continue without us all. But you have two fine sons to live for.' The tone had been kind enough to bring tears to Diana's eyes, and perhaps noticing them, Violet hardened her voice and concluded, 'Besides, it is vulgar to appear with the signs of weeping about one's face. Particularly in wartime. Do not do so again.'

Diana bit her lip and turned her face away, while she struggled to banish the forbidden thoughts.

'You think me harsh?' Violet asked unexpectedly.

'No – no,' Diana mumbled.

'You do,' Violet contradicted. 'But you will find that I am right. Giving in to sadness only prolongs it. Suffering is largely in one's own control. Dedicate yourself to duty, and you will find comfort. And,' she added, in a different voice, 'I shall help you, for as long as I am spared. It may not be long.' She raised a hand to stop Diana from protesting. 'Sir Maurice Enderby likes to flatter me that I am indestructible, but I feel the change within me. I shall not be able to help you for much longer, but I am conscious that I have not done my duty by you in the past. I have neglected you. For that, I apologise, and I hope that you will forgive me, not from any affection you feel for me, for I have no illusions about that, but for the help that I can give you.'

'But I do—'

Again the raised hand. 'You have joined a different stratum of society from that in which you were born, and its responsibilities are largely strange to you. And soon you will be alone to bear them. You must manage and preserve your son's estate until he comes of age. You must fulfil certain public and court duties. You must conduct yourself as a countess and mother of an earl. All of this is daunting to you.'

'Rupert was helping me—' Diana began, but broke off as the dowager closed her eyes, seemed to sway, looking as though she might faint. Diana flung herself to her knees in front of her, taking one of her hands and patting it. It was icy cold. The blueness of the lips had darkened. She controlled the first reaction of panic and said, keeping her voice low and steady, 'What can I do? Shall I ring for Pickering?'

Violet gestured towards her handbag. 'Drops,' she said. Diana found the bottle, uncorked it, held it to the cyanotic lips. Violet, brushed her hand away, took the bottle, dosed herself, and leaned back, hands in her lap, breathing shallowly and rapidly. But in a moment her colour improved, and she opened her eyes. 'Better,' she said.

Diana re-corked the bottle and put it back in the bag, expecting any moment to have her head bitten off. She had touched the dowager, had seen her in her weakness, was even now in an undignified posture – all punishable offences. But, to her astonishment, she found her hand, now resting on the arm of the chair, taken, first in one, then in both of the dowager's. Startled, she met her eyes.

'You have a kind heart,' Violet said, and seemed almost surprised to hear her own words. She hesitated, frowning, and then said, 'I have never cared for anyone to be kind to me. It gives them false expectations. And I do not like to be weak. But you and I . . .' A long pause. 'You and I have both suffered, and we have only each other now. I think perhaps we both need a friend.'

'I – would be honoured to be your friend,' Diana said flinchingly, expecting wrath.

But the dowager said, almost with a smile, 'Good girl.'

311

And then the smile disappeared, the hands were pulled away, and she said, 'Now get up from that ridiculous position and ring for luncheon. And after luncheon, we will walk a little in the garden – Enderby says I must have fresh air – and I will explain one or two things to you.'

It was not to be expected that the dowager would change completely: she was not built for warmth or confiding. But Diana did find it a help to feel that she could go to her for advice, that she was not all alone with her new and heavy responsibilities; and as she grew more confident in her dealings, the dowager seemed to trust her more, and was easier in her presence. And the imperious old woman was certainly fond of her grandsons, allowing herself to unbend with them as she never had with anyone before, not even her own sons. In the children, Diana had a link to her; and it became not unpleasant to spend time in her company. Not a delight, but certainly no longer a penance.

CHAPTER TWENTY

The strike of the entire Metropolitan Police force on the 29th of August took everyone by surprise.

Edward's sister Sonia found herself without someone to complain to. Her husband Aeneas was in Scotland, looking into a business opportunity, and in his absence she was accustomed to rushing to Edward to be reassured. Luckily, she remembered that the Hunters now had the telephone, and she rang Beattie, keeping her standing in the hall when there were dozens of things needing her attention.

'We shall all be murdered in our beds,' Sonia cried. It was her first reaction to most crises, and Beattie wondered vaguely why it was always 'in our beds' when surely at the first hint of riot you would be up and dressed and seizing the nearest poker for self-defence.

The police were poorly paid, being assessed at the level of an agricultural worker or unskilled labourer, and it was galling to the constables to see van boys and bus conductorettes nowadays earning more than they did. They had only one day off a fortnight, and frequently worked ninety-six hours for a week's pay.

The usual view of the public was that they were lowly public servants who didn't deserve more, but their sudden disappearance from the streets made the population of the great city so nervous that the Prime Minister quickly called in troops to guard key points for reassurance. There had been a lot of industrial unrest lately, and the feeling in the government was that if the police could strike no one was safe. Who would quell the unrest if the police would not? Calling on the army to control unarmed civilians was not the British way. That was how the Russian Revolution had started.

Lloyd George met the strikers' leaders the following day and settled with them: a pay rise, a war bonus, a child allowance, a reduction in the pension qualification period from thirty to twenty-six years, and a widow's pension. The Metropolitan Police went back to work, but other cities in the country eyed their forces nervously, and thought they had better see about a pay increase before there was trouble. The commissioner, Sir Edward Henry, was sacked for not having seen it coming, and was replaced by a military man, General Sir Nevil Macready, who it was hoped would get more of a grip on things.

The general concern about the situation, with its underlying fear of revolution, almost eclipsed the good news from the Front: that Bapaume had been taken at last on the 29th – the honour finally fell to the New Zealanders – and Péronne on the first of September with the Australians in the van. Péronne was forty-one miles from Amiens, where the Allies had begun on the 8th of August, less than a month ago. It was heartening progress.

Emily had not returned from holiday. Annoyance was the first reaction. Beattie assumed the girl had made a mix-up, missed the boat or lost her ticket. Cook, too, thought the absence as due to incompetence – or, as she put it, being 'daft as a brush'.

'Couldn't catch a bus at a bus stop,' she grumbled. 'She'll come traipsing back with some excuse, and how am I supposed to manage until then?'

She had to make do with Beryl, who was 'as much use

as a boxing kangaroo', she said, when Beryl managed to knock three eggs off the table with her elbow, then dropped a lump of butter, trod in it and walked it all over the kitchen floor before noticing. It maddened her that Beryl was not upset by these mishaps, and did not quake before Cook's wrath. She only grinned foolishly, said, 'Sorry,' as if it were nothing, and carried on. Cook lamented inwardly the loss of Emily who, after years of training, at least knew her ways.

It was Beryl who revived the idea that the ferry ship might have been sunk by U-boats. She opined with relish that Emily couldn't come back because she'd been 'blown to bits by a torpedo'.

'Don't be silly,' said Ada. 'We'd have read about it in the papers.'

'Might not,' Beryl said stubbornly. 'If there's lots of boats sunk, they can't write up all of 'em, stands to reason.'

When days passed without news, others in the servants' hall began to fear for her. Emily would surely have sent a letter explaining her absence. Ada wondered if perhaps she hadn't the money for a stamp; but if she was that penurious, how was she living at all?

And then Munt reminded them in his usual dispassionate way that Ireland was not a peaceful place: full of German spies, sympathisers and rebels. Lawless, too. 'Could have got caught up in some riot and shot,' he mentioned over the bread-and-jam one mid-morning. 'Or knocked on the head by a robber after dark. Either way . . .' And he shrugged and left it at that. *Either way, we won't be seeing her again.*

Gradually fear for her safety spread, but since there was nothing anyone could do, the only option was to wait and see.

'I don't like to give up hope, madam,' Cook said to Beattie as they discussed the week's meals, 'but we'll have to think about replacing her at some point. Beryl's not really suitable, and while she's helping me, Ada has to do her work as well as her own.'

'Yes, I know it's difficult for you all,' said Beattie. She did not favour the more dramatic suppositions, but was coming round to thinking that, finding herself back 'home', Emily had simply decided to stay there. She had taken everything with her – though that did not mean much, since she had very little except her clothes: it would all go in the one bag.

In fact, Ethel had slipped into her room and seen on the windowsill the china shepherd with the nose missing that she had given to her. It was Emily's most precious possession and Ethel didn't think she would have left without it, knowing she wasn't coming back.

But, of course, she could have had every intention of returning, and changed her mind once she was over there. Being Ethel, she didn't share these thoughts. Let people think it out for themselves, was her motto.

'We'll leave it to the end of the week,' Beattie decreed, 'and then I'll engage a new kitchen-maid.' It shouldn't be too difficult, she thought, even in wartime. Kitchen-maids were the lowest level of servant, and typically started at twelve, when they were too young to work at the more attractive jobs in the factories or on the buses. There was a large Irish population in the narrow roads behind the high street, which was always eager to send its daughters into service to ease the family finances. She'd have a word with Father O'Malley of Our Lady of Perpetual Sorrows – she knew him from several committees in which they both had an interest.

'If she comes back after that,' Beattie concluded, 'she'll have to find herself another place. I gave her one second chance. I can't have my household constantly disrupted by her.'

Events moved so fast that Laura and Ransley didn't have a chance to meet in Amiens, or near it. Ransley's field ambulance followed the troops forward; but once the action reached the old Somme battleground – as pitted as the surface of the moon – the terrain was too rough for the X-ray ambulance and its precious equipment, and they were sent northwards instead towards Arras. Laura and Ransley had to make do with scribbled letters, forwarded by the excellent army postal service. In them, they assured each other that 'it couldn't be long now'. Along an extended front, the Germans were being pushed back towards the position from which they had launched their spring offensive, the Hindenburg Line – a series of defensive fortifications stretching from Cerny, south of Paris, all the way to Arras. To break through the Hindenburg Line was the new objective. Once that was penetrated, the enemy would really be on the run, and it could only be a matter of months before they sued for peace, or were forced to surrender.

Edward often thought of his captain's words – that they were out of the trenches and wouldn't go back in. Morally, spiritually, it was cheering to be on the move, but it took its toll, particularly of those like him who were not in their first flush of youth. He was fitter now, and could cope with the hard marching, the physical exertion and the indifferent food, and like his men he had consigned fear to a sealed compartment in the back of his mind, but he never managed to sleep properly lying on the hard ground. He got up so horribly stiff it was sometimes minutes before he could move, except to stagger in circles and rub the bits of him that hurt worst. His servant, Tillotson, always tried to be on hand with hot coffee – or what passed for it when supplies from home ran out. Edward had had to grow used to Bovril as a substitute, preferable, at any rate, to coffee too weak to taste. Tillotson was young enough to sleep anywhere and rise refreshed, but he was really tactful about putting Edward's boots on for him when he couldn't bend that far.

But like the lady who ran off with the raggle taggle gypsies,

Edward had to get used to sleeping in the cold open field. The Germans were not exactly on the run but retreating steadily; and chasing them, Edward's company was moving forward every day, which meant no billets, no shelters, having to sleep wherever they could, under hedges or in shell holes. The enemy, as they fell back, were burning farms – and since the average French farm was made mostly of wood, there was little left afterwards to the service of the pursuing British. The Boche were looting, too, carrying off whatever they could, and destroying the rest, slaughtering animals, burning crops, and even contaminating or blocking up wells, something that was anathema to any civilised person. It was no wonder, Edward thought, they were so hated.

His letter of the 4th of September said,

I am writing this in comparative comfort, as we have come across some old trenches, beaten down at some point by artillery fire so they are only four feet deep, but there are dug-outs scooped out of the side, which give us better shelter than we have had for a while. Mine has a corrugated-iron roof, and when we hung the oilsheet over the opening and lit the candle inside, we were quite cosy. Somebody left behind a stove made out of an old biscuit tin, and my servant has promised burgoo tonight, which is crushed biscuit and bully beef, fried. I promise you it is a treat, much better than bully and biscuit "au naturel". I have a little coffee left, so I think I shall celebrate all this luxury and have a cup afterwards – I've been keeping it for a special occasion.

I must tell you that two days ago we were sent to attack a German position. We were in the second wave, and were to relieve the first wave, which went over at dawn. We arrived about midday, and found no Germans and none of our men. It seemed Fritz had not waited for the attack but had slipped away in the night and our chaps

318

had gone on. We followed, but marched all day without finding the enemy. We kept meeting men coming back, and they all said the same: "We've lost Fritz." Fritz was retreating so fast, it was evening before we caught up with our own first wave and found the new position where Fritz had stopped and turned at last. He gave us a hot welcome, however. There is hard campaigning ahead, but we all feel that the war is approaching a conclusion and we shall have them down and out for the count next spring, or soon afterwards.

The success was not without cost. The next morning dawned fine and clear, a little chilly, warning that autumn was coming, and at five twenty a.m. Edward's company, led by Captain Campion, attacked the new German position.

They had been sheltering in a ditch behind what was left of a hedgerow, and it was rather like 'going over the top' to stand up, when the minute hand of his watch reached the appointed hour, and say, 'Come on, my lads!' They climbed out after him, and he was struck, not for the first time, with the realisation that they would follow him without question for as long as they remained on their feet. Their trust in him ought to have been daunting, but instead it gave him a curious courage. He would not flinch, because if he didn't, they would not. And out in front was Campion, who would not flinch either, for the same reason. The men advanced into German machine-gun fire as calmly as though it was nothing but a swarm of gnats bent on spoiling a picnic.

They took the machine-gun post that was causing them trouble and barring the way for the rest of the advance, but Edward lost six of his remaining men. And Campion was badly wounded. A runner brought Edward to his side. Campion, white and sweating with pain, said, 'I'm afraid I'm out of it.'

Edward did what he could to make him comfortable until

319

the stretcher bearers reached them. He knelt beside him, aware that blood was seeping through his trouser knees.

'Gaunt's dead,' Campion said, referring to one of the other platoon commanders. 'That makes you senior. You'd better take over the company. Send word to HQ. They'll confirm. Damn it,' he added weakly, 'I was hoping to see it through to the end. I've been out since 'fifteen. Never been wounded. Led a charmed life.' He gripped Edward's arm and met his eyes earnestly. 'Stick it out, old chap. But keep your head down. Be at the end for me.'

Edward nodded, and patted his hand, then men wanting orders forced him to move away. When he returned, Campion had gone, taken back to the regimental aid post. Edward heard later that he had died there soon afterwards.

He had sent a message to HQ, and received a reply by return confirming that he was now Acting Captain Hunter and in command of the company. He did not feel any satisfaction in the promotion just then, coming as it did. And there was no glory in it, just distracting responsibility. He was surrounded by men asking him what to do.

'We dig in here for the moment. They'll be sending up food.' He set the sentries, and passed on Campion's most important advice, 'Keep your heads down.'

He was determined to be at the end for him.

It was not as easy at home to believe that the war was heading for a conclusion. Everything there seemed depressingly the same – the same shortages, the same rationing, the same steady influx of wounded, the same notices of death. Committee meetings, collecting for causes, helping in canteens, bandage-rolling, knitting, making up parcels for the Tommies – that was the reality for those who did not have jobs; and for those who did, it was hard work in usually uncomfortable conditions. Women in trousers with scarves round their hair, or hard-wearing skirts and tough lisle stockings; few men around, except the very young and the very old. Soldiers in the streets in uniform, or hospital blue; or, hardest to bear, out of uniform for good, in wheel-chairs, on crutches with one empty trouser leg, or with hopeless eyes selling matches on street corners. It was in the nature of things that, back home, they saw the bad consequences of the war, rather than any of the triumph.

Everything seemed to be getting shabby, too. In London the bomb damage remained unrepaired or crudely patched. No-one had time to wash buses or lorries, clean windows or sweep the streets. Gardens and window-boxes were devoid of flowers. People needed new clothes, shoes were worn out because the cobblers had gone to the Front, and shop windows displayed only dull, utilitarian things. There was a sense that the pleasure had gone out of life. And for so many, of course, it had, with the death of a husband, father, son, nephew, cousin. The population at home had not got out of the trenches. For them it was the same old slog, with no end in sight.

Beattie had not followed the war news with great attention in the past, but she was learning now that it was Edward who had kept her up to scratch, passing on what was impor-tant and, more pertinently, explaining it to her. Now she had to try to catch hold of the war's tail, just as it was becoming more elusive than ever. When the Front had run in a static line of trenches from Switzerland to the sea, it was easy enough to grasp what was happening: one or other side made an attack and was repulsed or advanced a mile or two. Now the Front was fragmented, the army seemed to be operating in small, almost discrete units, and the place names in the despatches were mostly unfamiliar.

Since that one emotional screed when he had asked her if they could start again, Edward's letters had gone back to being not exactly formal but at any rate neutral, as if penned for the whole family to read. She hardly knew what she had replied to it: the outpouring of feelings was not in her nature. Even if she had managed to gush, she thought he would have found it suspicious. She hoped she had managed to indicate receptiveness; she hoped, at least, that her reply had not been cold. But whatever it had been, it could not have been what was wanted, because he did not refer to the question again, and wrote instead about the war and his part in it. She felt a sickening sense of opportunity missed – like the misjudged step at the end of the flight that has you plummeting through a void.

They still had no word from Emily, and, nudged out of her distracted thoughts by Cook, Beattie had acquired a new kitchen-maid with the help of Father O'Malley: a diminutive, skinny child called Eileen, who claimed to be twelve but, presumably from under-nourishment, looked more like eight or nine. She was awed into silence by the sight of the Big House where she was to live and work, and for the first few days she crept about with enormous eyes and lips clamped shut, starting like a deer when anyone spoke to her. For once made sympathetic by her own woes, Beattie imagined her sobbing into her pillow at night.

But Eileen was lucky in that, the day before her arrival, Cook had had a letter from Fred, which had put her in such a good mood she was loftily kind to the child rather than fierce, told her if she was a good girl and did what she was told, she had nothing to fear, and tutted at her thinness rather than regarding it with suspicion. She did enquire rather sharply if Eileen had worms, and on being assured that she didn't, she set to making sure that the child had proper nourishment.

'Not like you to care,' Ethel commented sourly one day, when Cook pressed an extra potato on the kitchen-maid with the words 'Got to keep your strength up.'

Cook looked dignified and said, 'She'll be more use to me if she's bigger and stronger, stands to reason.' She didn't want anyone to think she was turning soft.

Eileen had much less imagination than Emily, and so was prepared to take Cook at face value, and behaved before her as she did before any authority figure: humble and obedient. As for the hard work – rising early, scrubbing the floors, blackleading the range, peeling stones of potatoes, fetching in the coal, washing mountains of dishes – she had got used to that at home. Here was better than home, more comfortable, quieter, and with much more food; and though she missed her family, they were only a mile away, and she could walk over and see them when she had her time off, so she was content.

She was naturally curious about the girl who had had her bed before her, and it was Beryl who told her Emily had been blown to bits by a torpedo. The china figurine on the windowsill had belonged to the unfortunate Emily. Eileen didn't like it: its nose was missing, and she got it into her head that Emily's nose had been blown off when the torpedo struck. She wondered whether Emily's ghost would haunt the house – not because she was imaginative, but because ghosts were part of her national heritage, from the Holy Ghost downwards, and their visitations were only to be expected. But nothing happened in the first few nights, and once she had turned the figurine round so she couldn't see its face, she didn't mind it, and sensibly put all thoughts of former maids, torpedoes and ghosts out of her head.

The war news was galvanising to David, who came down to breakfast every day now, and rattled his way through the newspaper, reading bits out to whoever else was there. If Beattie asked questions, he would gladly explain to her what was going on, but he had not Edward's knack of trimming the information to fit her, so she tended to stop listening

323

after a bit, just nodding and murmuring encouragement when he seemed to need it.

It was wonderful to see him so much better. He was walking now, leaning heavily on a stick – he had not yet learned to trust the wounded thigh – but at least it was not a crutch. It did not hurt him directly to walk, though it ached afterwards, and there were sharper pains if he overdid it. Highwood Road had to get used to the sight of David Hunter limping slowly up and down the pavement for his daily exercise, from The Elms to the corner and back. Little Hilda Lane, the butcher's delivery girl, fell off her bike with excitement the first time she saw him – though as the bike was too big for her, falling off it didn't exactly need a reason – and he stopped to help her. To have him carefully push the errant packages of meat towards her with the end of his stick, while apologising that he couldn't bend to pick them up, just as if she were a lady, had her all of a dither.

Between the better war news and his undeniable progress towards normality, he was more cheerful than he had been in two years. Antonia felt the difference, and was sometimes caught singing under her breath as she went about the house. He was beginning to discuss the future with her, where before he had assumed that there wouldn't be one. 'I don't know if I want to follow my father into the bank,' he said to her one Sunday, as they walked slowly together back from church. The rest of the household had gone on ahead, because he would need to rest two or three times, sitting on convenient garden walls. 'It would probably be the sensible thing. He could arrange a good start for me.'

'Wouldn't you like to go back to university, finish your degree?' she asked. With her hand resting on his arm, she felt as though they were a normal couple.

'I don't think so. I'm too old – I'd be too far behind the others. But I have wondered about the academic life. Perhaps teaching is the way for me. I could combine that with study.'

324

'Teaching little boys their Latin grammar?' she said, trying not to sound doubtful.

'They don't have to be *very* little,' he said. 'There are older boys at school as well, you know. Sixth-formers.'

Antonia suspected you would not be able to choose, if you worked in a school, and that a certain basic love of the boyish mind and habits would be a prerequisite to being happy as a schoolmaster; but these were early days. Once he was walking with confidence, the whole world would be open to him. No need to decide yet.

One day she was giving him his massage. She usually did it after he had his bath, to save him having to undress and dress again. He lay on the bed, with a towel over his middle for decency's sake, and she worked on the damaged leg as Sister Horrocks had taught her. Horrocks was no longer with them, having left two weeks ago. It was now twelve weeks since the operation, and since Horrocks had said that after three months they ought to be able to be confident of a recovery, Antonia was choosing to be confident. She usually massaged the other leg as well, for it took extra strain and the muscles tightened up. She was just about to begin on it when she became aware of David's eyes on her, and looked up to see an unusual expression on his face.

'What is it?' she asked nervously. 'Did I hurt you?'

'Do you remember,' he said slowly, 'on our wedding night, when you said we would just have to manage somehow?'

She blushed at the reference. 'Yes, I remember,' she said.

'Well,' he said, 'how do you feel about managing again?'

'What – now?' she exclaimed.

'Right now. The door's locked, isn't it?'

'Yes, but – at this time of day?'

He took her hand and laid it on the towel. 'Seems a shame to waste an opportunity.'

She flooded with joy. She had never had any illusions that he loved her romantically. Lately, she had believed he viewed her more as a nurse than a wife, and she had supposed that side of their life together was over. She had even wondered, nervously, in those haunted moments in the middle of the night, whether when he was well again he would fall in love with someone else – someone more like his ideal, more like Sophie, his first love, who had jilted him – and leave her.

So she was grateful to find that she was still a woman to him – and even more than that, she was delighted because it showed how much better he was feeling.

'I'll just pull the curtains,' she said.

He smiled. 'Do you think a blackbird will come and look in at us?' he teased.

But it seemed wrong to her to be doing it in broad daylight. She closed the curtains and, in the kindly gloom, came back to the bed and began undressing herself with nervous, excited fingers.

She hoped she could remember how to do it. She hoped she could still please him. She hoped she would manage not to hurt his leg.

She hoped no-one would come tap-tap-tapping on their door in the middle of it.

It was not unusual for an RAF squadron to receive visitors. Most of their flying was done by day, and in the evenings, pilots liked to exercise their sociability. Sometimes they drove into the nearest town, and sometimes groups from other squadrons came over for a mess dinner.

What surprised William was to be asked for by name by the visiting pilot, who he was told was chatting at that moment to the CO. It turned out to be a tall, lean, bronzed American, who swivelled as William came in and flashed a huge, white smile at him.

'William! Cousin William!'

'Fergie! I wouldn't have recognised you! I haven't seen you since – what was it? – the Easter of 1914.'

'You haven't changed much,' Fergie said. The cousins shook hands vigorously. 'Just the same long rasher of wind, as our old nanny used to say. How's Aunt Beattie?'

'Pretty well,' William said. 'Busy with war-work.'

'And Uncle Edward's over here, I believe? That's a queer start.'

'It was a bit of a surprise. But he's made captain already. We're very proud of him. How's—'

The CO interrupted him: 'Why not take the conversation to the bar? I'm sure our visitor would like to wet his whistle.' William realised the Old Man needed to get on with some work, and apologised. The CO shook Fergie's hand, said he would be the guest of honour in the mess that evening, and gently shoved the two young men out of his office.

Outside, William hesitated. It seemed a bit early for the bar, especially as they had all evening. 'Like to go down to the sheds?' he asked, as one offering a great treat.

Fergie's face lit. 'I was hoping you'd ask. What've you got?' They turned together and walked off briskly.

'Mostly SEs,' William said, 'but we've just had a couple of Camels delivered.'

'Yes, that's what I heard,' Fergie grinned. 'The timing of this visit wasn't completely coincidental. Have you tried one yet?'

'No, but I'm hoping to. They're the best, if you can handle them. What have *you* got?'

'SEs and Spads,' said Fergie.

They had a long and enjoyable technical discussion, first walking down to the sheds and then with the ground crew. The Camels had tremendous torque, which meant they could turn astonishingly fast, but by the same token they could easily go into a fatal spin. You had to know how to handle them. William was determined to be one who did.

'Well, good luck,' Fergie said. 'They say they kill as many pilots as Germans. But I'd love a shot at one.'

327

On the way back to dinner, William asked after his uncle and aunt in Ireland.

'Oh, they're pretty well, I gather,' said Fergie. 'I haven't been able to get over there yet. I will as soon as I have some leave. But I get letters, of course. Ma's a great writer. She's pretty cheesed off with Johnnie and me for coming back, after all the trouble she and Pa took to send us to the States. But, honestly, how could we stay there when all this was going on?'

'I'd have felt just the same. Where's Johnnie now?'

'He's still with the infantry. He didn't make the switch when I did – didn't fancy flying, can you imagine?'

William shook his head. 'It beats me.'

'He's somewhere on the other side of Amiens, next door to a French unit. He seems to like it on the ground. But he was always mad about guns, right from a kid, so I suppose it suits him. Me, I don't care about the armament side of it, though I'll shoot a Jerry when I have to, of course. But if I couldn't fly, I wouldn't touch this war.'

William thought the years in America had changed his cousin, who had seemed, if memory served him, a rather dreamy child, a bit of a Mummy's boy. And, of course, he reflected, having lived all his life in Ireland before going to 'the States', as he'd called it, he wouldn't have the same fierce sense of patriotism that had driven William, and David and Bobby before him, to volunteer. William was glad to be a flier rather than a foot-slogger, but he would have served in the infantry if that was the only way he could serve. Saving his country came first.

When they reached the mess, they found word of the visitor had spread, and most of the pilots were assembled, ready to give him the squadron's traditional greeting. Silver tankards were the custom, filled with beer for ordinary guests, and with champagne for honoured guests. The pilots' taste for champagne, set by the CO (there was a saying, 'A mess

328

takes the complexion of its colonel') meant that a large proportion of visitors ended up designated as 'honoured'.

They had a piano in the mess, and one of the pilots was a talented player; another had a clarinet, and a third could play the drums, though the best they could muster for him was a pair of biscuit tins. Between them, they could knock out ragtime well enough to please all but the fussy. Champagne was quaffed to 'The Darktown Strutters' Ball', while conversation rose until the noise was as thick as the cigarette smoke.

They were all young, most of them under twenty; and the squadron lost men at the rate of at least one a week from death, injury or capture. A pilot's life in France, it was calculated, typically lasted no more than six weeks. So they made merry while they could, and to the top of their bent.

Since David was recovering, Diana was a more frequent visitor to The Elms, having herself driven over with the children, which pleased Beattie greatly. And she showed herself a more thoughtful sister than had always been the case by offering the car and chauffeur to Antonia and David, if he would like to go out somewhere, for a change of scene. It was the sort of invitation – 'Just ring up whenever you want it' – that is not usually acted upon, out of diffidence or politeness, but Antonia could be ruthless when it came to David's comfort, and she bullied him into taking advantage of it. He had spent most of the last two years inside the same four walls, so it did wonders for his spirits to see a wide horizon and a long view.

Diana received a letter one day at the end of September, from the Front. It gave her a jolt, for she didn't expect any good news from that quarter. She wondered for a moment if it was her father writing to her, but a moment's reflection told her it was not his handwriting. Reluctantly, with an odd sense that the action was going to provoke some unwelcome change in her life, she opened the envelope.

It was from Ivo Rainton, written from 'Somewhere in France', and it was short. His brother, Lord Teesborough – who had been Rupert's best man at their wedding – had been wounded.

It must have been a bad one, because he was sent back to Blighty, and I've been trying to find out where he is. I've just learned that he is at Dene Park. I can't get any leave just yet, the way things are, so please, Diana, could you find it in your heart to visit Guy and make sure he has everything he needs? And, if it's not too much trouble, write and let me know how he is? My mother, as you know, is with the hospital in Malta so there's no-one to keep an eye on him, or I wouldn't trouble you.

Diana recollected hearing that Rupert's godmother, Lady Teesborough, who was a driving force in the Red Cross, had gone abroad to improve the administration of some hospital or other. She hadn't taken much notice at the time, and had not realised it was Malta, but she quite saw one could not get back from there in short order.

Guy, here at Dene? She never went into the hospital wing, and beyond seeing medical people and convalescents sometimes in the grounds, would hardly have known it was there. The private gardens, where she took the air, were off-limits for all hospital personnel, and the servants were ferocious about keeping them out of the wing retained for the family. Even so, she felt slightly ashamed that she had not known Guy was in her house. She got up at once to go and visit him.

She was dressed for home, in a plain black frock, with no jewellery, and with her hair drawn back into a simple chignon; even so, she was surprised to be addressed by a doctor, as she passed into the hospital wing, with friendly informality.

'Hello! What are you doing here?' he said, looking her over in a way that she had not encountered in a long time. It put her slightly off balance.

'I live here,' she found herself answering.

'Oh, really? One of the maids, I suppose,' said the doctor, misunderstanding her plain black dress. 'Well, don't let your mistress find out you're over this side. Our landlady's a real Tartar, so I hear. The dowager. And she's mustard on keeping us apart.'

Diana blinked in surprise, then realised he must be talking about her mother-in-law – probably didn't know there were *two* dowagers. He was young – in his late twenties, she supposed – and quite good-looking, or she might have been haughty with him. As it was, it rather tickled her to be mistaken for one of her own maids, and she hadn't felt tickled for a long time.

'So, what brings you here?' the doctor pursued. 'Come to give us a hand? There are quite a few chaps who would love to be visited by a pretty girl. Boost their spirits no end.'

'Yes,' said Diana, deciding on the instant. Why hadn't she thought of it before? 'I would like to visit. I've done it before, at Mount Olive, at the beginning of the war. But just now, I need to see one particular patient, if you could tell me where he is.'

The doctor, hearing her accent, was beginning to wonder if he had made a fool of himself. 'What's his name?' he asked, looking her over again with a more discerning eye.

'Lord Teesborough,' Diana said, and, with a sense of mischief she hadn't known she had, 'He was my husband's best friend.'

'Yes, I know him. I'll take you to him,' said the doctor. 'I say, I hope I haven't been – that is, I didn't know—'

'Perhaps I should have introduced myself. I'm your land-lady – the dowager.'

'Oh, I say! Look here,' he began to apologise.

'My mother-in-law is also dowager countess,' she said kindly. 'And she *is* a Tartar. You're wise to be careful of her.'

'I should have known. I'm sorry,' said the doctor. 'Please come this way – er – your ladyship.'

She walked beside her chastened guide and, as the amusement drained out of her, asked, 'Can you tell me in what way Lord Teesborough is wounded?'

'It was a shell blast. He has a broken arm and some minor cuts on the face, but it's his leg that was badly messed up. He had one lot of surgery in the general at Étaples, before they sent him home. We've had another go, and we've managed to save it, I'm glad to say, so as long as infection doesn't set in . . .'

'I understand,' Diana said. She thought of David's long struggle, and didn't have the heart to ask for any more detail.

It was strange to see the ballroom full of beds and screens, with white-veiled nurses bustling about among them. Down the centre there was a row of tables and chairs at which ambulant patients were sitting, reading or playing cards.

She was led up to a bed, in which Guy Teesborough was lying, propped on pillows, his right arm in plaster and a sling, a sticking-plaster on his forehead under the crest of his hair, and a healing cut down his right cheek. The bedclothes, she noticed, were raised on a cradle over his right leg. His eyes were closed in his white face, and he seemed to be dozing.

'He might be a bit groggy,' said the doctor. 'He had surgery yesterday, and he's been given quite a lot of morphine since then.'

'Oh,' she said. 'Then I won't disturb him. I can come back another time.' She was about to turn away, when his eyes opened.

'I'm not asleep,' he said vaguely, and looked at her so

332

blankly, she was afraid his mind had gone. But he said, 'Diana,' which relieved her of one fear. Then he said, 'What are you doing here?'

It was the second time she had been asked that. 'I live here,' she said.

'In France?'

'No, at Dene Park.'

'I'm not in France?' His voice was creaky with disuse. 'I thought I was at the big hospital in Étaples.'

'You were, but they sent you home,' she said patiently. 'You're at Dene Park now. You know they've turned half of it into a hospital?'

'Dene Park,' he repeated. The doctor had brought her a chair, and she sat beside him. 'Dene Park?'

'That's right,' she said.

She watched his face as consciousness seeped back in, and then memory. His left hand gripped her forearm. 'Diana, tell me,' he said urgently, his voice much weaker than his grip. 'You'll tell me the truth. They've taken my leg, haven't they?'

'No,' she said, as calmly as she could. 'They managed to save it.'

'You can tell me,' he said, scanning her face with desperation. 'I can take it.'

'Truly, Guy,' she said. 'I promise I'm telling the truth. Your leg's still there.'

He closed his eyes. 'Thank God,' he whispered. Then he opened them, surveyed her face again. 'Rupert,' he said. 'Oh, Diana, I'm so sorry.'

'I'm – coming to terms with it,' she said. 'Life goes on.'

'Yes, it does,' he said, gazing at her intently. Then he sighed, and his eyelids drooped. 'Sorry,' he said. 'They've got me doped up. Not making much sense.'

'Go to sleep,' she said. 'I'll stay until you drop off.'

'You'll come again?' he asked anxiously.

She smiled. 'I live here, remember? I'll come and visit you every day.'

He nodded, and closed his eyes, and she watched his breathing. She thought he had dropped off, and tried to withdraw her arm, but his hand clenched on it; so she sat quietly until it relaxed and she was sure he was really asleep.

CHAPTER TWENTY-ONE

Christopher Beresford's sister Catherine had come home on leave, and he invited Sadie to lunch with them both.

'I know you'll love her,' he said. 'She's a tremendous sport – just like you.'

Sadie had always felt that being told you were going to love someone was the surest way to make you dislike them on sight, but there was no way to refuse without being rude, and she didn't want to hurt Beresford's feelings, so on Saturday the 5th of October she went up to Town on the train and took the Underground to Piccadilly Circus, where the Beresfords met her.

She guessed he wanted to show her off to his sister, so she had done her best for him by wearing the rust-coloured linen jacket and skirt, which she knew suited her colouring, with a cream blouse and the little pearl brooch Diana had given her at her wedding. It was unusually warm for October, with pleasant hazy sunshine and no sign of rain, so she had been happy not to wear an overcoat or carry an umbrella. She hoped she looked, if not pretty, at least as if she was making an effort.

Sadie would have known Catherine even had she not been standing beside her brother, because she looked very like him, with wiry fair hair, cut very short, blue eyes and freckles. She was very tall and her hands and face were tanned by weather. She was wearing FANY uniform – hard-wearing khaki skirt and tunic – complete with the khaki puttees and brown shoes, and the soft hat, which Sadie thought must be rather stifling in this mild weather. The stern outfit also made Sadie's feel rather frivolous.

She gave Sadie a beaming a smile and thrust out her hand. 'I'm delighted to meet you at last. Kit's written so much about you.' She had an unusually deep voice and a forthright manner. 'Can I call you Sadie? Call me Cat, won't you? Everyone does.'

Sadie shook the hand, noting the hardness of the palm, the short-cut nails, the indelible oil stains, the calluses and grazes. This was the hand of a working woman, like her.

'Kit?' she queried mildly. She had never heard him called that.

'I know – Kit and Cat! I suppose we thought it was funny when we were children, and it's stuck. You mustn't hold it against us.'

'Cat's really quite sensible,' Beresford said. 'Almost as sensible as me.'

'You? You're the dreamer of the family!' Cat cried, with a fond smile. 'Has he shown you his watercolours, Sadie? When the gifts were handed out, he got the artistic talent and I got the practical skills. The only oils I understand are the ones in engines.'

'I thought he was an expert on tractors,' Sadie said, enjoying her rather exclamatory style.

'It's all on paper,' Cat said seriously. 'I doubt if he'd even recognise one if he bumped into it in a field.'

'Oh, what a calumny!' Beresford protested. 'If it was in a field, it would have to be either a cow or a tractor, and I know what a cow looks like.'

'Kit tells me you're driving an ambulance too,' Cat said to Sadie, as they began to walk down Piccadilly.

'Oh, it's nothing like your sort of driving, I'm sure,' Sadie said. 'I just ferry the wounded from the station to the hospital.

Nice, safe suburban roads and nobody shooting at me. You must have had some exciting adventures.'

'I don't know that they're exciting, exactly,' Cat said, 'but I wouldn't change my life for anyone's, even though my poor mother disapproves.'

'We have to keep the worst of it from her,' Beresford said, 'or she'd have a conniption.'

'My father felt the same way about my aunt when she went to France to drive an ambulance,' Sadie said, 'but he got over it. He's terribly proud of her now.'

'Is she still out there? What's her name?'

'Aunt Laura? She's driving an X-ray ambulance now. The last I heard she was somewhere near Arras.'

'Oh, Laura Hunter? Handsome, dark-haired woman, ambulance called Matilda?'

'Do you know her?' Sadie said in surprise.

'I've met her. It's a small world over there, especially for us women,' Cat said. 'And everybody knows about Laura Hunter anyway, because of Artemis House. It was a damned shame it got bombed out. She was doing something very valuable for the cause of women.'

'Are you a suffragist?' Sadie asked.

'Of course. Aren't you?'

'Well, in *spirit* I am, but I've never done anything about it. I was too young before the war – and there's never time for anything *but* the war nowadays.'

'What you're doing is just as good as any banner-waving,' Cat said emphatically. 'Better, in fact. We are *proving* that we're as good as men.' She caught Sadie's glance at Beresford, and laughed. 'Oh, don't worry about Kit. He's one of us. And when he goes into Parliament, he's going to get us the equal franchise – aren't you, little brother?'

'No politics over luncheon!' Beresford ordered. 'Now, Sadie, I hope you're happy with the Ritz. I wanted us all to have lunch at the flat, but I'm without a housekeeper temporarily.'

'And that would have meant *me* cooking,' Cat interrupted.

'*Do* you cook?' Sadie asked, impressed.

'I have two dishes, and they're both sausages.'

'*Two* sausage dishes?'

'Sausages with onions, and sausages with no onions.'

They had a pleasant and lively luncheon at the Ritz, which was full, as always, with soldiers on leave and their families, the London-based, and a multitude of women eating together unchaperoned in the benign safety of the famous dining-room. Cat recounted some of her more interesting and exciting adventures, and made Sadie tell her at length about her work with the horses; and Beresford revealed, as an excuse for ordering champagne, that he had just been promoted to head of his department.

'It means a pay increase as well,' Cat said. 'He won't tell you, because it's indelicate to talk about money, but it's a substantial one. And, best of all, it comes with a real increase in influence.'

'Congratulations,' Sadie said, a little at sea.

'One has to think about what happens after the war,' Cat enlightened her. 'And it's my firm intention to see him stand for Parliament.'

Beresford laughed. 'You make me sound like a noddy, ruled by my sister. Tell her it's been my ambition too, for a long time.'

'I didn't know,' Sadie said. 'You've never mentioned it.'

'I wouldn't have, either, until it was more likely to be fulfilled. But this promotion is a good start.'

He changed the subject then, with a firm look at his sister, who, Sadie suspected, might be a bit of a 'blurter' – certainly not someone dedicated to tact above all considerations. When they had finished pudding, Beresford suggested that they go back to the flat for coffee, rather than take it in the restaurant. 'I've got some very nice beans that someone gave me.'

338

'And he makes it strong enough to taste, thank God,' Cat put in. 'The worst part of the war is not being able to get a decent cup. And,' she added, as if it were the clinching argument, 'if we go to the flat, I can show you his paintings because *he* won't. Too modest.'

The flat in Baker Street was the one Beresford and Cat had shared since the family home had been sold, though since joining the FANY Cat was not often there. She insisted on showing Sadie around, while Beresford made the coffee. It was large, light, and pleasantly furnished in the modern style. There was a handsome marble-floored entrance hall, a large drawing-room, and an adequate dining-room. There was a large bedroom, a smaller second bedroom, an even smaller third bedroom that Beresford used as a study, a bathroom, an enormous kitchen, and behind the kitchen a maid's bedroom and lavatory, by the back door onto the service balcony and stairs.

'It isn't grand,' Cat concluded, 'but it's very comfortable, and so handily placed – two minutes' walk from the station.'

Sadie agreed, wondering why she sounded as though she was trying to sell it to her.

They drank their coffee in the drawing-room, while Sadie looked through a folder of Beresford's watercolours that Cat had brought to her, despite his protests. Sadie didn't know much about art, but she thought they were very good, with a flowing style and well-chosen colours. They were all rural subjects, ranging from wide landscapes to groups of farm buildings, cottages and village scenes. She particularly liked one of a village green with the church in the background and a working horse being watered at the pond. He hadn't got the horse right, she thought – horses were terribly difficult to paint – but the buildings and the trees were well done, and the sky was very convincing, milky with hazy cirrus clouds.

When they finished the coffee, Cat excused herself, saying

that she must go to her bedroom and sort out some things to take back with her when she left the next day; and Sadie said she should be getting home. She shook hands with Cat, who said she hoped she would see a great deal of Sadie in the future, and then Beresford said he would go with her to the station.

'The good thing about the flat,' he said, as they walked, 'is that it's so close to Baker Street station, which means an easy journey home for you.'

Sadie assented, wondering why he and Cat had both said it.

'For the future, I mean,' he added.

'I don't follow you,' Sadie said vaguely. They had reached the station entrance, and she was feeling in her pocket for her return half. As her hand emerged with the ticket, it was taken by Beresford, who then captured the other hand, too, and turned her to face him.

'I wasn't really meaning to do it here,' he said, with an embarrassed look, 'but it's so hard to find time to be together, and alone, isn't it? Sadie, I'm asking you to marry me. We've been seeing each other for a long time now. I suppose I ought to have waited until the war was over, but I've just had that promotion, which means I am in a position to support a wife. We can live in the flat to begin with – Cat's getting married next year, so she won't be there for long – which will be handy for you for visiting your family. And, of course, after the war, we can find a house somewhere, anywhere you like, as long as I can travel into London all right, for work. I expect you'll want to live in the country, for the horses, but the Metropolitan Line's very good. I mean, it could even be in Northcote, if you wanted. As to my prospects,' he went on as Sadie drew a breath to speak, 'the Civil Service is very safe, and promotion is steady, if you don't blot your copybook, with a gong at the end of it. And there's always the possibility of getting into Parliament, which would mean, as well as the influence and prestige, some lucrative directorships, so I think I can promise to be able to keep you in comfort and horses – and as many children as you'd like.'

He stopped at last, and it was a good thing, really, that he had spoken at such length, because it had come as a great shock, and she had needed time to assimilate it. She had not expected a proposal – well, not *now*, although she had suspected that one might come at some time in the future. And she had decided, since John had lapsed into his silence, that if he did propose, she had to be level-headed about her life, do the sensible thing and accept him.

In a single flash, like a landscape revealed by lightning, she saw that future. She saw herself a bride leaving the church on his arm, pelted with flower-petals by beaming well-wishers. She saw them living in that nice flat, a Town couple, going to concerts and the theatre, gathering a circle of educated friends for intimate suppers. She saw them in the country, with a house, a dog, stables at the back. He would learn to ride, they would hack together. They would drive out in an open car. People would come to stay at weekends. She saw herself a mother, with two fair-haired children. She saw the children leave home, and herself and Beresford sink into comfortable, be-cardiganed middle age, still good companions. He would play golf. She would be a pillar of the church, arrange flowers, head committees, do good works. A pleasant life, useful, comfortable, normal, fulfilling every human need.

She looked up into his eager face, and knew she couldn't do it. It was the rational, level-headed choice, and she was extremely lucky to be offered it, but she couldn't do it *to him*. She didn't love him. She liked him, was fond of him, could probably live her whole life with him without great unhappiness; but to withhold from him something she had pledged already to someone else, something she saw in his eager eyes he wanted from her, would simply have been wrong. She could live, she thought, with being unhappy, but not with being wrong.

'I can't,' she said. It was like hitting a puppy – his eyes flinched, his smile wavered. 'I'm so sorry. I like you awfully, but I don't love you in that way.'

He still had hold of her hands. 'Don't say "no" without thinking about it. I don't need an answer right away. I've surprised you, you weren't ready. I can wait as long as you like. We're awfully good together, and the rest will follow. You haven't thought, perhaps, what it means – love, and so on. I love you, Sadie, and it would make all our people so happy if we married.'

Gently she disengaged her hands from his, with an ache in her chest like a pulled muscle. 'I do know what love means,' she said, 'and I wish I loved you, but I don't. I'd rather do anything than hurt you, but I can't marry you, so please don't ask me again. And please don't think I'll change my mind, because I won't. And now I must go or I'll miss the train. Thank you so much for a lovely luncheon.'

She turned away, took a few rapid steps; then went back, reached up and kissed his cheek, and said, 'I think your paintings are awfully good. And I'll always be your friend.' And then she almost ran.

In the train on the way home, she tried not to think about any of it, for fear of crying in public. But the rhythmic chant of train wheels translated itself in her mind into the words, 'You've lost a friend; you've lost a friend.'

And I didn't have very many to start with, she thought miserably.

William's whole squadron had gathered in the mess for the briefing. The CO had a riding-crop that he carried some-times, to give his hands something to do, and he slapped his thigh with it rhythmically as he spoke, the sign of his inner tension.

'Right, chaps, pay attention,' he said. 'We've got a big show on today. There's an all-out attack in progress on the Hindenburg Line. The Boche is taking it in the neck, and our job is to stop his reinforcements coming up, and to hinder and harass his retreat. Bombing and trench-strafing – you all know what to do. Your flight commanders will brief you separately. Good luck.'

They left at intervals in flights of three, loaded with ammunition for the guns and four bombs each. William was still flying an SE5A – to his disappointment, he had not been assigned to one of the Camels and, as they were too valuable to risk mishaps, he hadn't even had a go on one. His group, led by a senior pilot, took off and crossed the lines near Cambrai at two thousand feet, then circled the country to the south of the town looking for targets.

There was a tremendous battle going on down below, and the air was bumpy with percussions, but because of the noise of the engine and the wind across the rigging, he could not hear any of it. It was strange to see a mass of earth suddenly leap into the air, a whole church collapse in a cloud of dust, and not to have heard anything of the shell that caused it. Farms burst into flame and blazed furiously, whole villages collapsed and disappeared into rubble and smoke, and since the pilot's brain automatically edited out the constant roar of the engine, it all seemed to happen in silence. It was like watching a film: almost, he expected to hear the click-click-click of the celluloid passing through the projector.

The first target the leader chose was a small railway station. They flew in low through some Archie fire, and William saw, a hundred feet below, half a dozen Germans standing on the platform, motionless, as though waiting for a train. Their grey uniforms blended like camouflage with the platform, but their faces were white ovals as they looked up.

The bombs made a heavy metallic sound as they dropped, and black smoke appeared. Circling back in formation, William saw the waiting room half demolished, smoke pouring from the signal box, and a gouge out of the end of the platform, like a giant's bite, with debris scattered across the lines. Of the Germans, there was no sign.

They flew on, looking for more targets, and found a group of about twenty Germans behind a village, who seemed to be setting up camp. They dived to five hundred feet and strafed. Fire was returned, and the three twisted and side-slipped away from each other to avoid it. William felt oddly annoyed at being fired on, and turning he saw that they were struggling to mount a machine gun. *You won't get me with that*, he thought, and came in lower. All the faces turned up to him again; he saw rifles aimed at him. He concentrated on the machine gun, and let go one of his bombs right over it. When he looked back, there was just a hole where it had been. A lucky hit.

But his two companions were nowhere to be seen – presumably had spotted other targets and headed for them. William didn't mind. He rather liked flying alone. You could concentrate on harrying the enemy, rather than on keeping the right distance from the other pilots and pulling out of the dive at the exact moment the leader did. His heart lifted at the feeling of freedom. It was a beautiful autumn day, warm, just a little hazy, and what could any man ask for more, than to be flying? Quite soon, he found a column of about twenty Germans marching briskly down a lane, and attacked. Most of them scattered – he thought he only hit two or three – but the effect on their morale made it worth while.

Circling, he flew over another lane, and saw a farm-cart drawn by two horses. It had a tarpaulin drawn over the load, which made it likely it was supplies of some sort for the Germans. The driver looked up in fear at the sound of his approach – a civilian in faded blue overalls and a soft cap – and whipped up his team, though there was nowhere he could go except straight along the lane. William knew he ought to destroy the cart and its cargo, but he couldn't hit it without hitting the Frenchman or the horses, and he didn't want to kill either. The horses were bays. He thought of what Sadie would say.

Either the driver's urging or the sound of the approaching aeroplane frightened them, and they bolted in a panic. When the lane curved round they charged straight ahead, bursting through the hedge at the side of the road. The cart overturned and the load fell out and bundles rolled down a shallow slope into the stream at the bottom. He hoped they were not waterproof. He couldn't see the driver, but hoped he had jumped clear.

He climbed again. Up ahead was a copse of trees, from inside which he saw several yellow flashes, signifying gunfire. Now that, he thought, was exactly the sort of target he wanted. The enemy had concealed a gun post in the trees, which could cause a lot of trouble to advancing troops, as well as to over-flying aeroplanes. He had two bombs left for the job. He dived to three hundred feet, leaned over the side with his hand on the bomb-release, and pulled.

The explosion was not just that of his bombs. There must have been a fuel dump, or something like it, down there, because there was a huge roar and blast of air, and the tail of his aeroplane shot up like a football being kicked. It threw the nose into an almost vertical dive. The machine screamed through the air, William with the control stick as hard back as it would go, seeing the ground hurtling towards him and knowing he had no control.

In that moment, he passed beyond fear, beyond despair, and into a calmness of fatalism. There was nothing he could do. He was going to die. It might have happened any time, but he knew now it had come.

The SE smashed into the earth, and there was a noise of splintering and rending that was like the end of the world. William felt the safety-belt cut into him as he was thrown forward, and his head hit the windscreen; warm blood gushed over his lips and chin; but he was not dead. The near-vertical dive had moderated in the few seconds of the fall. The SE was trying to obey the stick, trying to climb, and the ground that had met her was down-sloping, falling away. The disparity between the two was just enough to allow her to bounce clear, having ripped off her undercarriage. The engine staggered and caught; the SE was still flying, though barely above the ground.

He wasn't dead. William shook his head to clear it. The control stick was heavy and stiff in his hand; he could feel there was something wrong with the tail, and the rudder bar felt both unresponsive and fragile. He risked a glance back, and saw that one side of the tail-plane and elevator had been ripped off, and the rudder was partly jammed by the debris. He had no undercarriage, the tip of a propellor blade had been broken off, and the vibration of the engine was shattering. *How the hell was she flying at all?* The fear that had left him when he knew he was going to die returned full-force now he might be going to live. Oh, he wanted to live! With the help of the slope he had staggered up to ninety feet, but he could hardly steer; with only half a tail-plane she tried to pitch horribly, and the engine vibration made him fear it might break away entirely. He had to land soon, or face a worse crash; but he could not land in German territory. The compass was still working. With infinite care, pressing the fragile rudder bar as if trying not to break an egg, he brought her round inch by inch to face towards the lines. He was managing to keep her more or less level, and had got the speed up to eighty miles an hour, though the vibration was terrifying. All he could do was to fly on and hope for the best.

346

Now he could see trenches, ruined houses, shell holes, and grey uniforms huddling in them, their backs to him, while the earth erupted in fountains of mud and stones, and clouds of smoke drifted across like oily curtains. He was only just clearing the tree-tops, and prayed no-one would bother to look up, for he was so low and so slow now he was a real target. He was so near the ground, he could even hear the shuddering thunder of the guns. The battleground crawled by underneath him as he sagged lower. He tried to climb a little but the engine threatened at once to stall. Fifty feet, forty, still losing height. How long could it take to cross a battlegound? For God's sake, would it never end?

But now there were dead men below, scattered about, and some were in khaki and some in grey. No man's land. Now more trenches – and, oh, thank God, the men in them were facing towards him, and their uniforms were kindly, lovely, blessed khaki! Now he could land – and God help him again, for he had no undercarriage and would have no control. But at least if he survived he would not be captured.

The pock-marked ground was speeding past just below him. He tried to pull the nose up a little, the speed fell to seventy-eight, and there was nothing left to do but switch off. She struck the earth, jolted, slithered along on her belly with a hideous screeching sound, hit one of the craters, dug her nose into the ground, and flipped over, thudding heavily down onto her back. William thought, *Home!* And blacked out.

Arriving back at Valheureux after dark, in a tender, William limped into the squadron office, to be greeted rather sourly by the clerk. 'Oh, it's you, sir! I've already completed the returns. They're just about to go off to Wing. We thought you'd gone west, sir. You've been put down as missing.'

'Awfully sorry,' William said, rather hoarsely. 'Would you mind awfully altering them? I'd sooner not die tonight.'

The clerk huffed grumpily, but he had to say, 'Of course, sir. Glad you made it back. CO's at dinner in the mess, sir.'

William crossed the orchard towards the big tent, lit from within and glowing in the dark, like a pearl. The air smelt cold and fresh, of grass and overripe apples. He was aware that he was desperately hungry, but he also felt stupid and dead tired, incapable of going into any long narrative or explanation of what had happened. He wished he could go straight to bed – perhaps have something brought him on a tray, as when he was ill in childhood. Tomorrow would be early enough for telling. But he had no choice in the matter.

He entered the mess tent. The whole squadron was seated around the long table at dinner, with stewards moving about in the background, and a murmur of conversation. There was a smell of bruised grass, canvas, lamp oil and stew. Those facing him broke off their talk with expressions of surprise, and others turned to see what they were looking at. Now the whole company was staring at him in silence, whether approving or disapproving he didn't know. It was like being on stage without knowing the lines – or even what play he was in. Unsure what else to do, he limped past them to the end of the table where the CO was sitting, his face expressionless.

William's mouth was dry, and he felt nothing but weariness. He was dirty, bruised, his uniform was smoke-sullied and torn, and there was dried blood on his chin and down the breast of his tunic where his nose had bled.

He licked his lips, and said, 'I'm sorry I'm late, sir.'

Slowly, the CO smiled. 'Have a drink,' he said.

All across France, the British, French and American armies were moving forward. The front line, once drawn as if with a ruler from Switzerland to the sea, now wavered and lurched, sometimes crawling and sometimes racing, but always in the same direction, herding the Germans back towards their

348

own land. They fought desperately, and the Allies faced not only artillery but machine-gun posts that the enemy would not yield short of death.

And the Allies were hampered by the fact that they were advancing into unknown territory. All they had to go by was pre-war maps, often inaccurate and always inadequate, from which rivers, canals and dykes they had to cross were frequently missing, contours and woods sketchily described, villages and farms misplaced or not mentioned at all. And these farms, villages and small towns were still occupied by the original inhabitants, on whom the enemy had billeted themselves, and whom they had repressed for four years. These anxious civilians were waiting to be freed, and it was an impediment to the Allies' advance that they had to avoid as far as possible hurting them or damaging their houses and farms, whereas the Germans had no such limitations.

Autumn fogs were commonplace now, and smoke added to the confusion. Everyone was fatigued, and Edward sometimes felt such a sense of unreality caused by a combination of the three that he seemed to be operating in a dream. Now he was a captain, his responsibilities towards his men were greater, and he had to worry about water, food and shelter as well as combat. The further they advanced, the longer the supply route, and it seemed to him something of a miracle that ammunition, food and mail kept managing to find them when they were rarely in the same place for more than two days at a time.

But to counteract the difficulties, there was the pleasure of liberation. They were marching into villages that had received little damage, but where the population had been so repressed that they greeted Edward and his men with cries of welcome, '*La victoire!*' and '*Liberté!*' Prominent citizens would come forward to shake hands and express thanks. Everywhere he saw street names that had been changed to German ones, German signs over buildings that had been appropriated for enemy use, and public notices pinned up with *'Achtung!'* in heavy black print, and much use of the word *'verboten'*. When he had the chance to speak to the locals, he found that on the whole they had been treated fairly, though movement had been strictly controlled, and there had been dire shortages to cope with; but the enemy were still loathed, they were still the *'sales Boches'*, dirty pigs, barbarians. It didn't help that in some villages, when the Germans retreated, a few of the village girls went with them.

He wrote, on the 17th of October,

We have just had a real battle, of the sort you see on news-reels, in contrast to the skirmishes that mostly make up our lives these days. It began with a barrage from our side, too close behind us to be pleasant, so we had to lie flat with our faces in the grass. Once the barrage lifted we jumped up and advanced, but there was such a dense fog we could not see anything or anyone in front of us. All I had was a map and a compass. But we had not gone many yards when three tanks came lumbering out of the wood behind us, and we dashed after them feeling comforted by their presence. The barrage seemed to have done its work, because there were only a few Germans popping up here and there out of shell holes and dugouts. They all seemed inclined to fight, but a few rounds of rapid fire soon had them throwing up their hands and shouting, 'Kamerad!' I sent them off with an NCO and two men – there must have been twenty or twenty-five in all. Once, a German officer popped up and pointed his pistol at me, but I had my own pistol drawn and aimed it at him, and while he hesitated the men nearest me swung their rifles in his direction, so he saw he had no chance and put his hands up. He had a fine pair of field glasses round his neck which I took as a prize of war – they are most useful, my own having been damaged several days ago.

We are now out at rest for a few days, and are billeted

350

at a farm, so that we can get under cover for the first time in ages, and we officers actually have proper beds to sleep on, in the farmhouse. The inhabitants are so grateful to be liberated, they are treating us very kindly, though they have little to give after the occupation. But the farmer had some barrels of cider he had managed to keep hidden from the Boche, and has regaled us with them. Every man got a cupful, which helped our cold rations down – tins of bully and loaves of rather stale bread that arrived shortly after us. It was enough to have the men singing before they went to sleep. Still, I hope you people at home are not too optimistic about the chances of an early peace. There is much hard fighting to be done before Germany is brought to its knees, and I personally believe that only by occupying German soil can we force them to accept unconditionally our terms of peace. We cannot and must not compromise, or it will be no peace at all.

He did not tell Beattie, in his letter, that he had been wounded, for it was only a slight wound – the side of his left hand torn open by the bullet that had broken his field glasses. It was a nasty gash, but it had not damaged any of the tendons. He'd had it sewn up at the aid station, and though it hurt abominably, he'd carried on, with the help of a bottle of brandy pressed on him by the mayor of one of the villages they passed through.

He also did not tell her that the farmer who had given them his cider had a daughter, a young woman in her early twenties. When she had served the cider to him and his lieutenants in the farmhouse kitchen, he had addressed a few kind words to her in French. It had worked too well, for she had come into his room in the night and tried to get into bed with him. It had taken all the French he could dredge up from memory to rebuff her kindly. She told him her fiancé had been killed at Verdun, and begged him to take her with him, for fear that the Boche might come back. He had managed to reassure her and send her away, but for the rest of the stay he was on tenterhooks, and slept only fitfully, though he had wedged a chair under the bedroom door handle.

Now that the army was past the old battlefields, the X-ray ambulance could once again follow it. For Laura it was the most exhilarating part of the war so far, and Annie agreed with her. The boys, too, cheered up enormously now they were seeing parts of France that had not been pulverised and splintered. Sometimes they would recognise a place name with which they had some connection, exclaim that they had known a boy who came from that village, or had visited this town in peacetime. A rapid change of scene was more interesting than bumping up and down the same stretch of road. They still had to dodge the shells now and then, and were always in danger from gunfire, but with the Front moving ever away from them, they were able to get up to the battalion aid stations at an earlier stage, making them more useful.

They had the same difficulties as everyone else, in that they were relying on wholly inadequate maps, and though they were, broadly speaking, following the army, they could not stay close enough to be always in sight or earshot. They were lost one day in mid-October in a maze of small roads, from the junctions of which the signposts had either been removed or had never existed.

'I know we're somewhere between St Quentin and Cambrai,' Annie said.

'Not much help,' said Laura, holding the map out of the window to get the best light on it. It was foggy again, which did not help with the sense of direction – you could not tell which way the sun was, and even when you could hear gunfire, it was hard to tell where it came from. 'You know,' she concluded, after a bit, 'I don't think that river was the St Quentin Canal at all. I think it must have been the Oise. We must have turned the wrong way. In which case, we're somewhere here.' She circled an area with her forefinger.

One of the boys got down and scouted ahead. Laura was always worried about driving into a ditch – there were often deep ones on either side of these narrow roads – and of running out of petrol by driving about in circles where there was little chance of refilling. They lit cigarettes and waited, listening intently. They could hear gunfire, which they judged to be about fifteen or twenty miles away. Somewhere nearer to hand a cow lowed mournfully, and the fog condensing on the leaves of the tree above them dripped monotonously on the roof of the cab. Eventually, Morgan came back, looking brighter.

'I found an old man in a field,' he said. 'There is a village up ahead, Brancourt. He says if we go left at the first cross-roads and right at the second, we will come to the main road. Eventually,' he added with less certainty.

Laura was scanning the map. 'Brancourt! I have it! So the main road, if he's right, is the one to Le Cateau. That must be where the fighting is.'

It took a few more turns than the two mentioned to reach the main road, but once there, they saw the cheering sight of army vehicles and marching men in khaki. An ambulance coming down from the Le Cateau direction stopped at Laura's signal and confirmed that there was a battle going on there.

'Where's the aid station?' she asked.

'Go on up this road,' said the driver. 'Past the next village, big barn on the left at a crossroads. You can't miss it.' And he roared away.

Laura drove on, receiving some cheerful waves from parties they passed. Most of them knew the names of the civilian ambulances by now. And the aid station was indeed easy to find despite the fog. The artillery fire was louder now, and the fog was reinforced by smoke, but the activity around the aid station was impossible to mistake.

Laura leaned out of the cab to ask an orderly where to set up, and as soon as she had parked, she jumped down to see if she could help anywhere. She heard her name being called, and there was Ransley, just crossing the beaten space between two tents.

'I wondered if I might see you,' he said, taking possession of both her hands. He was wearing a pony-skin jacket over his uniform and under his apron, but its bulk did not disguise that he had got even thinner. His aquiline nose looked ready to break right through his skin. 'I thought you'd be following the action.'

'I've missed you a couple of times,' she said. 'Turning up not long after you'd moved on.'

'Well, you're a sight for sore eyes – you *and* your X-ray machine. I won't scold you for going into danger, because the Boche are on the run all right, so there's not much chance they'll be coming this way. Dearest girl, are you well?'

'Of course, never better,' she said. 'Don't you know I thrive on adventure? But you look as if you haven't eaten for a week.'

He pretended to consider. 'I'm not sure I have. Or slept. But you're a tonic in yourself – I shall keep going for a while yet, now I've seen you.'

Someone popped a head out of the tent and shouted urgently, 'Major – sir!'

'I must go,' he said. 'But I've got a good team and we're trying to be sensible and take breaks, and relieve each other. Are you staying here?'

'I'm the driver. If I say we stay, we stay.'

'Then I shall be off duty in . . .' he consulted his watch, '. . . in two hours, give or take.'

She freed her hands to free him. 'I'll be here. We'll share rations. Now go. Go!'

At least, she said to herself – as he hurried away, forgetting her existence entirely, she thought, while there were wounded to tend – at least she could make sure he ate something. They had begun quite some time ago to make sure they kept food supplies in the ambulance in case they got lost or stranded, and in the box in the back of the cab there were tins and jars and packets enough to make a decent meal for all of them several times over. And in another box, well padded with an old blanket, there were bottles of wine. Her heart sang at the thought of sitting down with him, talking to him – just being near him. Meanwhile, she would make herself useful. There was always something to be done, from carrying a stretcher to putting pressure on a bleeding wound until the doctor came, or comforting the dying.

CHAPTER TWENTY-TWO

Sadie had ample time to regret her decision, or at least to wonder, in the stilly watches of the night, if she would live to regret it.

The war would not last for ever, and when it was over, she would be cast up like driftwood on the dry shingle of a new world, whose shape and customs no-one could guess, a world that might be as different from before-the-war as a foreign country. And though when she was younger she had resented the idea that the only thing a girl could do with her life was to get married, she knew, when she thought about it, that she didn't want *never* to get married. She wanted to do that as well as other things. She didn't want to be alone all her life, to cope with the strange new world and its unknowable demands on her without a companion.

But who would there be for her to marry? The men would come back from the war, but thousands upon thousands would not come back, and many thousands more would come back utterly changed, perhaps unable to adapt. Already she had heard the girls up at Highclere talking about it in low voices. Two had lost their intendeds, and it had made the others nervous. They were wondering if there would be a shortage of men after the war. It seemed to Sadie that there must be. And she had been offered marriage by a very nice, very suitable man whom she really liked. What had got into her, what ingratitude towards the Fates, that she had refused him?

Meanwhile, with the new type of action going on in France, the ebb and make of the tide of wounded that they had become accustomed to had changed to a steady, unrelenting stream; and to add to the anxieties of the season, the influenza had come back.

It was worse than the July episode: it spread more quickly, was more virulent, and resulted in more deaths – and it did not affect only the poor and weak. There were as many deaths in Mayfair as in the East End; and a significant number of victims were under thirty-five.

Inevitably, given the traffic between the two places, it arrived from London in Northcote. Mouth and nose masks reappeared in the streets, chemists were besieged for nostrums, doctors were on constant call. The Northcote cinema – the New Empire in Upper Church Street - closed, and several celebrations booked into the rooms at the Station Hotel were cancelled.

The first death was that of Alfred Clulow, the piano tuner, a much-loved character. He had lodged with the Bellflowers, and passed the disease to the Bellflowers' younger son Cyril, who also died. Northcote was shocked – Cyril was only fourteen, and had just joined his father Eric in the family joinery business. Eric's aunt, Joyce Hicks, also lodged with them, and was soon heard to be laid abed with the terrible affliction. She was better known to Northcotians as Madame Mentallo, in much demand at parties and fêtes for her fortune-telling. Perhaps she had some communication line to Higher Powers after all, for though she was desperately sick, as the district nurse Connie Parling told Ada at The Elms, she didn't die of it, but settled in, pale and other-worldly-looking, for a long recovery.

The ambulance depot lay between the cottage hospital and Darvell's factory, and opposite Brewer's, the undertaker's establishment. Sadie, driving, saw the hearse pulling in and out of his yard all too often. Next door to Brewer's was the Coach and Horses – many was the joke that had been made about that, given the propensity of the pub's clients to fall over at closing time and hurt themselves – and next door to the Coach was the blacksmith's shop. Ben Chaplin, the blacksmith, had a long talk with the undertaker while he was shoeing his horses, and reported the conversation to his aunt Effie, who was the Hunters' charwoman.

'Fancy! Mr Brewer says they can't make the coffins quick enough, nor get people buried quick enough,' she told the servants, round-eyed. 'He says in places like Church End and those Irish streets behind the old high street, there's six and seven people all in one family, all lying dead in the house waiting to be put away.'

Cook hissed and rolled her eyes meaningfully at Mrs Chaplin. Eileen's family lived in one of those mean streets, Water Lane.

Trying to be tactful, Ada said, 'But it's not only the poor folk that get it.'

'Ooh, I know,' said Mrs Chaplin. 'Poor Mr Clulow!' She siphoned tea noisily through her teeth. 'And there's that Edna Sharpe, who works at Hadleigh's – she got took. Felt queer in the morning, Hadleigh's sent her home, and she was dead by the evening. It's that quick.'

'Fancy!' Beryl said, her mouth hanging.

'And my Ben says Nurse Parling stopped by yesterday and told him Mrs Prendergast of Maple House is down with it and not expected to live. That's only two streets away,' Mrs Chaplin concluded, pleased with the effect she was having.

'Well, that's enough talk about that,' Cook decreed hastily. Oddly enough, the creeping advance of the plague, which would have had her in hysterics a couple of years ago, was having no effect on her now. She had been blown up by a bomb dropped from a German aeroplane, and somehow that made other risks seem insignificant. And she'd just had a field postcard from Fred, saying 'I am quite well' and 'Letter follows', so all was as it should be in her own world.

Ethel was anxious, though, about her baby. Mrs David had gone back to helping at the Hastings Road canteen, now that Mr David was so much better, and the canteen's customers were all poor people: not poor like the Church End people or the Water Lane Irish, but poor enough to spread disease. And Mr David was taking pupils again – not too many, just one or two to get him into the swing of things – and everyone knew how school children were always covered with germs. She watched Peter like a hawk for any sign of sickness, and did her best to keep everyone away from baby Marcus, but of course she couldn't stop his own parents touching him, though she tried to discourage it in every way she could think of.

On Friday the 26th of October, Ada answered the door to a small boy, who doffed his cap politely and said, 'Is Mr Hunter at home, please?'

Ada knew him, of course, little Philip Cornwallis-Yorke, who had been being crammed by Mr David for several weeks now – according to Ethel, who eavesdropped when she passed the door, with little effect. He was an angel of a child with golden hair and rosy cheeks, but according to what Ethel had overheard Mr David say to Mrs David, he had the intellect of a house brick.

But Ada liked good manners, especially in children, and she smiled at him and said, 'Yes, he's expecting you. You can go on up. You know the way.'

'Thank you,' said Master Philip, and pattered away up the stairs.

Ada was about to shut the door when she saw the postman approaching, having come out of next door's gate, and she waited to see if he had anything for them. He turned in at their gate and came up the path, sorting the letters in his hand as he did so, but when he looked up and saw her, his face froze. He licked his lips nervously, and said, 'There's one for you here, Mrs Armstrong.'

He sorted one to the top of the pile and gave them all to her. She saw the army postal-service stamp, the educated handwriting, and turning it over, the name of a captain and his battalion address. Len's battalion.

'I hope it's not bad news,' the postman said, and when she didn't reply, he hurried away.

Ada went in, mechanically closed the door behind her, placed the bundle of letters on the hall table, and stared at her own envelope. If she opened it, her life would be different. She would prefer just to stand there for ever, and never move again. *But,* one part of her brain told her, *perhaps it isn't the worst. Perhaps he's in hospital. You have to find out.*

So she opened it.

Dear Mrs Armstrong,

I regret very much to inform you that your husband Sgt. L. E. Armstrong, No. 62732 of this Company, was killed in action on the night of the 21st instant. Death was instantaneous and without any suffering.

The Company was taking part in an attack and your husband's platoon was one of those which advanced against the enemy. The attack was successful, and the Company reached and established new positions. Later in the night the enemy shelled our lines and one shell fell on your husband's section, killing him and wounding a comrade. It was impossible to get his remains away and he lies in a soldier's grave where he fell.

I and the CO and all the Company deeply sympathise with you in your loss. Your husband was a much-loved colleague and friend. He did his duty in an exemplary way, and now has given his life for his country. We all honour him, and I trust you will feel some consolation in remembering this.

His effects will reach you via the Base in due course.

In true sympathy,

(Capt) I. K. Hislop

Ada walked towards the kitchen, not feeling the floor beneath her feet. She went in, and then stopped, unable to think what to do. At last Cook glanced up from the table, where she was mixing something in a bowl; stared, and said, 'Whatever is it? You're as white as a sheet.'

Ada couldn't speak. Cook's eyes went to the letter in her hand, and her own cheeks paled. 'Oh, my Lord,' she breathed. 'It's not bad news, is it?' She hurried over, put her arm round Ada's shoulders, urged her towards a chair. 'Sit down, dear, that's right. Oh, Lord! Ada dear, tell me what's happened!'

Ada only stared at nothing. She was thinking, *I'm a widow. I've been a widow nearly a week, and I didn't know. He's dead, and I didn't know.* But they were just words. They didn't seem to mean anything. They didn't *sink in*.

Cook gently prised the letter from her fingers, smoothed it out and read it. And cried, 'Oh! Oh!' She sat down on the next chair, still crying, 'Oh! Oh! Oh!' Eileen came in from the scullery to see what the noise was about, eyes round as coins, and stood wringing her hands in her apron, not knowing what to do.

Then Ethel came in, took in the scene, and the letter, and snapped at Eileen, 'Kettle, quick. Make 'em tea – strong! Lots of sugar.'

The mistress was out; she went to fetch Mrs David.

'Poor Ada,' Antonia said to David that evening. 'It could have been any of them – that's what I kept thinking. Your father, William, Cook's fiancé—'

'Cook has a *fiancé*?' he interrupted in astonishment.

'Yes – how did you not know? A very nice sergeant.'

'How *should* I know?' David countered. 'How do you know, come to that?'

'Goodness, one hears things,' Antonia said.

'But *Cook*? What sort of a man would—' He stopped himself, realising he was being perhaps needlessly ungallant. 'Well, it was Ada's husband, in the event. What a damned shame. At her age, she's unlikely to get a second chance.'

'It could have been your father, or William,' Antonia said again, staring at space. 'We all live with that, don't we? All the time. Even your aunt is in danger. The letter could come at any time, for any of us.' She closed her eyes briefly. 'Thank God you're here,' she said, very quietly.

His mouth thinned. Yes, but the 'thank God' included his wounding and the years of suffering, during which he had often wished to die. Still, he was here, the pain was mostly gone, there was a good chance of his being able to live a normal life.

Bobby was dead. And William: how long did they say was the average life expectancy of an RAF pilot at the Front? It was hard to be thankful when the war went on and on, and the threat never went away.

But he had to allow her her prayer. 'Yes, I'm here,' he said, and tried to make a joke of it. 'Of course, there's always the 'flu—'

'Oh, don't!' she said hastily, and he pretended not to see her cross her fingers.

Beattie had a quiet talk with Ada, and asked if she would like time off. Ada said drearily, 'Thank you, madam, but I wouldn't know what to do with it. I'd sooner keep busy, if you don't mind.'

'Just as you please,' Beattie said.

But then their eyes met, just for a moment, and the awful

emptiness of death looked out of each into each. There was nothing to be said, nothing to be done. You just went on.

Beattie nodded, and Ada went away.

Diana went to see Guy Teesborough every day. He was soon out of danger, but the recovery was going to take a long time, and would be tedious for an active man, as well as painful. But he bore it stoically, answered every question as to how he was with. 'Oh, pretty well, considering,' and a change of subject.

He was supremely easy to talk to. Diana had not generally got on very well with the Wroughtons' friends, for they came from a different stratum of society. They all knew each other, generally from childhood, or were related to each other, and not to recognise the nicknames they bestowed so freely on each other, not to remember the amusing incident or to share the old, favourite joke, left you struggling for firm ground under your feet. Diana, moreover, had never been a great one for small-talk, having something of her mother's reserve; and being a great beauty had meant she had never had to develop it. It had been enough that she was there, to be looked at.

And if the women in Rupert's circle were hard to get on with, the men were often worse, brought up in a tradition where men talked to men for pleasure and women only for duty. Rupert had been different. He had been interested in feminine things – clothes and hairstyles, furniture and curtains – and he had been a talker. Often Diana hadn't understood what he was talking about, but as he evidently intended to amuse her by his chatter, she'd been glad to listen and smile when it seemed appropriate.

But in Guy, for the first time, she met someone with whom she could converse freely. He encouraged her to talk about herself, was interested in her life, even the day-to-day details. He was well-informed on general topics, and answered all her questions but in a way she understood. She never felt mocked, or humbled, or an outsider with him.

She had to remember he was recovering from a serious wound, and not to tire him. But when she noticed him flagging, and made to leave him, he begged her to stay and forgive him for not talking for a while. Then *she* talked to *him*, telling him about her own childhood, and her family, her wishes and dreams and how they had changed. Sometimes he preferred not to talk, but to play cards, and once, when he was obviously in pain and all else failed, she sang to him, very quietly, some of the old folk songs Nula had sung to her when she was a child. She didn't know what made her try it, but it had seemed to soothe him. He had eventually slipped into sleep and she had felt a quiet happiness that she had been able to be of use to him.

One day she received a letter from Erskine Ballantine, Rupert's erstwhile best friend, the son of Courtland Ballantine the MP. He had been serving at the Front, but the letter came from a war hospital in London. The handwriting was so bad, she couldn't make out large sections of it. She gathered he had been wounded – how badly she did not know; frankly, she hardly cared, for she had never liked him, and believed he had disliked her even more. Why was he bothering her when he had family of his own?

But when she turned the sheet over, she found the rest of the letter was about Rupert. Even where she could read the words – the paper seemed to have got damp at some time, either with sweat or tears – she couldn't understand them. There was something about a 'secret' and, much underlined, an assertion that Diana had never understood him. He, Erskine, had been Rupert's only true friend. And Rupert had never loved her, only married her to 'look respectable'. It was Erskine that he had truly loved, and Diana had driven him away, so that his only choice was to go off to war and be killed. His death was *all her fault*.

It was a stupid, vulgar letter, but it made her hands shake. How could he *say* such things? If he *had* loved Rupert, how could be so cruel to his grieving widow?

And yet . . .

A thoughtfulness came over her. There had been something . . . Rupert had tried once or twice, quite earnestly, to tell her something about himself, and then, when she couldn't understand what he was saying, had dropped it and covered it up with a joke or a change of subject. A secret, as Erskine said?

If he had only married to be respectable, there were dozens of more suitable girls of his own class he could have chosen. But she remembered, when he had proposed to her, he had said she was the only one he could possibly marry because only she would 'understand'. It was frustrating, especially now when it was too late, to admit that she hadn't, and didn't.

For some reason, the story of Bluebeard came to her. If Rupert had had a secret, probably better to forget all about it. No use opening forbidden doors, letting out who-knew-what plague. On the other hand, there were the children to think about . . .

With a surge of determination, and damp hands, she took the letter to Guy. He had known Rupert all his life. If anyone could put her mind at rest, it would be him.

Guy was sitting up, and looking a little better when she reached his bedside. 'You look very pretty this morning, if I may be allowed to say so,' he said. 'There's colour in your cheeks.'

'I'm afraid it may be due to vexation,' Diana said, drawing up her accustomed chair. 'I've had a letter from Erskine Ballantine – a rather upsetting letter.'

Guy's smile faded. 'I'm sorry to hear that. I shouldn't set any store by anything he says, you know. He's rather mad.'

'Is he? The letter does sound rather mad – and apparently,

he's wounded and in hospital, so he might be feverish or in pain.'

'I'm sure that's it.'

'But you don't know yet what he says,' Diana objected. 'Please read it.'

Guy took the letter reluctantly, and perused it slowly. 'He's raving,' he said at last. 'None of it makes sense. I should pay no attention, if I were you.'

'He says Rupert had a secret – and he and Rupert were close friends, so I suppose he ought to know.'

'Trying to make himself important, that's all.'

Diana regarded him suspiciously. Was Guy anxious to deflect her? 'There *was* something, wasn't there? Guy, I wish you would tell me the truth. Was he hiding something from me?'

'If he was hiding something, he hid it from me, too.'

She frowned in thought. 'He said to me several times that he married me because only I could understand him. I wish I knew what that meant. And Erskine says he never loved me, that he only married me to be respectable.'

Guy took her hand and pressed it. 'Now, I know that's not true. Rupert certainly loved you. Erskine is an odd man, and he's been getting odder for years. He's just trying to stir up trouble.'

'Rupert did say some strange things,' Diana said doubtfully. 'I don't think I *did* understand him, not all the time.'

'He had a lively sense of humour,' Guy said. 'He was always joking. *I* didn't understand half his jokes. But when he married you he made the best choice of his life. He went to the Front because he wanted you to be proud of him. And he died a hero's death. That's all you need to remember.'

She looked at him uncertainly. 'If I were you, I would throw that horrid letter away and not give it another thought. And if Erskine should write again, or try to see you, you let me know, and I'll make sure he doesn't bother you any more.'

She sighed. She couldn't help feeling there was still something she hadn't got to grips with. But it was so nice to have a man defend her again. And even though Guy was in bed wounded and unable to stand, she believed him to be more than a match for Erskine.

'You really think Rupert loved me?' she asked, in a small voice.

'What man wouldn't?' he said. He discovered he was still holding her hand, and gently disengaged himself, hoping she hadn't noticed; and at that moment, fortunately, a nurse came up with a thermometer and broke the mood.

A letter from Fred.

Now Margaret my girl I dont want you to get all steamed up but theres a lot of talk going around that the Huns are putting out feelers for peace. Everybodys heard a rumour, not generally the same one ha ha, its properly given us the wind-up. The reason being that if the rumours are right and the end is coming you don't want to be copping a packet at the last minute, I never seen men so edgy, its all you can do to make them stand up let alone go over the top. Well we went into attack two nights ago, right on Jerrys tail and him sucking every last blessed bit out of the egg I can tell you. We done four miles under fire down a valley and over a river and men copping it wholesale, then got to shelter in a barn but the Hun started chucking wizzbangs and opened it up like a sardine can. We got clear somehow but with very bad wind-up. Then we had to get across a turnip field with no cover and Jerry had two lewis guns sweeping it. We made it to a slit trench but lost seven before we could get in and knock them out. I wish to God Jerry would chuck it quick before we lose more men. Whats the bloody point eh? All the Huns we capture just want peace, must be the brass hats holding things up. Well we are resting up just now and I hope to God the

nobs get the peace signed before we have to shift again, if I
cop one this near the end I shall be bloody mad I can tell you.
Be good pretty Peggy, with any luck your soldier boys coming
home soon. xoxo Fred.

There was a card game that was very popular among the Tommies, called 'House'. When the top line was filled and the game was nearly won, the player naturally got nervous, and they had an expression – 'sweating on the top line' – which had migrated from the game to be applied to any nerve-racking situation.

Edward knew it, and heard it these days among his men – sweating on the top line for the armistice, which they had all heard rumoured, but which didn't seem to come. The enemy just kept on fighting, as fierce and cunning as ever, determined to extract the highest price if he was forced to retreat. Now every man who was hit was the unluckiest bloke in creation.

They seemed to be in almost continuous action, pursuing hot on the enemy's heels, sometimes within sight of them. Now the men hated the Hun as never before for not giving in. They had killed as a matter of duty, but not hated much, professionals among professionals. Now they all had the wind-up.

Edward had too much to do to have time to think about what a sickening irony it would be to fall at the last fence. But at night, before he fell into a dead black sleep of exhaustion, he often thought of Captain Campion. 'Be at the end for me.' What a request! God, God! Every day he saw men cut down, and it could just as easily be him. Every morning, wrenched out of sleep that was never enough, to face a new day of hazard, he suspected God was laughing at him, playing with him: death or life, which is it to be? He was sweating on the top line, all right.

★ ★ ★

On Sunday the 3rd of November, Frank Hussey came to The Elms for his dinner, and announced that his employer, Sir George Pettingell, Bt, was ill with the flu.

Ethel, who had just come into the kitchen, moved rapidly backwards, like a cat that had stepped in perfume. 'How dare you come here with your germs?' she cried. 'Don't you come near me!'

Frank spread his hands. 'Come on, now, Ethel! D'you think I been anywhere near him? I've never even been in the house.'

'You may not have,' she said, 'but there's others have. They talk to somebody, and somebody talks to somebody else, and that's how it spreads. I got my baby to think of.'

'I haven't seen Sir George since last Sunday, and that was only him passing in the car on the way back from church. I'm clean as a whistle, inside and out.'

Cook felt the honours of the kitchen weren't being done. 'We're very glad to see you, Frank dear,' she said, 'and I'm sure we're very sorry your master's poorly.'

'I'm afraid it's a bit more than that, Mrs D,' he said. 'He's mortal sick, not expected to recover. My lady's in a terrible taking.'

'Oh, deary me,' Cook said. 'It don't seem fair, what with having to cope with the war, and now there's this terrible flu on top of it. Who inherits if he does die – hoping, of course, he don't?'

'His son Martin,' said Frank. 'He's at the Front, but he's on the staff, so he's got a better chance of coming back all right.'

'And then what happens to you?' Ethel asked suspiciously. New brooms had a habit of sweeping clean.

'Oh, I'll be all right. Mr Orwell's retiring at Christmas, so I'll be first gardener. Bigger cottage, and a pay rise,' he added, looking significantly at Ethel. She turned her head away, determined not to encourage him. 'I got lots of good ideas about the gardens for after the war. Mr Martin won't want to get rid of me.'

'And when *is* this war going to end, Frank dear?' Cook asked. 'You always seem to know things.'

'The Germans are suing for peace,' he said, 'but our government won't want anything less than complete surrender, so I reckon there'll be a battle or two more in it before the Hun gets the message. Next spring, I'd say.' He looked at Ethel again. 'And then a lot of people will have to start making decisions.'

Ethel sniffed derisively, and went out.

The letter with the official stamp did not strike Ada with fear because there was nothing more the army could do to her. It had taken her husband, after a marriage of two days. She went about her work now with a numbness that seemed to reach from the centre of her to the ends of her fingers. She watched her hands performing their tasks as if they were someone else's. The work was the same, the house was the same, her future expectations were the same, as if he had never existed. Except that she didn't sing now, as she had sometimes done, while she worked. She didn't think she would have the heart to sing again.

So she opened the letter indifferently, and then stared, feeling the blood rush away from her head. She thought she was going to faint.

'Oh, my Lord!' Cook said. 'What is it now? Ada, dear, you've gone white as a sheet.'

'More bad news?' Beryl asked, in a voice that half hoped it was – not for dislike of Ada, but because any excitement was better than the days all being the same.

Munt looked up from his bread-and-jam – eternal bread-and-jam, never any cake, such as a hard-working man had the right to expect! – and growled, 'Talk sense, can't yer? How can it be bad news? They already got him.'

Cook gave him a minatory look for his tactlessness.

Ada pulled herself together, and said, 'No, it's not bad news. Just – a shock. It's –' she licked her dry lips, '– they're giving me a war widow's pension.'

Cook winced at the word 'widow', which ought never to have been applied to her friend, poor Ada, and said, 'Well, that's . . . nice. I suppose. Isn't it?'

Ada handed the letter to her, with an air of resigning responsibility for it. Cook read it, her lips moving, and then she turned almost as pale as Ada had. She looked up. 'It can't be,' she whispered. '*Seventeen and six a week?*'

It was more than Cook got working at The Elms. It was certainly more than Ada got.

Munt jerked his chin at them impatiently. 'Struck all of a heap!' he complained. 'So they should pay. Not much for a man's life!'

Eileen stared as if she couldn't comprehend such riches. Beryl's mouth hung open with the primary stages of mastication clearly visible in it. She only got ten shillings and sixpence a week, and had thought herself lucky.

'You could leave, give up work,' Cook said, almost in a whisper. Ada nodded in a frightened way. She didn't like decisions being thrust upon her.

Ethel snorted. 'You get a pound a week in the factories. Who'd be in service anyway?'

'Well, you are,' Beryl pointed out, puzzled.

'I got my baby to think of,' Ethel snapped.

'She's in love,' Munt said mockingly. 'Think any o' that lot notice you even exist?'

'You mind your own business, you horrible old man,' Ethel said, goaded.

Cook and Ada had attention only for each other. They had been together a long time. 'You could live on seventeen and six,' Ada said uncertainly.

Cook nodded. 'But you're all found here, you got to think of that. There'd be rent and food and suchlike.'

'You can get a room in the village for three and six,' Eileen said helpfully. 'I seen one advertised in the sweetie shop.'

'I could rent, get a little cottage, just two rooms, like the one opposite the blacksmith's, for five shillings,' Ada said. 'And I don't eat much.' Suddenly her face twisted in misery. 'I don't want to go. I've been here since they came from London. I like it here. I don't want to be on my own.'

'For God's sake!' Ethel muttered in disgust.

Cook reached over and patted Ada's hand. 'Then don't you go. You don't have to.'

'But all that money! More than my wages! What'll I do with it?' How could she stay here and take wages from the missus when she was receiving an independent fortune? It didn't seem honest, somehow. The missus might not even *let* her stay. Who ever heard of a servant with private means?

'You could save it,' Cook said, after mature consideration. 'Put it aside, for a rainy day. For when you get old, like, and can't work. A nice little nest-egg.'

Ada took out her handkerchief and applied it carefully to her eyes. 'I wish I knew what to do.'

'Keep your mouth shut, that's my advice,' Munt said. 'Wait till the war's over. You don't know what'll happen then.'

'He's right,' said Cook – perhaps the first time she had ever uttered those words. 'No need to decide anything now. Quick decisions is bad ones. You stay here with us, Ada dear, till you know what's what.'

'I've got to tell them upstairs, I suppose,' she said doubtfully. 'They'll find out.'

'Nobody here's going to open their mouths,' Ethel said, and glared at Beryl and Eileen. 'And if a word of it gets out of this kitchen, I'll know who's blabbed about it, and I'll slap them so hard they won't see straight for a week. Understand?'

'I wouldn't say anything,' Beryl said indignantly.

'You run at the mouth like a babbling brook,' Ethel said contemptuously, 'but this time, you got me to think about, so keep your lip buttoned up.'

'Thanks, Ethel,' Ada said. 'I didn't expect you to care what happens to me.'

Ethel shrugged. 'It's still us and them,' she said. 'And I don't want any disruptions. I got my own job to think about.'

Munt gave her a malicious grin. 'That's right, girl. Maids is the first to be let go when the money's tight.'

'Why should money be tight?' Cook asked.

'War's expensive. Somebody's got to pay. While we're fighting, it's all on tick. Once it stops, the bill comes in. The 'ole country'll be bankrupt, you mark my words.'

'Oh, you always got something bad to say,' Cook snapped. 'Why don't you try having a happy thought for a change?'

Munt jerked his thumb at Ada. 'Ask her. Seventeen and six for a husband. That makes everything all right, don't it?'

Ada got up and left the table. 'I got polishing to do,' she said, and went out.

CHAPTER TWENTY-THREE

Still the wounded came in, and Sadie drove the ambulance every afternoon, except on Sunday. Sometimes she felt bad about taking Sunday off – the wounded didn't – but both her mother and Mrs Cuthbert said she must, or she'd get ill and be of no use to anyone.

'With the dreadful influenza so rife,' Mrs Cuthbert said, 'you have to keep yourself in tip-top condition to resist it.'

'Oh, I never get sick,' said Sadie.

'A lot of people who never get sick have caught this flu. It's not like the usual sort,' said Mrs Cuthbert.

On Wednesday the 6th of November she was driving back from the Walford Road hospital when she heard a motor horn honking, and in the mirror saw a car behind her, the driver gesturing out of the window. She frowned in annoyance. The Red Cross on the rear doors was apparently no guarantee of consideration from others. She stuck her arm out and beckoned him past, but he only hooted again. Up ahead was a wider spot where there was a farm gate, so she edged into it and stopped to let him by. But instead, he pulled in behind her.

'Oh, so he wants to remonstrate, does he?' she said to Nailer, who was keeping her company, standing with his forefeet on the dashboard. 'Well, I shall get mine in first!'

You watch your step, girl, said Nailer in the growly, country voice she imagined for him. *There's some queer folk about these days.*

She scratched the top of his head briefly. 'If he attacks me with a tyre iron, you can jump out of the window and come and rescue me,' she said, sprang down from the cab and marched aggressively towards the rear. The driver got out of the motor, and she felt a momentary twinge of anxiety before she realised that it was John Courcy. He was scarecrow thin – his uniform hung on him – and he looked worn out and much more than eight years older than her.

They stopped a few feet apart. 'I went to the depot, looking for you,' he said. 'And then I missed you again at the hospital.'

'Whose car is that?' Sadie asked.

'One of the doctors in Le Touquet. He said I could borrow it. I picked it up from his garage in London.' He stopped, and didn't seem to know how to go on.

It had never been difficult to talk to him. But there had been that long epistolary silence. 'What are you doing here?' she asked.

'I've got a forty-eight. I'm due for leave but it's too hectic for more than a short break.'

'It's barely long enough to get home and back,' Sadie observed.

'I know. I travelled all night. And I have to leave tomorrow at noon.'

She waited, not knowing what question to ask. Her heart felt painfully tight in her chest, just at being near him again. She wanted to gaze and gaze, but it was hard to do that when you were standing right in front of someone. She lowered her eyes and fiddled with her cuff.

That seemed to release him. He said, 'When I was home last time – when I was injured – you were so sweet to me.'

'Oh! Well – I—' She felt herself colour.

'I know. You would be sweet to any wounded soldier,' he

375

filled in for her. 'And mine was such a sorry sort of wound. A horse bite! Not a glorious battle injury. But you made me feel . . . heroic, anyway.' He gave an uneasy, deprecating smile. 'And afterwards, I was afraid I'd – misinterpreted. Made too much of it. No! Let me finish what I've got to say or I shall lose my nerve. I've been practising my speech on the journey for hours.'

'You don't need—'

'Please. Let me say it. I decided when I got back that the best thing was just to sever all contact. I didn't want to embarrass you or – or play on your pity.'

'Pity?' she exclaimed.

'It was hell, wondering. My mind went back and forth. And then Mrs Cuthbert wrote and said you were hurt that I had stopped writing, and that started up my hopes again, which was immensely painful. So when I got the pass, I thought the only sensible thing to do was to come and see you and find out. And then I'll know, and be able to go on with my life. One way or the other.'

'Find out what?' she asked, in terror that *she* was misunderstanding *him* now. All the blood seemed to have left her head, and it was inexplicably hard to breathe.

'How you feel about me,' he said awkwardly. Was this the smooth, capable John Courcy, able to cope with any emergency? He looked as much at ease as a man trying to balance on a moving sea of marbles. 'I've had feelings for you for a long time, but I wouldn't allow myself to follow them up because, well, I'm a lot older than you, for a start, and I'm just a poor vet with no prospects. I'm no catch. Whereas you . . .' He made an eloquent movement of his hand, signifying the entirety of Sadie Hunter, mind, character and body. 'But sometimes I've thought that perhaps – perhaps you *did* feel something for me. Other than friendship, I mean.'

He stumbled to a stop. Sadie was waiting in agony for

him to come to a conclusion, or at least ask a question that she could decently answer. Her silence seemed to make him even more nervous.

'Now it's your turn to speak,' he prompted. 'Let me down gently, there's a kind girl.'

'I'm not kind,' she began.

'You are,' he asserted. 'Kind and beautiful and funny and – and everything a sane man could want in a woman.'

'You want *me*?'

'Didn't I say that? Have I gone and left out the whole point? Oh, Sadie, I'm an idiot, you'll have to forgive me. What I'm trying to say in my clumsy way is that I love you, and it would make my life complete if you happened to love me, too. Lord!' He shook his head at himself. 'I'm so much better at communicating with animals!'

'No, you're not! I mean, you *are* wonderful with animals, but I've always found you easy to talk to.' *It's only on this one subject I haven't understood you*, she thought. 'You – you really love *me*?'

'Pretty much the whole time since I met you,' he said. 'I couldn't help it, you know.'

'But why didn't you *tell* me?'

'Because I haven't anything to offer you. I'm too old, too poor, too plain—'

'Now you're talking like Jane Eyre,' she objected.

'Who's Jane Eyre? No, don't answer that. Just please, for God's sake, tell me.'

'That I love you? Of course I do. I just can't believe you love me too.'

'Oh, God! Come here.'

He opened his arms, and she walked into them, and let her head down with a sigh onto his shoulder, felt his arms close tightly round her, smelt the scent of his skin, closed her eyes and thought, *I could never be happier than I am at this moment*. It was like coming home after long exile, when you had thought you would never see your native land again.

He rested his cheek against her hair, and they stood silently in a close embrace at the roadside, just breathing. After an unknown time, an army lorry went past, and the soldiers, leaning out, whistled and shouted, 'Oy-oy!' and broke the spell.

He released her, but took hold of her hands, and they gazed at each other.

Sadie traced with her eye every line in his face. His short-cut hair was grey over the temples, and there was a healing graze on his forehead. His skin was roughened and dry, as if he had shaved with a blunt razor. His eyes were slightly bloodshot, and the sockets were bistred. She wouldn't have exchanged him for the most glamorous film star in America. 'When you stopped writing, I thought I should never be happy again,' she said.

'I'm sorry. I did it for the best.'

'I tried going out with other men, but it was no good.'

He was taken aback. 'Other men?'

His response prompted her to devilry. 'One of them proposed to me. Actually, I think the other one would have as well.'

'You brazen hussy,' he said. 'I can see I came back just in time.'

'It was no good, though. I knew I couldn't love anyone but you. So I decided there was no point in thinking about marriage and so on, and after the war I was going to devote my life to spinsterhood and good works.'

'And I was going to become a cow doctor and live in a tiny damp cottage and become eccentric and irascible.'

'It seems we've both had a narrow escape.'

He grinned. 'Oh, Sadie! What did I ever do to be so lucky?'

'I can't believe—'

'Believe what?'

'That I don't have to be miserable any more.'

He took her in his arms again, and this time it was Nailer barking from the cab window that brought them back to the present.

He laughed. 'My old friend Nailer. I do hope he's going to live with us when we're married.'

'No-one else would have him,' she said happily. 'Are we really going to be married?'

'I have to save you from all these other men.'

Nailer barked again. She looked stricken. 'Oh dear! I'm still on duty. I have to go. The wounded—'

'I understand. What time do you finish?'

'Half past five.'

'I'll come and meet you at the depot.'

'We have all evening, and tomorrow morning,' she gloated.

'Next year, when this wretched war's over—'

'I was forgetting you have to go back. Oh, John, what if something happens?'

'We haven't been bombed or shelled yet. And the Germans are far away now. Unless they have a resurgence, it's the horses you have to worry about. I could get bitten again.' Nailer barked insistently, like the voice of conscience. 'Go,' he said, releasing her hands. 'I'll see you at five thirty.'

She decided not to tell them at home. It was too precious to have anyone else making comments, asking questions. When the war ended, that would be the time for public declarations.

They spent an evening of bliss, telling each other everything, marvelling at the mistake on both sides that had kept them apart – he thought she hopelessly underestimated her many wonderful attributes while seeing worth in him he simply didn't have; and she felt exactly the same about him.

'Fine pair of fools, we are!' he said, with a grin.

They talked; and, in the car in a secluded lay-by, there was an agreeable amount of kissing as well. Sadie, having worked with animals most of her life, knew about sex in theory, but nothing prepared you for the feelings aroused when the man you loved kissed you so long and so passionately. At one point he drew back his head to look down into her drowning face and said huskily, 'You look ruffled, like a bird.'

She *felt* ruffled. She wished they were already married, because she wanted to go with him right then to a room of their own with a bed and take off all her clothes and press every inch of her bare skin against his and do what the ache inside her commanded. She understood at last why it was that girls 'got into trouble'. When John kissed her like that, she needed only opportunity to abandon all society's teachings and embrace 'trouble' with glorious abandon. Oh, when the war was over . . . ! She pulled him to her and kissed him, and he groaned, and she was satisfied he felt the same way.

When he took her home and said goodbye to her at the gate, they parted in a seemly manner, with a handshake, not knowing who might be watching. She would be up at Highclere early tomorrow, and he would meet her there, and they would have the morning together. John had promised, in the middle of the kissing, that they would talk 'seriously' tomorrow. Which meant, she supposed, plans for after the war.

After the war! It had always seemed a doubtful concept that there could be anything after the war. Certainly it would be something unrecognisable. But now she had hope that it would be delightful, too.

She let herself in with her latch-key, like a modern girl.

Ada came out from the kitchen passage. 'Oh, it's you, miss. I was just going to bed, but there's some cocoa left in the pan if you was to fancy it. I could hot it up for you.'

380

'Thanks, Ada. You go on up – I can warm it for myself.'

And she thought, *Poor Ada!* She looked so sad, so beaten. That was the other side of the coin, the risk you ran when you let love in. Poor Ada had only been married for two days.

But for two days of being married to John, she felt she'd be willing to pay such a price. Though naturally, she hoped – and, with the optimism of twenty, she trusted – that it would never be asked of her.

Sadie had been going to ask if she and John could go for a ride together, but Mrs Cuthbert had anticipated, and by the time he arrived, she had two of the horses saddled and ready. 'Don't hurry back,' she said, with a look of great satisfaction. It had taken her a while to realise that Sadie was hopelessly in love; but she had always suspected Courcy favoured her. It was nice to have been able to play Cupid. Something good might come out of this beastly war after all.

They rode over the hill, down the valley and up the other side, to the high place where there was a magnificent view, back over Northcote towards London, where the distant spire of Harrow poked up from its pudding-basin hill. They had ridden in silence, content after the feast of yesterday simply to be together; but up at the outlook they dismounted, tied the horses where they could graze, and sat down together on the grass, arms round their knees, the breeze stirring their hair.

'It's so quiet,' he said. High up, a hawk was circling noiselessly on an updraught; somewhere far off, some jackdaws nattered. 'After Le Touquet . . .'

'Is it bad?' she said, construing the tone of his voice.

'More awful than I could ever tell you,' he said. He took one of her hands and ran a finger over it, as if trying to memorise it. 'I thank God that you will never see anything like that.'

'I'm not made of glass,' she said.

'There are some things no human being should see.'

'But it will be over soon?' she asked hopefully.

He didn't answer for a moment, watching himself learning her hand. 'I'm afraid your parents won't approve of your marrying me,' he said, after a bit. 'I'm not a proud father's dream.'

'I don't think they're proud of me,' she said, without emphasis.

'You've said that before, but I don't believe it.'

'They don't see me as you see me. I'm just Sadie. I'm not special, so they never had to be ambitious for me, and I don't get in the way, so they never had to worry about me.'

He gave a painful sigh, and put his arm round her, to draw her against him. She leaned into him, resting her head on his shoulder as they stared at the rolling green woods and quiet fields. 'When the war's over, as soon as I get back, I'll ask for your hand properly.'

'I'll be twenty-one in January, so I can do as I like. But it will be polite to ask.'

He laughed. 'Polite!'

'Where will we go? The world will be our oyster.'

'I thought, perhaps South America. Lots of horses there. Or Australia. Or perhaps Yorkshire. Where would you like to go?'

'I don't mind,' she said. 'As long as I'm with you.'

Edward overheard two subalterns talking about victory. 'They know they're beaten,' one said. 'It's in the air.'

He wished he felt either of those things. They kept moving forward, but they kept having to fight, and every day, when men fell, he cursed inwardly that the war had not ended a day sooner, a week sooner, a month, a year, so that those men could have been allowed to live. He was tired, and he was no longer always sure where he was. He did what he had to do mechanically; but the men seemed exhilarated by the rumours of peace, and by the fact that the Germans, however hard they fought, were going backwards, always backwards.

On Saturday the 9th of November, a rumour reached them, which seemed to be authentic, that the Kaiser had abdicated. Germany had become a republic. 'What do you think it means, sir?' one of the subs, Rice, asked him. 'Does it make peace more likely, d'you think? Or less?'

'I don't know,' Edward said. 'The war might have been all the Kaiser's idea in the first place, but it was politicians that carried it on. I'm not sure republican politicos are any less addicted to blood and glory than imperial ones.'

Rice's pleading look faltered. 'You don't think it's coming?'

'Oh, it's coming all right. They can't win now. But I'm afraid it may not be as easy as people think. We will have to beat them all the way back to Germany, make them know they're defeated, make them roll over, otherwise they'll just get up as soon as our backs are turned and it will all start again. There's probably a hard winter ahead of us.'

The next day, they found themselves next to a Canadian corps, serving with the British Army, with the prospect of more action. The Germans were just ahead. He had called his lieutenants together and was trying to smooth the creases out of a very battered map, when Vickers, who had been murmuring to Rice, said, 'I say, do you know where we are?'

'I'm just about to enlighten you,' Edward said wearily.

'No, sir, I mean – that's Mons up ahead. Mons! Where the war started, back in 1914. The first big battle was the Battle of Mons – we did it at school.'

Edward looked at his fresh young face with mingled hilarity and horror. He was so young that Mons was now history to him! And they had got back, after four agonising years, to where they had started! He feared he was going to laugh, but managed not to. They'd have thought him mad. Mons, tomorrow: fighting, and another chance to die. It would suit God's sense of irony, he suspected, if he were to meet his death at the war's starting-point.

On Monday the 11th of November, William's squadron was at breakfast, chatting about this and that: a murmur of young voices punctuated here and there by laughter; mouths busy in eager young faces.

'I say,' said Anderson, a piece of sausage halfway to his lips, 'something's up.' One of the ground staff had come in at the far end of the tent and was talking urgently to two of the stewards.

'Somebody's bus has gone wonky,' said Griffin. 'Bags not mine.'

'Here's the Old Man,' William said, looking the other way. The CO had just come in from the mess, with a piece of paper in his hand. His expression was always hard to read, but he looked this morning particularly reserved. 'Bad news?' William muttered, and Anderson shrugged.

'Gentlemen,' said the CO, and silence fell. 'I have here a communication from Wing. There will be no operation this morning.' A mutter of disappointment rose, and he spoke over it. 'An armistice was agreed at five this morning. All hostile activity is to cease at eleven a.m.'

Puzzled looks were exchanged. 'Is it peace, sir?' Jackman asked.

'Conditions have been laid down, and the Germans have thirty-six days to comply,' said the CO. 'I suspect they have neither the heart nor the ability to resume after that, but every man must speculate for himself.'

'Oh, gosh, darn,' said Wilkinson, a Yank who had only

arrived on Saturday 'I've never had a chance to bag me a Hun. Now I'll never get my name on the board.'

Conversation broke out all around, but William was thinking that his last Fokker fight, yesterday, looked like being his last ever. But it was not the fight he was remembering. After it, he had dived down to look for targets on the ground. There was a grey country road, running straight as a dyke towards the east, between untended fields, with sentinel poplars bordering it at intervals. It was a still day, and the yellow leaves were hanging limp; so still that the smoke from a burning farmhouse was rising straight up. Down below half a dozen Huns in shabby grey uniform were pushing and heaving a laden handcart along the rutted road – laden, he supposed, with what they had looted before burning the house. He recognised only the shape of a brass bedstead. This, then, was what had become of a mighty military nation, of the pomp and glitter, of the bombast that had claimed sovereignty over the whole world. One of them glanced up at the sound of his engine, but they only increased their efforts, determined to get away with their paltry haul. William did not fire on them. They were no longer worth it.

Swinging north and then west, he had passed over some shallow trenches, smashed and deserted, littered with bits of equipment, corrugated iron, barbed wire, broken timber, and one machine gun, presumably rendered useless before the evacuation. Behind it sat one grey soldier, and William, flying low to the ground, drew a breath of caution before he realised he was dead. He was helmetless, fair-haired, and some shell fragment had severed one arm and torn open his chest, so that William saw a glimpse of his ribs gleaming through the bloody tatters. His face was turned upwards, and his mouth was open as though he had gasped for breath before he died. An unknown soldier, unimportant, forgotten by everyone, left behind – one dead youth that the war had passed over before rolling on unheeding.

William had been out here for over four months, when they said a pilot's life expectancy was six weeks. He had been downed twice, and lived. His luck could surely not have lasted much longer.

Now, it seemed, he was going to live.

Someone was speaking to him. 'Eh?' he mumbled.

'I said,' Anderson intoned carefully, as if to the deaf, 'what do you think you'll do when you're demobilised?'

'Try to get a flying job somewhere, I suppose,' William said. 'Flying's the only thing worth doing, really. I might stay on in the RAF.'

'If they'll have you,' said Anderson, 'after the CO caught you split-arsing the other day, in defiance of regs.'

Chubby Partridge leaned across the table and gestured towards the sausage on Anderson's plate. 'I say, are you going to eat that barker, or can anyone have it?'

Timmy came into the kitchen, breathless, his face red, his hair wild. 'It's over!' he cried. 'The war's over!'

Cook, boning meat at the table, looked up in annoyance, and waved the bloody knife at him. 'You wicked boy! Don't you come in here spreading rumours like that, or I'll give you such a smack.'

'But it's *true*,' he protested. 'The postman shouted it over the gate. The war's over at eleven o'clock this morning. He said rector's trying to find bell-ringers.'

Cook stepped backwards, knife still in her hand, felt blindly behind her and sat down heavily. 'If I find out you're lying . . .' she began, still unable to believe.

Munt appeared behind Timmy in the doorway. He looked at her across the boy's head.

'It's true,' he said. 'Armistice, eleven t's morning.'

Their eyes met, and everything the war had meant seemed to slide down the air between them, like a frost.

Timmy looked from one to the other eagerly. 'Did we

win? Does it mean we won?' Neither of them replied. 'Did we win?' he insisted.

But Cook and Munt only stared at each other.

Diana was in her sitting-room, dictating letters to her secretary, Miss Greengross, when she heard some disturbance outside in the house. 'See what that is, will you?' she said.

Before Miss Greengross could reach the door, it opened, and Padmore came in, ruffled out of her normal professional calm.

'Oh my lady, the news has just come,' she cried without preamble. 'The war's over!'

Diana frowned. 'It can't be! So soon? They were saying next year some time.'

'Apparently the Germans have had enough. Their generals were talking to our generals all night, and they announced this morning that the guns would fall silent at eleven o'clock.'

'It's over?' Diana said. Her thoughts went first to the hospital ward. 'Have the men been told?'

'Yes, my lady. It was one of the doctors who told me.'

Diana was at a loss. 'You'd better make sure her ladyship knows,' she said.

'Yes, my lady. It's wonderful, isn't it? Now the boys will come home.'

'Have you someone over there?' Diana asked, in surprise. It occurred to her that she didn't know anything about Padmore's private life.

'Two nephews, my lady,' Padmore said, and she was actually *grinning*.

Diana waved her away. 'I had better go to the hospital side, and see if there's anything I can do,' she said to Miss Greengross. She didn't think there was. But she didn't know what else to do. She wished Rupert were there to tell her.

* * *

To begin with Laura had heard the noise of voices. The X-ray ambulance was parked in a field by an aid station, just outside a village, and they had been sleeping, for once, in proper beds, though without sheets, in an abandoned house they had been guided to by the local mayor. It was not Ransley's field hospital – she had no idea at the moment where he was. She leaned out of the window when she heard the noise, fearing the Germans were attacking, but realised it was cheering, not panic. People were hopping about in the street, hugging; others were running this way and that.

'What's happening?' she shouted down. 'What is it?' An old man looked up and shrugged, not understanding, but grinned too. Another waved at her exultantly and shouted 'Good Tommy! God save the King!'

She raided her mind for French. '*Que'est-ce qui ce passe?*' she shouted, as a group of women ran by, one of them clutching a bottle and another with an apronful of apples.

'*Guerre finie!*' was the shout that came back.

Soon she and Annie were downstairs, just as Morgan and Jean-Marie reached the door, looking as though they had dressed by guess, and told them the news. The boys seized their hands and jigged them around in a silly dance, overwhelmed with excitement.

War *finie*, Laura thought. We'll be going home. Ransley will come home. And the future will hold – what? It was impossible to imagine.

'It's queer,' said Annie, 'but I'm going to miss Matilda.'

'I'm going to miss you,' Laura countered.

'No need to,' said Annie. 'I'll be there too.'

The bells of Holy Trinity were ringing now, with wild enthusiasm if not skill – so much enthusiasm that Beattie worried they might be turned right over and dismounted, and someone would be killed, an unlikely victim to an excess of joy. She was standing by the window in her bedroom, to get away from questions and exclamations. She could hear the noise of the servants being happy downstairs; outside, when the bells stopped for a moment for the ringers to get their breath, she could hear other bells in the distance; and factory hooters; and locomotive whistles; and car horns. Everyone seemed to want to make a noise.

Down in the street people had come out of the houses, were standing by their gates talking, most of them with dazed smiles on their faces. Servants were gathering in the road to chatter and laugh, children were racing up and down, dogs were barking – she feared Nailer must be down there somewhere, leading the riot as usual. Every now and then a motor-car came past, and hooted its horn, and everyone cheered and waved. It was the maddest thing she had seen.

For now all was celebration. But there would be visitors soon, and telephone calls. She would have to be sociable. She would have to make decisions: people would want to know what to do, and some things would not stop just because there was an armistice. The canteen would have to continue to serve food, the hospitals to tend patients. And the hardship committees would surely not go out of business, for the hardship of families who had lost their breadwinner would not magically cease. She wondered what would happen when the soldiers began to come home. After so long away, would they be able to settle in? Would their wives, who had learned to do without them, be able to find space for them? Some, she knew, had taken new men to their hearths. She foresaw trouble in many quarters.

Would she go on being as busy as she had been these last few years? She thought back in amazement to her life before the war: a life of ordering meals, arranging flowers, washing the valuable china, hosting the occasional party. And in between – acres, it seemed, of time. What had she done with it? She couldn't remember. She couldn't even remember what she used to think about during those long, empty days.

It filled her with dread and panic that she might have to go back to it. She could no longer cope with an empty mind, because it would fill with unbearable memories.

Edward would come back. What would happen to them? Would he still want her, still want to 'try again'? *Could* they live together? So much lay between them, not only the shadow of Louis, but now his experiences at the war. She remembered how impossible David had found it to talk about, and how resentful he had been that he could not. *David!* What would happen to him, now? He would want to seek a career, and set up his own establishment. He would take Antonia and the baby and go away. And she would be left with an empty house and a life she no longer knew how to live.

Edward would come home, and William, and thank God for that. But Louis was dead, and Bobby; Charles Wroughton, and Diana's Rupert; poor Ada's husband; lads from the village that she had known since they were children; so many, so many. The war was over, but the dead were dead and they were never coming home.

Edward was standing in a field, talking to his subalterns about the day's action to come, when the news reached him. A journalist attached to the Canadian Army came, grinning so hard it looked as though his face might fall in half, looking for someone else to tell. He had heard it over the wire. A German delegation had crossed the line during the night, and a conference had been held in Maréchal Foch's personal railway carriage, in a gun siding in the Compiègne Forest. Terms had been discussed, and a document had been signed.

Edward saw the ripple of excitement that eddied around and ahead of the journalist, but he was overtaken by a runner with a message from Brigade, and by Edward's servant, who pre-empted them all with the news in soldier-language: 'It's over, sir! War napoo!'

The journalist arrived and added detail; the message from Brigade made it official. All hostility was to cease at eleven a.m., and officers were to look to the welfare of their men, and to keep military order. They would not be pursuing the Germans as previously planned. They would be staying put, until further instructions could be sent.

'Is it true, sir? Is it true?' one of the subalterns, Broad, was asking him

'Yes, it's true,' he said.

It was over. No more slaughter, no more maiming, no more blood. No more disembowelled horses, no more putrid corpses, mud, barbed wire, deafening noise of guns and exploding shells; no more damp beds and horrible food and wondering if you would see another dawn. He was going to live. He and all these men around him had a future.

'What are we going to do, sir? Today, I mean,' Broad was asking.

They would have to get the men together and tell them – officially, because he doubted anyone was still in ignorance – and then there would be fatigues and, he supposed, general 'slacking off' for the day. He ought to think about arranging some activities to keep them in hand. A football match, perhaps.

War napoo. Behind him, across France, he had left dozens of men, whose names he had known, dead and maimed. He had seen them fall. He had knelt in Campion's blood as he promised to be at the end.

'Sir? Orders, sir?' That was Russell, adding his urging.

The sky was low and misty grey, and a fine rain was falling. He turned his face up into it, so that the raindrops would fall on his cheeks and they would not know he was crying.

Sadie was riding one of the horses in the paddock, using one of her favourite training ploys, the row of empty bottles, along which the horse had to weave in and out – it taught them handiness and balance. She saw Mrs Cuthbert coming – she was almost running. Dread gripped her heart. It must be bad news. Her father – William – *John*. The war still had so many ways to hurt her.

She slipped from the saddle and led the horse over to the gate. She saw, as Mrs Cuthbert drew nearer, that her face was pale with shock, and fear settled coldly in her chest. 'What's happened?' she asked, to get it over with. Always better to know than not to know.

'It's peace!' Mrs Cuthbert cried. 'Horace had a telephone call from Colonel Barry at the War Office. They've agreed a cease-fire. Fighting stops at eleven this morning. Oh, Sadie, it's over!'

Sadie found she had no words. They would come back, then, her father and brother and John. She felt she ought to want to grin and clap and jump for joy – and perhaps she would, later, but just now all she felt was solemn. It was over, but the cost had been so high. She remembered that summer, 1914, the hot days, the talk of war as though it were a treat to come, like an ice-cream. She remembered the boys playing soldiers, Germans and English, pointing twigs for guns and crying, *Bang bang, you're dead!* Dreams of glory. National pride. The peace should have come at Christmas 1914, when they could have rejoiced wholeheartedly, in their innocence. They were all different people now. They knew too much.

She felt the warm velvet of the horse's muzzle brush across the back of her neck, and then the nudge as he rubbed an itchy eye against her shoulder. *Well, at least you won't have to go and be blown to bits*, she thought.

The bells of Rustington's church, St Mary's, started to ring, making the horse start. It was not a proper carillon or change, they were being pulled crazily, anyhow, just to make a noise. It was a clamour of madness – but, in this case, mad joy. Mrs Cuthbert was looking at her, waiting, she supposed, for a response, but she still had no words.

'It's over,' Mrs Cuthbert said again. And suddenly her eyes filled with tears. 'Oh, Sadie, all those boys. And the horses!'

Sadie stepped closer, and they clasped hands silently on the gate-top, while the horse sighed, and shifted his weight from foot to foot.

As soon as Beth heard the news, she rang the Palfreys' house, needing someone to share it with. Sonia answered, and was so excited it was hard to understand her. In between breath-less sentences, Beth could hear voices in the background, high with excitement, and laughter, and every now and then, the doorbell ringing.

'So many people!' Sonia gasped. 'Everybody's coming round. Aeneas is going to shut the factory for the day. He and Audrey are coming home. We're going to have a party. Do come! You must come! Come *now*.'

'I'm on my way,' Beth cried. 'I'll be there in no time.'

She took a taxi, too disturbed to cope with public trans-port. The war was over! Jack wouldn't die! He'd be coming home! She was driven through streets thronged as never before. People leaned out of omnibus windows and cheered. They stood on roofs or hung out of upstairs windows, some waving flags. Shop assistants were out in front of their shops; factory girls still in mob caps were wandering among the crowds, having left their benches; men in uniform were kissing girls, whether their own or someone else's, who knew? People were linking arms and singing, people were dancing, people were blowing whistles, children were racing up and down, mad with excitement. And, this being London, the barrows were out selling hot chestnuts, hot sausages, hot potatoes, and Union Jacks on sticks to wave.

Eventually, the crowd got so thick, the taxi was reduced

to crawling. The elderly cabby opened his glass slide and shouted, 'You might as well walk from here, missy – it could take all day. You all right to walk?'

'Yes, of course.' Beth laughed. 'I don't mind. How much do I owe you?'

He turned his whole body round so she could see his grin. 'What – today? Can't charge yer today! You got someone over there?'

She knew he meant France, the war. 'My husband. He's been in since the beginning.'

'Well, he'll be home soon, then,' said the cabby. 'Gawd bless yer, love.'

Beth was so moved, she felt like kissing him. But she didn't. She eased herself into the mad, cheering, laughing crowd, and hardly felt the pavement under her feet.

Victor Sowden never heard that the war was over. The news of the cease-fire hadn't reached his unit. They were pursuing some Germans who had crossed a canal and set up a machine-gun post in the village beyond, trying to gain every last inch of territory before they were routed.

A German aeroplane, whose pilot also had not heard, flew in low up the road and strafed the Tommies to defend his own side. Several bullets hit Victor in the chest, and one of them penetrated his heart. He fell backwards, and lay face up to the soft sky. His expression was surprised, as though death was not at all the way he had expected.

It was 11.08 a.m.